Simpkinsville and Vicinity
Arkansas Stories of Ruth McEnery Stuart

Simpkinsville and Vicinity

Arkansas Stories of
Ruth McEnery Stuart

Edited and with an introduction
by Ethel C. Simpson

The University of Arkansas Press
Fayetteville
1983

Library of Congress Cataloging in Publication Data

Stuart, Ruth McEnery, 1856–1917
    Simpkinsville and vicinity.

    Bibliography: p.
    Contents: The woman's exchange of Simpkinsville—An
Arkansas prophet—The unlived life of little Mary
Ellen—[etc.]
    1. Arkansas—Fiction. I. Simpson, Ethel C., 1937–
II. Title.
PS2960.S45 1983   813'.4   82-16160
ISBN 0-938626-12-4

This project is funded in part by a grant from the
Arkansas Endowment for the Humanities.

For Vergil—
my most critical admirer
and most admiring critic

Acknowledgments

The impetus to write this book came from a weekend trip to southwest Arkansas in the spring of 1980. Walking along the streets and paths of Old Washington and visiting the home of Ruth McEnery Stuart confirmed my notion that her stories would find an appreciative audience in the 1980s. I owe a primary debt of gratitude to several people for that weekend: to Mary Medearis, Coordinator of the Southwest Arkansas Regional Archives, my hostess; to Marguerite Smith Moses, a native of Washington, who welcomed me into her home, the Stuart house itself, and shared her memories with me; to Harriet Jansma, Ellen Shipley, and Bill Baker, for convincing me that I should undertake the project.

Thanks to Sandy Williamson and Wendy Schacter who typed the manuscript, picking their way through thousands of apostrophes and quotation marks in the dialect stories, and to other members of the staff of the University of Arkansas Library for their help in locating and copying research materials. Thanks also to the staff of the Center for Instructional Media, University of Arkansas, and to Joyce Gralak, for preparing the photograph for the frontispiece.

Contents

Introduction

The imaginary southwest Arkansas village of Simpkinsville provides the setting for most of the stories in this selection of Ruth McEnery Stuart's Arkansas fiction. These stories describe the day-to-day lives of white rural Southerners sometimes referred to as the "plain folk." Many of the characters appear in more than one story, and the effect is that of a chronicle of small-town life. The one exception in the group, "Queen o' Sheba's Triumph," is set not in Arkansas but in New York City. But Sheba comes from Broom Corn Bottom, Arkansas, and her life story is determined by her origins and connections there.

Ruth McEnery Stuart was born into the world of Southern gentility that sets the tone of much of her writing, indeed of a whole generation of Southern writers. The values she celebrates in her stories, sketches, and poems rise from a tradition of family life and pride in one's origins that is apparent in her own life. Her grandmother, Mary Routh, was reared in St. Francisville, West Feliciana Parish, Louisiana, and was connected by marriage with other distinguished Louisiana families.[1] In 1818, Mary Routh married John Stirling, a Scot. She died not long after Mary Routh Stirling, mother of Ruth McEnery Stuart, was born.[2]

Mary Routh Stirling married James McEnery, a member of the Irish gentry from County Limerick, whose family property had been confiscated in Cromwell's time. James's parents had emigrated to Virginia with their six children. One of the sons, the Reverend John McEnery, who died in 1841, had a slight reputation as a geologist. Two others, James and Henry, left Virginia for Louisiana. In her biography of Stuart, Mary Frances Fletcher cites a family story that they left because their sister made what they considered an unworthy marriage. Henry O'Neill McEnery settled at Monroe, Louisiana, and eventually acquired large holdings in land and slaves. Two of Henry's sons were governors of

1. Mary Frances Fletcher, "A Biographical and Critical Study of Ruth McEnery Stuart," p. 4.
2. Ibid., p. 5.

1

2 · Ruth McEnery Stuart

Louisiana. John was elected in 1873; Sam, who assumed the office in 1881 when Gov. Louis A. Wiltz died, was elected in 1884. Sam also served in the United States Senate and on the Supreme Court of Louisiana.[3]

James McEnery, Ruth's father, settled first at New Orleans but subsequently moved to Marksville in Avoyelles Parish in central Louisiana. Ruth was born in Marksville on 19 February 1852.[4] Her name was Mary Routh McEnery, and she was called Routh. She was the eldest of eight children.[5] In 1852, the year of her birth, her father was the mayor of Marksville.

Sometime before 1860, the McEnerys moved to New Orleans, where James McEnery was on the staff of the Customs House. From that time until her death, Ruth always had family connections in New Orleans, and made frequent and often lengthy visits there. The McEnery children were educated there, attending both public and private schools.[6] The members of the large family remained close, often traveling together as they grew older. Mr. McEnery's health failed in later life, and the daughters as well as the sons had to work to support themselves. The records of Ruth's life at this period are indefinite, but it appears likely that before her marriage she was a schoolteacher at the Locquet-LeRoy Institute, a finishing school for young ladies.[7]

When Ruth was growing up, New Orleans was a thriving, cosmopolitan city, inhabited by a growing immigrant population. The turmoil of the Civil War doubtless accentuated the markedly contrasting levels of society and behavior that already existed. Ruth and the other women of her family took a daily constitutional, walking through the Creole and Italian neighborhoods, along the river, through the Negro sections, as well as in the more sedate streets above Canal Street and in the Garden District.[8] The color and style Ruth absorbed during these walks are reflected in the many stories of New Orleans life that she published in later years.

3. Ibid., pp. 5–7.
4. This is the date she gave on her marriage license, but some sources give other dates, as early as 1849. See Ina Rebecca Howell, "A Critical Biography of Ruth McEnery Stuart," p. 7.
5. Ibid., p. 8.
6. Ibid., p. 11.
7. Ibid., p. 17.
8. Ibid., p. 15.

Ruth's cousin, James McEnery, was married to an Arkansas woman named Mildred Stuart. In 1879 when Ruth was twenty-seven years old, she and her sister Susie were invited by Mildred to visit her in Columbus, Hempstead County. Susie returned to New Orleans, but Ruth remained in Columbus to teach. By most accounts, Mildred McEnery was interested in making a match between Ruth and her brother, and she succeeded. Four months after her arrival, Ruth and A. O. Stuart were married.[9]

Alfred Oden Stuart was fifty-eight years old in 1879. He had already been widowed three times and had eleven children. "A successful farmer who lived in town," he had stayed at home during the war to raise food for the troops and the civilian population.[10] He was interested in politics, although he did not hold public office himself.[11] After they were married, the couple moved to Washington, the seat of Hempstead County, Arkansas. Their house had been built in 1852 by a relative of A. O. Stuart. The L-shaped, one-story frame dwelling with gable ends was a common type in Washington.[12]

In the nineteenth century, Washington was an important town, and the numerous members of the Stuart family were among the earliest leaders of the community. A. O. Stuart had farm properties on either side of Washington and was a partner with his son-in-law in a mercantile establishment, Stuart and Holman.[13] He and Ruth lived in the midst of the little town, where her talents as a hostess and an organizer attracted a wide circle of friends. She had her own seamstress living in a house on the property and gave a great deal of time and attention to designing clothes and supervising their construction.[14] She organized a reading club and a social group called the D.O.T. (Dear Old Town) Club. Charlean Moss Williams recalls that Ruth arranged a Pink Tea, considered to be a very successful innovation at the time.[15] The Stuarts had a son, Stirling, in 1882, but Ruth

9. Ibid., p. 20.
10. Ibid.
11. According to his daughter, Mrs. Elise Stuart Spragins, quoted by Fletcher, "Biographical and Critical Study," p. 30.
12. A. O. Stuart Family File. Southwest Arkansas Regional Archives, Old Washington State Park.
13. Fletcher, "Biographical and Critical Study," p. 33.
14. Ibid., pp. 25–30.
15. Charlean Moss Williams, The Old Town Speaks, p. 295.

McEnery Stuart's time in Washington was to be very short. On 5 August 1883, A. O. Stuart died of a stroke at the age of sixty-three. He is buried in the Presbyterian Cemetery in Washington.[16]

At this juncture in her life, Ruth returned with her little boy to the family home in New Orleans. She may have returned to teaching in the New Orleans schools, but the information about her life at this time is not definite.[17] She moved in the social circle of other New Orleans literary figures, including George W. Cable, Mollie Moore Davis, whose father was editor of the *Times-Picayune*, Dorothy Dix, a columnist for that paper, and Katherine Nobles.[18]

However, a trip to North Carolina in 1887 marked the real beginning of Stuart's literary career. She and her sister Sarah went to a summer resort where they met Charles Dudley Warner, then the editor of *Harper's Magazine*. After her return to New Orleans, she sent Warner two stories anonymously: "Uncle Mingo's Speculations" and "Lamentations of Jeremiah Johnson." Warner kept "Lamentations" for *Harper's* and sent "Uncle Mingo" to the *New Princeton Review*, the first magazine to publish a story by Ruth McEnery Stuart. "Uncle Mingo" appeared in February 1888, "Lamentations" in May.[19]

In 1888, following the acceptance of two other stories,[20] Stuart moved to New York. After this, she began to spell her first name *Ruth*, considering the family spelling *Routh* too likely to be mispronounced. She lived at first in a boarding house, having left Stirling with her family in New Orleans. She soon became as popular in New York as she had been in Washington or New Orleans.[21]

In 1893, Harper and Brothers published a collection of eleven of Stuart's short stories and two of her poems under the title *A Golden Wedding and Other Tales*. With the exception of "Camellia Riccardo" and "The Woman's Exchange of Simpkinsville," the

16. Ibid., p. 47.
17. Fletcher, "Biographical and Critical Study," p. 35.
18. Ibid., p. 40.
19. Ibid., p. 38.
20. "Camellia Riccardo" appeared in *New Princeton Review*, September 1888. "A Golden Wedding" was published in *Harper's New Monthly Magazine* in December 1889.
21. Fletcher, "Biographical and Critical Study," p. 44.

stories in the collection are about black characters. For the next twenty-nine years, Stuart was to develop stories about blacks, New Orleans, and Simpkinsville in a successful career as a writer and platform speaker.[22] In fact, some of her published stories and sketches appear to have been written particularly for oral presentation. The title of one collection, for example, is *Moriah's Mourning, and Other Half-Hour Sketches* (1899). *The Plantation Songs*, collected in 1916, and *Daddy Do-Funny's Wisdom Jingles* (1913) also provided material for her programs.[23]

For the rest of her life, Stuart traveled widely in the United States, giving public readings from her works. Scrapbooks in the Stuart Papers contain countless clippings and handbills describing her performances. In 1895 she read for three weeks in Chicago, where she enjoyed very favorable reviews. Nearly every winter she returned to New Orleans for an extended visit, and often gave readings there to benefit charitable causes. She also gave many readings in New York at the YWCA, the Carnegie Lyceum, and the Fifth Avenue Theatre. In New England she appeared at the Worcester Women's Club, at Radcliffe, and before the New England Women's Press Association. In 1898 Stuart made a western tour that included readings in Colorado Springs and Denver, where she read to an audience of "about 2,500 people."[24]

When she was not traveling, Stuart lived in New York with Stirling and her sister Sarah, who joined them in 1897.[25] Stuart's experiences during the early part of her career are described in a substantial series of letters collected in the Stuart Papers at Tulane, which were written between 1897 and 1912 to Drs. C. Augusta and Emily F. Pope of Boston. The Pope sisters were twins, both physicians. Their brother, Col. Alfred Augustus Pope, a leading manufacturer of bicycles in the United States, advised Stuart on business matters. Stuart frequently stayed with the Doctors Pope when she toured New England.

Although she eventually became a financial success, she did have some lean years. In 1901 she wrote to her "Dear friend,"

22. Ibid., p. 45.
23. Fletcher, "Biographical and Critical Study," p. 75.
24. Ruth McEnery Stuart to Dr. C. Augusta Pope, 25 April 1897. Stuart Papers, Tulane University Library, New Orleans, La.
25. Howell, "Critical Biography," p. 45.

(one of the Popes): "I have got all my jingles done and away. . . . I have great hope of making some worth while money out of these trivial rhymes. Pray that I may, for I need it."[26]

In addition to financial difficulties, Stuart also suffered from poor health. Because she did not have a strong constitution, and pushed herself too hard, she was frequently ill and tired. In October 1904 she went to Onteora, a resort in New York, for rest. In February 1905 she went to the Jackson Health Resort in Dansville, New York. While she was away, her son Stirling was seriously injured in a fall outside their home at Flushing. He was hospitalized for more than a month, and the letters from his mother to her friends the Popes in Boston reveal the depths of her grief. Stirling died on 21 April 1905. He was buried in the family plot at the Metairie Cemetery in New Orleans.[27] The death of Stirling was a devastating blow to Stuart, and her literary output diminished appreciably afterward. She returned to the Jackson Health Resort for several months in February 1906.[28]

However, by this time she had become financially comfortable. In a letter to her sister in New Orleans, she wrote: "I have no fear of financial pressure. I make money fast enough when I am at work. I shall . . . be busy again. I worked yesterday and the day before at a story, the first for much over a year."[29]

In July 1906 she traveled to Europe, returning to New York in January. She spent part of the winter of 1907–1908 in New Orleans, as had generally been her habit, and gave a reading at Newcomb College in April 1908.[30] Gradually she began to pull out of her depression, and to resume her earlier routine of writing and public readings. By March 1909 she was back at Dansville, where, as she wrote to the Popes, she was "deep in work."[31] She went to New Orleans in the spring of 1910 and again in 1911, but in July 1911 she was back in New York, and in August on a trip abroad.[32] On her return, she continued her routine of public appearances, residing in New York and wintering in New Orleans. In June 1915 she was awarded an honorary degree of

26. Stuart Papers.
27. Fletcher, "Biographical and Critical Study," pp. 92–94.
28. Ibid., pp. 98–100.
29. Stuart to Sarah Stirling McEnery, 9 May 1906. Stuart Papers.
30. Fletcher, "Biographical and Critical Study," pp. 100–105.
31. Stuart to the Drs. Pope, 29 March 1909. Stuart Papers.
32. Fletcher, "Biographical and Critical Study," pp. 117–18.

Doctor of Letters by Tulane University.[33] Shortly thereafter she went to New York one last time. She became ill and entered a sanitarium, where she died on 6 May 1917. After a funeral in New York, she was buried in the Metairie Cemetery, near her son.[34]

Although Ruth McEnery Stuart is virtually unknown today as a writer, in her own time she enjoyed considerable popular and critical recognition. During the years between the publication of "Uncle Mingo's Speculations" in 1888 and her death in 1917, Stuart published more than seventy-five stories in addition to her dialect verse. These stories and poems appeared in many of the major magazines of the period, *Harper's Bazaar, Harper's New Monthly Magazine, Century Magazine, New Princeton Review, Delineator, The Outlook,* and *Lippincott's Magazine,* and were collected in twenty-three volumes.

Her work was widely reviewed in England as well as in the United States. The Stuart Collection at the Tulane University Library contains scrapbooks of clippings that attest the popularity of her work. An article published in 1893 associates her with the "Harper Set"—an informal group, including Mark Twain, who wrote for the magazine—and she worked temporarily as an editor for *Harper's Magazine.*[35]

Early in her career, Stuart's dialect works received critical notice. An article in *The Critic* compared her writing favorably to that of another New Orleans author, Grace King,[36] while a Boston paper compared her work to that of the New England local colorist, Mary E. Wilkins Freeman.[37] When Stuart gave a series of readings in Chicago, a local columnist said, "Mrs. Stuart's Negro dialect comes nearer to perfection than that of any other contemporaneous writer."[38] An article in 1896 summarized the beginning of her career and her continued success: "Eight years ago a new writer came out of the South. . . . Since then Mrs. Stuart has written constantly, and she is now recognized as one of the leading writers of America."[39] In 1904 she was invited to membership in the Lyceum Club of London, which had also invited

33. The certificate is in the Stuart Papers.
34. Fletcher, "Biographical and Critical Study," p. 173.
35. *The Recorder* (New York), 2 December 1893. Scrapbook, Stuart Papers.
36. 10 June 1893. Scrapbook, Stuart Papers.
37. *The Courier,* 8 July 1894. Stuart Papers.
38. "Sharps and Flats," *Chicago Record,* 19 March 1895. Stuart Papers.
39. John D. Barry, "A Chat with Ruth McEnery Stuart," *The Illustrated American,* 6 June 1896. Scrapbook, Stuart Papers.

other American authors, including local-color writers Sarah Orne Jewett and Mary E. Wilkins Freeman.[40]

In addition to her facility with dialect, critics frequently praised Stuart's humor. In a letter to her family in August 1894, Stuart quoted a review of *Carlotta's Intended* by R. H. Stoddard that appeared in the *New York Mail and Express:* "The book is equal to any recent work of short stories, and superior to most in its quality of humor. . . . Mrs. Stuart understands what only great humorists understand, that pathos and humor are inseparable."[41] Stuart's pathos is another quality often praised by critics. A clipping from the *Watchman* refers to the sweetness, tenderness, and purity of her descriptions: "Such literature helps us to sanctify the imagination and deepen the channels of the domestic sentiment through which only a pure national life can flow."[42] In a review of *In Simpkinsville,* an anonymous critic described "An Arkansas Prophet" as "pretty, pathetic, and delightful." He further noted that "The Unlived Life of Little Mary Ellen" was "so harrowing as to have been untellable but by so delicate a pen as this."[43]

Stuart's success is further reflected in the quality of her books as physical objects. Her stories were often collected and presented in handsomely designed volumes. In addition to collections of short stories, some of Stuart's longer stories were published separately, for example, *The Woman's Exchange of Simpkinsville* (1899), *Napoleon Jackson, Gentleman of the Plush Rocker* (1902), and *Carlotta's Intended* (1909). Both the individual stories and the collections included illustrations by some of the outstanding magazine artists of the day: Arthur Burdett Frost, well known for his *Uncle Remus* drawings and his careful depiction of rural America; Edward Windsor Kemble, who specialized in Negro characters and had illustrated *Uncle Tom's Cabin* and *Huckleberry Finn;* and Jessie Willcox Smith, illustrator of *Little Women.* The books had patterned covers and Art Nouveau bindings stamped in gilt. Many of the titles appear to have been published for the gift-book market, especially those containing Christmas stories.

40. "The Lounger," *Critic* (New York), June 1904. Scrapbook, Stuart Papers.
41. Stuart to Sarah Stirling McEnery, postmark 11 August 1894. Stuart Papers.
42. *Watchman* (Boston), 27 December 1894. Scrapbook, Stuart Papers.
43. *Chicago Times Herald*, 23 July 1897. Scrapbook, Stuart Papers.

When Ruth McEnery Stuart died in 1917, she died with the era about which she had written. The World War and the social changes that followed it made fiction of the local-color school hopelessly out-of-date. As time passed, readers rejected its sentimental and romantic tone. A copy of *Sonny* in the Arkansas Collection at the University of Arkansas Library demonstrates the changing views toward this type of fiction. Beneath the printed dedication, "To my son Stirling McEnery Stuart," is the following inscription: "Written by my Aunt. Often I've enjoyed her fine Southern hospitality in Washington, Ark. home of her married life where my first coz 'Sterling' [sic] was born." On the verso of this page is an inscription in another, more modern, hand: "Sonny's wedding is a lotta baloney!" And beneath that, in a wavering old-fashioned script: "Sonny's wedding was *sweet* & lovely— down with Baloney." Despite this sentiment, for many years the baloney theory has prevailed.

Several reasons can be advanced for the rapid decline of Stuart's popularity. The Great Depression, the Dust Bowl, and the dislocation that accompanied World War II made it impossible to romanticize the life of the plantations, small black settlements, and white villages of the South. People like the Simpkins sisters could be poor but proud; however, the next generations might be just poor and seek a brighter future through higher education and life in the city. For these people, Simpkinsville represented the dead past, and the more dead the better. Furthermore, developments in American race relations after World War I also influenced negative attitudes toward Stuart's stories. Some of her black characters are gross caricatures, and many of her stories of plantation life are marred by a tone of ironic condescension. The paternalistic benevolence that passed for liberalism in race relations in Stuart's stories was repugnant to readers of the younger generation of both races.

Whatever the reasons for it, the decline of Stuart's popularity coincided with the decline of the sentimental tradition in American literature and of the myth of the Old South. That being the case, why should anyone at this date try to revive interest in Simpkinsville and its chronicler? In the first place, Ruth McEnery Stuart was a nationally known and successful writer who contributed to an important development in American literature. Her contribution to the local-color tradition as well as to Southern literature merits closer attention. The particular locales of her stories, her narrative method, and her techniques of characterization demonstrate the trademarks of the most successful local-color writers.

Topographic features and vegetation, as well as the dialect, ethnic traits, and the mores and habits of thought of a specific region provide the material for local-color fiction. Stuart's fiction falls into three main groups, each set in a different locale: New Orleans, the plantations of south or central Louisiana, and the imaginary Arkansas village of Simpkinsville. Within each group are stories and sketches of varying lengths, from brief monologues intended for presentation from the speaker's platform to book-length novellas. All these stories belong to the local-color tradition. The material for the New Orleans stories is drawn from Stuart's years in that most cosmopolitan of Southern cities. Her stories celebrate the romantic qualities of New Orleans. The architecture of its distinctive "quarters" forms a backdrop for the well-to-do Creoles, the poor immigrants and blacks, and the "Americans" of the uptown district.

The second group of Stuart's stories depicts the life of blacks on the plantations. Of all her stories, these appear to have received the highest critical acclaim.[44] Many of these works are set in the Cane River country of Louisiana, not far from Stuart's home town of Marksville. This is a broad flat country of fertile cotton fields. Other stories in this group are set in the cane and cotton plantation country below New Orleans, the bayou region bordering the Gulf of Mexico. However, the stereotyped characters and sentimental plots make them less palatable to modern readers. From the vantage point of the 1980s, the most artistically successful group of Stuart's fiction is that represented in this selection, the stories and sketches associated with the imaginary town of Simpkinsville. These stories are collected in *In Simpkinsville Character Tales* (1897), *Sonny, A Christmas Guest* (1894), *The Woman's Exchange of Simpkinsville* (1899), *Sonny's Father* (1910), and *The Unlived Life of Little Mary Ellen* (1910).

The Simpkinsville locale is based on Washington, Arkansas, where Stuart lived after her marriage in 1879 until 1883. Earlier in the nineteenth century, Washington had experienced something

44. Reviews. Scrapbook, Stuart Papers.

of the excitement of the nation's Southwest expansion, for the town lay at the junction of two important national roads. The Chihuahua Road from St. Louis to Mexico served as a mail route in the 1820s and was a major trail to Texas and the Southwest. The Fort Towson Road led from Louisiana through the Oklahoma Indian Territory to Fort Smith. Washington was the mobilization place for military operations during the Mexican War, and Texas heroes such as Sam Houston, Stephen Austin, and David Crockett passed through the town.[45] During the Civil War, Washington was the state capital for two years, and its population swelled to forty thousand, of whom the majority were refugees or soldiers camped in the vicinity.[46]

But by the time Ruth McEnery Stuart got there at the end of the seventies, Washington was much like the Simpkinsville she describes in her stories: a rural village circled by farms and plantations whose occupants go into town to buy their supplies and visit their friends or to attend church or social gatherings. Like the roads of Washington, the roads of Simpkinsville and vicinity are unreliable; in "An Arkansas Prophet," the New Year's Eve party has to take place in spite of the week-long rains that have reduced the roads to hub-deep "gumbo mud." But, on still, quiet summer afternoons when the deep galleries and high-ceilinged sitting rooms provide cool, dim havens, the characters living along hot, dusty roads hear the passers-by, recognizing the sound of the doctor's buggy or of Ol' Proph's wagon and listening to the songs of the field hands on their way to work.

In present-day Washington, Ruth Stuart's own Greek-Revival house still stands, surrounded by the shrubs and trees described in her stories—crepe myrtles, jasmines, and the larger magnolias and oaks. The climate supports the lush vegetation of the yards as well as of the fields and woodlands surrounding the little town. The long growing season, mild but rainy winters, and hot summers affect the way people live, as well as how they make their living. The land around the town is still devoted to farming, and, although there is some evidence of modernization, the atmosphere is much the same as it was at the turn of the century. This atmosphere was of paramount importance to the develop-

45. Mary Medearis, *Washington, Arkansas: History on the Southwest Trail*, p. 4.
46. Williams, *Old Town*, p. 111.

ment of the regional character of Stuart's stories. The predominantly rural physical setting of the stories was the basis for many of the cultural values they reflect.

In Simpkinsville, the people live off the land or by providing goods or services to those who do. Stuart's characters are not often the landed aristocrats of the plantations, but, like A. O. Stuart, farmers and their families who live in town. The Simpkins sisters, for example, belong to a planter's family that lost its land and most of its money after the Civil War. Some of their women friends are married to storekeepers, preachers, or doctors, as well as to farmers. Deuteronomy Jones, the garrulous old narrator of the "Sonny" stories, is an elderly planter whose son now manages the family's farms, even while making a large income from his nature books. Some of the men in the stories are called Judge or Colonel, indicating some connection with local politics, government, or the military. The few women who are working outside the home are usually schoolteachers, although occasionally Stuart portrays a woman as a missionary or a public lecturer.

Stuart's stories, like much Southern fiction, give a large place to family life and family activities. In a series of monologues, narrated by Deuteronomy Jones, Stuart depicts the life of the Joneses from the birth of "Sonny," in his parents' old age, describing Sonny's baptism, his schooling, his courtship and marriage, and other events in the family's life together. The "Sonny" stories describe a network that stretches from Deuteronomy Jones's mother-in-law, who shared the Jones home when Jones was a young man, to the youngest of his seven grandchildren, born when he was an old man sharing the home with his married son. In other Simpkinsville stories, characters include an unmarried sister making a home with her brother's family, a widow who looks after her own children as well as those of the widower next door, and twin sisters living in the old family home alive with memories of their parents and brother.

Since the Southern rural communities did not enjoy many secular entertainments, home and church activities filled an important need in people's lives. The Simpkinsville stories contain descriptions of Christmas dinners, a New Year's Eve party, weddings, and commencements celebrated by the whole community.

All decent Simpkinsville people go to church, and church activities and personnel, such as preachers or deacons, are important topics of daily conversation.

An important pastime in rural communities is storytelling, and Stuart takes full advantage of this fact. First, she includes many colorful, interesting stories subsidiary to her main narrative. More important, however, the storytelling tradition provides one of her narrative devices. She employs a storyteller or narrator whose presence in the story allows Stuart herself to assume a more distant posture from her material. This is a popular device in regional fiction because it allows the author to be an *outsider*, like her readers, observing the distinctive behavior of her fictional locale and characters with a certain detachment. The most obvious instances of this detachment are in the stories of blacks. The narrator of these stories is usually condescending, presenting them as childish and ignorant, or else idealizing their faithful devotion to their white master.

"Queen o' Sheba's Triumph" has a considerably more objective point of view than many of Stuart's stories about black characters. The narrative is in an ironic mode, and Sheba's comical shortcomings in taste and sophistication are emphasized in the first section of the story. But her character develops out of the situation in which she lives, and the later details of the narrative contribute to the development of a serious theme, the triumph of the heroine over every obstacle, by means of the very standards of taste and behavior that brought her low. The story has a grimly humorous undertone, but the dominant emotion is sympathy for Sheba's lonely struggle.

"An Arkansas Prophet" and "The Unlived Life of Little Mary Ellen" draw from the tradition of storytelling to employ another common local-color device. An objective narrator lays out the opening scene, describing the local types as they sit swapping stories. Then the narration shifts to one of the characters who tells the story of a significant and, in these instances, sad local event. In "An Arkansas Prophet," several men are gathered around the stove in the village store, and Dan'l McMonigle tells the story of Ol' Proph' for the benefit of Simpkinsville's new parson. "The Unlived Life of Little Mary Ellen" is set in the summertime, and the men are out-of-doors. The two "leading physicians" and a preacher discuss Mary Ellen's case, each supplying details from his own speculations or experience. In each story, when the reader at length has the background, the objective narrator returns for the denouement.

Many of Stuart's Simpkinsville stories are in fact monologues narrated by Deuteronomy Jones, Sr. He is, of course, an insider, having lived all his more than seventy-five years on his father's farm. Even in these "Sonny" stories, however, Stuart sometimes gives Jones the outsider's role, as when he describes a trip to the Northeast and to New York, or when he attends a women's meeting.

The Simpkinsville stories reveal the same approach to character development that many other authors used in local-color fiction. Dialect and local manners and mores fill in the broad outlines of a regional "type." This approach is very clearly visible in local-color stories about blacks. Some common stereotypes are the black preacher, the ladies' man, the old man full of folksy humor and wisdom, the adorable little pickaninny with a touch of larceny. These are all characters in Stuart's fiction, as well as in much other Southern writing before World War II. However, Stuart's best work portrays highly particularized versions of the types. The hero of *Napoleon Jackson* appears to be the stereotype of the shiftless black man, living off the labors of his wife. But in the mock trial conducted by the white "regulators," Napoleon's wife and another witness testify to his many outstanding qualities as a father and husband.

Among her white characters, too, Stuart transcends the types with many deft touches of characterization. In the best stories, the situation provides the means of character development. For example, in their struggles with genteel poverty and changing times, the Simpkins sisters are like many a pair of old-maid ladies. Yet they display an atypical resourcefulness in adjusting to their circumstances, as well as an unusual kindness and tolerance of outsiders, including even Yankees.

Dialogue is the chief means by which the characters are revealed to the reader. Stuart describes the circumstances of the Simpkins sisters, but the ladies characterize themselves in their many anxious conferences about how to survive without disgracing their family position. As a result, the reader is led along the sometimes tortured path of their reasoning, as in this example: "Ef Sonny had o' lived, an' married—which, for a man, as long as they's life they's hope—they might in time o' been sech as would care for they ol' auntie's valedict'ry. That ribbon cost five dollars a yard, in Confed'rit money, an' tain't all silk, neither." Stuart's use of punctuation and sentence structure conveys not only the vocabulary but also the stresses and rhythms of her Southern speakers. Modern prejudice against reading dialect is no doubt grounded in the abuses of the local-color school. But Stuart was very highly regarded for her rendering of black speech. Joel Chandler Harris wrote her, "You have got nearer the heart of the negro than any of us."[47] One of her best stories about blacks is "Napoleon Jackson, the Gentleman of the Plush Rocker." Napoleon is charged with neglecting his duty toward his family, but an old granny-woman defends him in court.

"Yas, sir. Fust an'fo'most, I know 'Poleon don't work beca'se he can't he'p hisse'f. He can't work. His mammy—why, you-all chillen, you 'member his mammy, ole 'Hoodoo Jane.' Ef you don't, you oughter. But Jane warn't no hoodoo. She was a hard worker, an' when she labored so hard for her las' marster, Eben Dowds, Jedge Mo'house's Yankee overseer, wha' bought him out, she was so overdriv' dat she swo'dat de chile dat was gwine come to her th'ough all dat endurin' labor shouldn't nuver lay a hand to a plow. *She marked him for rest.*

"I ricollec' same as ef't was yesterday, she say she was gwine leave one rockin'-cheer nigger to tek her place when she died, an'she done it. An' I'm her witness to-day, befo' Gord."

Her rendering of other Southern dialects is equally consistent and accurate. She avoids most of the excesses of spelling that irritate modern readers, such as writing *wuz* for *was* or *gon* for *gone*. Several elements of Stuart's consistent treatment of dialect are illustrated in this passage from "The Dividing Fence":

"Well, they's some ketchin' diseases thet I'd send my child'en after in a minute, ef they was handy; an' then, agin, they's others thet I wouldn't dare to, though, ef they *was* to come, I'd be glad

47. Edwin Lewis Stephens, "Ruth McEnery Stuart," *Library of Southern Literature*, ed. Edwin Anderson Alderman et al., 11:5145.

when they was over. Any disease thet's got any principle to it I ain't afeerd to tackle, sech ez measles, which they've been measles, behavin' 'cordin' to rule, comin' an' goin' ef they was kep' het an' sweated correct, ever sence the first measle."

Here Stuart reproduces the dropping of final sounds common to many dialects: *kep'* for *kept*, *an'* for *and*. She also spells out certain variant pronunciations: *sech ez* for *such as*, *afeerd* for *afraid*, *ef* for *if*. A third element of her dialect style is recorded in distinctive grammar and syntax: *they's* for *there is*, the use of *ain't*, dialectal forms of the past participle, such as *het* for *heated*, omission of the adverbial ending, such as *correct* for *correctly*.

Furthermore, this snatch of Mrs. Carrol's opinion on measles illustrates another quality of Stuart's dialect style. The sentences are loosely structured by parenthetical elements, concession clauses, condition clauses, and other interruptions of thought. The second sentence in the passage contains a free-floating clause, loosely connected to the main idea by *which*, a construction that occurs often in Stuart's dialogues, and reflects the rambling conversational style of the speakers. In addition, this passage builds upon one of the most distinctive and successful techniques Stuart used. In these few sentences, measles is analyzed in minute detail, practically personified in its having principles and its "comin' an' goin'." It is the measles, not the patient, that "was kep' het an' sweated." Stuart's characters have a passion for detailed discussion. They mingle scientific or historical wisdom with folk sayings or religious maxims and string it all together with connectives like *jest ez, which, ef,* and so on. Their attention to detail is largely responsible for the humor of the dialect passages, and, at the same time, their discussions are remarkably faithful to real conversational speech.

In addition to their technical qualities, and their importance in the history of local-color fiction, Stuart's stories of Simpkinsville evoke that connection between the past and the present that many Americans are in the process of discovering. There is much delicious humor in these rural characters and incidents, as well as pathos and sentimentality. Despite their shortcomings in attitude, some of her stories about blacks provide a detailed picture of their life after the Civil War. Finally, the Simpkinsville stories assert the values of rural family life and closeness to the land, values still prized in the present generation.

The American Bicentennial celebrations encouraged Americans to investigate the past. In earlier times, the descendants of those who arrived on the *Mayflower* and of the Revolutionary soldiers claimed nearly all of the genealogical attention. Since the Bicentennial, however, other Americans are also searching for their roots, not just the white Protestant majority, but blacks and other ethnic groups as well, learning that their ancestors, too, were "a legacy" as Deuteronomy Jones says, worth tracing through census and court records and cemetery lists. The South is learning at last that its history did not come to an end at Appomattox Court House, but that life went on and that the lives of grandparents and parents are worth attention.

The humor of the Simpkinsville stories comes from several sources, and in the best stories, it offsets the sentimental note that often threatens to drown out everything else. Most of Stuart's humor is gentle mockery of the foibles of human nature and of the attitudes and tastes of the rural South in the Gilded Age. In "The Women," for example, Deuteronomy Jones provides a commentary on this early stage of the women's movement that is generally sympathetic. But his description underscores several ironies: most of those attending the mother's meeting are single women because the mothers are too busy. Indeed, the speaker herself is a single woman who was raised in an orphanage. The early "Sonny" stories provide a humorous view of family life dominated by a spoiled child. However, as Sonny grows older, he mellows somewhat so that when as an adolescent he faces down the School Board and the entire community, he is a more sympathetic character.

Much of the best humor comes when Stuart allows the characters to reveal themselves. Miss Melissy in "A Note of Scarlet" feels that she has thrown over all the restraints of her religious training and indeed of human decency when she makes a red wool mat without counting the stitches and goes fishing on Sunday. The contrast between her perception of the situation and the reader's produces the humor. Grandpa Jones's experiences in

New York provide examples of classic frontier humor based on the country bumpkin in the big city, amazed at everything he sees.

In two of the Arkansas stories, as well as in others set in New Orleans, Stuart produces a more grotesque humor. "The Unlived Life of Little Mary Ellen" hovers between sentimentality and hilarity for much of the narrative. In fact, the community succumbs to hysterics at the climactic moment in the plot, when the fluttering white ribbons on the gatepost, traditionally used to signify the death of a child, announce the "death" of a wax doll. In "Queen o'Sheba's Triumph," the humor derives from the fact that the heroine plans and presides over her own funeral, and then dies in the middle of it.

Like other local-color writers, Stuart also develops her characters' dialects and personal idiosyncracies of speech for humorous effect. Her famous character Deuteronomy Jones, Sr., is an entertaining speaker in many ways. Not only does he display sound judgment, but he also expresses himself very pungently. For example, he has an "obnoxion to automobiles" because they lack the companionability of horses. When he visits the city, he uses the "alleviators" to get to his hotel room on an upper floor. He remarks about the "crystalizin' effect of old age" in the Simpkins sisters: "them old maiden sisters ain't changed a ioto in any conceivable way for twenty-five year." Sally Ann Brooks, the twice-widowed scatterbrain, is criticized for her "conspicuosity" of dress. And when Sonny is awarded his diploma, the old man remarks about the "unanimosity" of the board's decision. One word of Deuteronomy's speech is so idiosyncratic that it has puzzled many contemporary readers. He consistently says *thess* for *just*. In this edition, the spelling has been modified to *jest*, which is consistent with the usage of all Stuart's other characters.

Stuart's handling of black characters was very highly regarded by literate Americans of her time. In many cases, Stuart's black characters receive the same treatment as her white people. They desire respectability and its trappings, although the black aspirations may be more humorously described. The black families are closely knit, and the characters are frequently heroic in their ability to overcome the extreme limitations imposed on them for generations. They approach life with verve and enthusiasm and practice Southern hospitality of the highest order. The loyalty of servants in sentimental fiction can be very tiresome. But the ingenuity and courage of some of Stuart's black characters, like Rose Ann Jackson or Queen o' Sheba, are not so common-place in nineteenth-century fiction. The white characters recognize these qualities, even when they harbor the traditional racist attitudes. Ol' Prophet disappears and reappears amid mysterious circumstances in "An Arkansas Prophet," but the white men clearly understand where he has been and what he has done. The white "regulators" who have indicted Napoleon Jackson are forced to admit, if only to themselves, their own responsibility for his idleness.

In addition to providing pictures of the plain folk of Arkansas, Stuart's stories and sketches are celebrations of rural life. Although she often describes the more ridiculous effects of the closed structure of village life, the intimacy and charm of Simpkinsville come through. The natural beauty of the setting is emphasized in many of the stories, as well as the delight of the characters in such rural activities as fishing, farming, and bird-watching. Further, these stories affirm the values of family life. Deuteronomy Jones and the Simpkins sisters are vividly conscious of their long-dead parents, and the past is almost a living force in their daily routine. Miss Melissa Moore's duties as an aunt and sister-in-law provide her status in the family and the community, and Queen o' Sheba's family ties continue to exert themselves long after she has left Broom Corn Bottom for New York. Grandpa Jones realizes that his long association with the younger generation has allowed him to broaden his outlook beyond the narrow provincialism of some of his neighbors. From his experiences as both descendant and ancestor he has drawn the resources that enable him to meet the many changes that have occurred during his lifetime, resources that include a deep yet tolerant religious faith, a mind open to innovation and change, and a well-developed sense of humor.

Many readers may find Stuart's depiction of daily life and work appealing. Her characters tend their children and their gardens and manage their own affairs and those of their neighbors with fortitude and good humor. Their lives may be narrow, but in the best of these stories, they are enlivened in numerous small ways. Family celebrations and holidays build a sense of community. Blacks and whites alike know how to have fun, and pride in thrift and work is balanced with generous hospitality and the joy of fellowship. These idealized traits of country life engage the imaginations of readers who are seeking alternatives to the complex, alienating life-style of the late twentieth century. For many readers, Stuart's imaginary village of Simpkinsville offers a haven where life is slower and simpler, and where people know and care about one another.

Note to the reader: This edition follows the text reprinted in the books of Stuart's collected stories, which occasionally differ slightly from the magazine versions, and from each other. As a result, variant spellings occuring in the dialect passages have generally not been regularized, except when they seemed likely to confuse the reader.

The Woman's Exchange
of Simpkinsville

"I've been kissed once-t—with a reg'lar beau kiss—by Teddy Brooks." The puffs of smoke from old lady Sarey Mirandy Simpkins's pipe came faster after she had spoken.

"But I never kissed back. Hev you ever been kissed that a-way, 'th a reg'lar beau kiss, sis' Sophia Falena?" she continued, turning toward her sister, who sat, also smoking, beside her.

"Twice-t."

"Who by?"

"Once-t by Jim Halloway, time he spoken the word fo' me to marry 'im, an'—an' by another person for a far'well."

"An' you kep' two all these years an' never told 'em out, an' here I felt guilty a-hidin' one. Who was that various secon' smartie what done it to you, sis?"

"He weren't no smartie, Sarey Mirandy. He were Jim Dooley, an' it were time he 'listed in the army."

"Did you kiss back, Sophia Falena?"

"*Yas—I—did!* But what put kissin' into you' head to-night, sis? It's mighty funny, 'cause I was a-settin' here thinkin' 'bout kissin' too—an' I can't tell when I've studied about sech a thing befo'."

"I dunno. I was jest a-thinkin'. Sometimes it do me good to set an' think 'way back."

"Well, I tell you how I reckon kissin' come into *my* head. I was jest a-thinkin' *s'posin'.*"

"S'posin' what, sis?"

"Well, s'posin' all 'round. S'posin' Jim Dooley had of came back from the wah, fo' one thing."

A faint blush suffused the thin face of the speaker at the very audacity of that which her supposition implied.

"An' s'posin' Sonny hadn't of taken to birds—an' died. An' s'posin' the bank hadn't o' failed. Why, sis, I could set here an' s'pose things in five minutes thet'd make everything different. S'posin' time Teddy Brooks give you thet special an' pertic'lar kiss, *you* had jest—ef not to say kissed back, not *drawed away* neither. S'posin' that?"

"Well, sis, since we got on the subjec', I've supposened it more'n once-t—pertic'lar sence I see how ol' an' run-down the pore feller is. Sally Ann Jones ain't been even to say a half-way wife to 'im. Seem like ev'ry time she lays a new baby in the cradle fo' him to rock she gets fatter an' purtier an' mo' no 'count; an' pore Teddy he sets an' rocks the flesh clean off'n his bones. Yas, sis, I've thought o' *that* s'posin' many a time, but it's a vain an' foolish thought—ef not a ongodly one. But the one I've s'posened about most is Sonny."

Both women sighed. "Somehow I can't get used to thinkin' 'bout Sonny dyin', noways. No two girls ever had a better broth-er'n Sonny. Sonny was a born genius, ef th'ever was one. Perfes-ser Sloane down to Spring Hill say hisself they warn't a young man in the county thet helt a candle to Sonny fo' head-learnin'— not to speak o' Sonny's manners. An' when I set an' look at this houseful o' stuffed birds in glass cases an' think o' what Sonny might 'a' been—Well, maybe it was God's will for Sonny to take to birds, 'stid o' drink or card-shufflin' like some brothers."

"It's mighty funny, sis, for you an' me to be sett'n' up here s'posin' an' lookin' back at this pertic'lar time, when it so p'inted-ly behooves us to be lookin' ahead. Lemme see that paper ag'in. Yas, here it is in plain 'Merican: 'Failure of the Cotton King's Bank of Little Rock'—a whole colume. Nobody to read that would think of its sett'n' two ol' women to studyin' 'bout kissin', now, would they? What you reckon we better do, sis?"

"God on'y knows—an' He ain't tol' me—yet. Twouldn't be no use to try takin' boa'ders, would it?"

"Twouldn't be right, sis. They ain't noboby in town *to* boa'd out but them as are boa'din' a'ready, an' twould be jest the same as askin' 'em to leave an' come to us—'special as we got the fines' house."

"Twould look that a-way, wouldn't it? I thought about takin' in quiltin', but there ag'in, you know, th'ain't mo' quiltin' give out to be did than Mis' Gibbs can do—an' she half crippled, too. No, no. 'Fore I'd give out thet you an' me'd take in quiltin', I'd starve—*that* I would."

"I taken notice to a pertic'lar word you spoke jest now, sis, 'bout 'God knows.' You recollec' what the hymn say?

'Hev we trial or temptation,
Take it to the Lord in prayer.'

Seem to me like our trial's been followed by two temptations a'ready. It's mos' nine o'clock, an' I'm goin' to read my chapter an' then lay this case o' you an' me out clear, on my knees, befo' the Lord; an' do you do the same, sis, an' I b'lieve we'll be d'rected."

Lighting her candle, old lady Sophia passed noiselessly into her own room. Her sister sat for some time longer in thought, then she too, after shovelling some ashes over the coals upon the hearth, took her candle and went to bed.

The Misses Simpkins were twins, and at the time of the Civil War they had been fair blooming country maidens, both, and they were now, since the death, a year ago, of "Sonny," their bachelor brother, the sole representatives of a family that had stood with the best in the Arkansas community in which they lived; a family whose standards and traditions had been religiously observed in all things by the twin daughters upon whose frail maiden shoulders had developed responsibilities hitherto unknown to the women of the name of Simpkins. Their mother and grandmother had had slaves at their call, and by frugal care had accumulated what here in those days was counted as wealth.

They had worn their inherited frugality itself threadbare in the determination to "live like pa an' ma would like to have us live," and thus far they had succeeded.

Sonny, whose life, viewed retrospectively, seemed even to their loving eyes a failure, had been, when living, their pride and joy. Sonny was, in truth, a gentleman. His one year at college, which he left for the army in '61, had sufficed to introduce him into new realms of thought, and, it may be, had diverted activity from his hands to his brain. Certain it is that he never practically grasped the changed situation after the war, and the sisters and he had finally sold all the farm lands, reserving only the few acres surrounding the homestead. The proceeds, deposited in the failing bank, had yielded an income quite adequate to their modest needs.

Sonny had called himself a naturalist; and so he was—in a sweeter, broader sense than he knew. He was, as nature had made him, a true-hearted, unsophisticated gentleman. For more than twenty years he had been satisfied to pursue his chosen study, and take no note of time.

But Sonny was found one day, with a live bird still grasped in his hand, lying dead beneath a tree. Presumably he had climbed and fallen.

And now to the lonely sisters had come a second trial. Into their shadowed door had stalked unbidden and unexpected the informal guest called Poverty, with her startling command of "Work!"

It was dinner-time on the day following the conversation recorded before they reverted to the theme again.

"Well," said Miss Sarey Mirandy, "hev anythin' come to you, sis, thet we can do?"

"Hev anything come to you, sis Sarey dear?"

"Yas, it has. An' I'm 'fraid it's small comfort. Th'ain't but two things I can do, an' them's sewin' an' cookin'. Th'ain't any more sewin' needin' to be did in Simpkinsville'n them as are a'ready doin' it can do, an' as fo' cookin', you know how much chance they is in that—less'n a person'd hire out, which I *can't* do—not while ma and pa's ile-painted po'trait looks down from that chimbly at you an' me. Tell the truth, sis, what *to* do I *don't* know. Hev you thought 'bout it consider'ble?"

"Yas, I have, sis. You can cook an' sew, an' I can ca'culate figgurs, an' we got a-plenty o' houseroom, an' we're right on the public road, an'—"

"In the name o' goodness, sis hun, 're you wanderin', or what're you drivin' at?"

"Well, they's jest this much to it, sis Sarey Mirandy: I've got a idee; an' *my* idee is thet it's *the* idee—an' that's all they is *to* it."

Miss Sarey Mirandy readjusted her spectacles and scrutinized her sister's face. "Well, go on, honey. You've done got me wrought up!"

"Why, it's this—and I'd never o' thought o' sech a thing if it hadn't o' been for my trip to the city, along with me subscribin' to that magazine, both of which, you know, hun, you pretty solemn discountenanced. I seen it tried in the city, an' the magazine is continual tellin' how it works everywhere."

"But for gracious sakes alive, sis, what is the thing?"

"*It's a Woman's Exchange*—that's what it is!"

"But, sis hun, we ain't got nothin' to start it with."

"That's jest the beauty of it. They get started on nothin'. We jest give out thet the Exchange *is started*, an' everybody who does any sort o' work to sell sends it, an' we sell it for her an' *deduc'* ten precent. You see?"

"Well, I dunno as I do."

"Well, here: S'posin' ol' Mis' Gibbs, 'stid o' totin' her heavy comforters all 'round the county, an' losin' maybe two whole days' time a-sellin' one for two dollars, jest sends 'em in here, an' we sell 'em for her. She gets—ten from one dollar leaves ninety cents, an' nine an' nine's eighteen, eight an' carry one—She gets—"

"You don't mean she gets eight dollar? Twouldn't never do in the world. People wouldn't pay it. An', besides, I thought you said she wouldn't have to carry none?"

"Don't put me out, sis; I'm all frustrated—'f I jest had a slate! Now I got it! You don't carry at all. Ought's a ought, an' nine an' nine's eighteen. She'd get a dollar 'n' eighty cents, an' we'd get the two dimes. Then you could put any kind o' cooked things in an' sell 'em. Them lemon pies o' yours'd sell like hot cakes."

"An' who'd get the precent on them, sis?"

"Well, reely, hun, I—I hardly know. We got to deal fair. We might give it to charity. How'd it do to give it to Mis' Gibbs to make up the *deduc'* on the comforts?"

"That might do—if it's got to be give; but look's if it would nachelly *b'long* somewhere, don't it?"

"It do seem so. Maybe we might keep that fo' rent o' the room."

"Well, I dunno. Ef we do, we had ought to give it out, so every person'd understand."

"That's so. Of course. Well, how'll we start, hun?"

"Why not hev it called out in church? It's a good helpful work."

And so it was done.

When, on Sunday following, the minister stepped aside to read the notice, Miss Sophia Falena grew so flurried that she untied her bonnet strings and fanned vigorously. Her sister, however, though sniffling vociferously herself, nudged her, and she tied them again, and only cleared her throat at short intervals. The notice simply called a meeting of all interested in the project, which was duly set forth, on the next day at the Simpkins residence.

The response was most encouraging; all the chairs in the house and one from the kitchen being called into requisition to seat the attendants. Miss Sophia's voice trembled distinctly, as did the hand that held the paper from which she read, standing in the midst of the assembly, her "idees on the subjec'," which she had thought best to commit to paper.

The meeting was in all respects a success. Besides the assorted bits of advice which all gave freely on the spot, each promised to "enter" something. While Miss Sophia Falena, an atlas balanced upon her knee, made a note of articles promised, Miss Sarey Mirandy passed around raspberry-vinegar and crullers on an old silver-plated tray.

The two were similarly attired in gowns of shiny black silk, whose swishing sound at every movement seemed, with the clink of the high goblets against the silver waiter, reminiscent of a by-gone and more prosperous period.

The change wrought in the Simpkins household by the new enterprise was marvellous.

It was as if time had turned backward and they were young again, so quickly did they move about, so animatedly discuss the numerous details of preparation.

After considerable parley, they decided to use the mahogany centre table for cakes and articles of special showiness, while fancy-work could be advantageously displayed on the piano. If the time should come again when they cared to hear music in the house, they could move the things. Miss Sophia, who had been from home more than her sister, hated to open the old piano anyway. Indeed, she was once heard to say: "When that *piano* is shut an' kivered up, a person can look at it an' think music, 'cause the shape seems to favor it; but jest open it, an' I declare Methusalem ain't nowheres. It makes a person ponder on death an' *e*ternity."

The Exchange opened briskly. The centre table fairly groaned beneath its burden of cakes: "White Mountain," "Lady Washington," "Confederate Layer," "Marble," "Dolly Varden," "General Lee," and score of others, iced, and decorated with reckless elaboration; while in the centre, completing the effect of a spread feast, stood—under glass, it is true—a glowing pyramid of wax fruits.

The piano was a bazaar of many-hued zephyrs, from the miniature sacques and stockings of shrimp pink and kindred raw tints relegated by provincial taste to the adorning of babes, to the chinchilla and purple capes suggestive of grandmothers' rheumatic shoulders.

On a side table, wrapped in snowy linen, were heaped loaves of homemade bread, buns, rolls, lemon pies—the home contribution.

A stream of people were coming all day, examining things, pricing, but rarely buying. Indeed, nearly all had something in stock *to sell*.

The two old ladies flitted briskly about, ever and anon putting their heads together, only to dart off in other directions, as busy and buzzy as two happy house flies on a sunny day, only the bright red spots on their cheeks testifying to the unusual agitation of their minds. That they had need of tact, discretion, and judgment, not to mention patience, a bit of conversation caught up at random will perhaps best illustrate:

"An' who in the Kingdom sent in this curious cake, Miss Simpkins?" The querist was a patroness of influence.

"Kate Clark sent in that 'n', Mis' Blanks. It's a 'Will-o'-the wisp,' made out'n five times sifted flour, 'n' whites of eggs. She says she *made it up*, name an' all."

"Seem to me she'd have 'bout all she could do makin' up rhymin' po'try. What price does she put on it?"

"She wouldn't name no sum. She says she never prices the work of her mind in money, an' thet cake is jest the same to her as a po'try verse. She'll be grateful for whatever it'll fetch."

"Well, I vow! Time a person taken to writin' po'try, seem like they all but lose what little sense they got. How you goin' to sell it, 'thout no price?"

"Well, we 'lowed thet anybody thet'd wanted it'd deal *fair*. I s'pose, bein' as they's nothin' but eggs, an' only the half o' them, in it, they mus' be consider'ble flour. An' *siftin'* it five times, you know that's worrisome work. An' the eggs is well beat; you can see that. Don't you reck'n it's wuth two bits?"

"Maybe it is for them as are willin' to buy a quarter's wuth o' wind. When I want air, I'll go out dohs an' sniff it! That's all I'm askin' fo' mine, an' it iced all over, an' eight whole eggs in it, an' them beat sep'rate, an' a cup o' butter, not mentionin' the other things, nur the *extrac'*. They's a spoonful o' v'nilla extrac' in my cake if they's a drop, for I dashed it in by my eye—an' I've got what you call big eyes, come to measurin' food stuffs."

The speaker's little blue eyes snapped sharply, and she sniffed twice in hesitation, ere she proceeded, with some embarrassment:

"If you goin' to charge twenty-five cents fo' Kate Clark's pile o' baked bubbles—you can lift it an' see it's nothin' else—you better rub that twenty-five off o' my iced cake, an' put a forty on it. That's it, a four an' a ought, an' whoever buys *mine* gets four dimes' wuth o' good nour'shment, if I do say it." She moved on apace. "I see Kitty Baker's sent in a lot o' things. Well, them as want to eat after Kitty *can*—that's all *I* got to say."

"Kitty's a well-meanin' girl, Mis' Blanks, an' needy, too. S'posin' you don't say nothin' like that to nobody. I see the flour *is* caked some 'roun' the edges of her cakes, but that ain't sayin' they's anything wrong with her cookin'."

"Why, Miss Sarey *Mi*-randy Simpkins! I'm a perfessin' Christian, as you know—an' tryin' to live up to my lights. I wouldn't say nothin' to injure Kitty fo' *nothin'*. These remarks I make to you is jest 'twix' you an' me an' the bedpos'. One o' my motters is 'live an' let live,' an' another one," she added, with a laugh, " 'what don't pizen fattens.' What you askin' fo' yo' lemon pies, Miss Simpkins?"

"Twenty-five cents, Mis' Blanks."

"Mh-hm! I s'pose they're made by yo' ma's ol' receipt—three eggs to the pie, savin' out the whites to whip up fo' the top?"

" 'Deed, Mis' Blanks, Sis made 'em, an' I couldn't tell you jest how she po'tioned 'em, but I know she ca'culated thet they come to eighteen cents apiece, not countin' firewood, which, sence pore Sonny's gone, we hev to hire to have cut."

"Cert'n'y; an' yet I'd think a little thing like a pie you could slip in whils' other things are bakin'."

"That's so; we do; an' yet—Do you think two bits is too much for 'em, Mis' Blanks?"

"Law, child, the idee! I was jest a-thinkin' *this*. You know business is business, Miss Simpkins, an' I was jest a-thinkin'—they *can't noways* be more'n *five* eggs in a pie, even if they was guinea eggs—an' they's eight in my cake, *an' it iced an'* flavored. Jest rub that *four*, please'm, an' put a *five* on my cake, will you? 'Cordin' to the gen'ral valliation it's wuth a half a dollar if it's wuth a cent. Well, I mus' be goin'. What you chargin' fo' yo' bread, Miss Simpkins?"

The old lady addressed scarcely found voice to answer. "Ten cents a loaf, Mis' Blanks."

"Well, you better gimme a loaf, please'm. You see, makin' cake an' bringin' it to the Exchange, I didn't bake to-day. I s'pose you make with salt risin', don't you?"

"No, Mis' Blanks, we raise with 'eas'-cakes."

"Jest so it don't tas'e hoppy, I ain't pertic'lar; but from hoppy bread *de*liver me! Well, good-by, Miss Sarey Mirandy, honey—*good*-by, an' I'm going to pray for you to succeed. Lemme know who buys my cake. I do wish I could be there to see it cut. Well, good-by again. Law! here comes Mis' Brooks with a bundle big as a Chris'mas tree. I *must* stop an' see what she's fetchin'. I do declare this here Woman's Exchange does tickle me all but *to* death. Simpkinsville ain't been so stirred up sence the fire. Howdy, Mis' Brooks? I see you keepin' the ball a-movin'!"

"You better b'lieve I wasn't goin' to be outdid by all you smart seamsters an' fancy cooks."

And Teddy Brooks's wife, drawing off their loose wrappings of paper, set upon the table a gorgeous pair of old crystal candelabra.

"How's them for antics?" she exclaimed, resting her hands upon her fat hips, and stepping backward.

These candelabra had been the proudest possession of Teddy's mother to the day of her death. To sell them seemed sacrilege to the loyal mind of Miss Sarey Mirandy.

"Are they—for sale?" she asked, with an effort at composure.

"Why, yes, indeedy; of course they're for sale, Miss Simpkins. Ain't nobody else brought in no antics? They're the special specialities they sell *in* Exchanges, antics are. I wanted to fetch over Teddy's ma's gran'ma's belluses. The wind's all out of 'em, an' they're no good 'cept'n' *as* antics, which I nachelly *de*spise. But Teddy taken it so hard I had to leave 'em, to keep the peace. You asked if these're fo' sale—ain't everything here fo' sale, Miss Simpkins?"

"Ev'rything thet *is* is, of co'se, but they's some things thet *ain't*. Sonny's birds ain't, nor pa's an' ma's ile-painted po'traits, nor none o' them things which them thet are gone seem to stan' guard over."

"Well, the way I look at that is, if the spirits thet stan' guard over things, as you say, would jest keep 'em dusted an' cobwebbed off, so's we could be sure they *was* keepin' up with 'em, they'd be some sense in it. Teddy took on some over sellin' the ol' things, but I tol' him he hisself was the only Brooks antic I cared to keep. How much you reck'n I ought to get for 'em, Miss Simpkins?"

"I'm 'feered I was too ol' a frien' to ol' Mis' Brooks, Sally Ann, to put a price on them candelabras, but you're at liberty to put whatever tag you like on 'em; an' sis an' me'll do our part, fair and square. I see they's one dangle missin' on this one."

"Yes; I give it to the baby to cut 'is eye-teeth on, an' he dropped it, an' it snapped. The things're no manner of account. They cost a hundred dollars, an' I doubt if I'll get ten for 'em, but I'm goin' to start 'em at that, anyway. I'm dyin' for a swingin' silver-plated ice-pitcher, an' have it I will. I've got the price all to seven dollars. Teddy laid it by to have the children's pictures took, but I told him the young ones could see their pictures in the side o' the ice-pitcher." And Mrs. Brooks laughed heartily at her own humor. "When I can swing back in my red plush rockin'-chair an' tilt ice-water out of a silver-plated pitcher, I'll feel like some. I see you've got lots o' goodies for sale. I'm bound to have *somethin'* from th'Exchange for supper. What kinds have you got?" She slipped a piece of licorice-root from her pocket to her mouth as she began a circuit of the room, chewing vigorously the while. "Better do up that choc'late layer for me, Miss Simpkins," she said, finally. "Teddy don't eat choc'late, but I don' know but he's better off 'thout cake anyway. Jes' charge it, please, to Teddy—Mr. Theodore Brooks; that's it. Might's well open a 'count here first as last 'f you're goin' to have choc'late fixin's—that's the one thing I c'd get up in my sleep to eat. An' I don't know's I'll bother bakin', if you're goin' to have bread. Jest lay by a couple o' loaves every day, please."

When Mrs. Brooks passed out, the sisters, from their opposite corners of the room, managed to exchange glances, and both sighed.

When the first day was over, all the bread and rolls were sold; indeed, nearly all the housewives who had taken this first step in bread-winning went home with bought loaves under their arms. It was only after some days, when the gorgeous array of sweets was growing stale, that the sisters and their patrons began to realize that there were no buyers of luxuries in their frugal little village.

Besides several purchases of Mrs. Brooks there had been but one cake sold. The "Will-o'-the-wisp" had passed on the second day into the possession of a certain pale young telegraph operator—the same who was "keeping company" with its poetic fabricator.

Perhaps the materialistic circle of housewives, whose substantial contributions were further solidifying before their eyes, should be pardoned for the numerous pleasantries expended on this purchase. That the objects of their mirth, two ethereal young persons dealing professionally in commodities so unsubstantial as poetry and electricity, should choose "wind-cake" for nourishment, was a combination too prolific of humor to be passed by. The portly contributor of the still unsold eight-egg cake waxed especially facetious over it; and on the occasion of a unanimous vote of the "stockholders" to send the entire stale lot as a donation to the inmates of the poorhouse, she even went so far as to withdraw hers from them, and to bear it in her own hands as a gift to her friend the poetess, who, she declared, should have "one good bite o' solid substance, if she never had another."

The exclusion of confections, excepting those supplied to order, practically converted the Exchange into a bakery; for the fancy department, after passing through a fading process, had shrunken through many withdrawals, until a single glass case—an unused one among Sonny's possessions—held the entire stock.

Screened from the odium of professional bread-making by

the prestige of the "Exchange," the Misses Simpkins were thus enabled to earn in this simple manner a modest living. True, the vocation had its trials, but there were compensations.

If their delicate wrists and arms were decorated with a succession of bracelets in the shape of burns from the oven doors, if they agonized many nights over the intricacies of numerous receipts sent in by kind advisers, and were oft disquieted in spirit by the vicissitudes of salt rising, compressed yeast, or potato leaven, it was yet a new youth-restoring life to be always professedly and really busy with work that left no time for repinings.

It was a sweet secret pleasure to Miss Sarey Mirandy to make the loaves Teddy Brooks paid for as large as she dared without attracting notice. And sometimes, on anniversaries—which perhaps she alone cherished—of their young days, it pleased her tender maiden heart to slip a few raisins into his loaf, with a suspicion of cinnamon, in loving memory of his boyish fancies.

For some time she was tortured with a dread that some one should offer to buy the candelabra. Should such a time come, she would calmly reply that they were already sold, when from an old stocking she would produce one of the ten-dollar coins that represented her own funeral expenses. It should buy Teddy's wife a swinging pitcher, and the chandeliers would descend by will at her death to Teddy's daughter—his mother's namesake.

For a long time she scarcely left the house, fearing her sister should sell them during her absence. Indeed, at times she was in such a state of suppressed panic over the matter that she would gladly have bought them outright were it not for gossip. People would talk. In her calm moments she knew that no one in Simpkinsville would pay half the amount for the useless old-fashioned bric-à-brac that they had seen all their lives. In fact, she had often heard the women jokingly wonder who would buy "Mis' Brooks's antics," and "if because she'd visited in Washington"— a distant town in the State, noted for its social distinction—"she was the only person in Simpkinsville who knowed about swingin' ice-pitchers." When they "had change to fling away, they'd buy ice-pitchers for themselves, an' not swap it off for glass Noah's-ark dingle-dangles."

So in time Miss Sarey grew to feel pretty secure about the chandeliers, and at night, when her sister knitted or nodded beside her, she would often half close her eyes, and looking thus at the crystal pendants, seem to see, as the fire sparkled from the prisms, bright memory pictures of her youthful days. Herself, a rosy-faced girl with curls, often smiled at the retrospective old woman from the familiar scenes; and Teddy was there, and Sonny, and another—a boy who had not come home from the war—and every one was young, and the trees were green, producing nuts, berries, persimmons, or sustaining grape-vine swings, as reminiscence required. Only the missing dangle, on which Sally Ann's baby had cut his teeth, made a painful gap in the panorama. In this vacant place Teddy, grown palefaced and weary, seemed, somehow, always to stand, and while she looked at it, all the other pictures went out. So she would turn the defective side to the wall.

When the winter had passed, the Exchange had gone through some changes, shaping itself to the needs of the community by contraction or extension, according to indication. A few who seemed especially fitted to become at once its patrons and beneficiaries had resented its overtures as an insult, as did Mrs. Gibbs, the respected quilter of comfortables. From every point of view the Exchange was an offence unto her sensitive nostrils. To its bid for her patronage she had protested with a sniffle that "she hed never ast no mo'n they was wuth fo' her quilts, an' the day she took off two dimes on one, she'd own that she owed jest that much to every person as ever bought one. As fo' totin' the quilts around the country, she didn't know as 'twas anybody's business in special. The roads was free, and she reckoned her rheumatism was her own—not but what she'd be glad to give it to anybody that was honin' to take care of it. As to her time, she hadn't bound herself out to nobody but the good Lord, an' she 'lowed to claim the time He give her till He changed it for eternity, when she guessed she'd take that too, if the Simpkinsville folks didn't have no objections. The only vistin' she ever done was takin' orders in the spring o' the year and deliverin' her money's wuth *to a cent* in the fall. Them that thought she gadded too much was welcome to do 'thout comforts an' freeze, jest to give her the hint."

The truth was that the social side of Mrs. Gibbs's profession was her very life. A habit of spending a day with her patrons at both ends of each transaction kept her in touch with the home lives of the people. If she had conducted her business through an agent, she would long ago have shrivelled out of existence. There was much in her work to develop an interest in what to outsiders might seem trifles, such, for instance, as which among her patrons' families kicked in their sleep; and in her social rounds it became her pleasure to discover whether the solution lay in the eating of hot suppers or in guilty consciences.

If the Exchange failed to fulfil all its possibilities in some directions, it did unforeseen duty in others, especially supplying an oft-felt want in the open door which it soon offered to the passing stranger.

Simpkinsville had never boasted a hotel, and so it naturally came about that, in the common parlance of the village, travellers understood that "at the Exchange they could get comfortably et an' slep' " for a reasonable consideration. This was robbing no one, as previously it had been an unwritten law of hospitality of the town that strangers be entertained gratis. It seemed odd that its leading family, that which not only lent the dignity of its solitary gabled front to its highest eminence, but had bequeathed to Simpkinsville its name and traditions, should have been first to put a price on the bread broken with a stranger, but such is the irony of fate; for, with a sensitiveness revealed to the close observer by the slight pursing of their lips, which perhaps the wayfarer interpreted as having a mercenary meaning, these two old ladies did actually charge him twenty-five cents who consumed a hearty meal, reducing the bill with minute scrupulousness to fifteen, and even to ten cents, to such as failed in appetite. Further their most rigorous consciences did not lead them, as they agreed it was "wuth a dime to cook things an' then not see 'em et."

That they were sensitive to their changed social relations through the ever-present atmosphere of trade was evinced by a conversation one night, when Miss Sophia Falena broke a long silence by saying: "Sis hun, I been figurin' to see how we can contrive to move the Exchange out'n the parlor. When we *do* have outside comp'ny, I declare I hate to set 'em 'round that centre table piled up with sech as we been raised to offer our comp'ny free—an' it fo' sale. Time the Jenkses come in last week, an' we sat

round so solemcholy, every now 'n' ag'in glancin' at the table
which was covered up with mosquito-nettin', I vow if the thing
didn't seem to me like some sort o' corpse, an's if we were some
way holdin' a wake over it, an' oughtn't to laugh out loud."

Her sister chuckled nervously: "It's funny, sis, but, d'you
know, I thought about that too—an' maybe I oughtn't to say it,
but it 'minded me o' pore Sonny's buryin'—an' ma's an' pa's. But
I don't see how we can help it. We might clear off the table entire,
an' put the bread and rolls on shelves. I never knew of no dead
person bein' laid on a shelf—not literal, though the way they're
forgot they might's well be."

"Let's do it, sis, an' get shet o' that ghostly covered table.
Maybe you didn't take notice to it, but last Sadday when ol' Mis'
Perkins sidled up to the table so stately an' raised up the nettin',
she said the identical pertic'lar word that she said time she taken a
last look at Sonny. 'Jes' as nachel as life,' says she, jest so. Of co'se
she was referrin' to Inez Bowman's case o' wax fruits but it gimme
the cold shivers to see her standin' there ag'in a-sayin' them same
words. An' they's another thing strikes me, sis. When a day or a
night boa'der *do* drop in, it seems to me the house mus' seem sort
o' gloomy with nobody in it but a lot o' dead glass-eyed stuffed
birds an' two old ladies—which you know to outsiders we are,
sis—an' them dressed in black solid as Egyp'. Seem to me it's
enough to sort o' take away a travellin' man's appetite. How'd it
do fo' you an' me to baste a little white ruchin' in the neck an'
sleeves o' our black comp'ny dresses—not meanin' no disrespec's
to the dead, but in compliment to the livin'?"

"Well, ef you say so, sis hun. Seem like our first duty *is* to the
livin'. Maybe ef we *do* lighten our mo'nin' a little these worldly
drummers an' sech won't feel called to talk religion to us like they
do. I can see it comes purty hard on 'em."

"An' I declare, maybe it's foolish, but I *do* wish Tom wasn't a
black cat. He looks mighty doleful layin' asleep on the hearth of
evenin's. A pink ribbon 'roun' his neck wouldn't look too worldly, would it—not for the pore soulless beast, hun, of course, but
for us?"

"Why, no, I reck'n not—or a blue one. The blue bow on my
valedict'ry is purty faded, but ef you think it'd do, why, th' ain't
no use in keepin' it no longer. Ef Sonny had o' lived, an' mar-

ried—which for a man, as long as they's life they's hope—they might in time o' been sech as would care for they ol' auntie's valedict'ry. That ribbon cost five dollars a yard, in Confed'rit money, an' tain't all silk, neither—but for a cat—"

"Tain't any too good fo' Tom, sis. He's been a faithful ol' cat. But they's another p'int on my mind. Don't you think maybe we better open up Sonny's room, an' sun it good, an' reg'late it, so's ef we're pushed fo' room we could let comp'ny go up there to sleep? As tis, we can't sleep mo'n three strangers *no* way, an' if a crowd *was* to come—not thet they're likely—but I b'lieve ef we'd do it, we'd be relieved ourselves. As long as we keep it shet tight, jest the way Sonny left it, we'll feel like death is locked in—an' I don't know as it's Christian. What you say, sis?"

"Well, maybe you're right, dearie. S'pose we go up in the mornin' together. I've done started up there three times a'ready, an' my knees trembled so they give way under me—but if you was with me, maybe—You don't s'pose strangers would mind sleepin' with so many birds, do you?"

"Cert'n'y not. Why should they, less'n maybe they was high-strung, an' their minds got excited? Ef so, they *might* imagine they was all singin' at once-t, quick as the light was out. If *sech* a person was to try to sleep there—well, I dunno. They's thirty-one hundred an' sixty-three stuffed birds in that garret room, an' all in sight o' the bed."

"Shucks, sis! you're talkin' *redic'lous*—I vow ef you ain't! D'you s'pose any right-minded man would think o' sech as that? Of course we ain't goin' to put no skittish person to sleep in Sonny's room noway—jest reel gen'lemen, an' only them ef we're pushed."

"It cert'n'y do behoove us to take in all we can, hones', sis, for seem like the Exchange money don't mo'n, to say, hardly pay our boa'd somehow."

The truth was, the profits of breadmaking were steadily shrinking. Not only did Teddy Brooks's loaves grow larger and larger as he waxed paler and more careworn, but among the "customers" of the Exchange there was scarce one whose circumstances did not seem to the old ladies an appeal for generosity—hardly one who was not, as they said, "mo' in need'n we are."

It would have been a hopelessly weary business but for its rich perquisites in opportunities of sympathy and helpfulness.

The spacious garret chamber was thrown open none too soon, as only a week later it was called into unexpected requisition through the arrival, late one evening, of a party of five dust-begrimed travellers, whom the ladies would have feared to receive had they not been accompanied by a neighbor, who had taken charge of their horses, and who, in a whispered aside, announced them as "Uncle Sam's men, with a-plenty o' greenbacks," adding, *sotto-voce*, with a wink: "Kill the fatted calf for 'em, an' then charge 'em with a cow."

While the strangers sat at supper that night it was pathetic to see the solicitous scrutiny with which their hostesses scanned their faces in turn, eager for some sign by which to decide who of them all should be counted worthy to sleep in Sonny's bed. A chance remark settled the question.

"Well," said one, "I believe we are in the land of the myrtle and orange."

"Hardly," rejoined another; "but, better yet, we are in the country of the night-singing mocking-bird. Do you ladies ever hear them at night?" he added.

"From the upstairs bedroom," replied both sisters at once, while Miss Sophia continued:

"The winders open ri-ight out into the maginolia-trees, where they set and sing all night long some ni-ights."

The stranger's eyes beamed. "How delightful! If one might be so fortunate!" he replied, with a rising inflection, smiling.

"It's yore room, sir, for the night," said Miss Sophia, exchanging glances with her sister; "with whichever one o' the other gentlemen you choose. They's a wide easy-sleepin' bed in it, a-plenty broad fo' two."

"An' if you want to hear the birds sing," added Sarey Mirandy, "jest open any winder you like. They's four, not countin' the dormers, and they all open into trees, an' every tree's full of birds' nests."

"Isn't that rather remarkable? Are all the trees here full of nests?" the stranger asked.

"No, sir. Sonny—Mr. Stephen Decatur Simpkins, our brother thet's passed away—he had a gift. He got 'em to nestin' there."

"He was a lover of birds—do I understand?"

The sisters exchanged glances again, and Miss Sarey answered simply, "Yas, Sir. He was a nachelist."

"Ah, indeed!"

Around the speaker's mouth played that ghost of a smile which, being interpreted, means amused incredulity, while the conversation, becoming general, passed to other things.

With such an introduction, an hour later, Mr. John Saunders, of the Smithsonian Institution, of Washington City, accompanied by his associate Ezra Cox, proceeded, candle in hand, to the modest roof chamber that held the lifework of Stephen Decatur Simpkins, naturalist.

The next morning, though the twins appeared at breakfast in their spick white-ruched dresses, and Tom sauntered around the table resplendent in a blue neck ribbon, the ends of which hung to his knees, a distinct depression marked the spirit of the household. Despite their best efforts in the direction of cheerfulness, the twins were haggard and wan. The eyes of their guests, on the contrary, beamed with pleasure.

In the first interval of silence, after serving the dishes, Miss Sarey Mirandy, turning to the occupants of the room above, asked, timidly:

"May I ask, sir, what perfession you gen'lemen perfess?"

"Certainly, madam," replied Saunders, his eye twinkling. "The three at your left, Messrs. Green, Brown, and Black—men of color, you perceive—are members of the National Geological Survey, whom Congress has sent out here to hunt up some mineral specimens. My friend here, Mr. Cox, and I—my name is Saunders—are from the Smithsonian Institution at Washington City, at present loafers, as we are off on a vacation. We are called scientists, I believe. Naturalists is a name we like better, but really"—he hesitated for a moment as if to gain entire seriousness—"here, in the presence of your brother's beautiful work, we should appropriate the name timidly, with heads uncovered. Is this collection of birds known in the State, may I ask?"

"Well, yes, sir. I reck'n tis. Tain't never been to say *hid*. It's been right here. Th'aint nobody, black nur white, in the county, but *knows* they're here."

"It is not registered. I know of all the important recorded

collections in America. I wonder if you ladies realize what a treasure you possess? My friend and I studied it until our candle burned out. Then we crept down and begged those of our friends, and burned them up—besides one we found in the dining-room. I hope we didn't disturb you ladies?"

The sisters exchanged glances and colored.

"Th'wasn't to say 'xactly noise enough to disturb nobody, sir, ef we'd knew what it was, but th'ain't nobody slep' up in Sonny's room sence he passed away tell now, an' the sound of every footfall seemed like him back ag'in. So we nachelly kep' listenin' for 'em to stop, an' to tell the whole truth, sir, when we heard 'em so late, not knowin' nothin' 'bout you gentlemen, we got nervous an' scared like, 'n' we got up an' dressed, an' set up the live night long, 'th our vallibles all in reach—not thet you gentlemen look like peddlers, which even if you was, you might be hones'.''

The professional gentlemen present thought it unsafe to look at one another, while they expressed the sincere sorrow they felt at so unfortunate a misunderstanding. The occasion of their late hours, however, soon became the absorbing theme, resulting in a full restoration of confidence. Saunders's enthusiasm was genuine.

"I actually counted sixty-one beautiful specimens not existing in any registered collection," he said, addressing his companions.

"An' they wasn't all easy got, neither," replied Miss Sophia. "Why, Sonny slep' in a crape-myrtle tree ev'ry night for a week once't, jest to find out how a little he bird conduct hisself—ef he changed places with his settin' wife, or jest entertained 'er sett'n' on a limb beside her.''

Her interlocutor smiled. "And how was it—do you remember?"

"Well, reely—how was it, sis?"

" 'Deed, sir, I disremember. Either he did'r he didn't—one. I clean forget, but—but it's put down in the book."

"So there is a book?"

"They's five leather-backed books, sir, with nothin' but sech as that *in* 'em. Sis an' me've read in 'em some, an' for anybody that *cared* for sech, I s'pose it's good readin'. They's *one* thing, it's *true,* an' thet's more'n you can say fo' the triflin' novels thet folks pizens their minds *an'* principles with."

"You have indeed a valuable possession here, ladies. Have you ever thought of selling it?"

"Sellin' Sonny's birds? No, sir. No mo'n we'd sell pa an' ma's ile-painted po'traits, or Sonny's Confed'rit clo'es, *ragged* as they be."

"No, sir. They's some things thet money don't tech. We wouldn't sell them birds, not if we got ten cents a head for 'em an' that's mo'n most of 'em'd be wuth even if they was baked in a pie—'n' the crust an' gravy throwed in."

"But, my dear ladies," said Mr. Cox, "they are worth far more than that. As a collection they are worth considerably more than a dollar apiece—"

"Sis," said Miss Sarey Mirandy, "the gentleman don't understand. Them birds, sir, ain't nothin' but feathers an' skin, an' it full o' rank pizen arsenic. Th'ain't a blessed thing in 'em but raw cotton, an' it physicked, an' nine out'n every ten of 'em never was no 'count for either cookin' nur singin'. We wouldn't deceive you *'bout* 'em. But if they was birds o' Paridise, caught before the fall o' Adam, jest swooned away, an' li'ble to come back to life any minute, 'n' you offered us the United States Mint for 'em, even so, th'ain't for sale—*noways.*"

This was somewhat of a rebuff to the first overture of the Washington scientist, who indeed seriously meant that the Institution should become possessed of the new-found treasure, if possible. He had inserted the edge of a wedge, however, and was satisfied to wait before pressing it.

Breakfast over, it was but natural that Miss Sophia should follow the visitors into the parlor, while she, with evident and pathetic pride, exhibited the additional specimens there. When, a half-hour later, she rejoined her sister in the kitchen, she was so full to overflowing of this tender theme that some time elapsed before she remarked, in a tone betraying a secondary interest:

"Well, I reck'n Sally Ann'll have her swingin' pitcher, after all, 'cause I've done sol' the candelabras."

Miss Sarey stood kneading dough, with her back to her sister. She came near falling for a moment.

"Wh—what you say, honey? H—who bought—*what?*

She kept on kneading, and did not turn.

"That slim, light-complected one, I say, has done bought ol' Mis' Brooks's candelabras, 'n' I mus' say I never sol' a thing with a worse grace. I'm a-puttin' the ten dollars which he give for 'em here in this pink vase on the dinin'-room mantel, an' do you give it to Sally Ann, honey. I don't want nothin' to do *with* it, nor with her neither. She gets me riled enough to all but backslide 'th her 'extravagance 'n' super*flu*ousniss!'"

Miss Sarey had not realized until now how attached she had herself become to the old candlesticks. Their shimmering prisms were crystallized memories. Themselves, their long-familiar fantastic shapes, were friends antedating in association any surviving friendship.

When she had completed her task, great beads of perspiration stood upon her pale brow. Passing out, she nervously seized the ten dollars and hastened to the parlor. The purchaser stood admiring his new possession. Laying the money before him, she said, with a masterful effort at composure:

"They's been a mistake made, sir. Them candelabras is already sold."

"Indeed? I'm sorry," he said, bowing; and as she moved away, he added, "I should be glad to give five times the price—if they could be secured."

Miss Sarey Mirandy hesitated. "Sir?"

There was something almost tragic in the apprehension expressed in this one word.

The offer was repeated.

Fifty dollars! Half her secret hoard! In a twinkling the sum resolved itself into a difference in the quality of a shroud and coffin. Without apparent hesitation she replied, firmly: "The lady thet's bought 'em don't ca'culate to sell 'em. Thank you, sir." And, her old heart thumping absurdly, she went out.

Declining the fifty dollars had seemed a simple matter of decision and principle at the moment, and the offer a bribe to her loyalty; but all day, as she moved about the house, her secret kept growing, first naturally from the germ, as the extravagance seemed to grow in enormity, and then by accretion, as one by one the sundry deceptions it would involve gathered about it.

Of course, she would deal fair. Sally Ann should have the

fifty dollars. But this soon became the slightest consideration. She must not be known as the purchaser, not even to her sister. If she hadn't told her of that long-ago kiss, it would be different. Sally Ann would naturally tell every one the price she got, and she would ask questions.

For the first time in her life she was shamefaced and afraid, responding even to her sister's enthusiastic remarks about Sonny in an incoherent manner. In the midst of her greatest apprehension the front gate was heard to slam, and Sally Ann Brooks did actually appear coming up the path. Seeing her enter, however, Miss Sophia said:

"Sis, you set Sally Ann down in the parlor and talk to her, honey. I'm 'feared if I'd see her tickled over that ten dollars I might not be perlite. Maybe, if a more Christian spirit comes to me, I'll come in after whiles; but it's mos' supper-time, anyhow."

As she passed through the parlor to receive Mrs. Brooks, Miss Sarey was astounded to perceive the "red-complected" coveter of the candelabra still standing before them. If the devious ways of deceit had been an old-travelled road to her, her dilemma would have been less trying. Not to introduce those who chanced to meet in her parlor would be a social dereliction of which she was incapable. To do so in the present instance would invite disaster.

She did not hesitate. Come what would, she would be a lady worthy the name of Simpkins. What she said at the door was, "Walk right in the parlor, Sally Ann, an' I'll make you 'quainted with a gen'leman that's here from the North."

"Law, Miss Simpkins!" exclaimed Teddy's wife, shrinking back. "I ain't got on no corset nor nothin'. I jest run over in my Mother Hubbard as I was. I wouldn't go before a strange gentleman the way I am, nohow, for nothin'."

Miss Sarey Mirandy was saved. Trembling within, and with two solferino spots upon her thin cheeks, she invited her guest into her own room.

"We hear you've got a house full o' Yankees," said the guest, taking a rocking-chair; "but Mr. Jakes says they're real ni-ice, an' he says the way they're a-praisin' up Mr. Sonny Simpkins roun' town you'd think he might o' been George Washin'ton, or maybe Jeff Davis hisself."

"Yas, Sally Ann. It's been mighty gratifyin' to sis an' me to hear them a-praisin' of Sonny. One of 'em's been a-studyin' over Sonny's books the livelong day."

"Is that so? If they read them books, they mus' shorely be educated. Kitty Clark's beau says they been a-telegraphin' all day to Washin'ton City—an' he says the name o' Simpkins has gone over the wire more'n once-t, though neither he nor she nor I got any right to tell it. Three of 'em, you know, 's been out to Mr. Jakes's farm all day a-spyin' dug-up things with a spy-glass. Mr. Jakes is diggin' a new cow-pond, an' they do say he's dug up enough to undo the whole Bible. That's the way the talk's a-goin', but I'm thankful to say I was raised a good 'Piscopal Church woman—not sayin' nothin' 'g'inst the Baptists, Miss Simpkins— an' the Prayer-book don't, in no place I ever opened it, make no mention o' Mr. Jakes's cow-pond, nor the ins an' outs of it. An' talkin' 'bout the Church, Miss Simpkins, fetches me to what brought me here—not that I needed any excuse; but this is Lent, you know, in our Church, an' we're 'xpected to make some sort o' sacrerfice—if not fastin', some other—an' I thought, 'stid o' de-nyin' myself spring onions or maybe choc'let, since Teddy's mind seems to run on 'em consider'ble, I'd come over an' get them candelabras o' his ma's an' set 'em back on the mantel where she left 'em. Don't you think the Lord might take that the way it's meant, for a Lenten off'rin'?"

"I do indeed, Sally Ann, an' a good one." And she added, in a moment, "'Cause you know, honey, they *might* o' sold for what'd fetch considerable worldly vanities."

"Yes'm, so they might, tho' I doubt if th'ever would."

A moment's silence followed, broken finally by Miss Sarey.

"But I'd advise you, Sally Ann, child, to examine yore deed purty close-t before you offer it to the dear Lord, 'cause you know, honey, He sees the inside *inness* o' all our purposes. Suppose somebody, now, was to offer to buy them candelabras 'n' pay a big price, cash down. How 'bout Lent, honey?"

The old lady's heart was thumping furiously.

"Well, Miss Simpkins, tell the truth, *they couldn't get 'em*—not if they offered me the first price of 'em." Teddy Brooks's wife's eyes filled with tears as she continued: "Teddy seems right porely these days, Miss Simpkins. An' another thing I come to ask you was if you had any more o' that blackberry wine o' yores left. It helped him a heap las' spring. Some days I get so worreted the way he seems a-failin'. Seem like if he'd get good 'n' strong, I wouldn't care fo' nothin' else."

When Miss Sarey went for the wine, she moved with the alacrity of a happier and younger woman than she who had entered the room ten minutes before.

For the first time in years she kissed Teddy's wife at parting, and bade her "keep good heart, an' not forgit the good Lord loved her an' hers." And as she turned to go in, she drew a long free breath as she said to herself, "An' yet some folks'll set up an' say th'ain't no sech a thing as a special providence."

The entertaining of five strange college-bred men, who talked familiarly of things beyond their ken, albeit the bird theme was a bond of sympathy between them, was a somewhat formidable undertaking to these old timid women of narrow and hitherto protected lives, though they had congratulated themselves many times to-day that "the household was perpared for 'em, even down to Tom."

When supper was over to-night, and Mr. Saunders, with a formality that was significant, begged an interview with the ladies in the parlor, they were seized anew with a vague distrust.

These Yankee men who wore the United States initials "promiscuous" about their persons, and made so free with the telegraph, might be—what? Spies? Detectives?

Neither confided to the other what, in truth, was but a suspicion of a suspicion, as they repaired together to their chambers to secure their turkey-tail fans and fresh hemstitched handkerchiefs, and slip bits of orris root into their mouths.

The gentlemen were already assembled, and the meeting lost nothing, but rather gained, in formality on the entrance of the twins, who, bowing slightly, proceeded to seat themselves side by side upon the sofa.

"Ladies," said Mr. Saunders, rising, "yesterday a party of tired men came to your door asking for supper and a night's lodging. They had come from a distant brilliant city, with its art galleries, its institutions of learning, its glare, its music. Coming into this little inland Arkansas town, they expected to find rich, deep forests, and fertile fields tilled by true-hearted children of the soil. Within your hospitable door they hoped for what Solomon meant when he said, 'A dry morsel, and quietness therewith,' as they were both hungry and tired. Instead of a dry morsel, you have given us sumptuous fare, ladies; and for the quietness we sought, we have found—what shall I say?—the stillness of a temple, where, instead of sleeping, we have since sat in reverence. Two of us have spent a day and half a night in studying the beautiful lifework of Mr. Stephen Decatur Simpkins. Here we have found science, art, literature, romance, poetry—music, for the birds at our windows have filled the night with melody. There are in the world but two larger personal collections of birds than that we find here. There is none so exquisitely perfect in every detail. I have not found a gunshot in a single specimen, gentlemen, nor a ruffled feather—"

"Th'ain't but thirteen shot birds there," interrupted Miss Sarey Mirandy, "and them was give to Sonny. He spent five years livin' 'mongst 'em, so's they'd know 'im, before he ever ketched one."

"All the valuable known collections," resumed John Saunders, "are on exhibition in public institutions. As its representative, ladies, I am authorized to say to you that the United States government wishes to place the work of Mr. Simpkins in the Smithsonian Institution at Washington—"

Simultaneously, as if electrified, the twins rose to their feet. Miss Sophia first found voice. What she said, in a quavering tremor, was this:

"If I may please speak, sir, Sonny lived a peaceful an' law-abidin' citizen clean sence the wah—an' he hedn't no more hard feelin's to them he fit ag'in 'n we've got—not a bit. If, after all these years, the North see fit to converscate his pore voiceless birds thet show *theyselves* how harmless Sonny spent his time— not havin' even to say a shot *in* 'em—why, all we got to ask is jest wait a few more years, till two ol' women pass away, an' then, why, if the North cares for 'em, they'll be nobody lef' to claim 'em."

As she sat down, her sister spoke:

"Them words we let fall to you Northerners 'bout Sonny's Confed'rit uniform wasn't intended fo' no insult to you gen'lemen. We jest prize it, bein' his sisters, 'cause seem like it's got all his young shape in it yet—that's all. Th'ain't a livin' bit o' strife mixed in our feelin's 'bout it—not a bit. That's all we got to say, I reck'n—ain't it, sis?''

John Saunders was not the only man present who found it necessary to use his handkerchief before he could trust his voice again. There was a very tender note in it when he said:

"I have blundered shamefully, my dear ladies, and I beg you to forgive me. Your brother's property is yours. No power on earth can take it from you. The war and confiscation are no more. Were Mr. Simpkins living, he could desire no greater honor than national recognition as one of America's first naturalists. This is what we would accord him now. His work lies buried in this little town. In the national museum thousands will visit it daily. His portrait will hang beside it, and his poetic and exhaustive treatises adorn the public libraries. These books alone, describing numerous hitherto unclassified specimens, and giving original methods of capture and preservation, are worth several thousand dollars. I am not yet authorized to name a specified sum. We cannot always pay as we should like to, but I can guarantee that to the estate of Mr. Stephen Decatur Simpkins the United States will pay certainly not less than ten thousand dollars for the collection entire; it ought to be double that. We feel quite sure that when you ladies fully understand, you will not let any feeling stand in the way of his getting his full honor."

For answer the sisters turned to each other, opened their arms, and fell sobbing each upon the other's shoulder. Thus they sat for some moments, and when they raised their heads they were alone.

"I hope," said Miss Sophia, wiping her eyes, "I hope pa an' ma's been a-lookin' on an' a-list'nin', sis. Twould make 'em happier even in Heaven."

"Yas; an' Sonny too, dearie; I hope he's been present, though I doubt if he'd care so much. I b'lieve he'd 'a' cared more to be upstairs las' night a-studyin' the birds with them gen'lemen."

"I reck'n you're right, sis, an' maybe he was. I don't b'lieve the good Lord'd hinder 'im if he wanted to come."

If some supposed the fortune coming to the Misses Simpkins would prove a death-blow to the Exchange, they were mistaken.

A comfortable income gave its machinery just the lubrication it needed for smooth and happy working according to the pleasure of its proprietors.

Three years have passed since Sonny's collection of birds went to Washington, and every spring the sisters plan to go East to visit it at the Institution; but each season finds Teddy Brooks "lookin' so porely" that Miss Sarey Mirandy finds an excuse to put it off. When pressed, she did even say once to her sister:

"Though Sally Ann is growin' in grace every day, an'll make a fine woman in time if she lives, you can't put a ol' head on young shoulders; an', like as not, before we'd be halfway to Washin'ton she'd run out o' light bread an' feed Teddy on hoe-cake, which always was same as pizen to 'im even in his young days."

An Arkansas Prophet

If you would find the warmest spot in a little village on a cold day, watch the old codgers and see where they congregate. That's what the stray cats do, or perhaps the codgers follow the cats. However that may be, both can be depended upon to find the open door where comfort is. They will probably lead you to the rear end of the village store, the tobacco-stained drawing-room, where an old stove dispenses hospitality in an atmosphere like unto which, for genial disposition, there is none so unfailing.

From November to May the old stove in the back of Chris Rowton's store was, to its devotees at least, the most popular hostess in Simpkinsville. And, be it understood, her circle was composed of people of good repute. Even the cats sleeping at her feet, if personally tramps, were well connected, being lineal descendants of known cats belonging to families in regular standing. Many, indeed, were natives of the shop, and had come into this kingdom of comfort in a certain feline lying-in hospital behind the rows of barrels that flanked the stove on either side.

It was the last day of December. The wind was raw and cold, and of a fitful mind, blowing in contrary gusts, and throwing into the faces of people going in all directions various samples from the winter storehouse of the sky, now a threat, a promise, or a dare as to how the new year should come in.

"Blest if Doc' ain't got snow on his coat! Rainin' when I come in," said one of two old men who drew their seats back a little while the speaker pushed a chair forward with his boot.

"Reckon I got both froze and wet drops on me twix' this an' Meredith's," drawled the newcomer, depositing his saddle-bags beside his chair, wiping the drops from his sleeves over the stove, and spreading his thin palms for its grateful return of warm steam.

"Sleetin' out our way," remarked his neighbor, between pipe puffs. And then he added:

"How's Meredith's wife coming on, doctor? Reckon she's purty bad off, ain't she?"

The doctor was filling his pipe now and he did not answer

immediately; but presently he said, as he deliberately reached forward and, seizing the tongs, lifted a live coal to his pipe:

"Meredith's wife don't rightfully belong in a doctor's care. She ain't to say sick; she's heart-broke, that's what she is; but of co'se that ain't a thing I can tell her—or him, either.

"This has been a mighty slow and tiresome year in Simpkinsville," he added in a moment, "an' I'm glad to see it drawin' to a close. It come in with snow an' sleet an' troubles, an' seems like it's goin' out the same way—jest like the years have done three year past.

"Jest look at that cat—what a dusty color she's got between spots! Th'ain't a cat in Simpkinsville, hardly, thet don't show a trace o' Jim Meredith's Maltee—an' I jest nachelly despise it, 'cause that's one of the presents *he* brought out there—that Maltee is."

"Maltee is a good enough color for a cat ef it's kep' true," remarked old Pete Taylor—"plenty good enough ef it's kep' true; but it's like gray paint—it'll mark up most anything it's mixed with, and cloud it."

"I reckon Jim Meredith's Maltee ain't the only thing thet's cast a shade over Simpkinsville," said old Mr. McMonigle, who sat opposite.

"That's so," grunted the circle.

"That's so, shore ez you're born," echoed Pete. "Simpkinsville has turned out some toler'ble fair days since little May Meredith dropped out of it, but the sun ain't never shone on it quite the same—to my notion."

"Wonder where she is?" said McMonigle. "My opinion is she's dead, an' thet her mother knows it. I wouldn't be surprised ef the devil that enticed her away has killed her. Once-t a feller like that gits a girl into a crowded city and gits tired of her, there's a dozen ways of gittin' shet of her.

"Yas, a hundred of 'em. It's done every day, I don't doubt.

"See that stove how she spits smoke. East wind'll make her spit any day—seems to gag her.

"Yas," McMonigle chuckled softly, as he leaned forward and began poking the fire, "she hates a east wind, but she likes me—don't you, old girl? See her grow red in the face while I chuck her under the chin."

"Look out you don't chuck out a coal of fire on kitty with your foolin'," said old man Taylor. "She does blush in the face, don't she? An' see her wink under her isinglass spectacles when she's flirted with."

"That stove is a well-behaved old lady," interrupted the doctor; "reg'larly gits religion, an' shouts whenever the wind's from the right quarter—an' I won't have her spoke of with disrespect.

"If she could tell all she's heard, settin' there summer and winter, I reckon it'd make a book—an' a interestin' one, too. There's been cats and mice born in her all summer, an' birds hatched; an' Rowton tells me he's got a dominicker hen thet's reg'larly watched for her fires to go out last two seasons, so she can lay in her. An' didn't you never hear about Phil Toland hidin' a whiskey bottle in her one day last summer and smashin' a whole settin' o' eggs? The hen, she squawked out at him, an' all but skeered him to death. He thought he had a 'tackt o' the tremens, shore—an' of a adult variety."

"Pity it hadn't a-skeert him into temperance," remarked the man opposite.

"Did sober him up for purty nigh two weeks. Rowton he saw it all, an' he give the fellers the wink, an' when Phil hollered, he ast him what was the matter, an' of co'se Phil he pointed to the hen that was kitin' through the sto'e that minute, squawkin' for dear life, an' all bedaubled over with egg, an' sez he: 'What sort o' dash blanketed hens hev you got round here, settin' in stoves?' And Rowton he looks round and winks at the boys. 'Hen,' says he—'what hen? Any o' you fellers saw a hen anywhere round here?'

"Of co'se every feller swo'e he hadn't saw no hen, an' Rowton he went up to Phil and he says, says he: 'Phil,' says he, 'you better go home an' lay down. You ain't well.'

"Well, sir, Phil wasn't seen on the streets for up'ards o' three weeks after that.

"Yas, that stove has seen sights and heard secrets, too, I don't doubt.

"They say old nigger Prophet used to set down an' talk to her same ez ef she was a person, some nights, when he'd have her all to hisself. Rowton ast him one day what made him do it, and he 'lowed thet he could converse with anything that had the breath o' life in it. There is no accountin' for what notions a nigger'll take.

"No, an' there's no tellin' how much or how little they know, neither. Old Proph', half blind and foolish, limpin' round in the woods, getherin' queer roots, and talkin' to hisself, didn't seem to have no intelligence, rightly speakin', an' yet he has called out prophecies that have come true—even befo' he prophesied about May Meredith goin' wrong.

"Here comes Brother Squires, chawin' tobacco like a sinner. I do love a preacher that'll chaw tobacco.

"Hello, Brother Squires!" he called out now to a tall, clerical old man who approached the group. "Hello! what you doin' in a sto'e like this, I like to know? Th'ain't no Bibles, nor trac's for sale here, an' your folks don' eat molasses and bacon, same ez us sinners, do you?"

"Well, my friends," the parson smiled broadly as he advanced, "since you good people don't supply us with locusts and wild honey, we are reduced to the necessity of eatin' plain bread an' meat—but you see I live up to the Baptist standard as far as I can. I wear the leathern girdle about my loins."

He laid his hand upon the long leather whip which, for safe-keeping, he had tied loosely around his waist.

"Room for one more?" he added, as, declining the only vacant chair, he seated himself upon a soap-box, extended his long legs, and raised his boots upon the ledge of the stove.

"I declare, Brother Squires, the patches on them boots are better'n a contribution-box," said McMonigle, laughing, as he thrust his hand down into his pocket. "Reckon it'll take a half-dollar to cover this one." He playfully balanced a bright coin over the topmost patch on the pastor's toe.

"Stop your laughin', now, parson. Don't shake it off! Come up, boys! Who'll cover the next patch? Ef my 'rithmetic is right, there's jest about a patch apiece for us to cover—not includin' the half-soles. I know parson wouldn't have money set above his soul."

"No, certainly not, an' if anybody'd place it there, of co'se I'd remove it immediately," the parson answered, with ready wit. And then he added, more seriously:

"I have passed my hat around to collect my salary once in a while, but I never expected to hand around my old shoes—and really, my friends, I don't know as I can allow it."

Still he did not draw them in, and the three old men grew so hilarious over the fun of covering the patches with the ever-slipping coins that a crowd was soon collected, the result being the pocketing of the entire handful of money by Rowton, with the generous assurance that it should be good for the best pair of boots in his store, to be fitted at the pastor's convenience.

It was after this mirth had all subsided and the codgers had settled down into their accustomed quiet that the parson remarked, with some show of hesitation:

"My brothers, when I was coming towards you a while ago I heard two names. They are names that I hear now and then among my people—names of two persons whom I have never met—persons who passed out of your community some time before I was stationed among you. One of them, I know, has a sad history. The details of the story I have never heard, but it is in the air. Scarcely a village in all our dear world but has, no matter how blue its skies, a little cloud above its horizon—a cloud which to its people seems always to reflect the pitiful face of one of its fair daughters. I don't know the story of May Meredith—or is it May Day Meredith?"

"She was born May Day, and christened that-a-way," answered McMonigle. "But she was jest ez often called Daisy or May—any name thet'd fit a spring day or a flower would fit her."

"Well, I don't know her story," the parson resumed, "but I do know her fate. And perhaps that is enough to know. The other name you called was 'Old Proph',' or 'Prophet.' Tell me about him. Who was he? How was he connected with May Day Meredith?"

He paused and looked from one face to another for the answer, which was slow in coming.

"Go on an' tell it, Dan'l," said the doctor, finally, with an inclination of the head towards McMonigle.

Old man McMonigle shook the tobacco from his pipe, and refilled it slowly, without a word. Then he as deliberately lit it, puffed its fires to the glowing point, and took it from his lips as he began:

"Well, parson, ef I hadn't o' seen you standin' in the front o' the sto'e clean to the minute you come back here, I'd think you'd heerd more than names.

"Of co'se we couldn't put it quite ez eloquent ez you did, but we had jest everyone of us 'lowed that sence the day May Meredith dropped out o' Simpkinsville the sky ain't never shone the same.

"But for a story? Well, I don't see thet there's much story to it, and to them thet didn' know *her* I reckon it's common enough.

"But ez to the old nigger, Proph', being mixed up in it, I can't eggsac'ly say that's so, though I don't never think about the old nigger without seemin' to see little May Day's long yaller curls, an' ef I think about her, I seem to see the old man, somehow. Don't they come to you all that-a-way?"

He paused, took a few puffs from his pipe, and looked from one face to another.

"Yas," said the doctor, "jest exactly that-a-way, Dan'l. Go on, ol' man. You're a-tellin' it straight."

"Well, that's what I'm aimin' to do." He laid his pipe down on the stove's fender as he resumed his recital.

"Old Proph'—which his name wasn't Prophet, of co'se, which ain't to say a name nohow, but his name was Jeremy, an' he used to go by name o' Jerry; then somebody called him Jeremy the Prophet, an' from that it got down to Prophet, and then Proph'—and so it stayed.

"Well, ez I started to say, Proph' he was jest one o' Meredith's ol' slave niggers—a sort o' queer, half-luney, no-count darky—never done nothin' sence freedom but what he had a mind to, jest livin' on Meredith right along.

"He wasn't to say crazy, but—well, he'd stand and talk to anything—a dog, a cat, a tree, a toad-frog—*anything*. Many a time I've seen him limpin' up the road, an' he'd turn round sudden an' seemed to be talkin' to somethin' thet was follerin' him, an' when he'd git tired he'd start on an' maybe every minute look back over his shoulder an' laugh. They was only one thing Proph' was, to say, good for. Proph' was a capital A-1 hunter—shorest shot in the State, in my opinion, and when he'd take a notion he could go out where nobody wouldn't sight a bird or a squir'l all day long, an' he'd fill his game-bag.

"Well, sir, the children round town, they was all afeerd of 'im, and the niggers—th'ain't a nigger in the county thet don't b'lieve *to this day* thet Proph' would cunjer 'em ef he'd git mad.

"An' time he takin' to fortune-tellin', the school child'en

thet'd be feerd to go up to him by theirselves, they'd go in a crowd, an' he'd call out fortunes to 'em, an' they'd give him biscuits out o' their lunch-cans.

"From that time he come to tellin' anybody's fortune, an' so the young men, they got him to come to the old-year party one year, jest for the fun of it, an' time the clock was most on the twelve strike, Proph' he stood up an' called out e-vents of the comin' year. An', sir, for a crack-brained fool nigger, he'd call out the smartest things you ever hear. Every year for five year, Proph' called out comin' e-vents at the old-year party; an' matches thet nobody suspicioned, why, he'd call 'em out, an' shore enough, 'fore the year was out, the weddin's would come off. An' babies! He'd predic' babies a year ahead—not always callin' out full names, but jest insinuatin', so thet anybody thet wasn't deef in both ears would understand.

"But to come back to the story of May Meredith—he ain't in it, noways in partic'lar. It's only thet sence she could walk an' hold the ol' man's hand he doted on her, an' she was jest ez wropped up in him. Many's the time when she was a toddler he's rode into town, mule-back, with her settin' up in front of 'im. An' then when she got bigger it was jest as ef she was the queen to him—that's all. He saved her from drowndin' once-t, jumped in the branch after her an' couldn't swim a stroke, an' mos' drownded hisself—an' time she had the dip'theria, he never shet his eyes ez long ez she was sick enough to be set up with—set on the flo' by her bed all night.

"That's all the way Proph' is mixed up in her story. An' now, sence they're both gone, ef you 'magine you see one, you seem to see the other.

"But *May Day's* story? Well, I hardly like to disturb it. Don't rightly know how to tell it, nohow.

"I don't doubt folks has told you she went wrong, but that's a mighty hard way to tell it to them thet knew her.

"We can't none of us deny, I reckon, thet she went wrong. A red-cheeked peach thet don't know nothin' but the dew and the sun, and to grow sweet and purty—it goes wrong when it's wrenched off the stem and et by a hog. That's one way o' goin' wrong.

"Little Daisy Meredith didn't have no mo' idee o' harm than that mockin'-bird o' Rowton's in its cage there, thet sings week-day songs all Sunday nights.

"She wasn't but jest barely turned seventeen year—ez sweet a little girl ez ever taught a Baptist Sunday-school class—when *he* come down from St. Louis—though some says he come from Chicago, an' some says Canada—lookin' after some land mort-gages. An', givin' the devil his due, he was the handsomest man thet ever trod Simpkinsville streets—that is, of co'se, for a outsid-er. Seen May Day first time on her way to church, an' looked after her—then squared back di-rect, an' follered her. Walked into church delib'rate, an' behaved like a gentleman religiously in-clined, ef ever a well-dressed, city person behaved that way.

"Well, sir, from that day on, he froze to her, and, strange to say, every mother of a marriageable daughter in town was jealous exceptin' one, an' that one was May's own mother. An' she not only wasn't jealous—which she couldn't 'a' been, of co'se—but she wasn't pleased.

"She seemed to feel a dread of him from the start, and she treated him mighty shabby, but of co'se the little girl, she made it up to him in politeness, good ez she could, an' he didn't take no notice of it. Kep' on showin' the old lady every attention, an', when he'd be in town, most any evenin' you'd go past the Meredith gate you could see his horse hitched there—everything open and above boa'd, so it seemed.

"Well, sir, he happened to be here the time o' the old-year party, three year ago. You've been here a year and over, ain't you, parson?"

"Yes, I was stationed here at fall conference a year ago this November, you recollect."

"Yas, so you was. Well, all this is about two year befo' you come.

"Well, sir, when it was known thet May Day's city beau was goin' to be here for the party, everybody looked to see some fun, 'cause they knowed how free ol' Proph' made with comin' e-vents, an' they wondered ef he'd have gall enough to call out May Day's name with the city feller's. Well, ez luck would have it, the party was at my house that year, an' I tell you, sir, folks thet hadn't set up to see the old year out for ten year come that night, jest for fear they'd miss somethin'. But of co'se we saw through it. We knowed what fetched 'em.

"Well, sir, that was the purtiest party I ever see in my life. Our Simpkinsville pattern for young girls is a toler'ble neat one, ef I do say it ez shouldn't, bein' kin to forty-'leven of 'em. We ain't got no, to say, ugly girls in town—never had many, though some has plained down some when they got settled in years; but the girls there that night was ez pefec' a bunch of girls ez you ever see—jest ez purty a show o' beauty ez any rose arbor could turn out on a spring day.

"Have you ever went to gether roses, parson, each one seemin' to be the purtiest tell you'd got a handful, an' you'd be startin' to come away, when 'way up on top o' the vine you'd see one thet was enough pinker an' sweeter'n the rest to make you climb for it, an' when you'd get it, you'd stick it in the top of yore bo'quet a little higher'n the others?

"I see you know what I mean. Well, that was the way May Day looked that night. She was that top bud.

"I had three nieces, and wife she had sev'al cousins, there— all purty enough to draw hummin'-birds; but I say little Daisy Meredith, she jest topped 'em all for beauty and sweetness an' modesty that night.

"An' the stranger—well, I don't hardly know jest what to liken him to, less'n it is to one of them princes thet stalk around the stage an' give orders when they have play-actin' in a show-tent.

"They wasn't no flies on his shape, nor his rig, nor his manners neither. Talked to the old ladies—ricollect my wife she had a finger wropped up, an' he ast her about it and advised her to look after it an' give her a recipe for bone-felon. She thought they wasn't nobody like him. An' he jest simply danced the wall-flowers dizzy, give the fiddlers money, an'—well, he done everything thet a person o' the royal family of city gentry might be expected to do. An' everybody wondered what mo' Mis' Meredith wanted for her daughter. Tell the truth, some mistrusted, an' 'lowed thet she jest took on indifferent, the way she done, to hide how tickled she was over it.

"Well, ez I say, the party passed off lovely, an' after a while it come near twelve o'clock, an' the folks commenced to look round for ol' Proph' to come in an' call out e-vents same as he always done.

"So d'reckly the boys they stepped out an' fetched him in—drawin' him 'long by the sleeve, an' he holdin' back like ez ef he dreaded to come in.

"I tell you, parson, I'll never forgit the way that old nigger looked, longest day I live. Seemed like he couldn't sca'cely walk, an' he stumbled, an' when he taken his station front o' the mantel-shelf, look like he never would open his mouth to begin.

"An' when at last he started to talk, 'stid o' runnin' on an' laughin' an' pleggin' everybody like he always done, he lifted up his face an' raised up his hands, same ez you'd do ef you was startin' to lead in public prayer. An' then he commenced:

"Says he—an' when he started he spoke so low down in his th'oat you couldn't sca'cely hear him—says he:

" 'Every year, my friends, I stands befo' you an' look through de open gate into the new year. An',' says he, 'seem like I see a long percession o' people pass befo' me—some two-by-two, some one-by-one; some horseback, some muleback, some afoot; some cryin', some laughin'; some stumblin' ez they'd walk, an' gittin' up agin, some fallin' to rise no mo'; some faces I know, some strangers.'

"An' right here parson, he left off for a minute, an' then when he commenced again, he dropped his voice clair down into his th'oat, an' he squinted his eyes an' seemed to be tryin' to see somethin' way off like, an' he says, says he:

" 'But to-night,' says he, 'I don't know whar the trouble is,' says he, 'but, look hard ez I can, I don't seem to see clair, 'cause the sky is darkened,' says he, 'an' while I see people comin' an' goin', an' I see the doctor's buggy on the road, an' hear the church bells an' the organ, I can't make out nothin' clair, 'cause the sky is over-shaddered by a big dark cloud. An' now,' says he, 'seem like the cloud is takin' the shape of a great big bird. Now I see him spread his wings an' fly into Simpkinsville, an' while he hangs over it befo' the sun seem to me I can see everybody stop an' gaze up an' hold their breath to see where he'll light—everybody hopin' to see him light in their tree. An' now—oh! now I see him comin' down, down, down—an' now he's done lit,' says he. I ricollect that expression o' is—'he's done lit,' says he, 'in the limb of a tall maginolia-tree a little piece out o' town.'

"Well, sir, when he come to the bird lightin' in a maginolia tree, a little piece out o' town, I tell you, parson, you could 'a' heerd a pin drop. You see, maginolias is purty sca'ce in Simpkins-ville. Plenty o' them growin' round the edge o' the woods, but 'ceptin' them thet Sonny Simpkins set out in his yard years ago, I don't know of any nearer than Meredith's place. An' right at his gate, ef you ever taken notice, there's a maginolia-tree purty nigh ez tall ez a post oak.

"An' so when the ol' nigger got to where the fine bird lit in the maginolia-tree, all them thet had the best manners, they set still, but sech ez didn't keer—an' I was one of that las' sort—why, we jest glanced at the city feller di-rec' to see how he was takin' it.

"But, sir, it didn't ruffle one of his feathers, not a one.

"An' then the nigger he went on: Says he, squintin' his eyes ag'in, an' seemin' to strain his sight, says he:

" 'Now he's lit,' says he—I wish I could give it to you in his language, but I never could talk nigger talk—'now he's lit,' says he, 'an' I got a good chance to study him,' says he. 'I see he ain't the same bird he looked to be, befo' he lit.

" 'His wing feathers is mighty fine, an' they rise in mighty biggoty plumes, but they can't hide his claws,' says he, 'an' when I look close-ter,' says he, 'I see he's got owl eyes an' a sharp beak, but seem like nobody can't see 'em. They all so dazzled with his wing-feathers they can't see his claws.

" 'An' now whiles I'm a-lookin' I see him rise up an' fly three times round the tree, an' now I see him swoop down right befo' the people's eyes, an' befo' they know it he's riz up in the air ag'in, an' spread his wings, an' the sky seems so darkened thet I can't see nothin' clair only a long stream o' yaller hair floatin' behind him.

" 'Now I see everybody's heads drop, an' I hear 'em cryin'; but,' says he, 'they ain't cryin' about the thief bird, but they cryin' about the yaller hair—the yaller hair—the yaller hair.' "

McMonigle choked a little in his recital, and then he added: "Ain't that about your ricollection o' how he expressed it?"

"Yas," said old man Taylor, "he said it three times—I ricol-lect that ez long ez I live; an' the third time he said 'the yaller hair' he let his arms drop down at his side, an' he sort o' staggered back'ards, an' turned round to Johnnie Burk an' says he: 'Help me out, please sir, I feels dizzy.' Do you ricollect how he said that, Dan'l?

"But you're tellin' the story. Don't lemme interrupt you."

"No interruption, Pete. You go on an' tell it the way you call it up. I see my pipe has done gone out while I've been talkin'. Tell the truth, I'm most sorry thet you all started me on this story to-night. It gives me a spell o' the blues—talkin' it over.

"Pass me them tongs back here, doctor, an' lemme git another coal for my pipe. An' while I've got 'em I'll shake up this fire a little. This stove's ez dull-eyed and pouty ez any other woman ef she's neglected.

"Hungry, too, ain't you, old lady? Don't like wet wood, neither. Sets her teeth on edge. Jest listen at her quar'l while I lay it in her mouth.

"Go on, now Pete, an' tell the parson the rest o' the story. Tain't no more'n right thet a shepherd should know all the ins and outs of his flock ef he's goin' to take care o' their needs."

"You better finish it, Dan'l," said Taylor. "You've brought it all back a heap better'n I could 'a' done it."

"Tell the truth, boys, I've got it down to where I hate to go on," replied McMonigle, with feeling. "I've talked about the child now till I can seem to see her little slim figur' comin' down the plank-walk the way I've seen her a thousand times, when all the fellers settin' out in front o' the sto'es would slip in an' get their coats on, an' come back—I've done it myself, an' me a grand-father.

"Go on, Pete, an' finish it up. I've got the taste o' tobacco smoke now, an' my pipe is like the stove. Ef I neglect her she pouts.

"I left off where ol' Proph' finished prophesyin' at the old-year party at my house three year ago. I forgot to tell you, parson, thet Mis' Meredith, she never come to the party—an' Meredith hisself he only come and stayed a few minutes, an' went home 'count o' the ol' lady bein' by herself—so they wasn't neither one there when the nigger spoke. An' ef they've ever been told what he said I don't know—though we've got a half dozen smarties in town thet would 'a' busted long ago ef they hadn't 'a' told it, I don't doubt.

"Go on, now, Pete, an' finish. After Proph' had got done

talkin' of co'se hand-shakin' commenced, an' everybody was supposed to shake hands with everybody else. I reckon parson there knows about that—but you might tell it anyhow."

"Of co'se, parson he knows about the hand-shakin'," Taylor took up the story now, "because you was here last year, parson. You know thet it's the custom in Simpkinsville, at the old-year party, for everybody to shake hands at twelve o'clock at the comin' in of the new year. It's been our custom time out o' mind. Folks thet'll have some fallin' out, an' maybe not be speakin'll come forward an' shake hands an' make up—start the new year with a clean slate.

"Why, ef twasn't for that, I don' know what we'd do. Some of our folks is so techy an' high strung—an' so many of 'em kin, which makes it that much worse—thet ef twasn't for the new-year hand-shakin', why, in a few years we'd be ez bad ez a deef and dumb asylum.

"But to tell the story. I declare, Dan'l, I ain't no hand to tell a thing so ez to bring it befo' yo' eyes like you can. I'm feerd you'll have to carry it on."

And so old man McMonigle, after affectionately drawing a few puffs from his pipe, laid it on the fender before him, and reluctantly took up the tale.

"Well," he began, "I reckon thet rightly speakin' this is about the end of the first chapter.

"The hand-shakin' passed off friendly enough, everybody j'inin' in, though there was women thet 'lowed thet they had the cold shivers when they shuck the city feller's hand, half expectin' to tackle a bird-claw. An' I know thet wife an' me—although, understand, parson, we none o' us suspicioned no harm—we was glad when the party broke up an' everybody was gone—the nigger's words seemed to ring in our ears so.

"Well, sir, the second chapter o' the story I reckon it could be told in half a dozen words, though I s'pose it holds misery enough to make a book.

"I never would read a book thet didn't end right; in fact, I don't think the law ought to allow sech to be printed. We get enough wrong endin's in life, an' the only good book-makin' is, in my opinion, to ketch up all sech stories an' work 'em over.

"Ef I could set down an' tell May Day Meredith's story to

some book-writer thet'd take it up where I leave off, an' bring her back to us—she could even be raised from the dead *in a book* ef need be—my Lord! how I'd love to read it, an' try to b'lieve it was true! I'd like hm to work the ol' nigger in at the end, too, ef he didn't think hisself above it. A ol', harmless, half-crazy nigger, thet's been movin' round amongst us all for years, is ez much missed ez anybody else when he drops out, nobody knows how. I miss Proph' jest the same ez I miss that ol' struck-by-lightnin' sycamo'-tree thet Jedge Towns has had cut out of the co't-house yard. My mother had my gran'pa's picture framed out o' sycamo' balls gethered out of that tree forty year ago.

"But you see I'm makin' every excuse to keep from goin' on with the story, an' ef it's got to be told, well—

"Whether somebody told the Merediths about the nigger's prophecy, an' they got excited over it, an' forbid the city feller the house, I don't know, but he never was seen goin' there after that night, though he stayed in town right along for two weeks, at the end of which time he disappeared from the face o' the earth—an' she along with him.

"An' that's all the story, parson. That's three year ago lackin' two weeks, an' nobody ain't seen or heard o' May Day Meredith from that day to this.

"Of co'se girls have run away with men, an' it turned out all right—but they wasn't married men. Nobody s'picioned he was married tell it was all over an' Harry Conway he heard it in St. Louis, an' it's been found to be true. An' there's a man living in Texarkana thet testified thet he was called in to witness what he b'lieved to be a gen*uine* weddin', where the preacher claimed to come from Little Rock, an' he married May Day to that man, standin' in the blue cashmere dress she run away in. She was married by the 'Piscopal prayer-book, too, which is the only thing I felt real hard against May Day for consentin' to—she being well raised, a hard-shell Baptist.

"But o' co'se the man thet could git a girl to run away with him could easy get her to change her religion."

"Hold up there, Dan'l!" interrupted old man Taylor. "Hold on, there! Not always! It's a good many years sence my ol' woman run away to marry me, but she was a Methodist, an' Methodist she's turned me, though I've been dipped, thank God!"

62 · Ruth McEnery Stuart

"Well, of co'se, there's exceptions. An' I didn't compare you to the man I'm a-talkin' about, nohow. Besides, Methodist an' 'Piscopal are two different things," returned McMonigle.

"But, tellin' my story—or at least sence I've done told the story, I'll tell parson all I know about the old nigger, Proph', which is mighty little.

"It was jest three days after May Meredith run away thet I was ridin' through the woods twixt here an' Clay Bank, an' who did I run against but old Proph'—walkin' along in the brush talkin' to hisself ez usual.

"Well, sir, I stopped my horse, an' called him up an' talked to him, an' tried to draw him out—ast him how come he to prophesy the way he done, an' how he knowed what was comin', but, sir, I couldn't get no satisfaction out of him—not a bit. He 'lowed thet he only spoke ez it was given him to speak, an' the only thing he seemed interested in was the stranger's name, an' he ast me to say it for him over and over—he repeatin' it after me. An' then he ast me to write it for him, an' he put the paper I wrote it on in his hat. He didn't know B from a bull's foot, but I s'pose he thought maybe if he put it in his hat it might strike in."

"Like ez not he 'lowed he could git somebody to read it out to him," suggested the doctor.

"Like ez not. Well, sir, after I had give him the paper he commenced to talk about huntin'—had a bunch o' birds in his hands then, an' give 'em to me, 'lowin' all the time he hadn't had much luck lately, 'count o' his pistol bein' sort o' out o' order. 'Lowed thet he took sech a notion to hunt with his pistol thet twasn't no fun shootin' at long range, but somehow he couldn't depend on his pistol shootin' straight.

"Took it out o' his pocket while he was standin' there, an' commenced showin' it to me. An', sir, would you believe it, while we was talkin' he give a quick turn, fired all on a sudden up into a tree, an' befo' I could git my breath, down dropped a squir'l right at his feet. Never see sech shootin' in my life. An' he wasn't no mo' excited over it than nothin'. Jest picked up the squir'l ez unconcerned ez you please, an', sez he, 'Yas, she done it that time—*but she don't always do it.* Can't depend on her.'

"Then, somehow, he brought it round to ask me ef I

wouldn't loand him my revolver—jest to try it an' see if he wouldn't have better luck. 'Lowed that he'd fetch it back quick ez he got done with it.

"Well, sir, o' co'se I loaned it to the ol' nigger—an' took his pistol—then an' there. I give it to him loaded, all six barrels, an' sir, would you believe it, no livin' soul has ever laid eyes on ol' Prophet from that day to this.

"I'm mighty feered he's wandered way off som'ers an' shot hisself accidental'—an' never was found. Them revolvers is mighty resky weepons ef a person ain't got experience with 'em.

"So that's all the story, parson. Three days after May Day went he disappeared, an' of co'se he a-livin' along at Meredith's all these years, an' being so 'tached to May Day, and prophesying about her like he done, you can see how one name brings up another. So when I think about her I seem to see him."

"Didn't Harry Conway say he see the ol' man in St. Louis once-t, an' thet he let on he didn't know him—wouldn't answer when he called him Proph'?" said old man Conway.

"One o' Harry's cock-an'-bull stories," answered McMonigle. "He might o' saw some ol' nigger o' Proph's build, but how would he git to St. Louis? Anybody's common-sense would tell him better'n that. No, he's dead—no doubt about it."

"I suppose no one has ever looked for the old man?" the parson asked.

"Oh yas, he's been searched for. We've got up two parties an' rode out clair into the swamp lands twice-t—but there wasn't no sign of him.

"But May Day—nobody has ever went after her, of co'se. She left purty well escorted, an' ef her own folks never follered her, twasn't nobody else's business. Her mother ain't never mentioned her name sence she left—to nobody."

"Yas," interrupted the doctor, "an' some has accused her o' hard-heartedness; but when I see a woman's head turn from black to white in three months' time, like hers done, I don't say her heart's hard, I say it's broke.

"They keep a-sendin' for me to come to see her, but I can't do her no good. She's failed tur'ble last six months.

"Ef somethin' could jest come upon her sudden, to rouse her

up—ef the house would burn down, an' she have to go out 'mongst other folks—or ef they was some way to git folks there, whether she wanted 'em or not—

"Tell the truth, I've been a-thinkin' about somethin'. It's been on my mind all day. I don't know ez it would do, but I been a-thinkin' ef I could get Meredith's consent for the Simpkinsville folks to come out in a body—

"Ef he'd allow it, an' the folks would be willin' to go out there to-night for the old-year party—take their fiddle an' cakes an' things along, an' surprise her—she'd be obliged to be polite to 'em; she couldn't refuse to meet all her ol' friends for the midnight hand-shakin', an' it might be the savin' of her. Three years has passed. There's no reason why one trouble should bring another. We've all had our share o' trials this year, an' I reckon every one o' us here has paid for a tombstone in three years, an' I believe ef we'd all meet together an' go in a body out there—

"Ef you say so, I'll ride out an' talk it over with Meredith. What's your opinion, parson?"

"My folks will join you heartily, I'm sure," replied the parson, warmly. "They did expect to have the crowd over at Bradfield's to-night, but I know they'll be ready to give in to the Meredith's."

And this is how it came about that the Meredith's house, closed for three years, opened its doors again.

If innocent curiosity and love of fun had carried many to the new-year hand-shaking three years before, a more serious interest, not unmixed with curiosity, swelled the party to-night.

It was a mile out of town. The night was stormy, the roads were heavy, and most of the wagons without cover; but the festive spirit is impervious to weather the world over, and there were umbrellas in Simpkinsville, and overcoats and "tarpaulins."

Everybody went. Even certain good people who had not previously been able to master their personal animosities sufficiently to resolve to present themselves for the midnight hand-shaking, and had decided to nurse their grievances for another year, now promptly agreed to bury their little hatchets and join the party.

To storm a citadel of sorrow, whether the issue should prove a victory for besiegers or besieged, was no slight lure to a people whose excitements were few, and whose interests were limited to the personal happenings of their small community.

It is a crime in the provincial code-social to excuse one's self from a guest. To deny a full and cordial reception to all the town would be to ostracise one's self forever, not only from its society, but from all its sympathies.

The weak-hearted hostess rallied all her failing energies for the emergency. And there was no lack of friendliness in her pale old face as she greeted her most unwelcome guests with extended timorous hands.

If her thin cheeks flushed faintly as her neighbors' happy daughters passed before her in game or dance, her solicitous observers, not suspecting the pain at her heart, whispered: "Mis' Meredith is chirpin' up a'ready. She looks a heap better'n when we come in." So little did they understand.

If mirth and numbers be a test, the old-year party at the Merediths' was assuredly a success.

Human emotions swing as pendulums from tears to laughter. Those of the guests to-night who had declared that they knew they would burst out crying as soon as they entered that house were the ones who laughed the loudest.

"Spinning the plate," "dumb-crambo," "pillow," "how, when and where," such were the innocent games that composed the simple diversions of the evening, varied by music by the village string-band and occasional songs from the girls, all to end with a "Virginia break-down" just before twelve o'clock, when the handshaking should begin.

It seemed a very merry party, and yet, in speaking of it afterwards, there were many who declared that it was the saddest evening they had ever spent in their lives, some even affirming that they had been "obliged to set up an' giggle the live-long time to keep from cryin' every time they looked at Mis' Meredith."

Whether this were true, or only seemed to be true in the light of subsequent events, it would be hard to say. Certain it was, however, that the note that rose above the storm and floated out into the night was one of joyous merrymaking. Such was the note that greeted a certain slowly moving wagon, whose heavily clogged wheels turned into the Merediths' gate near midnight. The belated guest was evidently one entirely familiar with the premises, for notwithstanding the darkness of the night, the ponderous wheels turned accurately into the curve beyond the magnolia-tree, moved slowly but surely along the drive up to the door, and stopped without hesitation exactly opposite the "landing at the front stoop," well-nigh invisible in the darkness.

After the ending of the final dance, during the very last moments of the closing year, there was always at the old-year party an interval of silence.

The old men held their watches in their hands, and the young people spoke in whispers.

It was this last waiting interval that in years past the old man Prophet had filled with portent, even though, until his last prophecy, his words had been lightly spoken.

As the crowd sat waiting to-night, watching the slow hands of the old clock, listening to the never-hurrying tick-tack of the long pendulum against the wall, it is probable that memory, quickened by circumstances and environment, supplied to every mind present a picture of the old man, as he had often stood before them.

A careful turn of the front-door latch, so slight a click as to be scarcely discernible, came at this moment as the clank of a sledge-hammer, turning all heads with a common impulse towards the slowly opening door, into which limped a tall, muffled figure. To the startled eyes of the company it seemed to reach quite to the ceiling. Those sitting near the door started back in terror at the apparition, and all were on their feet in a moment.

But having entered, the figure halted just within the door, and before there was time for action, or question even, a bundle of old wraps had fallen and the old man Prophet, bearing in his arms a golden-haired cherub of about two years, stood in the presence of the company.

The revulsion of feeling, indescribable by words, was quickly told in fast-flowing tears. Looking upon the old negro and the child, everyone present read a new chapter in the home tragedy, and wept in its presence.

Coming from the dark night into the light, the old man could not for a moment discern the faces he knew, and when the little one, shrinking from the glare, hid her face in his hair, it was as if time had turned back, so perfect a restoration was the picture of a familiar one of the old days. No word had yet been spoken, and the ticking of the great clock, and the crackling of the fire mingled with sobs, were the only sounds that broke the stillness when the old man, having gotten his bearings, walked directly up to Mrs. Meredith and laid the child in her arms. Then, losing no time, but pointing to the clock that was slowly nearing the hour, he said, in a voice tremulous with emotion: "De time is most here. Is you all ready to shek hands?" Ef you is—*everybody*—turn round and come wid me."

As he spoke he turned back to the still open door, and before those who followed had taken in his full meaning, he had drawn into the room a slim, shrinking figure, and little May Day Meredith, pale, frightened and weather-beaten, stood before them.

If it was her own father who was first to grasp her hand, and if he carried her in his arms to her mother, it was that the rest deferred to his first claim, and that their hearty and affectionate greetings came later in their proper order. As the striking of the great clock mingled with the sound of joy and of weeping—the congratulations and words of praise fervently uttered—it made a scene ever to be held dear in the annals of Simpkinsville. It was a scene beyond words of description—a family meeting which even life-time friends recognized as too sacred for their eyes, and hurried weeping away.

It was when the memorable, sad, joyous party was over, and all the guests were departing, that Prophet, following old man McMonigle out, called him aside for a moment. Then putting into his hands a small object, he said, in a tremulous voice:

"Much obleeged for de loand o' de pistol, Marse Dan'l. Hold her keerful, caze she's loaded des de way you loaded her—all 'cept one barrel. I ain't nuver fired her but once-t."

The Unlived Life of
Little Mary Ellen

When Simpkinsville sits in shirt-sleeves along her store fronts in summer, she does not wish to be considered *en déshabille*. Indeed, excepting in extreme cases, she would—after requiring that you translate it into plain American, perhaps—deny the soft impeachment.

Simpkinsville knows about coats, and she knows about ladies, and she knows that coats and ladies are to be taken together.

But there are hot hours during August when nothing should be required to be taken with anything—unless, indeed, it be ice—with everything excepting more ice.

During the long afternoons in fly-time no woman who has any discretion—or, as the Simpkinsville men would say, any "management"—would leave her comfortable home to go "hangin' roun' sto'e counters to be waited on." And if they will—as they sometimes do—why, let them take the consequences.

Still, there are those who, from the simple prestige which youth and beauty give, are regarded in the Simpkinsville popular mind-masculine as belonging to a royal family before whom all things must give way—even shirt-sleeves.

For these, and because any one of them may turn her horse's head into the main road and drive up to any of the stores any hot afternoon, there are coat-pegs within easy reach upon the inside door-frames—pegs usually covered with the linen dusters and seersucker cutaways of the younger men without.

Very few of the older ones disturb themselves about these trivial matters. Even the doctors, of whom there are two in town, both "leading physicians," are wont to receive their most important "office patients" in this comfortable fashion as, palmetto fans in hand, they rise from their comfortable chairs, tilted back against the weather-boarded fronts of their respective drug-stores, and step forward to the buggies of such ladies as drive up for quinine and capsules, or to present their ailing babies for open-air glances at their throats or gums, without so much as displacing their linen lap-robes.

When any of the village belles drive or walk past, such of the commercial drummers as may be sitting trigly coated, as they sometimes do, among the shirt-sleeves, have a way of feeling of their ties and bringing the front legs of their chairs to the floor, while they sit forward in supposed parlor attitudes, and easily doff their hats with a grace that the Simpkinsville boys fiercely denounce while they vainly strive to imitate it.

A country boy's hat will not take on that repose which marks the cast of the metropolitan hatter, let him try to command it as he may.

It was peculiarly hot and sultry to-day in Simpkinsville, and business was abnormally dull—even the apothecary business—this being the annual mid-season's lull between spring fevers and green chinquapins.

Old Dr. Alexander, after nodding for an hour over his fan beneath his tarnished gilt sign of the pestle and mortar, had strolled diagonally across the street to join his friend and *confrère*, Dr. Jenkins, in a friendly chat.

The doctors were not much given to this sort of sociability, but sometimes when times were unbearably dull and healthy, and neither was called to any one else, they would visit one another and talk to keep awake.

"Well, I should say so!" The visitor dropped into the vacant chair beside his host as he spoke. "I should say so. Ain't it hot enough *for you?* Ef it ain't, I'd advise you to renounce yo' religion an' prepare for a climate thet'll suit you."

This pleasantry was in reply to the common summer-day greeting. "Hot enough for you to-day, doc'?"

"Yas," continued the guest, as he zigzagged the back legs of his chair forward by quick jerks until he had gained the desired leaning angle—"Yas, it's too hot to live, an' not hot enough to die. I reckon that's why we have so many chronics a-hangin' on."

"Well, don't let's quarrel with sech as the Lord provides, doctor," replied his host, with a chuckle. "Ef it wasn't for the chronics, I reckon you an' I'd have to give up practisin' an' go to makin' soap. Ain't that about the size of it?"

"Yas, chronics an'—an' babies. Ef *they* didn't come so punctual, summer an' winter, I wouldn't be able to feed mine thet're a'ready here. But talkin' about the chronics, do you know, doctor, thet sometimes when I don't have much else to think about, why, I think about them. It's a strange providence to me thet keeps people a-hangin' on year in an' year out, neither sick nor well. I don't doubt the Almighty's goodness, of co'se; but we've got Scripture for callin' Him the Great Physician, an' why, when He could ef He would, He don't—"

"I wouldn't dare to ask myself questions as that, doctor, ef I was you. *I* wouldn't, I know. Besides"—and now he laughed— "besides, I jest give you a reason for lettin' 'em remain as they are—to feed us poor devils of doctors. An' besides that, I've often seen cases where it seemed to me they were allowed to live to sanctify them thet had to live *with* 'em. Of co'se in this I'm not speakin' of great sufferers. An' no doubt they all get pretty tired an' wo'e out with themselves sometimes. I do with myself, even, an' I'm well. Jest listen at them boys a-whistlin' 'After the Ball' to Brother Binney's horse's trot! They haven't got no mo' reverence for a minister o' the gospel than nothin'. I s'pose as long as they ricollect his preachin' against dancin' they'll make him ride into town to that sort o' music. They've made it up among 'em to do it. Jest listen—all the way up the street that same tune. An' Brother Binney trottin' in smilin' to it."

While they were talking the Rev. Mr. Binney rode past, and following, a short distance behind him, came a shabby buggy, in which a shabby woman sat alone. She held her reins a trifle high as she drove, and it was this somewhat awkward position which revealed the fact, even as she approached in the distance, that she carried what seemed an infant lying upon her lap.

"There comes the saddest sight in Simpkinsville, doctor. I notice them boys stop their whistlin' jest as soon as her buggy turned into the road. I'm glad there's some things they respect," said Dr. Alexander.

"Yas, and I see the fellers at Rowton's sto'e are goin' in for their coats. She's drawin' rein there now."

"Yas, but she ain't more'n leavin' an order, I reckon. She's comin' this way."

The shabby buggy was bearing down upon them now, indeed, and when Dr. Jenkins saw it he too rose and put on his coat.

As its occupant drew rein he stepped out to her side, while his companion, having raised his hat, looked the other way.

"Get out an' come in, Mis' Bradley." Dr. Jenkins had taken her hand as he spoke.

"No, thanky, doctor. Taint worth while. I jest want to consult you about little Mary Ellen. She ain't doin' well, some ways."

At this she drew back the green barège veil that was spread over the bundle upon her lap, exposing, as she did so, the blond head and chubby face of a great wax doll, with eyes closed as if in sleep.

The doctor laid the veil back in its place quickly.

"I wouldn't expose her face to the evenin' sun, Mis' Bradley," he said, gently. "I'll call out an' see her to-morrow; an' ef I was you I think I'd keep her indoors for a day or so." Then as he glanced into the woman's haggard and eager face, he added: "She's gettin' along as well as might be expected, Mis' Bradley. But I'll be out to-morrow, an' fetch you somethin' thet'll put a little color in yo' face."

"Oh, don't mind me, doctor," she answered, with a sigh of relief, as she tucked the veil carefully under the little head. "Don't mind me. I ain't sick. Ef I could jest see her pick up a little, why, I'd feel all right. When you come to-morrer, better fetch somethin' she can take, doctor. Well, good-bye."

"Good-bye, Mis' Bradley."

It was some moments before either of the doctors spoke after Dr. Jenkins had returned to his place. And then it was he who said:

"Talkin' about the ways o' Providence, doctor, what do you call that?"

"That's one o' the mysteries thet it's hard to unravel, doctor. Ef anything would make me doubt the mercy of God Almighty, it would be some sech thing as that. And yet—I don't know. Ef there ever was a sermon preached without words, there's one preached along the open streets of Simpkinsville by that pore little half-demented woman when she drives into town nursin' that wax doll. An' it's preached where it's much needed, too—to our young people. There ain't many preachers that can reach 'em, but—Did you take notice jest now how, as soon as she turned into the road, all that whistlin' stopped? They even neglected to worry Brother Binney. An' she's the only woman in town thet'll make old Rowton put on a coat. He'll wait on yo' wife or mine in his shirt-sleeves, an' it's all right. But there's somethin' in that broken-hearted woman nursin' a wax doll thet even a fellow like Rowton'll feel. Didn't you ever think thet maybe you ought to write her case up, doctor?"

"Yas; an' I've done it—as far as it goes. I've called it 'A Psychological Impossibility.' An' then I've jest told her story. A heap of impossible things have turned out to be facts—facts that had to be argued backward from. You can do over argiments, but you can't undo facts. Yas, I've got her case all stated as straight as I can state it, an' some day it'll be read. But not while she's livin'. Sir? No, not even with names changed an' everything. It wouldn't do. It couldn't help bein' traced back to her. No; some day, when we've all passed away, likely, it'll all come out in a medical journal, signed by me. An' I've been thinkin' thet I'd like to have you go over that paper with me some time, doctor, so thet you could testify to it. An' I thought we'd get Brother Binney to put his name down as the minister thet had been engaged to perform the marriage, an' knew all the ins and outs of it. And then it'll hardly be believed."

Even as they spoke they heard the whistling start up again along the street, and, looking up, they saw the Rev. Mr. Binney approaching.

"We've jest been talkin' about you, Brother Binney—even before the boys started you to dancin'." Dr. Jenkins rose and brought out a third chair.

"No," answered the dominie, as with a goodnatured smile he dismounted. "No, they can't make me dance, an' I don't know as it's a thing my mare'll have to answer for. She seems to take naturally to the sinful step, an' so, quick as they start a-whistlin', I try to ride as upright an' godly as I can, to sort o' equalize things. How were you two discussin' me, I'd like to know?"

He put the question playfully as he took his seat.

"Well, we were havin' a pretty serious talk, brother," said Dr. Jenkins—"a pretty serious talk, doc' and me. We were talkin' about pore Miss Mary Ellen. We were sayin' thet we reckoned ef there were any three men in town thet were specially qualified to testify about her case, we must be the three—you an' him an' me. I've got it all written out, an' I thought some day I'd get you both to read it over an' put your names to it, with any additions you might feel disposed to make. After we've all passed away, there ought to be some authorized account. You know about as much as we do, I reckon, Brother Binney."

"Yes, I s'pose I do—in a way. I stood an' watched her face durin' that hour an' a quarter they stood in church waitin' for Clarence Bradley to come. Mary Ellen never was to say what you'd call a purty girl, but she always did have a face thet would hold you ef you ever looked at it. An' when she stood in church that day, with all her bridesmaids strung around the chancel, her countenance would 'a' done for any heavenly picture. An' as the time passed, an' he didn't show up—Well, I don't want to compare sinfully, but there's a picture I saw once of Mary at the Cross—Reckon I ought to take that back, lest it might be sinful; but there ain't any wrong in my telling you here thet as I stood out o' sight, waitin' that day in church, behind the pyramid o' flowers the bridesmaids had banked up for her, with my book open in my hand at the marriage service, while we waited for him to come, as she stood before the pulpit in her little white frock and wreath, I could see her face. An' there came a time, after it commenced to get late, when I fell on my knees."

The good man stopped speaking for a minute to steady his voice.

"You see," he resumed, presently, "we'd all heard things. I *knew* he'd *seemed* completely taken up with this strange girl; an' when at last he came for me to marry him and Mary Ellen, I never was so rejoiced in my life. Thinks I, I've been over-suspicious. Of co'se I knew he an' Mary Ellen had been sweethearts all their lives. I tell you, friends, I've officiated at funerals in my life— buried little children an' mothers of families—an' I've had my heart in my throat so thet I could hardly do my duty; but I tell you I never in all my life had as sad an experience as I did at little Mary Ellen Williams's weddin'—the terrible, terrible weddin' thet never came off."

"An' I've had patients," said Dr. Jenkins, coming into the pause—"I've had patients, Brother Binney, thet I've lost—lost 'em because the time had come for 'em to die—patients thet I've grieved to see go more as if I was a woman than a man, let alone a doctor; but I never in all my life come so near *clair* givin' way an' breakin' down as I did at that weddin' when you stepped out an' called me out o' the congregation to tell me she had fainted. God help us, it was terrible! I'll never forget that little white face as it lay so limpy and still against the lilies tied to the chancel rail, not ef I live a thousand years. Of co'se we'd all had our fears, same as you. We knew Clarence's failin', an' we saw how the yaller-haired girl had turned his head; but, of co'se when it come to goin' into the church, why, we thought it was all right. But even after the thing had happened—even knowin' as much as I did—I never to say fully took in the situation till the time come for her to get better. For two weeks she lay 'twixt life an' death, an' the one hope I had was for her to recognize me. She hadn't recognized anybody since she was brought out o' the church. But when at last she looked at me one day, an' says she, 'Doctor—what you reckon kep' him—so late?' I tell you I can't tell you how I felt."

"What did you say, doctor?"

It was the minister who ventured the question.

"What can a man say when he ain't got nothin' to say? I jest said, 'Better not talk any to-day, honey.' An' I turned away an' made pertence o' mixin' powders—*an'* mixed 'em, for that matter—give her sech as would put her into a little sleep. An' then I set by her till she drowsed away. But when she come out o' that sleep an' I see how things was—when she called herself Mis' Bradley an' kep' askin' for him, an' I see she didn't know no better, an' likely never would—God help me! but even while I prescribed physic for her to live, in my heart I prayed to see her die. She thought she had been married, an' from that day to this she ain't never doubted it. Of co'se she often wonders why he don't come home an' sence that doll come, she—"

"Didn't it ever strike you as a strange providence about that doll—thet would allow sech a thing, for instance, doctor?"

Dr. Jenkins did not answer at once.

"Well," he said, presently, "Yas—yas an' no. Ef a person looks at it *close-t enough*, it ain't so hard to see mercy in God's judgments. I happened to be at her bedside the day that doll come in—Christmas Eve four years ago. She was mighty weak an' porely. She gen'ally gets down in bed 'long about the holidays, sort o' reelizin' the passin' o' time, seein' he don't come. She had been so werried and puny thet the old nigger 'Pollo come for me to see her. An', well, while I set there tryin' to think up somethin' to help her, 'Pollo, he fetched in the express package."

"I've always blamed her brother, Brother Binney," Dr. Alexander interposed, "for *allowin'* that package to go to her."

"*Allowin'!* Why, he never allowed it. You might jest as well say you blame him for namin' his one little daughter after her aunt Mary Ellen. That's how the mistake was made. No, for my part I never thought so much of Ned Williams in my life as I did when he said to me the day that baby girl was born, 'Ef it's a girl, doctor, we're a-goin' to name it after sis' Mary Ellen. Maybe it'll be a comfort to her.' An' they did. How many brothers, do you reckon, would name a child after a sister thet had lost her mind over a man thet had jilted her at the church door, an' called herself by his name ever sence? Not many, I reckon. No, don't blame Ned—for anything. He hoped she'd love the little thing, an' maybe it would help her. An' she did notice it consider'ble for a while, but it didn't seem to have the power to bring her mind straight. In fact, the way she'd set an' look at it for hours, an' then go home an' set down an' seem to be thinkin', makes me sometimes suspicion thet that was what started her a-prayin' God to send her a child. She's said to me more than once-t about that time—she'd say, 'You see, doctor, when he's away so much—ef it was God's will—a child would be a heap o' company to me while he's away.' This, mind you, when he hadn't shown up at the weddin'; when we all knew he ran away an' married the yaller-hair that same night. Of co'se it did seem a strange providence to be sent to a God-fearin' woman as she always was; it did seem strange thet she should be allowed to make herself redic'lous carryin' that wax doll around the streets; an' yet, when you come to think—"

"Well, I say what I did befo'," said Dr. Alexander. "Her brother should 'a' *seen* to it thet no sech express package intended for his child should 'a' been sent to the aunt—not in her state o' mind."

"How could he see to it when he didn't send it—didn't know it was comin'? Of co'se we Simpkinsville folks, we all know thet she's called Mary Ellen, an' thet Ned's child has been nicknamed

Nellie. But his wife's kin, livin' on the other side o' the continent, they couldn't be expected to know that, an' when they sent her that doll, why, they nachelly addressed it to her full name; an' it was sent up to Miss Mary Ellen's. Even then the harm needn't to've been done exceptin' for her bein' sick abed, an' me, her doctor, hopin' to enliven her up a little with an unexpected present, makes the nigger 'Pollo set it down by her bedside, and opens it befo' her eyes, right there. Maybe I'm to blame for that—*but I ain't*. We can't do mo' than *try* for the best. I thought likely as not Ned had ordered her some little Christmas things— as he had, in another box."

The old doctor stopped, and, taking out his handkerchief, wiped his eyes.

"Of co'se, as soon as I see what it was, I knew somebody had sent it to little Mary Ellen, but—

"You say Brother Binney, thet the look in her face at the weddin' made you fall on yo' knees. I wish you could 'a' seen the look thet come into her eyes when I lifted that doll-baby out of that box. Heavenly Father! That look is one o' the things thet'll come back to me sometimes when I wake up too early in the mornin's, an' I can't get back to sleep for it. But at the time I didn't fully realize it, somehow. She jest reached an' took the doll out o' my hands, an' turnin' over, with her face to the wall, held it tight in her arms without sayin' a word. Then she lay still for so long that-a-way thet by-an'-bye I commenced to get uneasy less'n she'd fainted. So I leaned over an' felt of her pulse, an' I see she was layin' there cryin' over it without a sound—an' I come away. I don't know how came I to be so thick-headed, but even then I jest supposed thet seein' the doll nachelly took her mind back to the time she was a child, an' that in itself was mighty sad an' pitiful to me, knowin' her story, and I confess to you I was glad there wasn't anybody I had to speak to on my way out. I tell you I was about cryin' myself—jest over the pitifulness of even that. But next day when I went back of co'se I see how it was. She never had doubted for a minute thet that doll was the baby she'd been prayin' for—not a minute. An' she don't, *not to this day*—straight as her mind is on some things. That's why I call it a psychological impossibility, she bein' so rational an' so crazy at the same time. Sent for me only last week, an' when I got there I found her settin' down with *it* a-layin' in her lap, an' she lookin' the very picture of despair. 'Doctor,' says she, 'I'm sure they's mo' wrong with Mary Ellen than you let on to me. *She don't grow, doctor.'* An' with that she started a-sobbin' an' a-rockin' back an' fo'th over it. 'An' even the few words she could say, doctor, she seems to forget 'em,' says she. 'She ain't called my name for a week.' It's a fact; the little talkin'-machine inside it has got out o' fix some way, an' it don't say 'mamma' and 'papa' any mo'.''

"Have you ever thought about slippin' it away from her, doctor, an' seein' if maybe she wouldn't forget it? Ef she was my patient I'd try it."

"Yas, but you wouldn't keep it up. I did try it once-t. Told old Milly thet ef she fretted too much not to give her the doll, but to send for me. An' she did—in about six hours. An' I—well, when I see her face I jest give it back to her. An' I'll never be the one to take it from her again. It comes nearer givin' her happiness than anything else could—an' what could be mo' innocent? She's even mo' contented since her mother died an' there ain't anybody to prevent her carryin' it on the street. I know it plegged Ned at first to see her do it, but he's never said a word. He's one in a thousand. He cares mo' for his sister's happiness than for how she looks to other folks. Most brothers don't. There ain't a mornin' but he drives in there to see ef she wants anything, an', of co'se, keepin' up the old place jest for her to live in it costs him consider'ble. He says she wouldn't allow it, but she thinks Clarence pays for everything, an' of co'se he was fully able."

"I don't think it's a good way for her to live, doctor, in that big old place with jest them two old niggers. I never have thought so. Ef she was *my* patient—"

"Well, pardner, that's been talked over between Ned an' his wife, an' they've even consulted me. An' I b'lieve she ought to be let alone. Those two old servants take about as good care of her as anybody could. Milly nursed her when she was a baby, an' she loves the ground she walks on, an' she humors her in everything. Why, I've gone out there an' found that old nigger walkin' that doll up an' down the po'ch, singing to it for all she was worth; an' when I'd drive up, the po' ol' thing would cry so she couldn't go in the house for ten minutes or mo'. No, it ain't for us to take away sech toys as the Lord sends to comfort an' amuse his little ones;

an' the weak-minded, why, they always seem that-a-way to me. An' sometimes, when I come from out of some of our homes where everything is regular and straight accordin' to our way o' lookin' at things, an' I see how miserable an' unhappy everything *is*, an' I go out to the old Williams place, where the birds are singin' in the trees an' po' Miss Mary Ellen is happy sewin' her little doll-clo'es, an' the old niggers ain't got a care on earth but to look after her—Well, I dun'no'. Ef you'd dare say the love o' God wasn't there, *I* wouldn't. Of co'se she has her unhappy moments, an' I can see she's failin' as time passes; but even so, ain't *this* for the best? They'd be somethin' awful about it, *to me*, ef she kep' a-growin' stronger through it all. One o' the sweetest providences o' sorrow is thet we poor mortals fail under it. There ain't a flower thet blooms but some seed has perished for it."

It was at a meeting of the woman's prayer-meeting, about a week after the conversation just related, that Mrs. Blanks, the good sister who led the meeting, rose to her feet, and, after a silence that betokened some embarrassment in the subject she essayed, said:

"My dear sisters, I've had a subjec' on my mind for a long time, a subjec' thet I've hesitated to mention, but the mo' I put it away the mo' it seems to come back to me. I've hesitated because she's got kin-folks in this prayer-meetin', but I don't believe thet there's anybody kin to Miss Mary Ellen thet feels any nearer to her than what the rest of us do."

"Amen!" "Amen!" and "Amen!" came in timid women's voices from different parts of the room.

"I know how you all feel befo' you answer me, my dear sisters," she continued, presently. "And now I propose to you thet we, first here as a body of worshippers, an' then separately as Christian women at home in our closets, make her case a subjec' of special prayer. Let us ask the good Lord to relieve her—jest so—*unconditionally;* to take this cloud off her life an' this sorrow off our streets, an' I believe He'll do it."

There were many quiet tears shed in the little prayer-meeting that morning as, with faltering voice, one woman after another spoke her word of exhortation or petition in behalf of the long-suffering sister.

That this revival of the theme by the wives and mothers of the community should have resulted in renewed attentions to the poor distraught woman was but natural. It is sound orthodoxy to try to help God to answer our prayers. And so the faithful women of the churches—there were a few of every denomination in town in the union prayer-meeting—began to go to her, fully resolved to say some definite word to win her, if possible, from her hallucination, to break the spell that held her; but they would almost invariably come away full of contrition over such false and comforting words as they had been constrained to speak "over a soulless and senseless doll."

Indeed, a certain Mrs. Lynde, one of the most ardent of these good women, but a sensitive soul withal, was moved, after one of her visits, to confess in open meeting both her sin and her chagrin in the following humiliating fashion:

"I declare I never felt so 'umbled in my life ez I did after I come away from there, a week ago come Sunday. Here I goes, full of clear reasonin' an' Scripture texts, to try to bring her to herself, an' I ain't no mo'n set down sca'cely, when I looks into her face, as she sets there an' po's out her sorrers over that ridic'lous little doll, befo' I'm consolin' her with false hopes, like a perfec' Ananias an' Sapphira. Ef any woman could set down an' see her look at that old doll's face when she says, 'Honey, do you reckon I'll ever raise her, when she keeps so puny?'—I say ef any woman with a human heart in her bosom could hear her say that, an' not tell her, 'Cert'n'y she'd raise her,' an' that 'punier children than that had growed up to be healthy men an' women'—well, maybe they might be better Christians than I am, but I don't never expec' to be sanctified up to that point. I know I'm an awful sinner, deservin' of eternal punishment for deceit which is the same as a lie, but I not only told her I thought she could raise her, but I felt her pulse, an' said it wasn't quite what a reel hearty child's ought to be. Of co'se I said that jest to save myself from p'int-blank lyin'. An' then, when I see how it troubled her to think it wasn't *jest right*, why, God forgive me, but I felt it over again, an' counted it by my watch, an' then I up an' told her it was *all right*, an' thet ef it had a-been any different to the way it was under the circumstances, I'd be awful fearful, which, come to think of it, that last is true ez God's word, for ef I'd a-felt a pulse in that doll's wrist—

which, tell the truth, I was so excited while she watched me I half expected to feel it pulsate—I'd 'a' shot out o' that door a ravin' lunatic. I come near enough a-doin' it when she patted its chest an' it said 'mamma' an' 'papa' in reply. I don't know, but I think thet the man thet put words into a doll's breast, to be hugged out by a poor, bereft, weak-minded woman, has a terrible sin to answer for. Seems to me it's a-breakin' the second commandment, which forbids the makin' of anything in the likeness of anything in the heavens above or the earth beneath, which a baby is if it's anything, bein' the breath o' God fresh-breathed into human clay. I don't know, but I think that commandment is aimed jest as direct at talkin' dolls ez it is at heathen idols, which, when you come to think of it, ain't p'intedly made after the image of anything *in* creation thet we've seen samples of, after all. Them thet I've seen the pictures of ain't no mo'n sech outlandish deformities thet anybody could conceive of ef he imagined a strange-figgured person standin' befo' a cracked merror so ez to have his various an' sundry parts duplicated, promiscuous. No, I put down the maker of that special an' partic'lar doll ez a greater idolitor than them thet, for the want o' knowin' better, stick a few extry members on a clay statute an' pray to it *in faith*. Ef it hadn't a-called her 'mamma' first time she over-squeezed it, I don't believe *for a minute* thet that doll would ever 'a' got the holt upon Mary Ellen thet it has—I don't indeed."

"Still"—it was Mrs. Blanks who spoke up in reply, wiping her eyes as she began—"still, Sister Lynde, you know she frets over it jest ez much sence it's lost its speech."

"Of co'se," said another sister; "an' why shouldn't she? Ef yo' little Katie had a-started talkin' an' then stopped of a sudden, wouldn't you 'a' been worried, I like to know?"

"Yas, I reckon I would," replied Mrs. Blanks; "but it's hard to put her in the place of a mother with a reel child—even in a person's imagination."

There had been in Simpkinsville an occasional doll whose eyes would open and shut as she was put to bed or taken up, and the crying doll was not a thing unknown.

That the one which should play so conspicuous a part in her history should have developed the gift of speech, invested it with a weird and peculiar interest.

It was, indeed, most uncanny and sorrowful to hear its poor piping response to the distraught woman's caresses as she pressed it to her bosom.

To the little doll-loving girls of Simpkinsville it had always been an object of semi-superstitious reverence—a thing half doll, half human, almost alive.

When her little niece Nellie, a tall girl of eight years now, would come over in the mornings and beg Aunt Mary Ellen to let her hold the baby, she never quite knew, as she walked it up and down the yard, under the mulberry-trees, with the green veil laid lovingly over its closed lids, whether to look for a lapse from its human quality into ordinary dollhood, or to expect a sudden development on the life side.

She would, no doubt, long ago have lost this last hope, in the lack of progression in its mechanical speech, but for the repeated confidences of her aunt Mary Ellen.

"Why, honey, she often laughs out loud an' turns over in bed, an' sometimes she wakes me up cryin' so pitiful." So the good aunt, who had never told a lie in all her pious life, often assured her—assured her with a look in her face that was absolutely invincible in its expression of perfect faith in the thing she said.

There had been several serious conferences between her father and mother in the beginning, before the child had been allowed to go to see Aunt Mary Ellen's dolly—to see and hold it, and inevitably to love it with all her child heart; but even before the situation had developed its full sadness, or they had realized how its contingencies would familiarize every one with the strange, sad story, the arguments were in the child's favor. To begin with, the doll was really hers, though it was thought best, in the circumstances, that she should never know it. Indeed, at first her father had declared that she should have one just like it; but when it was found that its price was nearly equal to the value of a bale of cotton, the good man was moved to declare that "the outlandish thing, with its heathenish imitations, had wrought sorrer enough in the family a'ready without trying to duplicate it."

Still, there couldn't be any harm in letting her see the beautiful toy. And so, as she held it in her arms, the child came vaguely to realize that a great mystery of anxious love hovered about this strange, weird doll, a mystery that, to her young perception, as she read it in the serious home faces, was as full of tragic possibilities as that which concerned the real baby sister that lay and slept and waked and grew in the home cradle—the real, warm, heavy baby that she was sometimes allowed to hold "just for a minute" while the nurse-mammy followed close beside her.

If the toy-baby gave her the greater pleasure, may it not have been because she dimly perceived in it a meeting-point between the real and the imaginary? Here was a threshold of the great wonder-world that primitive peoples and children love so well. They are the great mystics, after all. And are they not, perhaps, wise mystics who sit and wonder and worship, satisfied not to understand?

Summer waned and went out, and September came in— September, hot and murky and short of breath, as one ill of heart-failure. Even the prayer-meeting women who had taken up Miss Mary Ellen's case in strong faith, determined not to let it go, were growing faint of heart under the combined pressure of disappointed hope and the summer's weight. The poor object of their prayers, instead of seeming in any wise improved, grew rather more wan and weary as time wore on. Indeed, she sometimes appeared definitely worse, and would often draw rein in the public road to lift the doll from her lap and discuss her anxieties concerning it with any passing acquaintance, or even on occasion to exult in a fancied improvement.

This was a thing she had never done before the women began to pray, and it took a generous dispensation of faith to enable them to continue steadfast in the face of such discouragement. But, as is sometimes the case, greater faith came from the greater need, and the prayer-meeting grew. In the face of its new and painful phases, as the tragedy took on a fresh sadness, even a few churchly women who had stood aloof at the beginning waived their sectarian differences and came into the meeting. And there were strange confessions sometimes at these gatherings, where it was no uncommon thing for a good sister to relate how, on a certain occasion, she had either "burst out cryin' to keep from laughin'," or "laughed like a heathen jest to keep from cryin'."

The situation was now grown so sad and painful that the doctors called a consultation of neighboring physicians, even bringing for the purpose a "specialist" all the way from the Little Rock Asylum, hoping little, but determined to spare no effort for the bettering of things.

After this last effort and its discouraging result, all hope of recovery seemed gone, and so the good women, when they prayed, despairing of human agency, asked simply for a miracle, reading aloud, for the support of their faith, the stories of marvellous healing as related in the gospels.

It was on a sultry morning, after a night of rain, near the end of September. Old Dr. Jenkins stood behind the showcase in his drug-store dealing out quinine pills and earache drops to the poor country folk and negroes, who, with sallow faces or heads bound up, declared themselves "chillin' " or "painful" while they waited. Patient as cows, they stood in line while the dispensing hand of healing passed over to their tremulous, eager palms the promised "help" for their assorted "miseries."

It was a humble crowd of sufferers, deferring equally, as they waited, to the dignitary who served them and to his environment of mysterious potencies, whose unreadable Latin labels glared at them in every direction as if in challenge to their faith and respect. To the thoughtful observer it seemed an epitome of suffering humanity—patient humanity waiting to be healed by some great and mysterious Unknowable.

It may have been their general attitude of unconscious deference that moved the crowd to fall quickly back at the entrance of the first assertive visitor of the morning, or perhaps old 'Pollo, the negro, as he came rushing into the shop, would have been accorded right of way in a more pretentious gathering. There was certainly that in his appearance which demanded attention.

He had galloped up to the front door, his horse in a lather from the long, hot ride from the Williams homestead, four miles away, and, throwing his reins across the pommel of his saddle, had burst into the drug-store with an excited appeal:

"Doctor Jinkins, come quick! For Gord's sake! Miss Mary Ellen *need* you, Marse Doctor—she need you—*right off!*"

He did not wait for a response. He had delivered his summons, and, turning without another word, he remounted his horse and rode away.

It was not needed that the doctor should offer any apologies to his patients for following him. He did not, indeed, seem to remember that they were there as he seized his coat, and, without even waiting to put it on, quickly unhitched his horse tied at the front door, and followed the negro down the road.

It was a matter of but a few moments to overtake him, and when the two were riding abreast the doctor saw that the old man was crying.

"De dorg, he must 'a' done it, Marse Doctor," he began, between sobs. "He must 'a' got in las' night. It was so hot we lef' all de do's open, same lak we *been* doin'—But it warn't we-alls fault, doctor. But de dorg, he must 'a' snatch de doll out'n de cradle an' run out in de yard wid it, an' it lay a-soakin' in de rain all night. When Miss Mary Ellen fust woked up dis mornin', she called out to Milly to fetch de baby in to her. Milly she often tecks it out'n de cradle early in de mornin' 'fo' missy wakes up, an' make pertend lak she feeds it in de kitchen. An' dis mornin', when she call for it, Milly, she 'spon' back, 'I ain't got her, missy!' jes dat-a-way. An' wid dat, 'fo' you could bat yo' eye, missy was hop out'n dat bed an' stan' in de middle o' de kitchen in her night-gownd, white in de face as my whitewash-bresh. An' when she had look at Milly an' den at me, she sclaim out, *'Whar my child?'* I tell you, Marse Doctor, when I see dat look an' heah dat inquiry, I trimbled so dat dat kitchen flo' shuck tell de kittle-leds on de stove rattled. An' Milly, she see how scarified missy look, an' she commence to tu'n roun' an' seek for words, when we heah pit-a-pat, pit-a-pat, on de po'ch; an', good Gord, Marse Doctor! heah come Rover, draggin' dat po' miser'ble little doll-baby in his mouf, drippin' wid mud an' sopped wid rain-water. Quick as I looked at it I see dat bofe eyes was done soaked out an' de paint gone, an' all its yaller hair it had done eve'y bit soaked off. Sir? Oh, I don't know, sir, how she gwine teck it. Dey ain't no sayin' as to dat. She hadn't *come to* when I come away. She had jes drapped down in a dead faint in de mids' o' de kitchen, an' I holp Milly lif' her on to de bed, an' I come for you. Co'se I had to stop an' ketch de horse; an' de roads, dey was so awful muddy an'—"

It was a long ride over the heavy roads, and as the good doctor trotted along, with the old darky steadily talking beside him, he presently ceased to hear.

Having once realized the situation, his professional mind busied itself in speculations as to the probable result of so critical an incident to his patient. Accident, chance, or mayhap a kind providence, had done for her the thing he had long wished to try but had not dared. The mental shock, with the irreparable loss of the doll, would probably have a definite effect for good or ill—if, indeed, she would consent even now to give it up. Of course there was no telling.

This question was almost immediately answered, however, for when, presently, the old negro led the way into the land leading to the Williams gate, preceding the doctor so as to open the gate for him, he leaned suddenly over his horse's neck and peered eagerly forward. Then drawing rein for a moment, he called back:

"Marse Doctor, look hard, please, sir, an' see what dat my ol' 'oman Milly is doin' out at de front gate."

The doctor's eyes were little better than his companion's. Still, he was able in a moment to reply:

"Why, old man, she is tying a piece of white muslin upon the gatepost. Something has happened."

"White is for babies, ain't it, Marse Doctor?"

"Yes—or for—"

"Den it mus' be she's give it up for dead."

The old man began sobbing again.

"Yes; thank God!" said the doctor. And he wiped his eyes.

The bit of fluttering white that hung upon the gate at the end of the lane had soon told its absurd and pitiful little tale of woe to the few passers-by on the road—its playful announcement of half the story, the comedy side, pathetically suggesting the tragedy that was enacting within.

Before many hours all Simpkinsville knew what had happened, and the little community had succumbed to an attack of hysteria.

Simpkinsville was not usually of a particularly nervous or hysterical temper, but a wholesome sense of the ludicrous, colliding with her maternal love for her afflicted child, could not do less than find relief in simultaneous laughter and tears.

And still, be it said to their credit, when the good women

separated, after meeting in the various houses to talk it over, it was the mark of tears that remained upon their faces.

But when it was presently known that their nerve poise was to be critically tested by a "funeral" announced for the next day, there was less emotion exhibited, perhaps, and there were more quiet consultations among the serious-minded.

When Miss Mary Ellen, prostrate and wan with the burden of her long-borne sorrow, had from her pillow quietly given instructions for the burial, the old doctor, who solicitously watched beside her, in the double capacity of friend and physician, had not been able to say her nay.

And when on the next day he had finally invited a conference on the subject with her brother, the minister, his fellow-doctor, and several personal friends of the family, there were heavy lines about his eyes, and he confessed that before daring his advice on so sensitive a point he had "walked the flo' the livelong night."

And then he had strongly, unequivocally, advised the funeral.

"We've thought it best to humor her all the way through," he began, "an' now, when the end is clairly in sight, why, there ain't any consistency in changin' the treatment. Maybe when it's buried she'll forget it, an' in time come to herself. Of co'se it'll be a tryin' ordeel, but there's enough of us sensible relations an' friends thet'll go through it, if need be." He had walked up and down the room as he spoke, his hands clasped behind him, and now he stopped before the minister. "Of co'se, Brother Binney"—he spoke with painful hesitation—"of co'se she'll look for you to come an' to put up a prayer, an' maybe read a po'tion o' Scripture. An' I've thought *that* over. Seems to me the whole thing is sad enough for religious services—ef anything is. I've seen reel funerals thet wasn't half so mo'nful, ef I'm any judge of earthly sorrers. There wouldn't be any occasion to bring in the doll in the services, I don't think. But there ain't any earthly grief, in my opinion, but's got a Scripture tex' to match it, ef it's properly selected.

A painful stillness followed this appeal. And then, after closing his eyes for a moment as if in prayer, the good minister said:

"Of course, my dear friends, *you* can see thet this thing can't be conducted *as a funeral.* But, as our good brother has jest remarked, for all the vicissitudes of life—and death—for our safety in joy and our comfort in sorrow, we are given precious words of sweet and blessed consolation."

The saddest funeral gathering in all the annals of Simpkins-ville—so it is still always called by those who wept at the obse-quies—was that of Miss Mary Ellen's doll, led by the good brother on the following day.

The prayer-meeting women were there, of course, fortified in their faith by the supreme demand laid upon it, and even equipped with fresh self-control for this crucial test of their poise and worthiness. Their love was deep and sincere, and yet so sensitive were they to the dangers of this most precarious situa-tion that when presently the minister entered, book in hand, a terrible apprehension seized them.

It was as a great wave of indescribable fright, so awful that for a moment their hearts seemed to stop beating, so irresistible in its force that unless it should be quickly stayed it must presently break in some emotion.

No doubt the good brother felt it too, for instead of opening his book, as had been his intention, he laid it down upon the table before him—the small centre-table upon which lay what seemed a tiny mound heaped with flowers—and, placing both hands upon the bowed head of the little woman who sat beside it, closed his eyes, and raised his face heavenward.

"Dear Lord, Thou knowest," he said, slowly. Then finding no other words, perhaps, and willing to be still, he waited a moment in silence.

When he spoke again the wave had broken. The air seemed to sway with the indescribable vibrations that tell of silent weep-ing, and every face was buried in a handkerchief.

"Thou knowest, O Lord," he resumed, presently, raising his voice a little as if in an access of courage—"Thou knowest how dear to our hearts is Thy handmaiden, this beloved sister who sits in sorrow among us to-day. Thou knowest how we love her. Thou knowest that her afflictions are ours. And oh, dear Father, if it be possible, grant that when we have reverently put this poor little symbol of our common sorrow out of sight forever, Thy peace may descend and fill her heart and ours with Thy everlasting benediction."

The words, which had come slowly, though without apparent effort, might have been inspired. Surely they sounded to the women who waited as if uttered by a voice from Heaven, and to their spiritually attuned ears it was a voice comforting, composing, quieting.

After this followed a reading of Scripture—a selection taken for its wide application to all God's sorrowing people—and the singing of the beautiful hymn,

"God shall charge His angel legions
Watch and ward o'er thee to keep."

This was sung, without a break, from the beginning clear through to the end, with its sweet promise to the grief-stricken of "life beyond the grave." Then came the benediction—the benediction of the churches since the days of the apostles, used of all Christians the world over, but ever beautiful and new—"The peace of God, which passeth all understanding, keep your hearts and minds," etc.

All the company had risen for this—all excepting Miss Mary Ellen, who during the entire ceremony had not changed her position—and when it was finished, when the moment of silent prayers was over and one by one the women rose from their knees, there came an awkward interval pending the next step in this most difficult and exceptional service.

The little woman in whose behalf it had been conducted, for whom all the prayers had been said, made no sign by which her further will should be made known. It had been expected that she would herself go to the burial, and against this contingency a little grave had been prepared in the family burial-ground, which, happily, was situated upon her own ground, in a grove of trees a short distance from the house.

After waiting for some moments, and seeing that she still did not move, the reverend brother finally approached her and laid his palm as before upon her head. Then, quickly reaching around, he drew her hand from beneath her cheek, felt her pulse, and now, turning, he motioned to the doctor to come.

The old man, Dr. Jenkins, lifted her limp arm tenderly and

felt her wrist, listened with his ear against her bosom, waited, and listened again—and again. And then, laying back the hand tenderly, he took his handkerchief from his pocket and wiped his eyes.

"Dear friends," he said, huskily, "your prayers have been answered. Sister Mary Ellen has found peace."

Queen O'Sheba's Triumph

When Queen o' Sheba Jackson came to New York from her plantation home at Broom Corn Bottom, she trod the plank from the Jersey ferry into Gotham like a tragedy queen, and if a little cloud, dark as her face, rising over North River, had swollen and spread before her eyes until the city about her was gray and then nearly black and then suddenly wet, she read in the incident no presage of disaster. She knew that hereabouts were the weather headquarters, and she had brought her umbrella, and the dash with which she ran it up and started forth, her Broom Corn stride in full action, fairly illustrated her spirit.

She had come against the separate and combined protestations of her family, friends, and church, who had coaxingly, prayerfully, and at last even abusively, advised against it. It takes great spirit to brook such opposition, and Queen o' Sheba had struck out to win.

As she entered the crowd that jostled her elbows on either side, she realized in her new environment a menace to both soul and body. She had been warned that she was "li'ble to be light-ning-stuck wid a live wire at any street-crossin'," and she knew that evil incarnate was rampant in the great city; but she dodged the telegraph-poles, sniffed at the populace, and feared nothing.

In her pocket there were eighteen dollars in money, tied in the corner of her handkerchief, folded in with a slip of paper on which was written the year-old address of a friend who had previously migrated from Broom Corn. Sheba would have ex-changed letters verifying this address, but for fear. Her fortune had come suddenly, and she dared not hold it lest it should melt. The manager of the narrow-gage road that handled Broom Corn's cotton had offered her fifty dollars for her cow, in the presence of witnesses, on the day before his train killed it on the track, and he was pleased to settle with her for transportation to New York and twenty-five dollars to boot. Five of the remaining seven dollars of the price of her happy disaster were bulging in a wad from Sheba's stocking now—a reserve for a rainier day; and as she strode along, and the sun came out, and she began to see things in the clear light, she was pleased to remember this reserve. It gave her license as to the eighteen in her pocket.

The first thing she realized concerning herself was that her clothes were all wrong. Of course, being second-hand, they were several seasons old even in Broom Corn, but they had come from Broom Corn's best. For one brief moment, feeling the tightness of her dolman over her arms, Sheba resented New York as daring to oppose Miss Minervy Cheatham in so trivial a matter as the shape of a wrap. Miss Minervy, the judge's daughter, was a traveled person, who used languages, and who rode the fields about Broom Corn in a riding-habit, the only one extant in the vicinity, and she easily set the pace for the community in all matters of dress and etiquette. Sheba had made Miss Minervy's spring garden two years before for this wrap—a seal plush, edged with fur—and as she pressed through the great-sleeved throng on this first gray day, she remembered that it had come from New York and she felt betrayed. It is like repudiating a debt—the way some cities do. Sheba had dug and hoed and raked, and even begun to gather, for this garment, chiefly because it had been brought from New York; and when she had found herself hither bound, one of her greatest pleasures was in realizing that the wrap question, at least, was happily settled.

But the dolman had begun to go out of fashion at the first town where the train stopped, and it had grown worse at every station until she got off the cars, and now, while she trod the city of its birth, she felt it shrink into the past with every step she took. She did not care for the motley crowd on the streets, but she did dread to meet the friend upon whom she was to depend for an introduction, "lookin'," as she mentally expressed it, "like a tacky from 'way back." And so, instead of following up the address she carried, she began to watch for shop-windows, and finally, after she had been walking for an hour or such a matter— no great walk for a Broom Corner—she suddenly disappeared at the door of a Sixth Avenue department-store, armed with her eighteen dollars and a mortal discontent; and when she came out, nearly an hour later, she was radiant in the coat of the multitude, stiff, fur-trimmed, double-breasted, balloon-sleeved, and with a storm-collar that in its flamboyant flare answered her most daring spirit.

She would have bought a hat, had hats not been so dear. She

had tried on several, however, and studied them to such effect that, watching her chance, she tilted her own, hind part before, on the back of her head, and the result was so gratifying that she decided to wear it just so; and when she had secured it in place with a nine-cent jeweled pin, it not only answered the challenge of the storm-collar but set the pace for even greater things. Its bows, arranged for the face, smiled promiscuous greetings on all who walked behind it, while its delighted wearer opposed them by a beaming front. When Sheba jostled the Sixth Avenue throng again a feather boa of fine presence graced her neck. She had swung it there quite as one who had habited with constrictors all her life. Of course, the storm-collar repudiated the boa as super-erogatory, but Sheba could not realize this. Still, to do her justice, she had bought it as a bargain rather than as a needed factor in her toilet. It had cost but two dollars and ninety-eight cents, the odd cents exactly expressing its recent "reduction" (from two dollars). And in this certainly no woman who knows how to shop can blame her. Have we not all done likewise?

Sheba had her friend in mind when she stepped into the street, but the windows were fascinating—in more ways than one. Not only were they glittering allurements in their offerings, but each, when taken at a happy angle, became a mirror, and in its reflection Sheba saw what to her prejudiced eyes was the figure of a stately and finished New-Yorker. The transition had been quick, it is true, but some of us are assimilative. Seeing herself thus, it was perhaps but natural that she should have hesitated in front of a photographer's, "just to look" at the beautiful tintypes of which his glaring advertisement promised to supply three copies in five minutes, and for only twenty-five cents.

Many of the sample pictures in the showcase were of persons of her own color, which was an added attraction, and—

Well, when her pictures were finished, they fully corroborated the flattering testimony of the windows, and as she slipped them reluctantly into her pocket and started on her way up-town, her expression was quite urbane and self-complacent.

She had asked a policeman to help her on her way, intuitively recognizing a uniform bravely worn in public as a sort of stamp of reliability.

"I don't know who you is, but you's *some*body, an' you ain't a-hidin' it." So she had addressed the seven-foot protector of the peace, who answered her with his index-finger, and sent her flying southward in an elevated train at Fourteenth Street. How could a stranger know the difference between Ninth Avenue and Ninth Street? The fact that Queen o' Sheba Jackson did not know was important inasmuch only as it made it late in the day when, having returned disappointed from the vicinity of the Battery after a vain pursuit, she found that the number which her friend's address called for in Ninth Street was nowhere indicated. The place where it belonged was what seemed to be a pit, out of which emerged ropes and pulleys, marked in the early twilight by a red lantern. The house had been torn down.

Now, for the first time, Sheba felt frightened. The street-lamps were lighting, and every one seemed suddenly to be hur-rying home—or somewhere. She did not feel inclined to ask a policeman to direct her again. She had discovered near the Bat-tery that these uniformed men were the police, having really witnessed one in action, and to be consigned to a lodging by such as one of them would have been too much like being in custody for her free spirit.

Her present dilemma, however, was not for long. There were plenty of colored people in the throng in Ninth Street, many of them evidently going home from work, and Sheba soon found herself in company with her kind in a stately tenement, where she easily got a bed by a small prepayment. Thus she entered upon her life in the great city.

It is no simple matter to get the best sort of position in a strange place when one has no recommendation, and so Sheba was constrained to begin by taking what even to her inexperience seemed a second-best. It afforded her a home, however, and the munificent wages of twelve dollars a month, so that she was soon able to write a letter to her people which, with the enclosed tintype, told so startling a tale of instant success that, but for the cost of the trip, many of them would have hastened to follow her. The average wages in Broom Corn was four dollars, payable generally, in part at least, in trade at one of its stores.

City life, as it is practised in New York, was trying to Sheba in many ways. She had been somewhat of a local celebrity as a cook at the Bottom, and her first ardor was somewhat dampened when she came to discover that here skill in making her specialties—buttermilk and beaten biscuit, for instance—counted for naught, and that her frying-pan was unavailable. The golden bread, fragrant at home with the sweetness of the Indian meal, was here a poor, sawdusty thing suggestive of the kiln, and needing to be sugared to become palatable. And there were other disappointments. Her toilets would not pass muster with people of any form whatever, and her speech would go not at all with them. When it was not too slow it was altogether too swift, which is to say that the picturesqueness of her drawl was insufficient to compensate for its acceleration under provocation. From a second-class place she was constrained to accept one of the third rate, which is a demoralizing experience. It takes but a short pedigree of such to constitute a plebeian in the ranking of metropolitan service, and a plebe on the down grade seems to have a poor chance to alter her course. At least, so it seemed in Sheba's case. She changed situations many times during the first year, and more than once she changed against her will and suddenly. Life was hard, and there were many times when, but for her challenged pride, which alone of her attributes seems to have remained unsullied, she would have returned to her native heath, if she had had the money.

At one time she fell ill, and there were days of experience and loneliness when she missed things. Even in the hospital, where everything was immaculate, she missed the personal attention of the home doctor, whose habit it was to "lump" the servants' bills in with the yearly accounts of his white patients whom they served; and she missed the visiting sisters of the church in the doubtful days of slow convalescence and of her "setbacks." She missed space and air and freedom. Indeed, it sometimes seemed as if she were missing everything. The even beds and the serene faces of the nurses palled on her, and she pined for the home air charged with emotion. One good moan or an "Amen!" at her bedside and a mustard-plaster that would weigh a pound—such as these were the things for which her soul hungered.

When she sent the prosperous-looking tintype of herself to her home people, Sheba had no intention of misrepresenting her condition any more than she had when she refrained from mentioning her illness, and the fact that she had lain for several weeks a charity patient in a city hospital. One has a right to one's reserves, surely, and indeed the bravest of us sometimes feel that in maintaining silence we are exercising our best part.

In sending the tintype she had meant only to say, "See how fine I look in my New York toggery!" And if the picture said, instead, "Behold! I am rich, and prosperous and superior, and the ring upon my finger is a diamond, and my fur-trimmed garment represents a small fortune!" the fault was hardly hers. Even if she had anticipated its telling so exaggerated a tale, she would not have suppressed it, if for no other reason, because she would not have expected it to be believed. But when one wrote her from the plantation that another had remarked that "Queen o' Sheba Jackson needn't to think that because she's set up in New York and can afford to sport fur coats and diamonds that she's the biggest toad in the puddle," she simply did not deny the allegation. Indeed, it is likely that the edifice of deceit that she had soon begun to build, and into which she at last moved bodily, was the direct result of home suggestion. The imputations of affluence, even negatively confessed, became interesting to her, and adversely as her fortunes declined did she build upon this foundation her castle of indolence and ease.

The city address which she gave at home, and to which her mail was sent, was the tenement where she paid twenty-five cents a month for trunk-space, with the privilege of making it a dollar a week when she was pleased—or displeased to occupy the bed beside the trunk.

During the first year, in which she many times changed her residence, the trunk address was only twice changed, and in both instances the letters sent to Broom Corn hinted that its removal— which, of course, was ostensibly hers—was in an ascending scale.

Sheba really told very few lies outright about herself and her fortunes in these days, and when she first found herself ostensibly writing from her own apartment, in which there were "stuffed chairs," "dumbwaiters" and "election bells" (the last needing only to be touched to produce almost any desired service), she scarcely knew how it had come about. Indeed, this deception was in the beginning only an accident. When the misleading letter was written, she was actually cooking for the family of a "floor-walker" in Fourteenth Street, and it was true that these attractive luxuries were there, as well as some elegancies which she also casually mentioned; and if she artlessly alluded to them as "ours," it was with no desire to deceive. It had been the habit of her life to ally herself thus with the white families with whom she lived.

After her illness, when Sheba came out of the hospital, she was but a shadow of her former self. She was not strong enough to stand the heat and fatigue of cooking, and after trying vainly for more attractive work, she finally found herself in the position of cook's assistant—otherwise scullion—in a Harlem boarding-house. She had presided over a better kitchen in her day, and she felt pretty blue when she first took the orders of the great Irish potentate, "Miss Bridget," and became conscious that of all the servants there, she was the very lowest in the social order. For the first time she now fully realized that there was absolutely nothing worth while in life for her in New York, and she knew that she would never go home. With this last realization came hopelessness—hopelessness which gradually found expression in a dogged compliance.

The servants all slept in cots on the basement floor, and naturally the last comer always had to take the worst place at night, at the head of the basement stairs, where the draft from the cellar blew over her cot; and when Sheba first placed hers here she felt more lonely than she had ever felt in all her life before. It was pretty close quarters when all the cots were down, but, as Maggie the left-handed dish-breaker, once remarked, "There's fun in ut when a person gets used to ut wanst—yis, fun and company," she laughed. But Maggie was blessed with a saving sense of humor, and on her very first night, when she had accepted the cellar draft, she bravely remarked in a loud voice, as she emerged from behind the clothes-rack, where she had repaired with her rosary for prayer: "Sure, there's no room to be lonesome in ut, ony-way"; to which the cook's voice had replied, from under the covers in the kitchen: "Sure, an' mony's the toime since, I'd pay a guinea a minute, if I had ut, for a half-hour o' the lonesomeness I dreaded comun' over."

The question of place was a matter of nightly scramble, excepting, of course, in the case of the cook, who located her claim according to her whim, and held it by prestige, backed on occasion by brawn and language. The servants made no complaint at this unavoidable crowding; and, indeed, it would have been unreasonable to do so, for did not the landlady, who would almost have tipped the scales with Bridget, sleep in the ostensible "escritory" in the little reception-room, and repair to the dish-closet for her afternoon changes of toilet?

Sheba hated the cook, and she hated the lesser maids—all but left-handed Maggie, through whose promotion she had come into her position. It is true, Maggie said the worst things to her on provocation; but, as she expressed it, Maggie "talked to her like a human," which was some comfort. It was she who put her up to securing a better place for her cot at night, and let her into the rule of the roost, which was that whoever made down her bed and *prayed by it* fixed her claim to the chosen location for the night, all excepting, again, the cook, who weighed three hundred pounds, and said her prayers in bed—"by a dispensation," so she said. Maggie assured her, too, once when she was in one of her friendliest moods, that she didn't mind colored people since she had got used to them, and that it was a holy relief, for when she first came over she crossed herself and called on the blessed Mother every time she met one.

The laundress was colored, and so was the bell-boy, who went home at night; but they had Eastern pronunciations, and were no company whatever to Sheba. It was the laundress, however, who unwittingly brought into her life the element of hope that makes it possible to write a sketch of her the title of which may hold so fine a word as "triumph."

When, one day, a well-dressed white man called to see the laundress, Sheba could not help overhearing part of his conversation before she knew who he was, and when the woman of the tubs approached her haughtily and said that Mr. Stein wished an introduction to her, she was glad to speak with him. Mr. Stein represented the Afro-American Funeral Insurance Company, Limited, and he had called to collect her dues from the laundress, who held a policy in his company. His desire to meet Mrs. Jackson was entirely in the character of solicitor, and if he had but known how eagerly she listened to his every word as he set forth the advantages of his corporation, he would not have felt it necessary to solicit quite so warmly. When she had lain so ill in the hospital, the prospect of an unmarked grave in potter's field had stared her in the face—a pauper's grave over in the mosquito country which she vaguely knew lay somewhere across the river. And yet, even while it seemed to near, she would have preferred it to an ignominious return home in a position where those who had most fiercely opposed her might come and stand over her and say things to her face, and she would not be able to answer them.

For a trifle paid monthly she was now offered assurance of decent burial. An added sum would guarantee a higher grade of service, with carriages and other accessories. The scale ran somewhat like this: Fifty cents, payable monthly before the third day, assured simple, silent burial, with no "grievers." This sum doubled would secure the plumed hearse. Twenty-five cents apiece, paid quarterly, would prepay mourners—a comfortable provision for the stranger—while a dollar a year would cover the cost of fresh flowers. The funeral oration was offered free to such as "took up" all the other advantages. There was a neat chapel on the floor above the undertaker's shop of the company—a chapel which might be inspected at stated times by such as wished to verify the representations of the company's agent. Indeed, for such "doubting-Thomases" there were occasional "sample funerals" given, when applicants for policies were treated without cost to an entire ceremonial, even to the ride in the carriage to the cemetery. Sheba did not know about this premium upon hesitation when she so readily decided to embrace the proffered terms, and, indeed, she was tempted to a quick decision by Mr. Stein's kind offer to advance the money for the first payment out of his own pocket. So within an hour after she had been introduced to the scheme she had mortgaged her precarious income for a full benefit: six mourners—the same being considered "a set"—music, flowers, the pomponed hearse and funeral oration, with a final bed of green, were now hers to contemplate. The policy crediting her with a first payment, which she signed in the presence of the laundress and the bell-boy—the latter didn't expect to die, and refused to insure—was delivered to her on the third day of the month following, when she paid double dues, making good the loan.

Strange to say, the taking of the policy revived her spirit and renewed her self-respect. The fact that she must die to win counted for nothing to her. She would win, even though she died, and the end would be triumphant, no matter how much of humiliation she might have to endure in the interval. The simple fact that she really did save the money to keep her policy paid up soon began to institute within her an upward tendency. She was obliged to do without many of the baubles which it had been her habit to buy, and she was obliged to guard her temper. It became necessary that she should keep her place. The ordinary chances of life, dealing with fairly amenable material, ought out of these elements to evolve a pretty respectable woman—in time. How much time is, of course, a question of the special case. Sheba was not vicious, although she did some things which are badly catalogued in the moral code of the best civilizations—but, if such a thing is possible, she did them innocently.

If she had been of a pious turn, no doubt the funeral insurance, with its formal presentation of death beyond contingency, would have instituted a revival of religion within her; but the fact is, she was not only not religious, but the opposition of the Broom Corn congregation had set her staunchly against the church even in her adopted home.

She had made an emotional connection with the Methodist Church when she was very young, but before she was well grown she had recklessly danced herself out of its fold, and had never resumed active membership with it, although she had generally gone to church at Broom Corn, and was enrolled as one of its straying sheep long before she had actually wandered beyond its jurisdiction.

On a certain morning several months after she had taken her insurance policy, Queen o' Sheba waked with a start before day, and, raising herself upon her elbow, looked about her. She had scarcely slept all night, and even in the dim light of the gas turned low her face showed marks of distress. It was evident that there was something on her mind, and that it was disturbing her sorely.

As she glanced from the clothes and shoes strewn over the floor to the faces of the sleepers, whose vociferous snorings almost deadened the sounds of the rats tumbling in the wall, a change came over her face and for a moment her eyes fairly twinkled with merriment. A sense of the ludicrous had come to her relief.

"For Gord's sake!" she chuckled. "No wonder I dremp about a boat-race." And then, fairly shaking with suppressed laughter, she added: "Name o' Gord! jes look at my cushioned cheers—an' my piany—an' my gilt sofy—an' my—"

She ducked her head suddenly under the cover, lest she should rouse the cook; for while she laughed she observed that one whistling steamer in the race had failed to come to time, and she was pretty sure it was the *Bridget*.

When she poked her head out again in a moment, however, there were only the old marks upon it, care lines and the deep-set eyes that tell of failing health and disappointment—only these, with the added shade of a new trouble.

Sheba was in trouble indeed—trouble of an altogether unexpected sort, which in its descent upon her tired mind had nearly stunned her. The blow had fallen early the morning before, and all day she had done her work in a perfunctory manner, half dazed and brooding, and when Maggie had sympathetically asked what ailed her, she had only shaken her head moodily and drawled, "Nothin' in p'tic'lar."

The thing that had really befallen her was a joyous letter from home—a letter which brought her only ostensibly "good news" from her people. Surely it ought to be good news to know that one's friends are coming!

It would have been good news to poor Sheba if things had been different.

The situation was this:

Delegates from all the societies of the various colored churches in and about Broom Corn had decided to take advantage of special rates to New York to attend a reunion, and at least half the delegates were Sheba's personal friends.

It was even likely that one or two members of her own family would make a break and come. Of course they were all delighted at the prospect of the visit, and the letter announcing their coming was the most personal and affectionate that poor Sheba had gotten since she had left home.

This added to her pain in the matter, if anything could have made it worse after the simple fact had reached her. Really the letter frightened her so that she trembled, and she had not quite realized its contents until she had sat and read it carefully again and again, "studyin' over it" between readings until it was all plain.

She had not the slightest idea what to do. Her first impulse was to run. She could easily take her trunk, leaving no new address behind it at the old place; but this would invite disaster as certainly as holding her ground. This last, however, she could not contemplate. The fact is, she had no ground to hold. If she could not allow her friends to go to the address through which she had received her letters, and to discover her fraud, neither could she invite them to visit her in the basement where she had during the day only right of way between the sink and the window where she peeled potatoes, and debatable cot-space at night.

No wonder she was troubled as she lay thinking the matter over in the early morning hours. Who that has suffered—which is to say, who that has lived—does not know this tragedy-time when life's fortifications are unguarded, and its lanterns cast green lights in which yesterday's trivialities get their innings as dancing imps of terror?

Sheba had been tormented by three-o'clock-in-the-morning visions before now. From her cot she had seen the little shouting corn-plaster man standing on a wheelbarrow, a giant above her head, and reaching down what seemed the distance of a block, with an arm that lengthened as she eluded it, he had tried to snatch her pocket-book from her hand, as she stood in the crowd and her eyes were blinded with light; and she had waked with a shriek on Sunday morning gaspingly to recover the memory that she had really spent a dime for a box of russet-shoe polish in Ninth Avenue, the night before, from the irresistible orator behind the corn-plasterer, when she had not a russet shoe to her feet and was twenty-five cents short on her insurance. She knew about this kind of filmy draped ghosts that change shape and finally melt and disappear in the light of day, leaving only the disposal of a trivial obligation to dispel them utterly.

But this was of another sort. It waked her with a sense of discomfort only, and a vague foreboding which took a far worse shape than the bugaboo of her dream as the mists of sleep cleared and left it before her frightened consciousness, a naked, horrible fact. Yes, it was true. Her people were coming. It was not a dream. They were coming, expecting to visit her in her own home. She had told them she had a home—she had even described it to them; and they were coming. Jake Byers, the preacher, was coming, and Sol Tyler, and maybe her stepsister Cely, and the Lord knew how many more. When she had gone over and over the fact in her mind, she suddenly dropped back on her pillow and closed her eyes, and as she drew the comforter up over her breast her hand touched an envelop which lay there. It held her funeral insurance policy. She always kept it about her person, to make sure that in case she should die suddenly it should be found—a wise precaution for one prospectively alone in death. And so, pinned inside her dress during the day, and at night attached to her chemise, the policy bore her company.

Excepting a few old clothes, it was the only thing she possessed in the world, and when her hand accidentally touched it this morning she clutched it with a pitiful, convulsive movement. In a moment, still pressing her hand over her treasure, she suddenly sat up in bed, and in another she had risen to her feet; and when she had picked out her things from the floor, she tiptoed cautiously out of the room. She was in so much trouble that it irritated her to see others asleep, and she even resented the snores by which they seemed to boast that they were sleeping.

As she went out she mumbled: "Do, fer Gord sake, lemme git out o' dis bedlam whar I kin hear myse'f think!" And when she had gotten quite beyond ear-shot she added: "Thank Gord I ain't no po' white! Deze heah Dutch an' Irish can out-sno'e a sugar-house in grindin' season."

When she had reached the laundry, she pushed up the window, and stood within it, breathing deeply. It was her habit thus to fill her lungs when she arose, the nights seeming to leave her weary and short of breath.

Day had not yet broken, and it was nearly dark. Still, she could discern the form of a black cat as it ran across the back yard, and when it uttered a low "Miaou!" she shuddered from the habit of fear. It was a bad omen—a black cat's crossing her vision and crying out to her in the dark. It was a sign of death. At another time she would have put down the window and come quickly away; but not so now. After her first shock she laughed almost bitterly as she muttered: "Miaou away much as you like. I on'y wusht to Gord you'd fetch me de fatal message about de middle o' nex' week. I'd show dem Broom Corners a sight."

She lit the gas as she spoke, and took the policy from her bosom and unfolded it, and as she looked over it she read aloud slowly: "A white cashmere shroud—an' a cherry-wood coffin—wid silver handles—dicorated wid flowers—an' six veiled mo'n-ers—an' a fun'al oration—an' de dead-march—an' a plumed hearse—an' fo' ca'iages—" And as she began nervously to refold it, she added: "Oh, Lord, send it quick—send it quick! Yas, kitty, I pray de Lord you come wid de fatal message, shore 'nough. *I'm petered out!*"

She was coughing a little from the chill air, and she turned from the window to the faucet, where she washed her face, and then she began putting on her clothes.

"Dis heah fun'al policy is a fus'-class chest pertector," she chuckled, as she presently laid the envelop inside her corset.

"Eh, Lord! ef I could on'y reelize on it nex' week I'd mek dem bottom'lan' delicates open dey eyes."

Her words were unmeasured, consciously expressing only her distress; but when they fell upon her ears a meaning beyond her thought startled her, and she held her breath. If she could only realize on the policy next week!

"What's de matter wid drawin' dis fun'al *in advance*, I'd like to know?" she muttered presently. "I ain't got much longer to live nohow, an' I kin pay on it long as I hold out, an' take to de potter's field when I die. It's as good a place to lay in as any, ef a pusson don't try to ca'y name an' station into it. Jes so I'm in hearin' o' Gab'iel's horn—"

It was a seed-thought that had come to her, and it had fallen into willing soil under forcing conditions. In ten minutes it had not only taken root, but was flourishing and throwing out tendrils of hope in every direction.

The scheme was great. It would eliminate the personal quantity absolutely, and her dignity would be vindicated in the eyes of her scorners. Of course, the Broom Corn delegates would be notified and invited to the funeral in a body. The company gave sample funerals sometimes on occasion. Why not give one now, and just name it after her?

If only Mr. Stein could be made to see it as she saw it!

At first, naturally enough, Mr. Stein could not be made to see it at all. Indeed, he virtuously denounced it on sight as simply "willainous," emphasizing his disapproval with a volley of polite profanity.

As the benefits of the exceptional attendance unfolded themselves to his alert ears, however, he began to veer a little and to ask questions.

Ten societies were to be represented. And there would be several delegates from each, nearly all of whom she would probably know, and who would come to her funeral.

Of course there were many difficulties.

For one important thing, her friends would wish to see the corpse. This, however, Sheba blew away with a breath. She would leave last requests. Indeed, every obstacle finally gave way under the pressure of her superior will, and it was soon Mr. Stein who was suggesting things. As a proxy, for instance, there were two customers on hand now, awaiting burial. One was a suburban lady whose family had sent her in, but he had found that her policy was not paid up. He had intended to put her quietly away, not because he was in any way obliged to do so, but simply because he considered her room better than her company. She was about Mrs. Jackson's color. "Y'unger, perhaps, but yest apout de face, py golly! Maybe, after all, ve could ugspose der corpse." So he developed the scheme.

When Sheba sat at the ironing-board in the laundry, that night, writing home, she was more than once obliged to lay down her pen and hold her aching sides for laughing.

Of course, the letter expressed her delight in the prospect of seeing her people. "She wrote only a few lines, because she was so very busy moving. The house where she had lived had just burned to the ground, and her things had been saved only by a chance. She would meet the delegates at the station, and take them home for dinner."

The letter closed with the casual remark that she was suffering a little with "palpertation of the heart," but she was otherwise well.

This was the edge of the wedge.

A later letter, which followed in a few days, although gay and hopeful in spirit, let fall another hint of heart trouble. She had

decided upon "heart failure" for her taking off. She had discovered that it was a swell New York method. Several distinguished people had been reported as dying of heart failure. It had
a good sound, and was sudden and unexpected.

When she had proposed the mock funeral, Sheba had not
dreamed of anything so audacious as attending it herself, but the
plan had scarcely assumed definite shape before she determined
to do so. Indeed, when the idea had once entered her mind,
nothing could dissuade her, and there was really no considerable
risk in it. She was emaciated in comparison with her former self,
and she had learned the Afro-urban art of effectively applying red
and white to a dark skin. Added to these screeneries, there was a
new bearing of which she was unconscious. She held her arms
nearer her body than of old, as people learn to do in a crowded
city, and she pitched less than she had done in her spacious field
life at Broom Corn.

When she entered the chapel, a full ten minutes before the
hour appointed for the obsequies, surely no one would have
known her, not even Bridget, the cook, had she met her suddenly, beplumed and veiled, in the hallway. Sheba had crept out of
her cot during the night before, and stealthily descended to the
basement, where she easily "borrowed" such finery as she
needed from several trunks in storage there.

Mr. Stein saw her when she came into the chapel, and when
he recognized her he came forward and politely led her to a front
seat. As she sat and looked upon the silver-handled coffin, covered with flowers, before the altar, and realized its implication,
her heart thumped so that it shook her body.

Mr. Stein was very busy putting last touches here and there,
and when he finally satisfied himself, he came and formally
invited Sheba to examine the decorations. He had evidently done
his best. Long sprays of smilax depending from the chandelier
found effective attachment in the handles of the casket, and there
were standing in every dirction ferns and palms galore, all chemi-
cally treated mummified affairs, waxed and awful, grim monu-
ments of death simulating life.

As Sheba stood beside the coffin, filled with admiration and a
gruesome triumph, she was suddenly seized with a wild desire to
see the face within. She had a mean feeling of resentment toward

it, as a usurper who was taking advantage of her in her extremity, and whose place in the potter's field she would herself have to occupy.

"Some folks is sho born to luck," she was maliciously reflecting, while Mr. Stein slid back the coffin lid; but when she peeped in she gasped.

"Who is it?" she whispered hoarsely , when at last she could speak, turning to Mr. Stein, whose soft hand supported her elbow.

"Nopoddy," he replied. "She's schust de tummy; she's vax. But ain't she a taisy, heh?"

The real presence of death in the garment of life was bad enough, but here was something even more gruesome and revolting in this second masquerade. Involuntarily Sheba shrank back, shuddering, from the ghastly thing.

Seeing her embarrassment, Mr. Stein hastened to explain: "Dot oder party vot loogs like you olready, her vamily hanks too close-t arount. Odervise ve vould have udilized her, und your friendts could haf looked upon der faze of der corpse. She vas schust your schtyle ugzactly. Some of her peoples got inwited to your funeral to-day, und ven dey see der peautiful ceremony I t'ink maybe dey put up de money. De tummy, ve put'er in for veight, schust, so de pallbearers dey don't sushpecd not'ing. She veighs a hund'ed und eighdy-nine pounds olready."

She had heard scarcely a word he said until now, but his last words startled her.

"Dat's de precise notch I weighed when I come f'om Broom Corn," she drawled, in an awed voice, "an' fer face an' features, look like I kin see myse'f layin' dar. I'm jes swathed in a col' sweat lookin' at myse'f. Tell de trufe, 'cep'n' fer de tightness o' dis frock an' de way it's got de spine o' my back on a strain, I'd think maybe it was me."

Mr. Stein turned and scanned her narrowly.

"*But der mout'!*" he exclaimed.

"You can jedge nothin' tall 'bout my mouf sence my toofs all drapped out. Dat Eighth Avenyer doctor he gimme a overdose-t o' calomon. When dey fell out, seem like my courage fell wid 'em, too."

Seeing him still dubious, Sheba bethought her of the tintype—one of the original three which she carried in her pocket-book. In a moment she had taken it out and held it up before him.

"Dat was me on'y jes but two yeahs ago," she said tentatively.

Mr. Stein was satisfied. With a wave of his hand he dismissed the subject, and when he arranged the flowers on the coffin again he placed them lower on the lid, as he chuckled, "Ve oggshibit de corpse."

While they spoke there came a flash of lightning, and presently another, and simultaneously with the first sound of low thunder Sheba heard footsteps on the stairs, and she staggered rather than walked back to her seat.

The comers were the hired mourners. They wore long black veils, and when they had reached the coffin, walking by twos, they separated, taking seats, four at the head and two at the foot of the casket. Of course they were not in the secret. Some secrets are for the principals only—and the fewer of these the better.

It was not long before the Broom Corn delegates came tramping up the stairs, their new brogans on the uncarpeted steps sounding like a drove of horses. Sheba recognized their tread, and she tried to fan herself carelessly when she knew they were entering, but her hand trembled so that she was obliged to lay down her fan.

She sat near the wall, and by turning a little she could see her own people when they came up the aisle. There were several women among them, and these hid their faces in their handkerchiefs with a proper show of grief. When the presiding minister appeared, arrayed in clerical robes, Sheba was much impressed; still her chief thought was of the effect upon her friends, for even in this critical moment her mental comment was, "I s'pec' dey'll all think I done turned High Church 'Piscopal up heah in New York."

But when the minister began to lead in prayer, and she heard the brave responses of her people, whose cries of "Amen!" and "Glory!" came clear and strong from several directions, she was strangely moved.

The service was imposing from the beginning, and if the sermon was short and somewhat impersonal as a tribute, it was pyrotechnic in its oratory; and when it came to a dramatic close,

Sheba knew by the breathless stillness that followed that the hour was ripe, and she raised her thin voice and sailed in with a plantation hymn which she knew she could count on for power. This was the only fillip she gave, but it was enough. The excitement which had flickered in ejaculations here and there now fairly burst into flame, sweeping everything before it. In the pauses, while they passed from hymn to hymn, the delegates rose one after another, and sometimes two at a time, to eulogize the lamented sister, who, while she listened to her imputed virtues, recognized her old self not at all, and there were critical moments when she almost lost her bearings.

It was only when they began to press forward to view the remains that they became quiet, and even then the silence was occasionally broken by a sob. "Brother Byers," the Broom Corn preacher, led the way, and, as a privileged character, lingered at the coffin to exchange a word with the others as they passed in turn. Sheba sat very near, and she could not help overhearing what they said. It was plain that all were deeply impressed with the splendor of the affair, and most of their comments were complimentary, which is to say that such as failed to declare that "Sis' Jackson" looked "puffec'ly nachel" found her improved in flesh—all excepting one. The only distinctly derogatory word uttered—and, paradoxically, it was this which pleased her most—was spoken by the Reverend Byers, him whose opposition had been a potent factor in her coming to New York.

As he leaned over the coffin, Sheba heard him whisper to Sam Simpleton, his presiding elder: "I don't want to wrong de dead, but f'om de way Sis Jackson's face looks *to me*, I s'picion dat her suddent *de*mise is the result o' *high livin'!* You know Sis' Jackson allus is hankered arter de flesh-pots." And when he shook his head mournfully, old Sam shook his, also. He thought so, too. His assent delighted Sheba especially because she had once been married to old Sam, and she hated him as few ex-husbands, even, are hated.

Sheba was standing it all very well, which means that she was keeping pretty well out of it. Although there were frequent crises when she choked up a little, she bravely maintained her position as a quiet observer almost to the end.

It began suddenly to be hard for her when she discovered

that the occasional suppressed note of real sorrow that had gone to her heart and almost upset her had come from her stepsister Cely. She did not know certainly that Cely had come until she saw her ashy face as she approached the coffin; and when she threw herself upon it, and, calling upon God to witness, accused herself of unsisterly conduct to her "beloved Queenie," for whose leaving home she freely blamed herself, Sheba trembled so that she could hardly sit up.

Cely was a shining light in the church at Broom Corn. The ultimatum of all her related experiences was always "Glory, halleluiah!" and her refuge did not fail her to-day.

Sheba knew her ways, and had no respect whatever for her religion. It was not that which moved her. The ties of blood and home are strong, even though they be attenuated. It was the familiar face and the thousand memories it wakened—this, with the note of genuine grief in the wail—that tore her tired, homesick heart asunder.

There was abject, honest remorse in the broken voice that begged the waxen face for forgiveness.

Sheba had begun to sob aloud, and was so evidently losing self-control that Mr. Stein was growing uneasy, when Cely reached her climax, and, with a shriek, threw herself over the coffin, falling in a swoon.

This proved but an anti-climax, however, for even while Cely was being carried into another room, Sheba, gaunt and wan, had risen from her seat and was trying to speak.

In this her darkest hour of guilt, when she had dared trifle with the dread mystery, a sudden light had broken upon her darkened spirit—a light which she interpreted as conversion—and she could not be silent another minute.

In a twinkling she had realized a saving grace and felt again the joy that had come to her but once, in her early religious experience, and she rose to proclaim her identity and her sin. She would make a full confession, and would go back home with her people, a prodigal daughter, but, by the help of God, for the rest of her days an honest woman.

As she opened her lips there came a blinding flash of lightning, accompanied by a clap of thunder.

Three times did she essay to speak, and three times was she

thus silenced. But the spirit was in her, and neither principalities nor powers could hold her now.

Seeing finally that words could gain no hearing in the bursting storm, she threw up her hands, shouting, "Glory! glory! glory!" again and again and again, with growing fervor and lessening voice, until, with a gasp, she fell into Mr. Stein's arms, and he hastened to bear her away. He carried her to the small antechamber opposite that in which the Broom Corn delegates were working over her sister, trying to bring her back to consciousness.

It had been his purpose, before starting to the cemetery, to call attention to this as one of his company's typical funerals, and to exploit its advantages; but the storm had demoralized his congregation, and the unprecedented conduct of his ostensible corpse had so demoralized him that he hastened to announce that, in consequence of the inclement weather, the interment, to which all the present company were cordially invited, would be postponed until the following morning.

He wanted to get them out of the way before Sheba should recover herself, not knowing what she might do or where he would stand. The deferred funeral would give him time to get her in order, and another opportunity to "work his business."

While he went about looking after his slowly departing guests, he stepped occasionally to the door and peeped in to see how Sheba was getting along, and he was pleased to observe that she seemed not to have moved from her position on the lounge where he had laid her.

Some of the delegates had not brought unbrellas, and they were somewhat nervous about keeping in a body, lest they should lose their way, so that it was perhaps an hour before the last one had gone; and Mr. Stein, turning the key in the front door, drew a sigh of relief and went to look after his patient. He had explained that she was an intimate friend of the deceased, and that she was being cared for.

When he reached the door he was surprised to see that she still had not stirred. This was strange, and yet the truth did not occur to him until he got quite near and saw her face.

The strain upon her tired nerves and heart had been greater than she could bear, and at the moment when the door of heaven had seemed open to her she had been allowed to enter in— shouting, triumphant.

This tragic ending at once simplified and complicated things for Mr. Stein.

It was an easy matter enough, a few hours later, to lift out the dummy figure, and to lay in its place her whose right it was to be there; and, to do justice, Mr. Stein made the change with a sentiment of satisfaction that was closely akin to real sympathy. He liked to deal fairly with his customers, and it pleased him to know that this forlorn one, to whom it had seemed to mean so much, was at last to get "full value." Even while he mechanically performed the last sad offices for her, he said aloud several times, "Poor t'ing! poor t'ing!"

Her tragic passing was a relief to him only in view of her sudden turn. The ordinary hysterical woman he knew from much experience; but while he had stood beside her in her last religious frenzy, he had heard Sheba's words, and they frightened him. Twice she had declared herself, and only fire from heaven had saved him from exposure. So far her taking off was a relief. But at the same time it set for him embarrassing limitations. For one thing, it put an embargo upon his advertisement. He dare not connect the name of his company with so irregular a burial. She would be missed, and then there might be a search; there could be no doctor's certificate of license without an investigation of the circumstances. The sample funeral had already been reported, and its postponement needed no explanation.

Sheba's name had not needed to be mentioned in the services, and for simple prudence it had been omitted.

For aught the Broom Corn delegates knew, the funeral was held in the church with which she had connected herself, and was being conducted at her expense—and they must think so still; they must go home thinking so.

The attendance on the first day was more than doubled on the next; but, shame to say, there were exactly one third of the promised dozen carriages in attendance. To do the company justice, however, there were all that were called for by the policy, which Mr. Stein would have given his hat to find, and which lay safely under Queen o' Sheba's hands, where she should hold it for all time.

The only jar in the morning funeral occurred when some friends who had not come the day before begged to see the face of the corpse, and Mr. Stein was constrained to decline.

Her face had changed so sadly during the night that they who had seen it the day before would not recognize it, so he said, and it would only be too sorrowful a sight—which was true.

Thus, after life's weary battle, did Queen o' Sheba achieve her full final triumph.

Sonny's Diploma

Yas, sir; this is it. This here's Sonny's diplomy thet you've heerd so much about—sheepskin they call it, though it ain't no mo' sheepskin'n what I am. I've skinned too many not to know. Jest to think o' little Sonny bein' a gradj'ate—an' all by his own efforts, too!

It is a plain-lookin' picture, ez you say, to be framed up in sech a fine gilt frame; but it's worth it, an' I don't begrudge it to him. He picked out that red plush around the inside of the frame hisself. He's got mighty fine taste for a country-raised child, Sonny has.

Seem like the oftener I come here an' stan' before it, the prouder I feel, an' the mo' I can't reelize thet he done it.

I'd 'a' been proud enough to've had him go through the reg'lar co'se o' study, an' be awarded this diplomy, but to've seen 'im jest walk in an' demand it, the way he done, an' to prove his right in a fair fight—why, it tickles me so thet I jest seem to git a spell o' the giggles ev'y time I think about it.

Sir? How did he do it? Why, I thought eve'ybody in the State of Arkansas knowed how Sonny walked over the boa'd o' school directors, an' took a diplomy in the face of Providence, at the last anniversary.

I don't know thet I ought to say that either, for they never was a thing done mo' friendly an' amiable on earth, on his part, than the takin' of this dockiment. Why, no; of co'se he wasn't goin' to that school—cert'n'y not. Ef he had b'longed to that school, they wouldn't 'a' been no question about it. He'd 'a' jest gradj'ated with the others. An' when he went there with his ma an' me, why, he'll tell you hisself that he hadn't no mo' idee of gradj'atin'n what I have this minute.

An' when he riz up in his seat, an' announced his intention, why, you could 'a' knocked me down with a feather. You see, it took me so sudden, an' I didn't see jest how he was goin' to work it, never havin' been to that school.

Of co'se eve'ybody in the county goes to the gradj'atin', an'

113

we was all three settin' there watchin' the performances, not thinkin' of any special excitement, when Soony took this idee.

It seems thet seein' all the other boys gradj'ate put him in the notion, an' he felt like ez ef he ought to be a-gradj'atin', too.

You see, he had went to school mo' or less with all them fellers, an' he knowed thet they didn't, none o' 'em, know half ez much ez what he did—though, to tell the truth, he ain't never said sech a word, not even to her or me—an', seein' how easy they was bein' turned out, why, he jest reelized his own rights— an' demanded 'em then an' there.

Of co'se we know thet they is folks in this here community thet says thet he ain't got no right to this diplomy; but what else could you expect in a jealous neighborhood where eve'ybody is mo' or less kin?

The way I look at it, they never was a diplomy earned quite so upright ez this on earth—never. Ef it wasn't, why, I wouldn't allow him to have it, no matter how much pride I would 'a' took, an' do take, in it. But for a boy o' Sonny's age to've had the courage to face all them people, an' ask to be examined then an' there, an' to come out ahead, the way he done, why, it does me proud, that it does.

You see, for a boy to set there seein' all them know-nothin' boys gradj'ate, one after another, offhand, the way they was doin', was mighty provokin', an' when Sonny is struck with a sense of injestice, why, he ain't never been known to bear it in silence. He taken that from *her* side o' the house.

I noticed, ez he set there that day, thet he begin to look toler'ble solemn, for a festival, but it never crossed my mind what he was a-projeckin' to do. Ef I had 'a' suspicioned it, I'm afeered I would've opposed it, I'd 'a' been so skeert he wouldn't come out all right; an' ez I said, I didn't see, for the life o' me, how he was goin' to work it.

That is the only school in the county thet he ain't never went to, 'cause it was started after he had settled down to Miss Phoebe's school. He wouldn't hardly've went to it, nohow, though—less'n, of co'se, he'd 'a' took a notion. Th'ain't no 'ca- sion to send him to a county school when he's the only one we've got to edjercate. They ain't been a thing I've enjoyed ez much in my life ez my sackerfices on account o' Sonny's edjercation—not a one. Th'ain't a patch on any ol' coat I've got but seems to me to stand for some advantage to him. Well, sir, it was jest like I'm a-tellin' you. He set still ez long ez he could, an' then he riz an' spoke. Says he, "I have decided thet I'd like to do a little gradj'atin' this evenin' myself," jest that a-way.

An' when he spoke them words, for about a minute you could 'a' heerd a pin drop; an' then ev'ybody begin a-screechin' with laughter. A person would think thet they'd 'a' had some consideration for a child standin' up in the midst o' sech a getherin', tryin' to take his own part; but they didn't. They jest laughed immod'rate. But they didn't faze him. He had took his station on the flo', an' he helt his ground.

Jest ez soon ez he could git a heerin', why, he says, says he: "I don't want anybody to think thet I'm a-tryin' to take any advantage. I don't expec' to gradj'ate without passin' my examination. An', mo'n that," says he, "I am ready to pass it now." An' then he went on to explain thet he would like to have anybody present *thet was competent to do it* to step forward an' examine him—then an' there. An' he said thet ef he was examined fair and square, to the satisfaction of eve'ybody—*an' didn't pass*—why, he'd give up the p'int. An' he wanted to be examined oral—in eve'ybody's hearin'—free-handed an' outspoke.

Well, sir, seem like folks begin to see a little fun ahead in lettin' him try it—which I don't see jest how they could 'a' hindered him, an' it a free school, an' me a taxpayer. But they all seemed to be in a pretty good humor by this time, an' when Sonny put it to vote, why, they voted unanimous to let him try it. An' all o' them unanimous votes wasn't, to say, friendly, neither. Heap o' them thet was loudest in their unanimosity was hopefully expectin' to see him whipped out at the first question. Tell the truth, I mo'n half feared to see it myself. I was that skeert I was fairly all of a trimble.

Well, when they had done votin', Sonny, after first thankin' 'em—which I think was a mighty polite thing to do, an' they full o' the giggles at his little expense that minute—why, he went on to say thet he requie'd 'em to make *jest one condition*, an' that was thet any question he missed was to be passed on to them thet had been a-gradj'atin' so fast, an' ef they missed it, it wasn't to be counted ag'inst him.

Well, when he come out with that, which, to my mind, couldn't be beat for fairness, why, some o' the mothers they commenced to look purty serious, an' seem like ez ef they didn't find it quite so funny ez it had been. You see, they *say* thet them boys had eve'y one had reg'lar questions give' out to 'em, an' eve'y last one had studied his own word; an' ef they was to be questioned hit an' miss, why they wouldn't 'a' stood no chance on earth.

Of co'se they couldn't give Sonny the same questions thet had *been* give out, because he had heerd the answers, an' it wouldn't 'a' been fair. So Sonny he told 'em to jest set down, an' make out a list of questions thet they'd all agree was about of a equal hardness to them thet had been ast, an' was of jest the kind of learnin' thet all the reg'lar gradj'ates's minds was sto'ed with, an' thet either he knowed 'em or he didn't—one.

It don't seem so excitin', somehow, when I tell about it now; but I tell you for about a minute or so, whilst they was waitin' to see who would undertake the job of examinin' him, why, it seemed thet eve'y minute would be the next, ez my ol' daddy used to say. The only person present thet seemed to take things anyway ca'm was Miss Phoebe Kellog, Sonny's teacher. She has been teachin' him reg'lar for over two years now, an' ef she had 'a' had a right to give diplomies, why, Sonny would 'a' jest took out one from her; but she ain't got no license to gradj'ate nobody. But she knowed what Sonny knowed, an' she knowed thet ef he had a fair show, he'd come thoo creditable to all hands. She loves Sonny jest about ez much ez we do, I believe, take it all around. Th'ain't never been but one time in these two years thet she has, to say, got me out o' temper, an' that was the day she said to me thet her sure belief was thet Sonny was goin' to *make somethin' out'n hisself* some day—like ez ef he hadn't already made mo'n could be expected of a boy of his age. Tell the truth, I never in my life come so near sayin' somethin' I'd 'a' been shore to regret ez I did on that occasion. But of co'se I know she didn't mean it. All she meant was thet he would turn out even mo'n what he was now, which would be on'y nachel, with his growth.

Everybody knows thet it was her that got him started with his collections an' his libr'y. Oh, yes; he's got the best libr'y in the county, 'cep'n', of co'se, the doctor's 'n' the preacher's—everybody round about here knows about that. He's got about a hund'ed books an' over. Well, sir, when he made that remark, thet any question thet he missed was to be give to the class, why, the whole atmosp'ere took on a change o' temp'ature. Even the teacher was for backin' out o' the whole business square; but he didn't jest seem to dare to say so. You see, after him a-favorin' it, it would 'a' been a dead give-away.

Eve'ybody there had saw him step over an' whisper to Brother Binney when it was decided to give Sonny a chance, an' they knowed thet he had asked *him* to examine him. But now, instid o' callin' on Brother Binney, why, he jest said, says he: "I suppose I ought not to shirk this duty. Ef it's to be did," says he, "I reckon I ought to do it—an' do it I will." You see, he daresn't allow Brother Binney to put questions, for fear he'd call out some thet his smarty grad'jates couldn't answer.

So he jest claired his th'oat, an' set down a minute to consider. An' then he riz from his seat, an' remarked, with a heap o' *hems* and *haws*, thet of co'se everybody knowed thet Sonny Jones had had unusual advantages in some respec's, but thet it was one thing for a boy to spend his time a-picnickin' in the woods, getherin' all sorts of natural curiosities, but it was quite another to be a scholar accordin' to books, so's to be able to pass sech a' examination ez would be a credit to a State institution o' learnin', sech ez the one over which he was proud to preside. That word struck me partic'lar, "proud to preside," which, in all this, of co'se, I see he was castin' a slur on Sonny's collections of birds' eggs, an' his wild flowers, an' wood specimens, an' min'rals. He even went so far ez to say thet ol' Proph', the half-crazy nigger thet tells fortunes, an' gethers herbs out'n the woods, an' talks to hisself, likely knew more about a good many things than anybody present, but thet, bein' ez he didn't know B from a bull's foot, why, it wouldn't hardly do to gradj'ate him—not castin' no slurs on Master Sonny Jones, nor makin' no invijus comparisons, of co'se.

Well, sir, there was some folks there thet seemed to think this sort o' talk was mighty funny an' smart. Some o' the mothers

acchilly giggled over it out loud, they was so mightily tickled. But
Sonny he jest stood his ground an' waited. Most any boy o' his
age would 'a' got flustered, but he didn't. He jest glanced around
unconcerned at all the people a-settin' around him, jest like ez ef
they might 'a' been askin' him to a picnic instid o' him provokin' a
whole school committee to wrath.

Well, sir, it took that school-teacher about a half-hour to pick
out the first question, an' he didn't pick it out *then*. He'd stop, an'
he'd look at the book, an' then he'd look at Sonny, an' then he'd
look at the class—an' then he'd turn a page, like ez ef he couldn't
make up his mind, an' was afeerd to resk it, less'n it might be
missed, an' be referred back to the class. I never did see a man so
overwrought over a little thing in my life—never. They do say,
though, that school-teachers feels mighty bad when their scholars misses any p'int in public.

Well, sir, he took so long that d'reckly everybody begin to git
wo'e out, an' at last Sonny, why, he got tired, too, an' he up an'
says, says he, "Ef you can't make up your mind what to ask me,
teacher, why'n't you let me ask myself questions? An' ef my
questions seem too easy, why, I'll put 'em to the class."

An', sir, with that he jest turns round, an' he says, says he,
"Sonny Jones," says he, addressin' hisself, "what's the cause of
total eclipses of the sun?" Jest that a-way he said it; an' then he
turned around, an' he says, says he:

"Is that a hard enough question?"

"Very good," says teacher.

An', with that, Sonny he up an' picks up a' orange an' a'
apple off the teacher's desk, an' says he, "This orange is the earth,
an' this here apple is the sun." An', with that, he explained all
they is *to* total eclipses. I can't begin to tell you jest how he
expressed it, because I ain't highly edjercated myself, an' I don't
know the specifactions. But when he had got thoo, he turned to
the teacher, an' says he, "Is they anything else thet you'd like to
know about total eclipses?" An' teacher says, says he, "Oh, no;
not at all."

They do say thet them gradj'ates hadn't never went so far ez
total eclipses, an' teacher wouldn't 'a' had the subject mentioned
to 'em for nothin'; but I don't say that's so.

Well, then, Sonny he turned around, an' looked at the company, an' he says, "Is everybody satisfied?" An' all the mothers an' fathers nodded their heads "yes."

An' then he waited jest a minute, an' he says, says he, "Well, now I'll put the next question:

"Sonny Jones," says he, "what is the difference between dew an' rain an' fog an' hail an' sleet an' snow?

"Is that a hard enough question?"

Well, from that he started in, an' he didn't stop tell he had expounded about every kind of dampness that ever descended from heaven or rose from the earth. An' after that, why, he went on a-givin' out one question after another, an' answerin' 'em, tell everybody had declared theirselves entirely satisfied that he was fully equipped to gradj'ate—an', tell the truth, I don't doubt thet a heap of 'em felt their minds considerably relieved to have it safe-t over with without puttin' their grad'jates to shame, when what does he do but say, "Well, ef you're satisfied, why, I am—an' yet," says he, "I think I would like to ask myself one or two hard questions more, jest to make shore." An' befo' anybody could stop him, he had said:

"Sonny Jones, what is the reason thet a bird has feathers and a dog has hair?" An' then he turned around deliberate, an' answered: "I don't know. Teacher, please put that question to the class."

Teacher had kep' his temper purty well up to this time, but I see he was mad now, an' he riz from his chair, an' says he: "This examination has been declared finished, an' I think we have spent ez much time on it ez we can spare." An' all the mothers they nodded their heads, an' started a-whisperin'—most impolite.

An' at that, Sonny, why, he jest set down as modest an' peaceable ez anything; but ez he was settin' he remarked thet he was in hopes thet some o' the reg'lars would 'a' took time to answer a few questions thet had bothered his mind f'om time to time—an' of co'se they must know; which, to my mind, was the modes'est remark a boy ever did make.

Well, sir, that's the way this diplomy was earned—by a good, hard struggle, in open daylight, by unanimous vote of all concerned—an' unconcerned, for that matter. An' my opinion is thet if they are those who have any private opinions about it, an' they didn't express 'em that day, why they ain't got no right to do it underhanded, ez I am sorry to say has been done.

But it's *his* diplomy, an' it's handsomer fixed up than any in town, an' I doubt ef they ever was one *anywhere* thet was took more paternal pride in.

Wife she ain't got so yet thet she can look at it without sort o' cryin'—jest the look of it seems to bring back the figure o' the little feller, ez he helt his ground, single-handed, at that gradj'atin' that day.

Well, sir, we was so pleased to have him turned out a full gradj'ate thet, after it was all over, why, I riz up then and there, though I couldn't hardly speak for the lump in my th'oat, an' I said thet I wanted to announce thet Sonny was goin' to have a gradj'atin' party out at our farm that day week, an' thet the present company was all invited.

An' he did have it, too; an' they all come, every mother's son of 'em—from *a* to *izzard*—even to them that has expressed secret dissatisfactions; which they was all welcome, though it does seem to me thet, ef I'd been in their places, I'd 'a' hardly had the face to come an' talk, too.

I'm this kind of a disposition myself: ef I was ever to go to any kind of a collation thet I expressed disapproval of, why, the supper couldn't be good enough not to choke me.

An' Sonny, why, he's constructed on the same plan. We ain't never told him of any o' the remarks thet has been passed. They might git his little feelin's hurted, an' twouldn't do no good, though some few has been made to his face by one or two smarty, ill-raised boys.

Well, sir, we give 'em a fine party, ef I do say it myself, an' they all had a good time. Wife she whipped up eggs an' sugar for a week befo'hand, an' we set the table out under the mulberries. It took eleven little niggers to wait on 'em, not countin' them thet worked the fly-fans. An' Sonny he ast the blessin'.

Then, after they'd all et, Sonny he had a' exhibition of his little specimens. He showed 'em his bird eggs, an' his wood samples, an' his stamp album, an' his scroll-sawed things, an' his clay-moldin's, an' all his little menagerie of animals an' things. I ruther think everybody was struck when they found thet Sonny knowed the botanical names of every one of the animals he's ever tamed, an' every bird. Miss Phoebe, she didn't come to the front much. She stayed along with wife, an' helped 'tend to the company, but I could see she looked on with pride; an' I don't want nothin' said about it, but the boa'd of school directors was so took with the things she had taught Sonny thet, when the evenin' was over, they ast her to accept a situation in the academy next year, an' she's goin' to take it.

An' she says thet ef Sonny will take a private co'se of instruction in nachel sciences, an' go to a few lectures, why, th'ain't nobody on earth that she'd ruther see come into that academy ez teacher—that is, of co'se, in time. But I doubt ef he'd ever keer for it.

I've always thought thet school-teachin', to be a success, has to run in families, same ez anythin' else—yet, th'ain't no tellin'.

I don't keer what he settles on when he's grown; I expect to take pride in *the way he'll do it*—an' that's the principal thing, after all.

It's the "Well done" we're all a-hopin' to hear at the last day; an' the po' laborer thet digs a good ditch'll have jest ez good a chance to hear it ez the man that owns the farm.

A Misfit Christmas

Well, well, well! Ef there ain't the doctor! At the steps befo' I discovered him! That's what I get for standin' on step-ladders at my time o' life. Ef you'd 'a' been a brigand you'd 'a' had me, Doc'—both hands up.

I was tempted o' the heathen by these big Japanese persimmons. Here, lay these on the banister-rail for me, Doc'—an' look out! Don't taste 'em, less'n you want yo' mouth fixed to whistle. That puckerin' trick runs in the family.

Yas, they're smooth an' handsome, but gimme the little ol' woods persimmon, seedy an' wrinkled an' sugared by the frost, character lines all over its face—same as a good ol' Christian.

Merry Christmas, ol' friend!—ef it is three days after.

This first shake is for "Merry Christmas," an' this is for thanks for yo' Christmas gif'. It did seem to be about the only one thet amounted—no, I won't say that, neither. They was all well-meant an' kind, an' I've been on the edge of cryin' all day, jest to think—although—

But come along into my room an' see the things. Oh, yas; I reckon it was a sort of "ovation" to celebrate my seventy-fifth Christmas this-a-way an' to make it a surprise party, at that.

It seems thet Mary Elizabeth, Sonny's wife, give out along in the summer thet this was to be my seventy-fifth Christmas, an' invited accordin'ly—all the village an' country-side. She jest give it out promiscuous, tellin' everybody thet the only person thet *wasn't* to know about it was me—*on pain of not havin' it*. That was what you might call a stroke of ingeniousness. They ain't a person in the county thet would miss havin' an unusual thing like that, an' so the secret was pretty safe-t.

She never wrote no invitations. She'd jest tell every person she met to instruct the next one. So nobody's feelin's was hurted. She declares she never hinted about presents; but it must 'a' been in her voice an' her intimations unbeknownst to herself, for not a mother's son or daughter come empty-handed.

'Sh-h-h! I notice the sewin'-machine has stopped an' she might—

But I tell you here—'sh!—I say, I tell you, doc', *I can't turn around in my own room.* An' sech ridic—I tell you, *I never was so miserable in my life!*

Oh, of course, they's exceptions. There's yo' present, f'instance. Sech a pocket-knife as that—why, it's a heredity! I've got it down in my will a'ready—that is to say, I've got it codiciled to my namesake. What you say? Oh, no; I wouldn't have no child named Deuteronomy, the way Sonny an' I was. I'm come to a reelization of it.

He an' Mary Elizabeth, why, they offered it through excess of devotional feelin'. I see you recall the circumstance now. He's named after a certain auburn-haired doctor—an' yet, as I say, he's my namesake—named something else, for my sake. We jes call 'im Doc' for short.

Yas, he'll get that knife, though I hope to season it a little an' get the blades wore down some before he receives it.

It was real white in you to send sech a thing as that. A person might 'a' supposed thet you'd 'a' sent a fresh box o' porous plasters, or maybe a bottle o' lithia tab—

Why, no; of co'se I didn't fear it. How could I—an' be surprised? But ef I had been anticipatin' the party, I'd 'a' thought o' yo' drug-sto' show-case, an' they ain't never anything appetizin' in it to me. You cert'n'y deserve credit not even to select sech a thing as a hammock or a head-rest, although ef you had, I'd never 'a' questioned it.

Yes, I got a few head-rests, some stuffed with hops an' some with balsam, an' one poor neck-roll perfumed with something turrible—asafetida, I reckon. I've laid that out to sun. Mary Elizabeth says they're good to ward off whoopin'-cough, an' I told her I'd rather have the whoopin'-cough than it.

Oh, yas; the party was fine, an', as I said, they was a lump in my throat from the arrival of the first visitor, although it was Moreland Howe, an' you know I never hankered after Moreland. I reckon the reason my throat lumped up so at him comin' was the thought thet *even* Moreland had come to wish me joy. You see, he give my emotions a back lick—an' it's jest like 'im.

He brought me that redic'lous thing hangin' from the swingin' lamp over my readin'-table in the hall there. What you say? "What is it?" God knows, doctor, an' he ain't told me. I suspicion it's jest a sort o' *eye-ketcher,*—to be looked at—although I'd ruther look at almost anything I know. It's a thing thet, ef a person was anyways nervous, would either help him or hender him. He might find ease in tryin' to count the red an' purple worsted tassels, or the flies thet light on 'em; but ef he did, seem to me he would come to realize thet there was holes in the perforated paper thet couldn't be counted, an'—well, I don't like to discuss it. It's the kind o' thing *she* or *I* never liked—not thet I've ever seen its exact match.

The only use *she* ever had for perforated paper was to make crosses for pulpit bookmarks—an' I've made 'em myself whilst she'd be darnin', jest startin' with one row o' between-holes an' cuttin' each one bigger until the desired size was reached, an' then pastin' 'em one on top o' the other, accordin' to size, so's the middle would rise up like sculpture. Then they're fastened on to the ends of ribbins to hang out in view o' the congregation. Now, there's a useful thing—an' suitable.

You know, Moreland was engaged to be married once-t, an' I suspicion thet this dangle is one of his engagement presents thet he's had laid away. I've got a consperacy in my mind thet'll rid me of it—in time. I'm goin' to tech it over keerfully with what attraction I can scrape off o' flypaper, quick as spring opens, an' when Moreland sees how they've ruined it, why, I'll drop it in the stove—*with regrets.*

He's dropped in twice-t a'ready sence it's hung there, jest to enjoy it, although he ain't crossed this threshold before but once-t in three year.

I tell you, doctor, they's nothin' thet stimulates friendship like givin'. Receivin' is cheap compared to it, ez the Bible declares.

Yes, but we were might sorry you couldn't come to the party, doctor; an' ef it had been anything but another birthday occasion thet kep' you away, we'd 'a' made a row about it. Of course the babies, bless their hearts! they must have all the attention thet they can't demand.

I tell you, things are a heap more equalized in this world than shortsighted mortals can discern.

But you ain't seen the bulk o' the presents yet, doctor. Wait a minute tel I have time to put on my hypocritical smile an' I'll take you in. We'll be ap' to meet Mary Elizabeth, an' I owe it to her particularly to be as deceitfully cheerful as I can over it; in fact, I owe it to all them thet took part in it.

I wouldn't mind it so much ef I could shet my room door an' get into bed an' see the interior landscape thet I'm used to, but—

'Sh-h-h! I hear her slippers. She's heared you an' she's comin' out.

Here's doctor, daughter. An' I'm jest takin' 'im in to view my purties.

So now, I s'pose my popularity is in a manner proved, as you say, an' it's all mighty fine an' gratifyin'. But after I've lived with my constituency for a while, so to speak, I'm goin' to get you to separate 'em, Mary Elizabeth, an' let the whole house feel it. No, don't say a word! It's got to be done. Do you think I'm that selfish thet I'd appropriate all the combined popularity of daughter an' son *an'* gran'child'en!

The truth is, Doc', this has got to be a turrible popular house sence Sonny has been elected school director an' little Marthy is old enough to have a choice o' hair-ribbins.

An' Mary Elizabeth she always was popular. An' I see she's lookin' at her watch: we're keepin' 'er too long. I s'pose a watch gets looked in the face the first week of its ownership often enough to lose countenance forever except it knew it would have plenty of retirement, later on. Most ladies' watches lead lives of leisure.

Yas, I give it to her. I think every lady should have a good gold watch an' chain, ef for nothin' else on account o' the children rememberin' "ma with her watch an' chain." An' the various daguerreotypes looks well with 'em. It's a part o' gentility, a lady's watch is, whether it's kep' wound up or not.

An' in case o' breakin' up a home, a watch looks well on the inventory. Little Marthy—her grandma's namesake—of course she's got *hers*, an' it ain't no mean timepiece, neither. It's got a live purple amethyst on one side, an' the chain goes around twice-t— an' ef the day comes when she wants to take my old picture out o' the case an' put in a younger man's, I'll be that much better pleased to know thet joy stays with us, along with time.

I wonder ef that ain't a purty fair joke, doctor, for a seventy-fiver—settin' amongst his troubles, too.

I'm glad she slipped away. She's sech a modest little thing—
went jest as soon as I referred to her popularity. I wouldn't 'a'
wanted her to stay an' look over my presents with you. It'd 'a'
made me tongue-tied. Come along, Doc'. That's right. You lif'
that an' I'll pull *this* back whilst I shet the door with my foot.

I tried to open that door yesterday from my bed the way I've
always done, but by the time I'd got the things out o' the way they
wasn't anything left to use but my teeth, an' ruther than resk my
plate on that glass door-knob I got up an' h'isted a few things on
to the bed—an' the rebellion thet came into my heart I'd like to
forget. I've doubted the doctrine of total depravity all my life, as
you know, but maybe it's so, after all—in my case, at least. I
reckon, like as not, all doctrines is true, more or less, in some
lights, or else so many people wouldn't see their ways to believin'
'em.

The way I've sinned over these presents has filled me with
regretful remorse.

Look out! Don't step! Wait a minute! Some o' the children has
wound it up. I hear it whir. Here it comes from under the bed. We
must've shook the floor. What do you think o' that, now? Sir?
Why, it's said to be a seed-counter. Jim Bowers brought it. He
says thet when it travels that-a-way it's prowlin' for food an' it
craves peas an' beans to count.

What's that you say? "Did I give it any?" No, I didn't. Not a
one. I was too nettled to give Jim that satisfaction. I know it's
some dod-blasted patent thet he's been took in with, an' he
thought thet bein' as I was in my second childhood, I'd be tickled
over it—an' I got contrary.

I really wouldn't care so much ef the thing wasn't so all-fired
big. It takes up as much floor-room as a chair, an' I'm compelled
to keep it in sight—for a while.

Who in thunder wants seeds counted, even if the fool thing
could do it? It's more like a toe-snatcher, to me; an' I intend to
have it chained to the table-leg, a safe-t distance from my bed. I
never did like the idee of havin' my bare feet nabbed in the dark.

Our littlest he's mighty mischievious, an' no doubt he heered
me an' you start to come in, an' he's sneaked in an' wound
up—Look out, there! I say he's been in here an' wound up things.
That ain't nothin' but a mechanical rooster, but you don't want to

step on it. See him stretch his neck an'—did you ever hear anything so ridic'lous! I s'pose I must ac' mighty childish for people to fetch me sech presents. An' yet, I ruther like that rooster. It tickles me to see the way he exerts hisself.

Hold on, Doc'! That's on the bureau an' it can't do you no harm. Yas, he's wound 'em all up, the little scamp, an' like as not he's watchin' us from somewheres.

Jest to think, Doc', thet we was boys once-t. It's the fullest-to-the-brim of happiness of all the cups of life, boyhood is, I do believe.

Don't start! Thet's jest a donkey savin's-bank, an' it'll "yee-haw!" that-a-way now tel a nickel's dropped in its slotted ear. He's the family favoryte of all the presents, an' he's heavy with money a'ready. What's that you say? "He'll bray tell he runs down?" But he don't never run down—not within the limit of human endurance.

They say they're the best money-savers on the market. They're so ridic'lous, 'most anybody'll spend a little change to see 'em perform. The feller showed his genius in makin' the deposit go to hushin' 'em. He knew thet once-t he got started, a man would give his last cent to silence him. Did you ever hear so much sound out of sech a little—An' his last bray is as loud as his first.

Here, drop this in his ear, for gracious' sakes, so we can talk.

Oh, them? They're picture-frames constructed out o' chicken-bones.

I s'pose maybe they's jestice in this museum, but they don't seem to be mercy.

It seems thet a lady down in Ozan has been givin' lessons in makin' 'em. Yas, chicken-bones steeped in diamond dyes; an' they say they's seventeen kinds o' flowers an' four fruits represented. I ain't studied 'em out yet, but I can see they've used drumsticks for buds, mostly. An' the neck-j'ints, unj'inted, they're wide-open perrarer-flowers.

The heads is seed-pods, an' so is the popes'-noses; an' I have an idee thet the chrysanthe'ums an' asters is constructed mainly of ribs. Of course it'd take a number, but on a farm—

Why, yas; I s'pose it is purty—uncommon purty—considerin'; but in things of beauty I don't like to have to consider, an' the thing don't appetize me worth a cent.

Them gum-ball frames, now, an' the sycamores an' pinecones do very well. But when it comes to framin' my relations, I sort o' like to put my hand in my pocket an' do 'em store-jestice. An' these nature-frames they ketch dust an' harbor spiders.

Between you an' me, I don't intend to give them graveyard chicken-frames house room more'n jest so long, an' the only real use I can think to put 'em to is a raffle; so I'll donate 'em to the next county fair to be raffled for expenses. You see, they'd be suitable for the flower, fruit, *an'* fowl departments, an' they pleg me, jest knowin' they're here.

Mary Elizabeth she ain't give no opinion of 'em yet, an' she may consider 'em suitable to frame a couple o' stuffed birds she's got; an' ef she does, why, she's welcome. She'd likely gild hers to match the pinecone frame round her mother. She's got it trimmed with a piece of her ma's favoryte silk dress, fastened in one corner by a little pin she used to wear. She considers suitableness in everything, Mary Elizabeth does.

These slippers I've got on was her present. She worked the initials, an' they're lined with a scrap o' one o' wife's old wool dresses, an' I like to know it.

That new readin'-lamp? Why, Sonny he give me that. The old one was good enough a-plenty, but it seems thet these new ones have special organdy burners—or no, I reckon it was the old one thet had the organdy burner, an' this one is to wear a mantle, he says. Either one reminds me of *her*—either the organdy or the mantle—an', of course, I need the best light now for my night chapter o' the gospel. The little feller—why, he made the stand it sets on, an' the mats was crocheted by the girls.

Oh, I got lots of nice suitable things, an' I appreciate every-thing, nice or not, exceptin' that seed-counter, an' I never will be reconciled to bein' made cheap of. I hate a fool, even when it's inanimate.

Yas, that's a map o' the world. Henry Burgess brought that. Yas, it does seem a nice thing, an' I said so, too, an' I'm glad I praised it befo' I saw the date on it. After that, I'd 'a' been compelled either to pervaricate or to fail in politeness, an' it's always easier to fall on a piller than into a brier-patch. Good hearted people has to look sharp not to become cheerful liars.

I've looked for places I know on the map, but it's either noncommittal or I'm not observant enough. They don't seem to be no Philippine Islands on it whatsoever, but like as not they wasn't thought much of then an' they're secreted somewhere.

I always did like the look of a wall-map—when I go into an office or court-house—but I doubt whether I'll ever fully relish this on my own wall. A clock thet won't keep truthful time always plegs me, an' this threatens me the same way.

Oh, no; that ain't to say a toy, exac'ly—that nigger doll on the mantel. It's a pin-cushion; an' the heathen Chinee, why, he's a holder of shavin'-paper; an' the stuffed cat it's a foot-rest. I notice it's mouse-e't at the corners, so the conno'ziers ain't deceived.

I see somethin' has stole the hickory-nut head o' the tooth-pick lady a'ready, an' I suspect it's the flyin'-squirrel I caught sniffin' at her yesterday.

An' that pile o' ribbins? Oh, they've come off o' all the things. That was the first thing I done, rippin' them off. They'd ketch in my hands so an' gimme goose-skin the len'th o' my spine.

I've passed them over to Mary Elizabeth, an' she'll likely work 'em into crazy-patches or hair-ribbins for the girls.

That? Excuse me whistlin'. That's *whisky*, doctor. An' who do you reckon sent it? Who but Miss Sophia Falena Simpkins, the twin—an' they both teetotalers! Shows their confidence in me.

"How old is it?" Well, she allowed it was as old as they was, an' of co'se that stopped my inquiry, but it's old enough to be treated with respect an' not abuse. Yas, that four-in-hand necktie was tied on its neck—from the other twin. Oh, it's the reverend stuff, an' that thimble-sized, hat-shaped glass over the cork seems to stand for their maidenly consciences, an' I won't never violate the hint.

That shoe-an'-slipper holder with all the nests in it was sent in by our chapter of the King's Daughters, each daughter contributin' one nest, as I understand it; an' it's ornamental on the wall, although my one contribution looks middlin' lonesome in it. Of co'se I always have on either my slippers or my boots, an' when I get into bed it's unhandy to cross the room jest to put either one up in style.

The first night it hung there the children all come an' put in their shoes for the night, but that was awkward. They had to go out barefeeted.

Yas, the motter is suitable enough. "Rest for tired soles" is about as inoffensive as a motter could well be. An' so is this, on one o' the umbrella-holders, "Wait tel the clouds roll by," although it seems a sort o' misfit for an umbrella. "When it rains it pours" would be more to my mind. Yas, I've got three. "Little drops of water," this one seems to have on it; an' this one says—I never can read them German-tex' letters. What's that you say? "Expansion for protection only?" It's well to be highly educated like you, doctor. I wouldn't 'a' made that out in a week. It sounds sort o' deep-seated to me, like ez ef more was meant than you see at first? I wonder ef it could refer to politics, some way. "Expansion for protection only." It cert'n'y sounds political. Why, of co'se, Jedge Whittemore, he sent me that—an' he's so opposed to annexin' the Philippines.

Yas, they did fetch a ridic'lous lot o' pen-wipers, for a person o' my sedate habits. I never did fly to the pen much. You see, when a present is more or less obligatory, why, a pen-wiper is an easy way out. Almost any cloth shape repeated an' tacked in the middle with some sort o' centerpiece, like an odd button, rises into prominence with the look of a present.

Of co'se I *have* wrote letters, from time to time, in days past. I was countin', only last Sunday, the letters I've wrote in my life, an', includin' my proposal-letter, which I wrote an' handed to her personal, on account o' the paralysis of my tongue—I say, countin' that, I've wrote seven letters all told; an' I regret to say, one of the seven was writ in anger, an' two in apology for it, so thet they's only four real creditable letters to my credit, an' one o' the four wasn't to say extry friendly, although it sounded well.

That was the one I wrote to Sally Ann, time her first husband, Teddy Brooks, died. Poor Teddy could easy 'a' been kep' livin' along a few years more, ef not permanent, ef he'd been looked after an' excused from so much motherly cradle service. Of co'se I knew Sally Ann, an' thet she was nachelly a public performer, an' would be readin' 'er letters of consolation out loud to whoever dropped in, an' I composed it accordin'. An' so she did, for she wrote me thet my note of condolence was the most eloquent of all she got—"so everybody said." She beats the Dutch, Sally Ann does.

I don't suppose she ever took a moment's comfort in seclusion in her life, no more'n a weather-vane. Poor Sally!

But talkin' about this excessive circulation of presents thet's come into fashion these last years, I don't approve of it, doctor; an' you know it ain't thet I'm stingy about doin' my part. I'll give a present, ef need be, an' I'll even command the grace to take one—I seem to've proved that—but it's the principle of the thing thet troubles my mind.

Some of our best-raised girls has got flighty that-a-way after goin' to boa'din'-school, where they learn a heap more'n Latin verbs an' finishin' behavior. Not thet I don't appreciate what they do acquire. It seems to lift 'em into a higher region of ladyhood, I know, an' it's a thing you can't locate.

Wife had a year at Hilltop Academy, an' I always thought she showed it, even in the way she'd gether eggs in 'er apron, or keep still tel another person quit speakin'. But of co'se they's boa'din'-schools *an'* boa'din'-schools, an' them thet fosters idle hands I don't approve of; an' the fact thet a parent may be able to pay for it ain't got nothin' to do with the divine responsibility as I see it. The idee of an earthly parent bein' willin' to put up big money to have his own flesh an' blood incapacitated for misfortune.

Oh, yas; they give me considerable books. They've complimented my education to that extent. This "pronuncin'-Testament," for instance, I seized with delight, hopin' to get the real patriarchal pronounciations. I wanted to see if sech jokes as "Milk-easy-Dick" an' "Knee-high-miah" and "Build-dad-the-shoe-height" was legitimate frivolity, but I ain't had no luck so far. I sort o' wonder what kind of a man would aspire to write a Bible-pronouncer.

You know sence Sonny's taken to writin' books, an' we've had an author's readin' here, I always seem to discern a person behind every volume.

Yas; they're usin' several of Sonny's nature-books in the schools, now, an' he has mo' orders'n he can fill, but he won't never hurry. You know he never did. He'll study over a thing tel he's satisfied with it, before any temptation would induce him to write about it. That's why he gets sech high prices for what he does. It don't have to be contradicted, an' no pleasure of the imagination will make him lead a dumb beast into behavior thet's too diplomatic or complicated.

He's done some jocular experimentin'—set eggs under inappropriate beasts an' sech as that—but he ain't had no luck. All our beasts-of-a-hair seem to flock together same as birds of a feather. He 'lows thet he's often seen expressions on our dog's face thet looked like ez ef he might be capable of intrigue or religious exaltation, but Sonny ain't felt justifiable in ascribin' motives jest on his facial indications—not even when it's backed by the expression of his tail.

You ain't goin'? Well, I'm a friend to all the sick, so I won't keep you. Yo' visit has done me good, doctor. I always did love to hear you talk. We agree an' disagree jest enough for sugar an' spice.

Oh, yas; it's been a merry Christmas; no doubt about that. An' the fun ain't fully over, either. I'll amuse myself with the presents thet's been adjudged suitable to my mind, when time hangs too heavy. I thought last night thet some time I'd empty that bottle o' iron pills I never took—I'd empty 'em into the seed-counter when it was on some of its migrations; an' ef it knew the difference an' spurned to count 'em, I'd try to have some respect for its intellect.

Good-by, Doc', an' a merry Christmas!

Surely, say it again: "Merry Christmas!" That lasts here tel we can say "Happy New Year!" They say our Christmas laughter was heared clair acrost Chinquapin Creek, an' ol' Mis' Gibbs, settin' there paralyzed in her chair, she laughed with us whilst she enjoyed the basket-dinner Mary Elizabeth sent over to her.

Yas, them's her cardin'-combs. She couldn't come to the surprise party, so she sent them to me. Her hands refuse to hold 'em any longer, an' she allowed no doubt thet I might while away my last moments that-a-way. But of co'se she didn't know me. I may be old an' childish, but even ef I was to turn baby again, I'd be a boy-baby. Yas, I know I *could* use 'em, but I *won't*.

It's true I made Bible book-marks, but they was for a man to preach by, an' a housewifey woman set beside me, sewin' whilst I made 'em. That was enough to difference me. Why, ef I was to get so sedated down thet I could set up here an' do feminyne work, I'd feel belittled, an' no man can stand that.

Well, good-by, ef you must. Here, ol' friend, gimme yo' hand an' lemme hold it still jest a minute. So much of our earthly hand-shakin' is jest touch an' go—an' I like to realize a friend's hand once-t in a while.

An' now I've got it, I want to keep it whilst I say somethin'. Settin' here these long hours sence this blessed Christmas day, which, after all my jocular analyzin', has moved me to tears, I've had a *thought*—a thought which has give me comfort, an' I'm goin' to pass it on to you.

Settin' amongst my misfit presents, yesterday, mad one minute an' chokin' with laughter an' throat-lumps the next, I suddenly seemed to hear a line o' the old hymn, "My Christmas will last all the year," an' then I was thankful thet my 'Piscopal experience had furnished me a ready answer to that: "Good Lord, deliver us!"

An' then, with my funny-bone fairly trimblin' an' my risible eye on the fly-catcher, the sweetest thought come to me—like a white bird out of a wind-storm.

Harassed as I was with all these presents, I couldn't seem to contemplate a continuous Christmas of peace, noways, when suddenly I seemed to see the words befo' me, differently spelled. Instid of "e-n-t-s" I saw "e-n-c-e," an' right befo' my speritual vision I saw, same ez sky-writin', "The Christmas Presence"— jest so.

Maybe it won't strike you, but it was a great thought to me, doctor, an' "Christmas all the year" had a new sound to my ears.

Think of that, doctor—of livin' along in the azurine blue, beholdin' the face of the Little One of the manger by the near light of the Bethlehem star!

Or maybe seein' the Beloved leanin' on a piller of clouds, illuminin' our listenin' faces with the gleam of his countenance whilst he'd maybe repeat the Sermon on the Mount from the book of his eternal memory. Think of what an author's readin' that would be—an' what an audience!

An' it's this Christmas Presence thet inspires all our lovin' thoughts here below, whether we discern it or not.

An' what we'll get on the other side'll be *realization*—a clair vision with all the mists of doubt dissolved.

This is the thought thet come to me yesterday, doctor, out o' the cyclone of playful good will thet got me so rattled. An' it's come to stay.

An' with it, how sweet it will be to set an' wait, with a smile to welcome the endurin' Christmas thet'll last "all the year" an' forever.

The Women

Well, doc', I don't wonder you wonder. That is, ef it's jest broke in on you—the stir among the women, an' what it's come to. I ain't quite so thunder-struck, because I've had time on my hands an' patience, an' I've been lookin' on an' watchin' whilst you've been tendin' the sick.

For perfessional lady speakers to come to Simpkinsville, an' for our women to go about wearin' badges an' to have their expenses paid aroun' the country ez delegates, ain't nothin' mo'n they've been havin' all over the continent for years. It's only come home to us, that's all.

It was funny, when you think of it, though, for 'em to let me into the "mothers' meetin'." I was determined to see what they was to it ef I could, so I engineered some—offered to take charge, an' light up the hall for 'em, free-gratis-for-nothin'; an' that carried it.

Of co'se they nachelly hesitated—an' me a man—but you know Sally Ann is great for savin' a dime, an' she laughed, an' says she, "Why, Grampa Jones he's man-woman-and-child, all in one, anyhow." Of co'se that made a laugh, an' they give in. So I jest handed ol' nigger Joe Towns a dollar—that's his gen'al fee for openin' up an' lightin', an' I wouldn't have him deprived—an' I see the whole thing from the openin' to the close. Yas, it cost some, but it was cheap—considerin' the show.

I tell you, it's an edjercation to a man to git into sech a crowd, an' to hear the women hol' fo'th. An' I heerd some things I hope to remember, an' to live by mo' or less, f'om this time on.

Of co'se I went on account o' the child'en mainly. I ain't denyin' all curiosity, mind you; but I knowed their mother she couldn't leave them at bedtime—most mothers can't—an' I allowed thet ef they was good words bein' distributed for mothers, I could collect 'em an' fetch 'em home about ez well ez the next one.

Sir? *"How many?"*

Well, I suppose they was maybe forty or fifty women there, all counted.

134

You ricollec' ten year ago come Christmas, when Abe Bosworth's sist'-in-law come down here f'om Ultima Thool an' lectured on women exhorters in the churches, they wasn't but *eleven* present, an' *they* was nearer the *froth* than they was to the *sediment* of Simpkinsville folks. The best ones wanted to go, but they didn't dast; opposition run too high.

Well, she said some good things thet's been quoted variously ever sence, an', ez Miss Phoebe Kellogg says, them 'leven women was the leaven thet leavened the whole lot. Miss Phoebe will have her joke on words, an' sometimes a little thing like that'll fix a number in yo' mind when it couldn't never be done in prose.

Yas, ten year ago only 'leven o' the light-weights floated into a woman's meetin', even when it had consider'ble Baptist sanction, an' now the best of our women rides up the middle of our roads astride of a wheel, an' most of 'em tagged at that, 'n' we don't think ez much of it ez we did of that argument for women to speak an' pray in meetin'.

Yas, I counted forty-three befo' some started to change seats an' I lost count, but I could come within one of countin' 'em now, *from memory*. I know everybody thet was there, an', ez I told you over the fence this mornin', they was mostly all maiden ladies.

Of co'se they wasn't nothin' to hender them attendin'; an', like ez not, most of 'em went to repo't to some home mother same ez I did—an' easier, not havin' no prohibition. You wouldn't chuckle that away ef you'd been there, doctor. It was a fine audience o' people, an' a lot o' good speakers.

Yas, the chief o-rater she was a single lady, f'om somewhere down East, I should jedge. I s'picioned her singularity soon ez I see her walk in, an' I 'lowed she was the paid one, too, which she was.

How'd I tell? Well, I don't claim thet I did tell exac'ly. She was that tall, slim one thet put up at the hotel—the one with short hair an' a certainty in her walk. I don't know ez that's much description, but it's the way she struck me.

You know they's short hair from fevers an' short hair from principle. You'd suppose they'd look about the same, but they don't. I know which is which in a minute. Now, they was somethin' in the cut of this one's head thet seemed to announce thet she'd burnt the bridges behind her—even in the front view.

But I'm sech a Miss Nancy thet ef I knowed a woman didn't

have no knot o' hair on the back of her head, I'd miss it, even in a full-face picture. Thank God, none of our women ain't took to the scissors, so far, though they do say sev'al of 'em went home from the meetin' an' th'owed away their gum-tragic bottles. I doubt ef they thowed 'em so far into the shrubbery, though, thet they can't find 'em befo' the nex' sociable. I hope not. I allus like to see young girls tricked out a little keerful. It speaks well for the young men of a place—shows they're popular.

Well, ez I was sayin', this short-haired one she come in with that slab-sided one with the big plaid basque on. Somehow it's been my lot in life, doctor, to see women o' her figger wear hit-an'-miss plaids. She was tagged consider'ble, an' she had a woolen bird on her bonnet.

They say she spoke fine down at Cedar Cliffs on the destruction of birds, an' she gives lessons in worsted birdmakin'. She 'lows, so they tell me, thet she don't wear that parrot—why no, I ain't shore it's a parrot, I on'y jedge by its color—she 'lows she don't wear it because she feels the necessity of wearin' a bird on her head, but jest to show the weak breth—sistren, I should say—thet, ef a bird *is* a necessity, it can be had without sin—fifty cents a lesson, worsteds th'owed in.

She says thet even ef the sheep was to be shorn out o' season, they have promise in Scripture of "tempered winds," a quotation not found in my Bible, so she ricommends wool-work without let or hindrance.

No, she didn't speak las' night. She only come along to survey the lan'scape o'er, an' see ef she could git scholars. She give a few samples of bird-songs an' mate-callin's whilst the mother speaker took a recess, an' I tell you she wasn't bad music, neither.

I s'pose *'tis* a sin, the way the men go out an' slay birds by the thousands, an' remove all the marks of death from 'em, an' offer 'em for sale—glass-eyed an' happy-lookin'. Of co'se 'most any woman would buy a thing like that, an' not give it a second thought, though *I* doubt ef you could find one engaged in the business.

Yas, I know, it's a cruel sex you an' me belong to, doctor. Even the most conscientious of us'll feel virtuous in killin' a bird, *jest so it's e't*, even ef whoever eats it is already surfeited.

They tell me thet at great ban-quets, where they have things

strung out in cou'ses, they never pass the birds aroun' tell everybody's chuck-full. That looks to me sarcastic, but of co'se it may
not be true. Ef every one thet had already e't enough could jest
blow on the superfluous bird an' sen' it back to life, they'd be
some sense in it.

But talkin' about the mothers' meetin'—where'd I leave off,
doctor? Oh, yas, I was sayin' the speaker was a singular number.
Well, an' that ain't all, neither. She was raised in a' orphan
asylum, so they tell me, an' she ain't never had no dealin's with
mothers, 'ceptin', of co'se, the visitin' mothers thet come once-t a
week an' fill the fatherless youngsters up with candy an' trash
enough to keep 'em puny tell next visitin'-day.

Of co'se I can see she might have an advantage in that, in
some ways. It's give her a chance to study the subjec' from the
outside. That's the side most critics has—the outside is.

Her chief objection to mothers seemed to be their partiality.
Sir? Why, their partiality for their own child'en, of co'se. She had
a heap to say about "universal motherhood"; that's a grand
soundin' term, "universal motherhood" is, an', for o-ratin', it
was the finest part of her discou'se, although I didn't quite git the
hang of it somehow—not clair. Yas, their partiality seemed to be
her principal objection to mothers—that an' their bigotry over old
maids.

But, takin' it from first to last, I should say she didn't have
much use for mothers, noways—that is, not for the common run.
Why, she didn't hesitate to say thet ef she was 'sponsible for a
population she'd ruther raise it on the incubator plan, ef possible,
than to trust it to the gen'al run o' mothers. But I reckon she was
inclined to be sarcastic in that. Sir? Oh, cert'n'y, they was other
speakers, but she was the only paid one.

She was fully primed with all sorts o' testimony ag'in'
mothers. Why, Doc', she had a whole set o' baby-clo'es, all heavy
with ruffles an' lace, an' she exhibited 'em one by one, displayin'
their faults, with the treachery of safety-pins an' all sech.

Then she showed fo'th the injurious motion of a cradle—
how it was shore to addle a young brain mo' or less. But the
damagin' shock of a knee-jostle was her favor-ite cruelty. Why,
she claims thet half the child'en have their constitutions jolted out
of 'em befo' they cut their eye-teeth—all on their mothers' knees.

Sir? Oh, she proved it—that is, she showed it fo'th—*with a doll.* She had one o' these with internal machinery an' vocal powers, an' she coddled it up an' kissed the supposed breath clean out of it, for all the world like you an' I've seen Sally Ann do hers, joltin' it all the while. An' then she opened it up an' showed us the condition of its internals—every vital either sprung or fractioned.

She 'lows she breaks up a ten-dollar doll every lecture, an' she considers it well broke ef it saves even *one* million-dollar baby. She says babies is dressed like ez ef they was millionaires, an' then treated same's ef they was three-for-a-quarter. You see they was times when it was necessary for her to git up a laugh.

Of co'se this is on'y a little scrap o' the lecture. She started with a child from the beginnin'—or befo' the beginnin', for that matter, goin' back the requi'ed time for all purposes. She seemed to know all about that. I s'pose likely she's read up on the subjec'.

An' she said one thing thet surprised me, doctor. She said thet the divinely intended chastisement was a spank. Of co'se this brought down the house for a few minutes. An' she ricommends a felt slipper, to be applied after a half to three quarters of an hour of meditation an' prayer, accordin' to how hot-tempered the mother is. What's that you say? Oh, yas, she got off that joke—a little joke goes a long way on the stage—an' it shook the house for a while. Of co'se it's true. Any slipper would be *felt* in the circumstances.

A frivolous word that-away, in the middle of an argiment, why, it frets me. Somehow I seemed to see the little one strugglin' acrost her knee whilst she stopped to crack a joke at his expense. That was the time I made up my mind, *for shore,* thet she wasn't no mother.

Some mothers'll do 'most anything when their dander's up an' they momentarily forget the helplessness o' the little one, but they'd hardly enjoy a scene like that in cold blood; so I was confirmed in my mind ez to her singularity from that minute.

Like ez not she was intended for a lecturer. I've allus thought preachin' an' practisin' was two sep'rate trades, an' no one person ought to be helt too strict to both.

I tell you, she said some good things, doctor. For one thing, she 'lowed thet the chastisement a mother administers for a misdemeanor is nine time out o' ten mo' a question o' the woman's temper'n what it is o' the child's fault; which we all know to be true.

Why, you an' I've known Sally Ann Brooks to box a child for spillin' syrrup on its frock, an' when it prevaricated direc' in other things, why, she'd jest dismiss it with a religious maxim 'way over its head.

Somehow the lady seemed *to me* to be whackin' away at Sally Ann about half her time, an' I'd find myself leanin' over to see how she took it; but she allus seemed to be all of a giggle, cranin' her neck to watch some other quarter.

You know she's a turrible gamemaker, Sally Ann is, an' they's nothin' she enjoys so much ez another person's expense.

Yas, the speaker she said a lot o' good things. They wasn't but one blame she put on mothers, though, thet seemed to fit our little Mary 'Lizabeth, an' I fetched it home to her intac'. She flared up a little over it at first, but she took it, all the same, an' I ca'culate it'll make some difference to her.

It was on the mistake of teachin' child'en too much an' tryin' to raise 'em too exact, on a set pattern. She's consider'ble inclined that away, Mary 'Lizabeth is, an' all the child'en seem to fall into line excep' little Marthy, the one I call mine. She seldom surrenders without a battle, that is, I mean where she's got her own notions, an' she gen'ally seems to know jest where she's a-headin' for, an' I want to have her let alone ez much ez possible.

Of co'se her mother she's for makin' a lady of her fo'thwith, an' I keep a-tellin' her it can't be did by no short cut. She'll git there all the same, but she's boun' to work out her own route.

She's one o' these mischievious, imaginative child'en, an' sometimes I call her an' git her to settle down, an' I reason with her a little, an' she never fails to come around all right.

She's a tur'ble little mimic, for one thing, for a child of eight year. Why, she can take off anything or anybody she's once-t see, tell you'd imagine it was befo' yo' eyes.

Ef you don't mind me tellin' you, doctor, that little midgit can take *you* off from the time you hitch up at the front gate, all the way up the gravel, hunchin' her lef' shoulder up so's I seem to see yo' medicine-case under yo' arm.

She can do that, an' then come an' set down befo' me an' tell me to poke out my tongue, in a voice I'm all but boun' to obey. You see, I've harkened to them words from you for so long.

She took off Brother Binney, the preacher, the other day, baptizin' a doll, an' when she come out with the words, Dicey seemed to think she might be struck by lightnin' for saterlege. But I wasn't noways afeard.

I never did believe thet God eavesdropped on little child'en at their plays much. He'd git hisself disliked by me ef he did, an' I knew it.

Sir? Oh, yas, Anna Wallace was there with her baby. No comprehensive child'en was allowed; but hers was so young they didn't take no notice to it. I spoke to her comin' in, an' she said she was 'most afeard it'd take its death in the damp night air, but she was boun' to come an' take lessons in how to raise it, *ef it lived*.

What's that, doc'? You say she called you in to see it befo' day this mornin'? Well, I'm not surprised. Croup, eh? Jest ez I thought. It coughed pretty metallic every now an' ag'in all the evenin'. Well, she was bent on attendin' the mothers' meetin' in character, an' she done it.

She allus was skittish, Anna was. Got it honest from her ol' daddy, Obadiah Emmett. He wrote po'try in odd hours, you ricollec', an' lost his farm by sheriff sale. His idee o' gittin' out o' debt was allus some scheme thet requi'ed mo' cash, an' he'd borry it with glee an' certainty.

It's jest about nachel to expect thet his daughter might be the sort o' woman thet'd all but kill a child experimentin' how to raise it. Things like that runs in the blood. Smart woman, though, Anna is. I'll never forgit her valedictory.

But, ez you say, doctor, I never did expec' to see the day thet's arrived—when the women would rise up in insurrection the way they're doin'.

Sir? Well, I don't know why not use that word. They talk about emancipation. Looks like they must 'a' felt in bondage to use a slave-term like that.

Sir? Oh, I'm for lettin' 'em have their way, doctor. I b'lieve in lettin' everybody have their way—lessen it's pernicious. Of co'se every woman or every individyal man can't have theirs, but I'd give in to *the bulk of 'em* every time.

I don't mind, jest so no partic'lar woman don't insurrect ag'in' her partic'lar man. That allus makes trouble. But so long ez it's general, an' the husbands is standin' off winkin' at each other, why, it only enlivens things up a little.

Of co'se a consider'ble part o' the agitators is insubordinatin' ag'in' imaginary husbands, which make it all the mo' harmless.

What's that you say, doc'? Did I go to the sufferage meetin' down at Cypress Swamp? *Didn't* I, though? You forgit, doctor. Of co'se I went, an' it opened my eyes, both uppr an' lower leds. I seemed to see the foundation-stone an' the cupalo o' the whole business that night.

"A Dozen Proofs of Woman's Superiority"—yas, that was the title o' that lecture. That's what took me twenty mile—the title of it. Not thet I wouldn't yield the blessed creatures a thousand superiorities, but I was curious to hear what particular dozen they'd lay claim to—in public. The argiment was purty much like any man lawyer's, far ez I could jedge—mos'ly spent in abusin' the opposite side.

She seemed to prove jest about everything ag'in' us thet could be proved ez she stood there brandishin' a fan.

Tell the truth, I felt too vile to live befo' she had done with the third superiority, an' I'd 'a' slipped out, only I didn't like to. It might 'a' looked like a confession, an' I like my closet for that.

Befo' I got to where my closet was, though, I seemed to git over my remorse, mainly. It was mo' on account o' my sex in gen'al, anyhow, thet I felt guilty—the way she exposed it.

When I cooled off, though, I see a heap of it was jest smoke. Somehow, when I hear a woman talk that-away, I wonder how she disposes of her father. She's *bound* to've had one, an' the Scriptures they mention him along with the mother ez entitled to honor—in the fifth commandment.

Yas, that's true; it *does* mention him *first,* but, like ez not, that was on account o' not havin' no woman mixed up in the framin' of it. I can't imagine thet either God or Moses intended any slight to women in that.

Sir? No, I'm not doubtful, doctor; I'm only forgitful, that's all. No, I don't know ez Mary 'Lizabeth ever werried over sech things. She's been purty well grounded. She's quick-witted enough to git into trouble, but she's too busy. But she's gen'ally one o' the first to see an advantage. She can see the value of a thing even through a shock, an' that's sayin' a good deal.

F'instance, her bicycle was the first ever rid down the Simpkinsville road. Ricollec' how it startled ole nigger Proph' so thet he fell on his knees an' commenced to prophesy when he see her? I can't say I liked to see her straddle it at first, but she never s'picioned it. She stays purty close-t at home, an' I saw exercise an' open air in it.

Besides, we'd see by the papers how women was takin' to the road in New York, an', tell the truth, I knowed the would-ef-you-could set o' women would all respect her still more for leadin' off. Otherwise I might 'a' been tempted to let her see me wince.

We've all got our weaknesses, an' I don't claim to be free from my share. But I would 'a' hated to see her hooted at.

'Stid o' that, she set the fashion, an' mo' butter-an'-egg money has gone into the bicycle-shops than to the heathen from this county from that time on, I'm proud to say. Yas, I said proud, doctor. I like the heathen, but I like our own folks, too.

But even ef I'd been reluctant to see her mount it, the way she rid would 'a' consoled me. Seem like *she* an' *it* was *one* from the time she got her first balance, an' that's where I draw the line yet. Any woman thet, after due practice, don't seem all of a piece with it ain't got no business on no wheel—that is, not for appearance. Mary 'Lizabeth she skirts an' skims for all the world like a chimbly-swaller, on'y mo' graceful.

No, ez I said, Mary 'Lizabeth don't think promiscuous, but she thinks to the p'int. I know when she heerd all the talk about female sufferage, an' so many was arguin' ag'in' it, claimin' thet all the lowest-down women would likely vote, whilst a heap o' the best wouldn't—same ez the men does—why, she didn't seem to be payin' no p'tic'lar attention, an' d'reckly, when they was a minute's silence, what did she do but up an' remark: "Why not jest let the *best* o' the women vote? Then them an' *the men together* might vote *out* the *bad* men, looks to me like, *an' start even.*" Jest that away she said it, whilst she was passin' the custard-glasses.

Sir? Oh, by good an' bad she jest meant the classes thet *ought* an' *oughtn't* to, that's all—them thet kin read, f'instance, or thet has property, or thet's been here long enough to have a say-so, or whatever. Seems to me, yet, thet that was a purty straight idee—

for Mary 'Lizabeth's size. Oh, yas, she figgered it out herself. An' I think maybe she's right.

The most fittin' of both sexes ought to rule the roost better'n the good an' bad of either one, seems to me.

Sir? Oh, I don't say you could stop them thet has a'ready voted—maybe not; but they might vote ag'in' any mo' ignoramuses comin' in. I don't know nothin' tall about it. Don't quiz me, doctor.

All I know is thet I'll be toted out to the polls, ef necessary, an' I'll drop in my ballot every time, an' so will Sonny. We'll speak out an' declare our principles. An' ef it ever was to come to us havin' to vote ez to who was to be qualified to vote, I'm afeard thet the sex o' the applicants would be the last thing I'd stop to consider.

Ez between Fitty Joe and Mary 'Lizabeth, f'instance, why, I'd discriminate in favor o' common sense an' goodness every time, ez you ricollec' I said to you the other day.

Didn't it never strike you, doctor, thet in a question like that maybe the women has *some* say, whether they wanted it or not?

Of co'se they could, anyhow, ef they'd a mind to. An' come to think of it, every woman is *half father* an' every man is *half mother*, more or less, an' jest because one sex declares in favor o' one parent an' the other in favor o' the other—

Truth is, I git mixed thinkin' about it. But my b'lief is thet them duties an' restrictions thet hinges on sex'll continue to hinge, an' them thet don't'll give way.

Some says ef women vote they'll haf to fight, but I can't say ez I see that. Tain't every man thet's built for battle. Some is constructed for poets, an' some, ag'in, ain't courageous an' can't write po'try, neither.

Sir? You say am I a woman's-righter? God knows what I am, doctor. I like that name, an' I'd like to be all the kinds of a righter thet it comes in my way to be, an' a wronger of no man.

That name seems to've stood a long time—to be fixed in the sand. I ricollec' when it first come how we all hated it. I was a young man then, an' ef my wife had 'a' mentioned sech a thing ez goin' ez a delegate anywheres, I'd 'a' looked for her to grow a beard nex' thing, an' I'd 'a' kep' 'er hid.

But settin' still in a back seat an' listenin' an' lookin' on all these years, why, let any doubter try it an' see ef it don't change his views—that is, ef he sets still enough, an' listens to both sides.

He may believe the way he b'lieved when he set down, but ef he does, he'll know the reason why, an' have some respect for his opponents, too.

Yas, I've lived to see a woman delegate rigged out in a dress made by a man dressmaker; an' he voted, an' she didn't. An' maybe it's right she shouldn't. I'm shore I don't know.

I ain't never been able to see anything appetizin' in the picture o' woman at the polls. But appetite ain't principle, of co'se.

Do you know what I sometimes think, doctor, when I jest look on an' consider? Why, I think of what the Bible says: "An' a little child shall lead them." Of co'se I know I'm movin' it out o' place a little, but I can fit it into things an' see how it's true in all this hubbub. I believe thet little child'en are the great leaders an' binders—or they're the *binders*, anyhow.

Why, I know a man thet's so flighty thet the next woman'll turn his head every time, an' he loses hisself so complete thet not even the motherliness of the mother of his child'en'll hold 'im. He turns fool every year or two, an' the little home-mother, why, she jest keeps eyes an' ears shet tell he gits the better of it, an' the call o' the child'en brings him back ag'in.

Of co'se he allus keeps the home supplied with marketin'—marketin' an' lies an'—Sir? Oh, this ain't no fairy-tale. I know the man. No, he dont' live here. He couldn't. I'd thrash him out myself, although I know likely he can't help his nature. Neither can a snake. That's why I always think, "Po' thing!" when I kill one. But I kill it all the same every time.

Sir? Oh, cert'n'y. Shore, you're right about that. The woman *might* be better shet of him, an' ef she lived here she *would*. But that ain't neither here nor there. This is only an extreme case—selected to p'int my p'int.

Yas, they's long stretches o' time thet I believe thet it's the child'en in this world thet's the great power—not the men or the women, but the child'en.

Why, I know a case of a baby rulin' Wall Street in New York for a whole week once-t—fixed the price o' cotton for six days an' set everything on a different basis for the entire season. They was seven new houses built in Simpkinsville that spring, more'n any season before or sence, an' it all come o' that baby.

What's that? "Whose was it? or where? or how old was he?" Well, never mind about that, but I don't mind tellin' you how old he was. He wasn't no age at the time. He was an old man's first, jest like Sonny was to me, an' he had been daily expected for a week, an' threatened not to arrive safe-t; an' for five days that man set in his back parlor, in call o' the doctors, an' dictated telegrams entirely different to what he would 'a' telegraphed ef he'd had his mind free, an' these telegrams they excited distrust on one side an' courage on the other, an' first thing you knew the old man's name was in all the papers for savin' his country from ruin.

You see, not knowin' jest how things was, he acted cautious, an' when, on the sixth day, that baby arrived, talk about silver spoons! Why, he had a whole set of gold ones in his mouth, he was that rich.

You see, the crisis in the market, why, it passed whilst the baby hesitated.

Yas, he's the man. I didn't intend to tell you, but sence you know—You see, he's nachelly techy about the circumstance hingin' on his timidity—that 'long with his ticklish fatherhood.

Of co'se the papers they all give him credit for jedgment, dubbed him the Napoleon o' the cotton-market an' all sech; an', the fact is, he lost his head complete an' jest held still, waitin' to hear that baby cry.

An' when it did cry, why, the newsboys was callin' out his name 'long the New York streets, so they say. Of co'se they named him for his daddy. Ol' man claired fo' millions for his firm in six days, so the story runs, an' ef it hadn't 'a' been for the youngster, he'd 'a' smashed the whole concern.

An' yit some says luck is a sinful word. An' maybe it is.

Of co'se I *know* where my faith is. 'T least, I know the top notch where it hangs; but the betweens, why, they often puzzle me.

Sir? Sonny's faith? Oh, I don't bother about that. Of co'se I reelize he's half mother, to start with, an' I know he believes in God an' Mary 'Lizabeth; an' betwix' that an' his book-writin', an' follerin' the little ones around, why, he don't have no time to reason out doubts. I never had time, neither, tell I was too old to enjoy 'em.

They do say, when folks spends too much time studyin' over things, they're ap' to git their religious views hind side fo'most, an' they tell me some has writ whole books to show they ain't got no religious views whatsoever. Looks to me like that's a thing a person could declare in a minute an' be done with it. But I know I'm ignorant of some things.

But talkin' about the women—what's that? Yas, that's true. Sonny does claim to be a sufferagette—in principle. He signed with Mary Elizabeth an' she signed first time the paper was passed 'round—not thet she advocates every man *or* woman votin'—but she 'lows to draw the line elsewhere.

By the way, it strikes me I hear tumblers a-clinkin', an' I s'picion she's fixin' you an' me a sinful drink now—'t least, mine'll be sinful. That drop out o' the bottle she puts into my glass o' raspberry syrrup has swelled from a teaspoon to a tablespoonful in two year, an' you ordered it an' never called my attention to it.

Of co'se I reelize a person has to len'then out his crutch at my age, an' you an' Mary 'Lizabeth has agreed to piece mine out on the sly. But I'm a sort of e-ter-nal vigilanter, doctor. It's hard to keep a thing hid from me. You're a tenderhearted man, an' that's one reason I like you—that an' yo' style.

Jest look at his starched cuff, slick ez a bishop's. It tickles me to see you sport white linen up an' down this dusty road. Somehow I wouldn't have confidence in a doctor thet didn't wear a starched cuff. It seems to go in with is di-plomy.

A starched cuff an' Latin diseases, why, they're about half the battle for a doctor. I obeyed a doctor for two years once-t, when I was a young man, jest because he treated me for *tic-douloureux;* an' one day I happened to be runnin' through the dictionary, an' I tripped on the word, an' found twasn't a thing but common neuraligy, *an' I quit.*

You know neuraligy it's different to most diseases. You either have it or you don't. It's come an' gone with me all my life. It ain't got no use for a strong man with a healthy appetite, but it's worse'n a vampire once-t it gits you down; so I've kep' shet of it mostly.

What? You ain't goin', doctor? Well, ef you must, jest step

over here with me to the end o' the piazzy an' look at the child'en a minute.

Ain't that a purty sight, now? Do you ricollec' when I used to look forrard to the time when they'd be swings in the branches o' that ol' oak, all goin' at once-t, jest like you see 'em?

Well, ez I set an' watch 'em ez the days pass so joyously, I reelize mo' an' mo' thet I'm approachin' the time when I'll be nothin' but a ancestor, an' I pray God to make me worthy. I tell you, doc', it's a great an' awful thing to be inherited.

Why, sometimes, when that nex' to the littlest one thows hisself down in a tantrum, I'm startled; it brings back my own youthful tumults so vivid. An' then, when d'reckly he gits over it, an' comes with his little wet face for me to kiss, I think about my ol' mother, an' I bless the Lord thet my ancestral responsibilities is so nobly divided. Her descendant would haf to be safe-t-guarded with sweetness, even ef he was skimped in his ol' gran'daddy.

How purty the sun is, doctor, where it frosts the edges o' them knotty oak-limbs that away, an' casts rainbows in the wet moss! It's a wonderful world, after all, an' I trust, when I pass along, it won't be shet out from my vision.

Jest look at little Marthy, now, an' see how she makes the boy give her her turn at the swing, an' she half his heft, an' then talk about women gittin' their rights. They'll git 'em when they're ready, don't you werry.

I did intend to put up a swing apiece for 'em, an' then says I: "No; that ain't the way o' the world. Let 'em learn fair play th'ough turn about, same ez they'll haf to later on."

Sir? Oh, they's only one swing short, not countin' the baby, of co'se. They's allus ap' to be one receivin' discipline; that is, unless his greatest pleasure is in seein' others swing, an' I ain't found no sech angelic natures among 'em yit. Ef I did, I'd feel his pulse an' sen' for you, yo' perfession bein' keepin' angels out o' heaven ez long ez possible. Did it ever strike you thet that was a sort o' frustratin' business, doc', for a Christian elder?

But ez I was sayin', talkin' about the women—I was werried, some, lessen in all this tumult they might git mannish, an' I'd be the last one to like that; but they tell me thet they's jest ez many organder-lawns an' furbelows sold in the States where they vote ez they ever was, an' no mo' small-sized pants.

I did hear thet the governor of some State or Territory—or the governess, maybe I should say—was inaugurated in a low-neck frock, but maybe tain't so? *Any*body kin say any*thing* ag'in' *any-body*.

My taste for sech an occasion would be a high-neck basque, an' black silk for the material—not thet I'm struck on the gover-ness idee in p'tic'lar, but jest s'posin'. Ef they was a good lady here runnin' ag'in' a bad man, why, I'd vote for her, of co'se. Sir? What's that you say? S'posin' it was six o' one an' half a dozen o' the other? Well, in that case I'd compliment the fair sex, of co'se. That's a matter o' raisin'. But—Sir? Ef she was reel wicked?

Oh, shoo, doc', I don't know ez I ever knowed one thet was; but I kin imagine thet she might be skittish or hysterical—they're the kind I dread.

One o' the best women I ever met gi'e me the fidgets every time I looked at her. She was both wall-eyed an' skittish-mannered, po' thing. I allus s'picioned she tried to make up for her eyes by her behavior, which was a great mistake.

She was the salt o' the earth, an' I knew it, an' yet, ef she was to come up that walk now, I'd suddenly ricollec' some errand in the kitchen, an' I wouldn't be able to help it.

Of co'se I'd return quick ez I could brace up, but back I'd go on first sight. Why, doc', you wouldn't b'lieve it of me, maybe, but they's been certain hens in the yard thet would gi'e me the creeps, allus actin' so agitated an' super*flu*ous—not comparin', of co'se.

There's Sally Ann Brooks, now; I hate to say it, but she kin git me about ez nettled ez anybody I *like*. What's that? Why, cert'n'y I like Sally Ann. Yas, I know she will whup her child'en constant an' dress 'em to kill; but she's one of our own girls, an' she means well.

You know she wanted to be 'lected delegate to the W. C. T. U., on account o' the stand she took to close the saloons; but our women is got too much sense to send the mother o' two sets o' child'en away f'om home.

Besides, you know how she is. Ez Mis' Blanks says, ef Sally Ann found herself app'inted to set on a platform befo' a audience o' people, like ez not she'd be for appearin' with her white ribbin rosette sash-width, or some other conspicuosity, an' I don't doubt she would. She's the sort thet'll second a motion she don't hear. Anything to be a-motionin' or a-secondin'.

The committee on delegations is goin' to come out here in the mornin' an' offer it to Mary 'Lizabeth; but of co'se she won't consider it. It's mo' of a compliment to her an' Sonny'n anything else, I reckon.

I feel like a secret society or a dynamite bomb, knowin' it an' not tellin' 'er, but I promised I wouldn't. Sir? How did I know it? Well, never mind; I was told, that's all. Somehow folks'll tell me 'most anything. That's a compliment they pay to my dumbness.

You nee'n't to laugh, doctor! Th'ain't nobody can play around a stake an' never tech it better'n I can. They're the best secret-keepers thet can do that. Yas, I'm a reg'lar magazine of explosives, an' you ought to know it an' never let a fever run too high in my system.

Yas, they've 'lected Miss Sue Sanderson delegate to the mothers' biennial, an' I think they've done mighty well. She'll enjoy the trip, an' she's free-handed, an' she's a good talker, an' I jedge she could build up an imaginary family an' raise 'em befo' an audience o' people ez slick ez the next one.

An' I tell you, doc', these meetin's all help along. Of co'se Sally Ann'll allus be herself, but I b'lieve thet after las' night's talk even she'll be herself *with restrictions*, f'om this time forrard. I doubt ef she'll ever box one o' her child'en ag'in—not in public, nohow.

Mary 'Lizabeth says the reason they picked Miss Sue Sanderson for a delegate is on account o' she bein' a Daughter o' the Revolution, an' she'll sort o' reflect double credit on Simpkinsville. What's that you say, doc'? Of co'se I know nobody don't b'lieve she's one; not but what she might be, for all I know. Anyhow, we-all know how she j'ined. When she heerd thet the Sandersons of Sand Hill was descended that away, why, she jest up an' claimed it, too, an' commenced to shorten her frock-waists an' to buy flowered curtain muslins for her dresses.

It's good she's ez purty ez she is. It takes consider'ble good looks to carry off that Marthy Washin'ton git-up in broad daylight. You know I ain't called her nothin' but "Lady Marthy" sence she adopted the costume. It pleases me to see her wear it, because it seems to make her so happy, an' the road is jest one picture purtier with her walkin' down it in garret frocks an' white kerchiefs.

She looks ez innocently proud an' delighted ez the wild roses she breshes with her skirts by the roadside.

To my mind, some women is so much like flowers thet for 'em jest to bloom seems all-sufficient. When a girl like Miss Sue wants to be a delegate to a mothers' convention, why, it's like a lily havin' medicinal qualities—an' they ain't nothin' ag'in' nature in that; they say some has.

Miss Sue says her only regret is thet the minuet can't be danced solitary. She craves to dance it, but she says they ain't nobody in Simpkinsville qualified to dance it with her.

Oh, yas, she said that to Mary 'Lizabeth's face, an' Mary 'Lizabeth she was turrible tickled over it, because she knows they's only three quarters o' my great gran'pa buried down in the Fayetteville cemetery, the rest of him bein' left on a Revolutionary battlefield; an' Sonny has got his swo'd an' crutch, both, an' his commission, too. An' she's got one on her ma's side, for that matter.

Sir? Oh, no, she never said nothin'. I did pleg Mary 'Lizabeth a little to send on her papers an' things an' git a badge, but she wouldn't. She 'lowed thet it was all she could do to keep up with her duties ez a mother, let alone settin' up to be a new kind of a daughter.

But I've got all the dockiments put by, an' ef any o' these little girls thet's comin' along should ever care to take advantage of bein' born Daughters of History, why, they'll find their title clair.

Little Marthy—funny for her name to be Marthy, now, ain't it? I never thought o' her an' Marthy Washin'ton together befo'— but our little Marthy is a born leader, an' it wouldn't surprise me none ef she'd be the sort thet'd some day enjoy puttin' ribbin bows on that ol' crutch an' swo'd, an' crossin' 'em over her mantel shelf.

Ef her mind should run that away, she won't haf to go to no junk-shop to git her relics, that's one thing shore. They say a heap of 'em does.

Sir? Oh, no, Miss Sue ain't got no badge. She says the name o' Sanderson is all the badge she needs, an' I reckon it's jest ez well she feels that away.

No, it's jest ez I said in the beginnin', doctor; they ain't no 'casion to fret about our women. They ain't banded ag'in' the men no mo'n the men has been banded ag'in' them all these years in their Odd Fellers an' Freemasonry an' all sech.

Of co'se they's some things in it all thet strikes a looker-on ez ridic'lous, now an' ag'in. F'instance, it plegs me to see our sweet young girls goin' roun' with what they call "Social Purity badges" on.

The dear child'en ain't no mo'n purity badges their selves, ef they on'y knew it, an' I hate to see 'em labeled. Seem like it might make 'em conscious.

Ol' Miss 'Tildy Ferguson is responsible for that. She was born plain-featured, Miss 'Tildy was, an' she's had a purty lonesome time all her life, with her eczema an' her deefness, an' when she started to wear the badge, why, I was pleased to see it—an' nobody can't say but what she's lived up to it strict. But it's only human not to know when to stop.

I s'pose they come a time when her own virtuous life ceased to satisfy her cravin' for virtue, an' so she app'inted meetin's an' got the girls all out an' tagged 'em, an' it seems they've made her president, an' she says it has renewed her youth like the eagle, she's that happy over it.

I reckon the truth is, everybody's life is bound to be a sermon, of one sort or another, an' the happy ones is them thet are convinced thet they've found their texts.

Of co'se white ribbins an' reelizations of goodness can't hurt our girls in the long run, an' ef it's brought happiness into the heart of one lonely ol' woman, that's somethin'.

No, don't let's you an' me fret over our women, doctor. The motters on all their banners is jest ez good for our sons ez for our daughters, an' we'll all do mighty well ef we try to live up to 'em.

The Child at the Door

Hold on there, Doctor! Don't shove that button! I'll come around an' let you in. She's asleep, at last, an' I reckon you better not disturb 'er, even you. I been waitin' out here on my side po'ch to intercept you, so's you wouldn't ring. Come right out an' set down, an' I'll tell you all about it.

It's little Madge, Doctor; yas, little Madge, the child of adoption, an' you know we're jest a leetle extry ticklish about her, less'n any harm was to come to 'er.

"When?" you say? Why, jest yesterday—come home from school with 'er face too flushed an' talkin' mo'n common—kep' up lively talk all th'ough 'er dinner an' didn't no mo'n pick at 'er victuals, all the time insistin' thet she felt fine. Ricollec' one thing she said was she felt like ez ef she could fly, an' when I felt of 'er pulse, she made game o' me an' says, "I'm all right, Gramper!"

Call me Gramper? Why not, I like to know? Bless her little heart! Why, Doc', ef I've got sech a thing ez a favoryte gran'child, after little Marthy, *her* namesake, an' little Doc' who requi'es it of me, why, it's little Madge Sutton Jones, dear an' adopted daughter o' the house. Well, I should say!

No, that's so, she ain't to say exac'ly little, although she's a child to be designated that-a-way. Some women is, an' it ain't always a question o' size. She's the tallest o' the brood now, an' ef I don't say she's ez purty ez any o' 'em, it's because I'm reticent.

Don't be impatient, Doctor. I'm a-comin' to that, now. Ez I keep tellin' you, she come home from school all petered out an' jest a leetle too frivolous; didn't eat no dinner an' asked an' was allowed to set up beyond 'er usual bedtime. I see that Mary Elizabeth had 'er motherly eye on 'er an' she follered 'er up stairs an' it wasn't no time befo' she come hurryin' back for Sonny to come an' feel of 'her pulse, an' first thing we knowed, the child was settin' up in bed, preachin' an' laughin' an' cryin' all at once-t. That was the time Sonny first tried to get you on the telephone—an' we ain't none of us got a wink o' sleep all night.

Sonny says she recited a number o' poems correct an' she's

sung like a nightingale, more songs than you'd think one bird would be able to turn. She's got a fine musical talent, an' Sonny said las' night he intended to have it cultivated.

Take it altogether, Doctor, it's been a turrible night—the storm outside so the house trimbled, an' the telephone detached by the elements, an' that little girl carryin' on what Sonny calls a Protean show, whatever that is—takin' one character an' then another the whole night th'ough, an' we-all doin' all the incapable things we knowed how for 'er relief, settin' beside the bed an' smoothin' 'er hand one minute an' complimentin' 'er on 'er elecution the next, an' Sonny testin' the telephone every little while in a vain effort to git you to prescribe. He knowed you couldn't cross Chinquapin Creek durin' the hurricane.

Well, it was a night of storm, in an' out doors, but jest befo' day, when he had finally got you on the telephone, why, she succumbed to sleep—an' she ain't stirred sence. No, we didn't have no time to foller no directions. When Sonny hung up the receiver, she was sleepin'. They-all advised me to go to bed then, but at my age, it's easier to rise at four than it is to go to sleep, so I urged Mary Elizabeth to go an' git a nap o' sleep an' Sonny, he's in the saddle, ridin' over the place ez he does every daybreak. Dicey's gittin' the coffee ready now, jest outside the bedroom door there an' keepin' an eye, an' I stationed myself out here to meet you.

Little Madge, she's layin' right inside there, an' ef she was to stir, we'd all hear her. No doubt it's jest as you say, Doctor. She's high-intellectual strung, an' a year out o' school would be the best thing for 'er. But I'd dread to see you tell 'er; she's sinfully ambitious, poor little human—an' gits only misdirectin' praise for it, on all sides.

She's got so robust these last three years, seem like we forgit how puny she was them first years of scant nourishment which have to be overcome, of co'se.

Adoption is a great an' honorable word in our family, Doctor, an' it has sort o' gilt-edged little Madge a leetle ahead o' the others—an' we want it so. It's hard to have things jest exac'ly right. They're ap' to shoot over or under the mark, so, in various little ways, we strive to give the adopted one the higher place. Better that than the lower one—an' otherwise, she shares every advantage an' obligation, share an' share alike. We let 'em foller their talents, mainly, an' Madge, she's the sociable one, with a tendency to cook. Sonny an' Mary Elizabeth, they were resolute in one thing: they wouldn't have no deception. That child learned to say " 'dopted" befo' she knowed the meanin' o' the word, an' thet she had some sort o' friendly advantage o' the rest in havin' a extry pair o' heavenly parents, same ez ef she had a kind of individual bank account to draw on in case o' need, an' she ain't never hesitated to use it, in argument. An' ef she was hard-pressed, I have known 'er to make a special p'int o' bein' *chose*, whilst the rest o' the child'en had to be took, hit an' miss, ez they come; I s'picion thet Mary Elizabeth give 'er that weapon of defense.

Mary Elizabeth is unusual. It ain't every motherly woman thet is at the same step-motherly, or adopted-motherly, the way she is. She seems to put 'erself in every child's place, an' to see its highest needs.

They's two distinctions in most families, two honors, so to speak—the eldest an' the youngest—an' in ours, they's three, eldest, youngest, *an' 'dopted*, an' I ain't shore but the last is first, ez it should be.

Our eldest has always been looked up to, *an' knowed it*, but we ain't never weighed 'im down with a sense of responsibility. I've seen oldest child'en all but robbed o' their youth in the constant demand to be "a livin' example" to the younger ones.

I notice Sonny an' Mary Elizabeth, they'll often say to the little ones, "See how pretty big brother does this or that," but that's the only challenge he gets—an' "big brother" 'll go through his paces like a merry showman, tickled over it. They's everything in how a thing's done.

They's one thing shore; if they's any element of total depravity in our child'en, it ain't never been challenged by opposition, an' I have an idee thet ef total depravity is let alone, *an' forgot*, it'll be gradually absorbed an' cast out o' the system. Oh, yes, I know I ain't quotin' from the catechisms, exactly—but you an' me, we are sort o' free-thinkers, within the lines, an' that's why I love to hear you talk!

But goin' back to the 'doption o' child'en, why, Doc', one o' the richest lives I can imagine would be jest to have a big, ample home an' to gradually fill it with adoptions—jest casual, ez the opportunity come along—an' seem like I'd never be so happy ez when I knew they was a child at the door.

I'd 'a' liked that to've been my fate, ef Sonny hadn't arrived an' been equal to any dozen to us. But like ez not, ef he hadn't come, an' opened our hearts *an' our eyes*, we might never 'a' reelized the blessedness o' child'en in the house. Yas, I'd 'a' been glad to've been a wholesale adopter of homeless child'en. I'd even liked to've put out a sign, "Needy child'en wanted an' no questions asked." I never could see the sense o' all the catechizin' they carry on over needy child'en. To me it's superfluous. There's the child, an' it's its own answer. Why, I've known cases for adoption quizzed out o' all countenance. Adopters seem to be so skeert less'n they'll adopt somethin' unworthy o' their dignity.

You ricollec' poor Steve Silverton, Doc'? Well, when little Madge's father died, it seems somebody went to Steve's wife about her—that was befo' we'd heard it—an' she was for takin' the child, Mis' Silverton was, but Steve wouldn't hear to it. He made some mean reference to "Old Slouch Sutton," the child's father, an' he 'lowed she wasn't *the right stripe* to annex to the Silvertons. I often wonder ef he thinks about that now, wearin' his own penitentiary stripes for high-class chicanery, after castin' slurs on poor old po'try-spoutin' Eli Sutton, who never did a de-liberate meanness in all his vagarious life an' is sleepin', honorably forgot, in a clean, weedy grave on the hillside.

What's that, Doc'? Oh, no. He ain't in the potter's field now. One o' the first things Sonny done after they 'dopted little Madge was to go quietly an' have his remains removed into a pay grave— an' it's all decently labeled, which ain't no more'n fair to the child.

Yas, she's been down there, once-t. You know, Sonny had him interred down in the Ozan where he was born. I took 'er down with one or two o' the child'en, an' she laid a flower there. It give 'er a sense o' dignity to do that. Yas, we wanted 'er to've been once-t, anyway, jest so she would reelize thet she could go.

I've often thought thet a graveless adult person must feel sort o' insignificant, an' I believe they do.

Yas, Steve Silverton, he turned little Madge down, I'm glad to say, an' so did sev'al of our best families, with well-meanin' prudence. Jedge Whittemore was one o' them thet shook his

head, "No," an' I ricollec' they say he related a fool story of a man
he'd heard about thet adopted a child of obscurity, an' when she
was fo' years old, it seems she slipped away from 'er nurse, an'
run an' stood on the street doorstep in 'er little birthday suit, in
great glee over 'er escape—like ez ef thet was a hyenous crime or
had anything to do with her bein' adopted.

Why, sir, when our Sonny was six, an' reely ought to've
knowed better, didn't he make a similar escape from the nigger,
Dicey, one day, in nature's scant apparel, an' he never stopped
till he got to the court-house, all the way th'ough Main Street,
befo' she caught him.

But we didn't consider it no indication of depravity—an' it
never occurred to us to try to git shet of him on that account, or
wish we could send 'im back where he come from.

What's that? Oh, yas, they returned that little fo'-year-old to
the asylum, on account of 'er escapage—'lowed thet they didn't
dast to take the resk of 'er morals, not knowin' but this "tendency," I believe they called it, might prove the beginnin' o' the end.

Yas, sir, they done that—an' she *four*. No doubt they was on
the lookout for indications o' total depravity an' were grateful for
havin' it revealed in time.

An'—what you say? Didn't the Whittemores—? Why, yes,
they did. After turning Madge down on account o' the story o' the
baby on the front steps, they 'dopted his wife's nephew, Archie
Atkinson, of Atkinsonville—'dopted him gleefully, knowin' all
about all the fine strains thet was united in his pedigree—an' jest
ez soon ez he was old enough, why Archie, he went out *in all his
clo'es*, an' disgraced the whole caboodle! Poor Archie! He was the
last of an enfeebled line, a nachel, well-dressed scapegoat, without a garment o' decency to clothe hisself with.

We-all felt mighty sorry for his aunt an' uncle. You see, it was
double humiliation. Mis' Whittemore was present at the closin'
exercises o' the High School last July, an' I couldn't help wonder-
in', when our little Madge was called up every few minutes to
take a prize, ef she remembered. Her whole name was called,
every time, Madge Sutton Jones. That's what she is—an' she
stands on it.

Of co'se, only the All-father knows what 'er fate will be. That
ain't for us—not with any o' the child'en. One mistake adopters

make, in my opinion, is in rushin' forward to results an' rewards. Jest the home-givin' an' the happy recipiency of a contented child might be its own daily reward, it seems to me.

I know, in our Sonny's most troublous days, we often said to each other, *her* an' me, "Ef he was took from us to-night, we'd be overpaid for all he's cost us—in the fullness of joy he's brought us," yas, an' that when he was thin-necked an' cantankerous with his stomach teeth, an' we was obligated to seize our joy chiefly in watchin' him sleep, an' oftentimes takin' turns at fannin' him, all the August nights th'ough.

But talkin' about family traits an' hereditary dispositions, I want to say right here thet we ain't got a thing to worry about in little Madge's family—an' ef we did, we'd refuse to worry an' try to crowd it out.

No, her father, Eli Sutton, wasn't no common man. He accepted town assistance, I know, an' his child has come to adoption, but they was some stuff in that man, an' whilst I couldn't never exactly openly uphold him, he always had considerable secret sympathy from me. I wish now thet I'd follered my instincts an' extended a hand to him in life.

The trouble is we expect the wrong things o' the wrong people. We ought to've been more friendly to Eli. When they found his garret full o' them perpetual-motion devices, an' that pitiful diary with them courageous entries of "almost perfected"—why, well—

I'd give a good deal ef he was back ag'in, poor, uncomplainin' worker, ef only long enough for us Christian neighbors to apologize to him for our mistrust. We often think of it—an' we try to make up to little Madge all we can, for neglectin' him, although, of co'se, she don't know it.

I don't call that bad blood for a child to inherit. They's some admixture of the martyr in it—with, of co'se a perponderance o' blame fool in finances, which he couldn't help.

Her mother was a woman of intelligence an' sperit, but I'm ashamed to say she cut out an' left Eli, although she must've knew about his perpetual-motion devices, an' the long night stretches o' work when all them candle ends was burned down. It seems she got tired with it all, an' 'lowed she was goin' down to Galveston to pass the school examination o' the state o' Texas, for a public school position, an' she intended to send for the child ez soon ez she could provide "a suitable home," an' you know she was drownded in the Galveston storm.

She could 'a' remained at home an' got less money here for teachin' our Simpkinsville primary longer hours, *an' looked after the old man.* Ef a wife won't do that, who will? No, she chafed under the style in which she was obliged to live with Eli, an' so she went off in search of refinement. That was when Eli first took to drinkin', an' I never blamed him. I can imagine what it was to be left in a cheerless house, for a man of inventive mind. Why, Doc', you know yo'self thet it took you an' me an' *her* an' the nigger, Dicey, all three, to wrastle with Sonny th'ough his teethin', an' ef his mother had up an lef' me then, I'd 'a' took to drink in a minute! They was moments when I'd 'a' done it, anyhow, ef I'd 'a' knowed how.

I tell you, Doc', now thet you scientists is describin' hookworms an' makin' allowances for "sleepin' sickness," an' treatin' it with somethin' besides moral persuasion, I reckon we'll have to change the classification of a good many of our unfortunate brothers who didn't seem to be able to keep up with the procession.

Yas, poor Eli Sutton proved in mo' ways than one thet he wasn't no common man. He had originality, an' the courage to express it. A holder of unpopular opinions, he didn't give a cent who listened or who reviled, an' they's somethin' not altogether despisable about that, although it's ap' to be tiresome.

Why, they was a time in Eli's youth when he edited an' printed a newspaper, our west—*an'sold it*—'t least, he *offered it for sale,* but it wasn't no best seller, ez they say. He told me about it, hisself. He run an entire series in that paper on the subjec' o' who wrote Shakespeare's works. Ricollec', he was for a literary man by the name o' Hogg, or maybe it was Bacon. Sence the child'en have been studyin' high school books an' I hear 'em their lessons, why, I'm gittin' so highly educated thet first thing you know, I'll be settin' fo'th theories myself. But somehow, Hogg an' Bacon, they seem to run together in a farmer's mind.

They was a po'try writer by the name o' Hogg. He's dead, now. I'm shore about that, because I ricollec' sayin' I'd 'a' thought he'd 'a' changed his name, jest for manners. Then, I see thet, on the contrary, he had affixed a second "g" to it, for emphasis—an' I see he was game, an' I took a likin' to 'im, on the spot.

Well, sir, that series run a year, an' it hurt the circulation o' the paper—in a farmin' community like that.

But Sutton did other things. For one thing, he invented a sort o' cement for the construction o' houses, jest takin' the dirt of a person's back yard an' combinin' it with chemicals, an' he believed in it so thorough thet he built a residential home out of it, an' they say it looked elegant an' substantial an' it reely was wind-an'-fire-proof, an' he saw his everlastin' fortune in it, but it seems one o' them western fall rains set in—a regular six-weeks' soaker—an' the house jest nachelly subsided during one night, an' befo' mornin' Eli an' his family foun' theirselves well placed for the study of astronomy.

It seems, he had left out some adhesive ingregent, so the stuff wouldn't hold out in a storm—somethin' like the man himself. Beyond the inconvenience o' the occurrence, it seems he wasn't fazed in the least. He 'lowed he realized the mistake he'd made an' he was for rebuildin' the place immediate, but his wife, she refused to occupy it with him, for which I exonerate her, entire. They's some experiments thet a person don't care to repeat.

Oh, no! We don't tell the child sech ez that. What good would it do? She's got 'er pa's set o' Shakespeare's plays entire, with no end o' "marginal notes," Sonny calls 'em, an' we encourage 'er nachel pride in it. Sonny says the notes is full o' ciphers, but I never could find no oughts to speak of in it.

What's that you say, Doc'? Wasn't I responsible for Jedge Townsend's adoptin' that boy? Well, s'posin' I was, what of it? Don't you think it was a good day's work? Yas, I knew you'd think so. I've often been tempted to tell you, then I'd put it off.

You're the only person in the county thet knows what blood's in that boy, Doctor, ef you do know an' from yo' continual lack of denial, I suspicion you do. An' I see you're still about it yet—which is straight goods.

An' you'd like to know how I worked the adoption, would you?

Well, partly by my nachel gift o' eloquence, I reckon. I don't mind tellin' you about it, seein' ez it's turnin' out so happy.

You see, his wife an' him, they both knowed thet I knowed thet you'd brought that child home "from the church door," an' was keepin' still about it. Whether you placed it there before or after takin' it inside an' privately baptizin' it or not, we'll never know. You whispered the one fact of the findin' to me, in confidence—an' ez you hoped I might do, I kep' a shet mouth on the outside an' let him an' his wife know, also "in strictest confidence." No, we'll never know jest how you found it, but we do know thet Moses's little sister never guarded the ancient law-giver amongst the bulrushes with more responsible care than that you give that little foundlin' befo' Pharaoh's daughter in the person o' Mis' Townsend, enfolded it in her queenly an' motherly arms.

So you'd like, after all these years, to know how I worked it, would you? I'll tell you, Doc', although I'd never 'a' mentioned it to you less'n you'd asked me. I'm a silent man—when they's need for it—an' I've always been here for you to question, ef you'd saw fit. I s'pose you thought thet the more you could say you didn't know on the subjec', the better.

I had sev'al things in my favor, with the Townsends, among other things an acquaintance thet runs back three generations. They believe me to be honest, an' I think likely they suspicion me to be fairminded an' not consciously cruel. An' then I knowed they needed a baby—an' needed it bad. Human hearts are like eggs. Ef they lay still too long, they git addled, an' a child, why it keeps things movin'—an' fresh.

Yas, we had often discussed adoption, they an' me, an' I knowed they was on a still-hunt for an adoptable baby, but I also knowed their prohibitions on the subject. You see, she's an aristocrat, an' in some ways, they're like camels, aristocrats is— that is when their aristocracy strikes outward. It's ap' to make a hump, so thet it's hard to git into the kingdom o' Heaven. I knowed the Townsends had both kinds—at least she had, or else I wouldn't never've entrusted one o' the Lord's little ones to 'er.

She's got the internal aristocratic *principle* in 'er which would prevent 'er from doin' a cheap or a mean act, an' ef she was a little humped on the outside with the consciousness o' superiority, why, I didn't mind, for I knew she could deliver the goods, an' no temptation would move 'er from integrity.

But of co'se, a woman like that, she's ap' to make a point of things, an' she said she'd never 'dopt no child of uncertainty. They had plenty o' money, an' so they even preferred to have the child penniless, which was a pardonable kind o' selfishness. They wanted to be everything to the little one.

Well, when you told me about this baby, I put on my thinkin' cap—an' when I laid eyes on the child—you ricollec' me comin' over an' kodakin' the little thing with Sonny's camera? Well, I never showed you that picture. Sez I, ef he can be shet-mouthed, so can I. I got a lovely picture, the little thing jest wakin' out o' sleep, with a smile on its face—an' I walked straight to the Townsends with it—an' left it with 'em to look at—an' kep' out o' their way for three days, so they'd live with it a while befo' anything was said.

An' on the fo'th day, Mis' Townsend, she wrote an' asked me to come over. They wasn't no telephones in Simpkinsville them days.

Well, I went, an' I went charged with success so thet nothin' else would do me. I made up my mind where that baby hailed from, an' I ain't never broached it to this minute—but I ain't never changed my mind, neither.

Well, I can't pretend to repeat a conversation, after so long. I went on the principle o' lettin' them do most o' the talkin', but little by little I called attention to things thet seemed attractive about the baby, not thet they was very much in a three-days'-old, beyond the fact thet it *was* a baby, an' healthy—an' happy. Do they often smile, I wonder, Doc', at three days? I s'pose they do. Sonny started in with all his functions so early, I don't seem able to differentiate.

Well, we talked along. I told 'er the down on his little head was a sort o' yaller, like corn silk, an', of co'se it didn't take long to strike the snag o' legitimacy, an' I ricollec', I remarked thet from the little I'd been able to gather, the baby's own folks was too proud an' haughty to receive it on the sly, at the back door, when circumstances for which the child wasn't in no wise responsible made it impossible for it to enter the front portal. You see, I used all the terms I could command thet I thought might appeal to 'er hump. I called attention to the baby's nose-line which happened to be high an' straight, for a newly-born—an' I ricollec' I told 'er it was attired in linen cambridge ornamented with valentia-lace—an' this set 'er laughin'. I ain't never told that on myself before, an' ef I mis-pernounced any o' that finery, why you are to blame, Doctor. It seems to me yet thet you said the goods was cambridge an' the lace valentia, an' they was somethin' else yo' wife said, about its bein' rolled an' whipped—but that sounded kind o' barbaric, an' I omitted it.

Well, I didn't seem to be makin' much impression, but I kep' on, casual. Told 'em thet ef they didn't want that child, we did, which you know to be true, in a general way. Of co'se, we didn't need the child the way they did. I didn't seem to be makin' no headway for about an hour or so. The Jedge, he had come in, meantime, an' whilst her an' me was discussin', he stood lookin' at the picture. His back is ez straight ez mine, Doctor, ef his ancestor did sign the declaration. No hump there. He's one of the Lord's aristocrats, all gentleness an' nobility. Well, after a while, somethin' rose up in me. I think it was the *success* I'd come for, an' I suddenly turned on my eloquent powers.

"My friends," I says, or words to that effect, "I've lived a long time, an' for the past few years I've been addicted to bio-graphical readin'. It's my favoryte branch o' literature," says I, "after the Bible, which is largely responsible for my biographical taste, for it's largely biography. An' I've noticed," says I, "thet the good Lord seems to take notice o' these little fatherless ones an' He bestows gifts upon 'em promiscuous, an' sometimes I wonder ef He don't maybe feel Hisself in some special way a Father to the father-less, who are so often also desolate and oppressed."

Well, they sent over an' got the baby. That was my maiden effort at eloquence, an' I won out. Ef I'd never done another day's work in my life, I'd almost be willin' to've lived to do that one thing—especially sence he's been readin' medicine with you, an' you tell me what a fine lad he is.

Talk about the sea givin' up its dead! I tell you, Doc', the revelations of the dry land'll outweigh the sea's dead, when the great day comes.

By the way, Doctor, do you ever hear from Dr. Cuthbertson's daughter, Charlotte, these days, I wonder? The first of Simpkins-ville women to take holy orders, an' a noble soul she was, God bless her.

"Died?" you say—in a cholera camp? You don't say! Well,

well! "Passed like a saint amongst 'em," you say, "an' died at the end of the season?" You don't tell me! What's that? You say they's men amongst the survivors who pray to 'er to this day—say their prayers at night to 'er jest ez ef she was a saint! It's a great world we live in, Doctor, an' not so much in need of theatres ez a person might think. Settin' back the way I've done these last years, an' takin' note o' the ins an' outs o' life, I often feel like ez ef I might be watchin' a great play.

The most beautiful young woman thet ever trod our Simp-kinsville lanes was Charlotte Cuthbertson, ez I remember 'er—an' it don't take much stretch of imagination to see 'er clothed ez a saint, walkin' amongst the sufferin' soldiers.

They say saints, to be real saints, has to suffer crucifixion—an' they's more than one kind o' crosses.

Did it ever occur to you, Doctor, thet poor little Mary, the Bethlehem mother, likely suffered 'er own personal crucifixion in a doubtin' community—besides the mortal pains through which she was endowed with the divine countenance? It wasn't no cinch—earnin' that slim ring o' gold around her innocent little head!

Seems to me they's more'n one lesson to be learned by them thet study over the story o' thet reverent and obedient little maiden soul. It's capable o' bein' looked at from every direction—an' ef the picture o' the little girl waitin' outside the stable gate don't make us jest a little less critical o' the child at our door, so's we'll be inclined to open it to him, in memory, ef we can't always do it in faith, then maybe we haven't studied it aright. That's the way it seems to me. Maybe ef I was mo' highly educated I might see it different, but that's the way it seems to me.

To my mind, every little orphan asylum child is in a sense waitin' outside our gates—an' the timid knock o' their little fists ought to keep us awake till we invite at least one to come in.

Here comes Mary Elizabeth, Doc'. Yas, daughter, here's the doctor! You say she's awake, now? Go right in, Doc', an' I'll wait out here for you. No doubt the fewer people she sees at once-t, the better.

* * *

Well, I thought you'd never come back, Doctor! Do you know how long you've been in that room? A hour an' seven minutes! Quite right, I'm shore, only I'm youthfully impatient.

An' you say it's jest the same thing—over-study, an' a disposition to undernourish which must be overcome—an' she must be kep' in bed a day or so, with anything she calls for to eat an' abundance of it—an' *no books, positive!* Well, ez Sonny says, *you're the doctor, Doctor!*

All she needs for the present is watchful care an'—what's that? "Amusement?" Excuse me conterdictin' a professional man, Doctor, but Madge ain't never needed to be amused yet. She'll amuse the whole crowd, let 'er alone. An' you say you're thinkin' out a scheme for 'er? Well, I've got patience. But did you take notice to Mary Elizabeth, Doctor? I often think with gratitude o' what a mother she has proved.

Why, she's motherly todes me, her father-in-law, an' to Sonny, hisself. I reckon any good wife is sort o' motherly to the husband of 'er choice.

Jest look at that hall hatrack, Doc', an' tell me ef you think I've got any occasion to kick. No, Mary Elizabeth an' Sonny, they ain't no mo' attracted to "race suicide" than you an' I are. Jest look at that collection o' hats—an' they ain't one, or a sunbonnet, there thet don't cover a lively intelligence, joyfully expressed, thank God!

Yes, an'—what's that you say? "An' yet I long for an orphan asylum?" Not much, I don't. Why, Doc', they's somethin' in the very name thet gives me the cold shivers! No, no! Ef half our people felt the way I do, they wouldn't be no sech desolate, homeless institutions on our American soil ez an orphan asylum.

They might have to be a few distributin' stations to which suddenly destituted child'en could be assigned for temporary care. Why, to my mind, a orphan asylum in a Christian community o' rich an' roomy homes is a sort o' national disgrace.

How can any institutional child have a fair chance o' being fully human? Think o' yo' boy, our little Doc', yo' namesake, bein' registered in one o' them awful books ez "No. 171," an' wendin' his lonely little way every night down the aisle between the rows o' cold, white cots to find his number, with no personal knee for his "Now I lay me"—an' havin' every last one o' his cunnin' little characteristics smoothed out flat by the daily iron of institutional rules—made exclusively for the rigid order o' the institution!

I never will forget the answer o' one o' the little asylum

inmates thet come to a Sunday-school class I taught whilst I was a youth. After callin' attention to a number o' Scripture mottoes thet adorned the walls, I ast 'er which of all the Bible texts she could remember influenced her the most, an' she chirped up, without a moment's hesitation, *"Keep off the grass!"* Poor little prohibited orphan!

Sech child'en always remind me o' the poor little incubator chickens thet ain't never nestled under a wing. Ef we was raisin' 'em to sell by the pound, it might do!

How's that, Doc'? You say you've done evolved a plan for little Madge? Mh, hm! Say that ag'in, Doctor, an' say it slow. Why, that sounds tremenjus! You say, it's important to git 'er away, but not so important ez to turn 'er mind away from 'er-self—an' so you propose to order little Doc' away for his health, an' to send Madge along to look after him, with instructions to live out o' doors—"any good place where they's hills an' springs," you say?

Well, you're a man of inventive genius, Doctor! An' I know the identical Methodist family thet'll be glad o' their board-money. But why limit 'em to two, Doc'? Eureky Springs has got the name o' bein' a sort o' fountain o' youth—what's the matter with me goin' along, an' exercizin' a grandfatherly eye on 'em! I couldn't renew my youth, because I ain't never parted with it, but I might recover my infancy, all right. But I'll promise to stop imbibin' before I need infant's care!

Well, I'll be jiggered! Shake!—"be jiggered?" Yas, I'll be doggoned! An' I ain't swore sech a swear ez that in thirteen year—not sence the little pitchers has had their big ears set for proper speech. But this tickles me, down to the ground! Go right in, now, Doc', an' consult with Mary Elizabeth about it—see how quick she can git us ready to start! An' fix the day.

You say the responsibility o' little Doc' will keep Madge's mind off'n 'erself—an' 'er strenuosity in follerin' him around will keep 'er actively in the open?

An', what's that? "Fishin'-tackle?"

Jerooshy! Why not! I wonder could I ketch a fish ag'in at my age, ef I was to balance myself keerful on a grassy bluff over a sedgy creek—with a old bakin' powder box with holes punched in the led, full o' wrigglin' bait beside me, an' a fryin' pan an' a piece o' bacon an' some cornmeal an' coffee in the basket at my elbow, propped ag'in' the cedar knees? An' matches handy!

An' ef I was to ketch a string o' goggle-eyed pyerch, instid o' rejoicin' over the recovery o' my youth, would I be ungrateful, I wonder, an' start a-grievin' for *her* ag'in, with the old regret thet time has begun to heal?

You see, in our youth, that was our favoryte debauch—jest droppin' every corrodin' care an' startin' out equipped for a day in the open, an' many's the time we've come home by starlight, so full o' sweet inflation an' gratitude thet any little bothers thet had been weighin' us down would seem to float away, same ez thistledown.

What's that you say, Doc'? "Is Madge a cook?" Haven't I been tellin' you all along? She's one o' these ornamental cooks, Madge is. Couldn't do a thing jest so, by rote, to save 'er life. It's like the Sutton eloquence, practically applied. Ricollec', I ast 'er to slip out in the kitchen an' bile me an egg, one day, when she was about six, Dicey bein' busy, an' what did she do but dye that egg green? Done it with peach leaves an' grass, an' a pinch o' sal sody, I believe. A thing like that is enlivenin', in a little youngster o' six.

Why, it was our Madge thet built that bridal couple on Amy Ames's weddin' cake, Doc'—done it every lick out o' her own head, an' whipped up eggs an' sugar!

No doubt, she'll have little Doc' an' me eatin' woods-cooked corn dodgers of every conceivable shape, an' the fried fish, balanced on their tails, beggin' to be devoured!

Ef you hurry an' git us off, Doc', we'll be there in time for the dogwood blossoms—an' we'll stay till the persimmons is sugary. I hate to be impolite on my own po'ch, Doctor, but why in the kingdom come don't you *rise up an' go in an' make arrangements with Mary Elizabeth—an' decide when we can start! Seems to me we're losin' time!*

Absent Treatment and Second Sight

Good for sore eyes you are, Doctor. I had about give you up for good. I was jest a-thinkin' yesterday thet like ez not you was ketchin' on to the new idee an' givin' me absent treatment!

That's right! Hang up yo' hat an' drop in that rocker an' give me some account o' yo'self! No absent treatment in mind, Doc'— not from you! They might be some doctors I'd welcome it from, but I'm too fond o' yo' conversational powers which help me ez much ez yo' physic.

D'you reelize thet you ain't set foot here sence jest after our return from our travels—seventeen days ago—an' me jest bustin' to confide all our escapages to yo' sympathetic ear. You see, you're the only man in the county thet's got a X-ray on my conscience—an' when I know you discern foreign things floatin' 'roun' in it, why, I like to have a chance to explain how they got there. Seems sort o' small of a man o' yo' size to take advantage of a family's health an' make hisself scarce. I always enjoy company mo' when I'm well than when I'm sick, an' yet I don't no sooner git down in the mouth than you come a-prowlin' round with a pill and powder expression on yo' face.

S'pose you've been out to the Simpkinses—to see ef the flutes is all prim in the old ladies' caps. They's somethin' mighty pleasin' in the crystalizin' effect of old age in some. Now, them old maiden sisters ain't changed a ioto in any conceivable way for twenty-five year, an' here I'm their senior by nearly a year an' ez variable ez a weather-vane an' ez open to conviction ez ever. Sometimes I think it's my continual association with childhood, that an' my nachel curiosity about every new thing thet turns up.

I s'pose ef they knowed about all our New York carousals, they'd be turrible scandalized, but they'll never know. We bought 'em both nice little presents from the north, exactly alike, of co'se, they bein' twins, a pair o' revised hymn-books in big print. Mary Elizabeth did crave to fetch 'em a pair o' new style capes. She says them dolman shapes seem to confine their elbows an' yet, she hesitated to do it, they bein' heirlooms of cut jet.

To my mind, antiquated fashions set becomin' on the folks they've grown old with. I wouldn't never've varied my clo'es the way I have excep'n for these growin' child'en. I reckon they'd be humiliated to have me dressed the way I'd feel most at home in, whilst I'd take especial delight in riggin' out like a cockatoo, ef it give them pleasure.

But I keep a-talkin' an' don't tell you what's on my mind. I want you to see New York, ez much ez I can present to you, th'ough my old eyes—an' some of it is so dazzlin' thet I feel like ez ef you must see it shinin' th'ough me.

There's that opera, now—what's that you say? "Did we go to the opera?" Ain't I tellin' you about it, ez fast ez I can? Yas, we did, an' my private opinion is thet we seen *an' heerd* the most corrupt operatic performance thet ever was looked at by a set o' Christian people.

You see, Sonny, he charged Mary Elizabeth to see everything she had been interested in by hearsay, an' sence we've had that talkin' machine, why the operatic singers is all household friends, so, she nachelly inclined to the opera, an' she consulted me, with all due respect an' timidity, an' I advised her to take a newspaper an' pick out the most correct-soundin' opera-play they advertised, which she done. In fact, she an' me, we picked it out together.

You see, most o' the opera-singers is these fureigners with sort o' heathenish names, an' the parts they play is open to criticism, but when she come to Mary Garden, why, we both seized upon it. Says she, "Now, that's a good American name." Mary always does seem sort o' saintly, an' a garden, somehow it put us in mind o' the garden of Eden. So we picked her out that-a-way, an' then when we see she was engaged in a Bible play, why our decision was complete.

The play was entitled Salome, you ricollec' the daughter of Herodias, an' tell the truth, we both felt like ez ef we was goin' to a religious service. I got out my New Testament, an' we read the fo'teenth chapter o' Matthew, all about how she danced befo' the king, an' we discussed the paganism of the ancient times, an' we resolved to go with reverent hearts to see the play played, an' half doubtful whether it was right to put such holy subjects on a theatre-stage.

Well, that was the sperit in which we went, but, ez I told you at the beginnin', ef I'm any jedge of corruption, that so-called Bible opera-play is the limit. An' the pore misguided girl thet does the part of Salome, well, the truth is, I don't think I'm competent to discuss it.

Of co'se, she was in a manner obligated to misbehave to the extent of rousin' the old king to all sorts o' brash vows, an' it may have seemed necessary for her to be about half stripped, to show them serpentine motions, but we was unprepared for sech exposure.

Of co'se, the words bein' all in French, an' sung at that which obscures their meanin' still more, we couldn't be shore but maybe they was in a manner explanatory. But ef the words matched her conduct, the whole thing was consider'ble out o' the way. I felt like ez ef it might be my duty to rise an' forfeit them five dollar seats, an' lead Mary Elizabeth out into the fresh air—that is, the best air we could git, in New York.

But I didn't. I'd glance at her every little while, an' she seemed so untouched by it all, I thought, like ez not, the unreality of the singin' conversation an' the over wrought behavior of everything in sight would likely make it like a dream to her—an' so we set it out. An' now, I'm glad we did.

They jest took the Bible narration ez a stake to play around, an' they wove licentiousness into it, right an' left. F'instance, they tried to prove by visual perception thet the girl, Salome, had fell in love with John the Baptist, at first sight, an' her askin' for his head was for spite, at his rejection. He cert'nly did act a perfec' gentleman when she fairly thowed 'erself at him. He was, to my mind, the only one thet reely looked his part. I'd 'a' knowed John, anywhere, not only by his raiment of camel's hair an' the leather girdle, but his look o' the wilderness an' the warnin' voice, all that was strictly scriptural. An' the scenery of the play, why that was reely worth the entrance money—all the grandeur of the Eastern court, an' the high color which didn't have to be translated.

An' that "dance o' the seven veils," why, ef it had 'a' been danced by a little child, I'd say it was one o' the most bewilderin' performances in the world. She shore is supple in the hinges, Mary Garden is, an' she must 'a' had consider'ble drillin' to be able to fling them veils exact, every time, a veil bein' about ez unmanageable a missile ez a person could try to throw at a mark.

I always liked a good game o' skill, an' I might've got over them seven veils, ef she hadn't acted so scandalous with John. An'—what you say, Doc'? "How about the audience?"

Well, I don't know ez the audience showed much mo' reticence than what Mary did, in a different way. It was a great sight, that immense half-moon o' chairs facin' the stage, all occupied by radiantly shinin' ladies, mostly, all mo' or less stripped.

"Respectable?" you say? Why, shore, that is, they was classed so—not only respectable an' wealthy, but high class, but—lean over here a minute, Doc', I can't speak this out loud, less'n Mary Elizabeth might git wind of it, but I want to say to you, both ez a friend an' family physician, thet whilst I set there, in that five dollar orchestral seat, an' borried Mary Elizabeth's little telescope an' surveyed that scenery of ladies occupyin' the front row of stalls right out in the glare of a thousand electric lights, it seemed to me I'd never seen so many nursin' mothers together, in my life.

I ain't disposed to criticize an' I won't say they was intentionally brazen about it. It might 'a' been forgetfulness, or it might 'a' been conformity to Parisian style. Mary Elizabeth, she seemed to attribute it to Paris, an' she says they do say the Paris rule for functional dresses is "the fuller the scanter," in other words, "the higher the style, the lower the cut."

Of co'se, in all sech ez this, I'd defer to the ladies theirselves, every time.

Mary Elizabeth, I could see thet she was mo' scandalized than what I was which was nachel enough. A person feels for her own sex. An' I didn't have no occasion to feel any too vainglorious about mine, neither, my pride in John's circumspection bein' over-balanced by my shame in King Herod, the Tetrarch.

Any ol' man turned fool over a girl is a humiliatin' spectacle, an' I wish it was rarer'n what it is. They ain't no better way for an ol' man to expose his decripitude than by contrast, an' yet, it's hard for a man in love to git far enough from his own folly to git any reasonable view of 'isself.

No, we didn't take the child'en, not to that. But Mary Elizabeth took Madge to a number o' matinee performances, to verify the Victor machine's performances. An' we all heard Harry Lauder sing, in his side-pleated skirt an' bare legs. I had to supply mountain scenery out o' my ol' head to make him appear allowable. We've got sev'al pictures of Highlanders at home here, an' they're all woods-surrounded. You see Madge is musical an' Mary Elizabeth, she never forgot it. She's had her voice tried—an' they bought some new records—an' I reckon they's some ambitious plans bein' hatched out betwixt her an' her mother.

When I heerd the reel singers, Doc', an' reelized the exactitude of the mechanical reproductions, I tell you, it set me a-thinkin'. All that musical an' emotional exactitude reproduced by the narrow pathway of a needle! Sech ez that makes me almost sorry I'm old. It seems to me we're on the ticklish verge of the full vision an' I'd like to be here for the revelation.

You know, we come home partly by sea, Doc', from New York to New Orleans, an' the rest o' the way by the Southern Pacific an' Iron Mountain, an' what I haven't had a chance to observe ain't worth mentionin'.

But the wireless telegraph, that, to me, is the century's achievement—so far. You never know what some student workin' in retirement has discovered over night. They're like patent medicines an' mortgages—inventors are. They work while you sleep!

But the WIRELESS!

Think o' bein' in mid-ocean an' gittin' messages addressed to the different passengers from Squedunk an' Moravia, an' no visible disturbance o' the air, even!

The Wireless man, aboa'd ship, he an' me, we got to be great chums, an' he all but adopted little Doc'. You see, electricity is a large part of our table conversation, sence the boys has been comin' along. An' these child'en have got all sorts o' electric contrivances, bells an' telephones, all about the place. Half the trees in our woods is mo' or less equipped with wires an' they ain't a tree-house nowhere but has its "system" in it, for some sort of experiment or harmless deviltry.

Well, it seems thet this man wasn't used to sech child'en an' he was inclined to rate little Doc' ez a progidy, tel I told 'im about his older brother an' his pa.

It seems, Doc', thet they jest turn out messages promiscuous, an' only the properly attuned machines can ketch 'em. Why, right now, whilst you an' me are settin' here, the air must be filled with live messages rushin' in all directions, from Maine to ships in the Pacific, or Hong Kong to Key West, an' even whilst they fairly tickle our ears, we don't reelize 'em, because we ain't adjusted to 'em.

I'd like to focus what little mind I've got left on the production of automatic receivers—receivers thet would ketch all thet was goin', or, at least, all thet was fitten for us. That would come near the attainment of divine power—an' my belief is thet it's comin'. They've dispensed with the wires an' the nex' thing will be dispensin' with the machines—an' by keepin' in tune with the infinite, we'll be enabled to discern the currents of love an' affection from hearts in accord with ours, not only on earth but in Heaven. To my mind, that'll be the dawnin' of the Perfect Day.

He was a polite young feller, that Wireless, an' mighty patient with my slow mind. I learned mo' of him in them five days at sea than I'd imbibe, settin' here on my loved po'ch, in ten year with yo' visits so sca'ce—that is, mo' specified knowledge.

The sweet lessons of full an' tranquil life have come to me here, an' I wouldn't exchange it—but I rejoice to've had this fresh illumination. I give the young man one o' Sonny's books, a signed one I happened to have aboa'd, an' you'd 'a' been proud to witness his delight.

Why, he knows all about our Sonny. An' when he found out thet *he* was little Doc's father, you should 'a' seen him. Nothin' the little feller could 'a' said would 'a' surprised him, then.

What's that you say? "I promised to tell you about seein' Sonny's books on sale?" Sure, I did. Seen people come up an' buy 'em, too, an' never let on. The first time we saw that was at the Waldorf. "Did we go to the Waldorf?" We've been to New York, I tell you, Doc'—to New York, with Mary Elizabeth ez pilot, aided an' abetted by Sonny, eggin' 'er on by every mail to see the last sight.

Yas, we put up at the Waldorf over night, registered in the office—I jest put down my initial there. I didn't want to humiliate Sonny by writin' myself down "Deuteronomy Jones, Sr." Although it's an old name, it seems to have a sort o' conspicuosity about it—so, I jest signed "D. Jones an' family."

Yas, we registered an' took a suite—that word's pernounced *sweet*, Doctor. We took a sweet, I say, an' went up in it in the alleviator, eleven floors—an' we stayed over night, an' the two

youngsters, they punched the buttons in the wall for every conceivable thing—an' the rest of 'em, they put their shoes out at
night to be shined, all but me. No, I wouldn't do it. I was like the
stranger in the castle who was afeerd to resk settin' out his shoes,
lessen they'd be gilded. An' besides, I never want nobody else
polishin' my boots. I like my own spit.

Well, we set in the Turkish room, an' we sauntered amongst
the pa'ms, an' we took that day's dinner, at supper-time, in the
main dinin'-room, all four of us at a little table together.

Then Mary Elizabeth, she 'lowed it would be nice for each
one to order what he wanted, but they all lingered in indecision
an' the list was long an' only partially intelligible. So, finally, she
see a mighty nice, well-behaved lookin' party of four at the table
catticornered away from us, an' they had jest give their order, an'
so she says, says she to the waiter, "Jest duplicate their order for
us, please, an' fetch it ez soon ez you can."

They was a mighty rigorous lookin' crowd for style, an' I
couldn't help applaudin' Mary Elizabeth's wit in seein' jest what
sech a party of average rich New Yorkers would order for a
ordinary dinner.

Well, I wush-t you could 'a' seen that dinner, Doctor! I won't
pertend to describe it to you, for it's beyond my vocabulary. I
know it cost thirty-one dollars an' thirty cents—an' I ricollec'
Mary Elizabeth, she 'lowed afterwards thet she didn't see no trace
o' the thirty-one dollars but she felt like thirty cents!

Yas, I know, it does seem a fabulous price, but you see, they
was tarrapin for four, for one thing, an' high-class duck—for
four—duck with the blood streamin' out of it so thet you had to
hurry an' mix it with the red jelly to deceive yo'self into eatin' it.
Then they was some kind o' round paddy-cakes of meat surrounded with br'iled toad-stools which I tried to summon sufficient fo'ce o' character to taste, an' did take on my plate. An', of
co'se, they was the usual amount of ornamental tricksy sweet an'
sour things, an' ice-cream which you unearthed from a hot choco-
late sauce. That was nice, I must confess, an' Mary Elizabeth's
delight in that one achievement was worth the price o' the whole
dinner. She's managed to git the recipe for that, somehow, an'
we've had it here, jest ez good ez the Waldorf's.

No doubt, it was a fine dinner, but when we had finished it, I hated to give extry trouble, but I felt sort o' empty, not havin' partaken of much, an' I asked Mary Elizabeth ef she'd be too much humiliated ef I was to order some pancakes an' syrrup an' a full-sized cup o' coffee, which I done. In fact, I got a pot o' coffee, an' drank it deliberate. That New York coffee, even at the big hotels, is inoffensive, an' I needed mild stimulation, leadin' the strenuous life the way we was.

Yas, ez I said, it was Sonny thet kep' a-writin' to Mary Elizabeth, eggin' 'er on to fetch home all sorts of New York experiences. He knowed she'd enjoy tellin' 'er friends about the opera, an' the Waldorf, an' so she does. I notice, sence she's come home, she don't resort to the curio-cabinet the way she used to, to make talk.

Yas, sence her backset with the last baby, when only yo' skill brought 'er th'ough the purple fever, Sonny, he's mighty lenient an' indulgent todes 'er. An' you know his new book is in the ninth edition a'ready, so thet the family expenditures has come to be a matter of discretion mo' than of necessity.

Yas, we was all sorry for him not to've been along, but you see, he's busy on another book, an' I tell you, Doc', the production of books bears consider'ble resemblance to child-bearin'. For the last ten years, I've noticed thet when Mary Elizabeth wasn't gittin' ready for a baby, why Sonny would be confined with a book. You nee'n't to laugh. I'm serious. He says he couldn't no mo' leave a book half done an' go gallivantin' than a hen could leave a settin' of eggs an' not know the life would be out of 'em, quick ez they got stone cold.

You see, life is life, an' the book thet ain't got life in it ain't no good, nohow. He made a joke on that, Sonny did. He's great on quiet jokes. He 'lowed thet nothin' could be expected to have circulation thet didn't have life—an', of co'se circulation is necessary for a book to do any good.

Yas, he's still hard at it, although he's got on mighty fast durin' the family exodus, so he says, although, from the number of surprises he's planned an' executed for us durin' our absence, I'd think that was all he did.

He says it was his only chance to administer absent treatment, an' he done it. He treated me to this sep-rate po'ch on the sunny side o' my room an' my own bathroom with tiles in it. I reckon he 'lowed we'd requi'e mo' luxury after we'd seen the world. An' he's got Mary Elizabeth a special bath 'j'inin' their room, likewise, an' a sun-parlor with a out-side place to sleep, an' a sort o' conservatorial annex, all on her floor, for her favorite plants. It seems, she had a suspicion of what he was doin' ez he wrote her she better select wall-papers in New York, ag'inst the time they'd be ready to use 'em, an' she didn't lose no time. She even advised him where to store 'em away, all the time full o' laugh, knowin' he'd have 'em hung, time she come home.

An' then, once-t awake, she described our Waldorf bath-room, an' 'lowered to him thet whenever she could affo'd it, she intended to have hers done like it, which was mo' of a knock-down than a hint, an' he tumbled.

Now, that sort o' absent treatment is to my taste. Of co'se when we come home, all the papers was up an' the parlor set recovered with the stuff she selected "for storage," an' of co'se, she bought a few things to conform. But she ain't no reckless buyer. She goes slow an' sure.

But about Sonny's books, ez I was telling' you, we was stand-in' close't to the book-stand there at the Waldorf, that night we put up there, an' a young man come up an' what does he say but "Have you got 'Nature's Overcoats,' by Deuteronomy Jones?" I don't know why, but would you believe I suddenly had a sensa-tion of goose-skin all over me, when I heerd it.

"Sure!" says the clerk, like ez ef he'd 'a' been ashamed not to've had it, an' I see him hand out the woods-colored volume an' take the dollar an' a half, an' when the man had started off, he turns back an' says he, "Any mo' of his books?" "All of 'em," says he, an' with that, he enumerated five, an' when he stopped, what does little Doc' do but chirp up, "Them ain't all. You forgot 'Thistles an' Armed Peace' an' 'The Dutchman's Pipe.' "

Well, sir, I wish-t you could 'a' seen that man. He jest turned an' looked little Doc' over, an' I could see myself thet our little man looked consider'ble of a young country greenie, an' says he, "What do you know about those books, my man?"

"I reckon you'd know about 'em," says he, "ef yo' daddy wrote 'em!"

Well, sir, with that he took the boy by the hand an' he led him into the office an' he called a crowd an' they catechised the little feller, an' when he come back, he was loaded up with candy an' fruit, an'—

What's that? Oh, no. I didn't make myself known. I'm considerate of Sonny, an' I know I'm jest a plain man. No, that was my absent treatment of him, not thet I think he'd want me to feel that-a-way, an' I ain't over-afflicted with undue humility. Only, I'd ruther meet strangers here at home, where I seem to fit my socket than in the glare of their electric lights.

I still have my pants cut by mother's ol' pattern, an' when I'm home, I don't never think about it, but I often had my attention called to 'em, somehow, walkin' the New York streets. The only man to give me comfort about my pants in New York was Abe Lincoln, an' him through that stature, in one o' the public squares. I reckon, like ez not, his wife made his.

Ain't it wonderful, the way ease an' comfort an' a loose fit can be conveyed in hard bronze? Ef the time should ever come when it might be interestin' to have statures of the father of Deuteronomy Jones, the nature-writer, I hope they'll be satisfied with my bust. I'd change my pants now for my livin' family, but I don't care to do it for posterity.

Yas, we've had a great time, Doctor, an' while it has changed my views on a few subjects an' made me mo' lenient in some o' my jedgments, it ain't no ways disturbed the foundations o' my faith.

I ain't never been troubled with no very rigorous sectarian doctrines, ez you know, an' even ef I had been, I'd 'a' had to widen out a little, after findin' so much good in all; an' I'm prepared to take what I find wherever I find it, ef it's genuine.

The fact thet you keep my rheumatism down the way you do with yo' ol'-fashioned alopathic salts an' ointments wouldn't prevent me lettin' a Christian Scientist aim any quantity of absent treatment at these j'ints which they declare ain't swole the way they seem to be to you an' me, an' I'd take a mud bath or an electric shower or a sun-soak or a water-cure, ef their advocates seemed sane-minded an' didn't requi'e *me* to deny the evidence of my senses which may be misguided, of co'se. But which in a good many things, seem to be faithful guides, so far ez they go.

I believe in absent treatment of the Scientists an' mind-healers to the extent of not abusin' 'em behind their backs. The avenues of the sperit don't seem to me to be limited to no one sect, an' it often seems to me thet one will git a-holt o' one side o' the truth an' one another, an' it takes 'em all to carry it along—or, maybe it does.

I can't help bein' jest a little on their side—I'm a-talkin' about them absent-treaters, now—I say I can't help bein' on their side when the newspapers all jump on 'em when one o' their number dies. They seem to forget thet our ol' graveyards are full o' the patients of our reg'lar doctors.

What's that, Doc'? "Am I goin' over to 'em?" Oh, no. But I want to treat 'em white, that's all. Any sect thet dwells upon the beauty of holiness an' thet challenges every soul to find God in itself has got a great truth, an' there's so much health an' wellbein' in that one reelization thet we might forgive 'em ef their heads gits turned a little an' they become imbued with the idee thet they've got a corner on the Grace of God. Listen at me, quotin' terms from the stock-market! You see, Doc', they ain't the first sect thet has considered itself especially divinely endowed, an' that sort o' delusion, ef it ain't carried too far, is a tower o' stren'th.

The thing thet we seem to me to need most is to unite on our agreements more an' not dispute about our differences quite so much. I've often thought thet at the last day the number o' sheaves we bring in might be mo' important than what kind o' scythe we cut 'em with.

Th'ain't no reputable religious denomination thet holds any doctrine opposed to brotherly love an' human helpfulness an' ef we keep busy with that, why we won't find much time to dispute about predestination or the Fo'teenth Amendment—I mean to say the Thirty-nine articles.

What's that you say? "Did I know thet Ol' Mis' Bradley has laid aside her specs, all th'ough absent treatment?" Why, yas, I heerd somethin' about it. Lemme see. Sarah Jane is two years younger'n what I am—an' I ain't had no need o' specs for a long time. In my case, it's second sight, the same thet my pa an' ma enjoyed, after they passed the sixty-nine mark, that, an' the *absence of treatment*. Our family eyes has always been reliable an' our sight ain't never been injured by no ambitious oculists.

"Don't I b'lieve in oculists?" Why, sure I do, an' I b'lieve in doctors, too, reg'lar doctors like you, but I'm always happier when my relations with 'em are purely friendly.

An' surgery, it never had no appetizin' effect on me. I never like to think about a surgeon's implements. I've always thought thet all doctors ought to be divinely endowed with a sort o' professional second sight, an' then they wouldn't be liable to err.

I never have been able to forgit that doctor thet put a patient to sleep with chloroform an' then took out the wrong eye—an' scissors is bein' sewed up in unconscious humans every day o' the week, ef we are to believe the papers. I've sometimes thought thet Dave Baily's wife might 'a' had sev'al pairs sewed up in her durin' all them operations she loves to talk about, an' maybe that's why she's so contrary an' argumentative.

No, I'll take my doctors sociably, whenever I can. They's nothin' I like so much ez to see yo' horse comin' down the road an' to know I'll have the pleasure of settin' down, like this, an' listenin' to yo' talk.

What's that you say? "Ain't our second boy thinkin' about studyin' medicine?" Cert'n'y he is, an' with my entire approval. He ought to've been yo' namesake. He got the idee from you, an' I approve of his so'ce of inspiration.

Some things are necessary evils—an' doctors seem to be one of 'em, doctors an' "healers" which of co'se is an interchange of terms. Ef you ain't considerable of a healer, you ain't got no business to be a doctor. I never could git at the consistency of that word among the Christian Scientists, though.

Ef they ain't no sech a thing ez disease, I can't exactly see what they profess to heal. Ef it's error, an' error is illness, then—? But, of co'se I'm antiquated an' maybe slow-minded. I was so curious thet I paid a five dollar bill for a soft-covered copy of *Science an' Health,* an' I don't say it ain't *science,* but it ain't *healthy,* not for me.

It's like sayin' the apostles creed an' the ten commandments backward—to me—the way we've been told to do to git to sleep. You can't say it ain't all there, but—well, I found it innocent enough. The only thing was I hadn't been sufferin' insomniously, an' didn't exac'ly need it. But for them thet need soothin', I'd ricommend it cheerfully.

An', when all is said an' done, we have to confess it holds a great truth an' that's why it's got sech a holt on some people. It seems to me to be an ancient truth, one o' the very oldest, a leetle fantastic in the way it's put, maybe.

Of co'se, our doctors an' preachers, they don' take to it. None of us don't like to be interfered with. But it has smoothed out some anxious faces in this neighborhood, an' ain't turned nobody vicious, an' that's somethin'.

Ef it hadn't did no mo'n to set po' ol' lame Tillie Fay dancin', I'd give it credit. What's that? Well, s'pose she does hobble jest the same! She says that's only reminiscent of error, an' she does look so happy! Give the devil his due, Doctor. You've treated Miss Tillie for thirty odd year, an' I'm not criticizin', but you never set 'er dancin'!

Yas, ez you say, Po' Molly Skinners did commit suicide in a spell of enthusiasm in it, but you ricollec' little Elsie Seaman jumpin' into Bramble bayou, from over-study, preparin' for 'er graduatin', an' none of us can ever forget our saintly little Mary Ellen Williams losin' 'er mind over that scoundrel jiltin' 'er at the altar, never turnin' up. Anything thet gets too much mastery over a mind is liable to th'ow it over.

I've often thought thet one o' St. Paul's most useful precepts was moderation an' temperance in all things. The trouble with us humans is thet we run so to extremes thet the very word *temperance*, itself, has come to stand for intemperate abstinence.

Mo' than one man has upset middlin' good minds, goin' looney over inventin' perpetual motion thet they couldn't invent. An' I ain't shore thet our Sonny ain't amusin' 'isself now over some sech machinism, in his garret workshop. He an' the blacksmith has consider'ble secrets together an' he's always fetchin' in some new contraption. But I ain't oneasy about him, because I know he don't run to intemperance.

Who is that drivin' by, Doctor? Nev' mind yo' specs, I see. It's Jim Toland's buggy with his third boy in it. I'm feerd Jim's porely. He sends the boys so often when he used to go hisself.

Talk about seein'! Why, I can discern the hue o' my red drawer th'ough the mesh o' this homespun on my kneecap, ez no glasses ever revealed it.

An' I see other things mo' clair, too, Doc'. I often seem to see beyond appearances, these later days, an' lookin' th'ough the criss-crossin' of some o' the troubled faces I've known so long, an' mo' or less misjudged, I see deep waters of patience an' silent endurance. Why, I've discovered mo' than one clair lake of peace in the waitin' soul of an ol' black man with a face ez wrinkled an' brown ez a raisin.

But most of all, I see beauty. Everywhere I look, it seems to be distributed. Of co'se, it has always laid thick along our country lanes an' over our hills. We sow it an' water it an' gether it, an' oftentimes unknowin'ly. Yas, I have a feelin' thet when we git ol' age's second sight, ef we'll open our souls to the vision, we'll find many a revelation of beauty thet's withheld from the eager eyes of youth. An' with that an' the wireless messages of love thet come to us, even from the Beyond, I ain't shore but old age is the most blessed season in life, ez well ez the richest.

A Note of Scarlet

Miss Melissa Ann Moore was a spinster who knitted green moss mats. She had learned how to make these mats when she was very young, and constant practice had kept her art perfect through many years.

There are two classes of needlework women: there are those who learn a pattern to honor it all their days—to whom it is a creed, and who would scorn a departure as they would scorn a heresy in religion; and others there are whom a design serves only as a hint, valuable chiefly as a point of departure into ways of their own without end. Even womanly women of this latter type have been known to confess a momentary grudge against a pair of tiny pink feet that demanded two of a kind from their all too adventurous needles.

Miss Melissa was an orthodox creature, and not more steadfast was she to the faith of her fathers than to the one moss pattern of her mothers. She fully believed that every perfectly constructed mat that emanated from her faithful fingers was foreordained to be, from the beginning of time, else it would never have been counted worthy to materialize.

There were examples of Miss Melissa's art in nearly every home in Simpkinsville—examples more or less faded and worn, according to circumstances, but all faithful witnesses of her entire worthiness to perpetuate the species. And, be it said to her credit, those that she made to sell were handled and their proportions verified with the same scrupulous care as were such as came into being for bridal or Christmas presents, or to adorn the marble base of her own evening lamp. You could measure the distance between the little moss clumps in the border of any of them, and find each one precisely as long as the index-finger of Miss Melissa's left hand, measured from the mole downward. She would no sooner have guessed at one of these intervals than she would have prevaricated in a statement of fact.

Miss Melissa lived with her married brother Caleb; and at the birth of each of his nine children there had been a pair of "aunty's lovely moss mats" ready as a welcoming gift to the little stranger, to be laid out for inspection among the pink and blue socks and sacks that were sent in by friends and relatives, after which they were withdrawn and packed away in camphor, to be kept until their owners should marry, when they would do double duty as wedding presents. Not that Miss Melissa was parsimonious. Far from it. But she was getting old, and, as she expressed it: "I'll be mos' likely passed away long befo' that time; an' so I put a envelop o' good wishes an' advice in with each set, which it seems to me'll be mighty impressive, comin' from a dear dead aunt, same as a voice from the grave."

She had even kept an extra pair of mats on hand, carefully wrapped and perfumed with sachet-powder, against the arrival of impending twins—the same "runnin' in both families"—so that, to quote again from her own lips, "the unexpected, ef it *should* come, should find itself expected in one quarter, at least." Indeed, she insisted that, for her part, she'd see to it that a duplicate baby shouldn't fall short of its welcome just for the sake of a few stitches she'd put into a duplicate pair of lamp-mats, "an' it jest as much a blood-relation to me as its twin, every bit an' grain."

She always made her mats in pairs, because they were "intended to be made in pairs"; and she set them, "as they were meant to be set, on each end o' the mantel-shelf, with a lamp all ready to light a-standin' in the center of each one." It is true, she used one of her own pair on the small center-table in her bedroom, but she always consistently borrowed it from its station opposite its mate and put it carefully back next morning.

For twenty years and more Miss Melissa had pursued her gentle art, and, as she herself was pleased to assert, she "hadn't never turned a mat out of her hand thet she wouldn't be more'n willin' to have raveled out an' counted, an' ef she ever should do sech a thing as to turn off one with a false stitch in it, it would run in her head same as a tune out o' tune, an' she'd look for a lamp to sputter quick as it was set on it."

There seems to be a serene pleasure in this kind of orthodox needlework. That there is joy in the other sort, with its fitful departures and sometimes eccentric creations, does not alter the matter. The even tenor of unquestioningly following a lead is conducive to length of days and a fair showing of good works therein.

It is the dweller upon the plain who has seen a mountain—either seen it with his mortal eyes or evolved it out of its antithesis—who becomes discontented and—does something. What he does is—is it not?—largely a matter of temperament. He may forsake the dead level of his native heath and go in search of his mountain, or he may mope and grow weary, and have nervous prostration or "low sperits," according to his social position.

No one knows, excepting the doctor, maybe—and of course we all know that he doesn't—what it is precisely that induces the condition so variously called, and which exhibits itself first in an ignoble discontent.

Why was it that, after all her years of faithful pursuit of it, Miss Melissa one day found herself restless in the practice of her art? When she wound the green zephyr for the moss border around the outsides of the parlor chairs, as she had so often done—"settin' each chair jest far enough from the wall to be walked behind, an' takin' in the top grape on the back o' the haircloth sofy"—why did she stop as many as three times on the third round, and raise the strands in her fingers, studying them thoughtfully until she finally said aloud: "'Tain't because it's green—though they do say green is forsaken; an' of co'se I know it's exac'ly the right shade, for I've matched it time an' ag'in by the livin' moss, an' it's, ef anything, even more natural. I 'spect it's my liver thet's torpid."

She started off again, though, and did not stop until she had wound the required number of strands. When she had finished, however, instead of cutting the zephyr, she hesitated and looked at it.

I've got half a notion to wind on another row!" she exclaimed. "I've often thought lately thet I'd like to see how that moss would look ef it seemed to grow a little thicker—or thinner." And even as she spoke she began her promenade around the horse-hair set; but there was a new look in her eyes, and she walked faster than on any of the earlier rounds.

Then came the tying of the strands preparatory to the cutting. At first she measured, as always, from the mole; but when she had tied one or two in this way, she suddenly thrust her hands behind her and exclaimed: "Lordy, how tired I am of it all! I'm a-goin' to stop an' guess at these spaces—that's what I'm a-goin' to do." And guess at them she did, tying faster and faster as she went.

It was her habit to take her work into the dining-room after supper, joining the family until they separated for bed; but to-night she stole into her own room, and locked the door.

That mat was never finished. Although she worked far into the night, and chuckled often over the irregularities that were so many expressions of her spirit of revolt, her joy was not full. The color wearied her. It was representative of a long way that had had no turning. Of course she could not know this. She knew only that, for some occult reason which she did not try to under-stand, she would have given her eyes, almost, if the strands had been red—"not none o' yo' pale pinky reds, neither, but jest a' all-fired red"; and the more she thought of it, the more the idea haunted her—the more the red invited and the green "tor-mented" her.

Two days afterward the center of the mat was done, and half of its irregular growth of greenery was already in place, when, in an access of impatience that surprised herself, Miss Melissa sud-denly threw it into the top bureau-drawer, turned the key, and, seizing her sunbonnet, started down the street. Within an hour a light and bulky parcel was lying, still wrapped, beside the un-finished green mat, under lock and key; and while she played with the baby in the dining-room, after supper, her brother remarked that he didn't know when he had seen Melissa looking so well or so young.

She did not wait for the family to separate, but, slipping away early in the evening, she escaped to her room, and turned the key in the door. Then she lighted the lamp and drew down the window-shade before she drew forth the parcel of scarlet wool and shook it out and held it before her, laughing aloud. Her brother was right. She did look young and pretty to-night—that is, young for forty-one, and pretty *for her.*

After admiring the hank of wool for some minutes, she laid it aside, hastily undressed, took down her hair and braided it in two long plaits for the night, and put on her flannel wrapper over her nightgown. Then she fastened one end of the red zephyr to one of her bedposts, drew back the rocking-chair until it stood in line for attachment, steadied it by slipping a shoe under its left rocker, passed over to the sewing-machine, took its spool for her next support, and so completed a circuit. Then taking a bit of sweet-gum into her mouth, she fairly flew round and round, until the thickness of the strands "seemed jest about right," when she recklessly bit the zephyr from the ball with her teeth, and sat down. The scissors lay within reach, but it suited her mood to ignore them. She even said aloud, as she glanced at them: "Lay still; I don't need you this time"; but when she had bitten the wool, she made a wry face, and added, "Reckon I better look out an' not bite that pivoted tooth out." But she chuckled as she said it.

The making of the red mat was the marking of a new era for Miss Melissa. The note of fine fresh color in her room, in her fingers, on her lap, and always in her consciousness, even when locked from sight, in some mystic way answered a need of her monotonous life. It appeased, if it did not satisfy, the weariness that was expressed as color-hunger of her eyes; and it is not suprising if in the joy of it she felt a sort of shame, and would not for all the world have had any one know about it.

She would light both lamps at night now, and turn them up to their full height, while she tried the effect of the mat on the mantel, putting its unfinished half in front under one lamp, while she laid the red zephyr around the base of the other, to get the effect of the balancing touch of red; and although she did not know it, the tune she hummed under her breath was one she had not sung for years. She never knew that the red mat took shape to the air of "Ever of Thee I'm Fondly Dreaming." To be fair to her, there really was no especial "thee" in her case. The term was generic, and even in this sense it was misleading. Miss Melissa had not been a woman of dreams or of imagination or regrets, nor was she in any sense sentimental.

She was acting under an impulse more lawless than any of her early girlhood, and while she experimented with the mat in various situations, she finally tried the color against her face, laying the unfinished mat as a collar on her neck. The picture pleased her, and she even pinched her cheeks till a faint color showed in them. Seeing this, she blushed to crimson from real

shame, and hurriedly turning out one lamp, she humbly removed the mat from her neck and went on with her work. But she
did not forget how she had looked to herself in that one brief
moment when she had blushed at her own vanity, and she
hummed another tune of her younger days, one called "The Rock
Beside the Sea," which had no more or no less application to her
case than the first. Both were simply bodily reminiscent, and
while she was turning backward they met her on the way.

But on the morrow, when she realized that it was Sunday,
and yet she took up her mat—she was on the second one now—
her song was still another, and there seemed to be a relation
between it and her mood as she sang gaily:

I'm going, going, going, going;
Who bids, who bids for me?

It had never been the kind of song she liked, and the girl who
had sung it at school exhibitions, twenty-five years before, was
one she had not admired. Yet here she was singing away at it, and
on Sunday! She sang it only because it was the most reckless song
she knew, and she was misbehaving as far as she could. And she
was having fun.

When the family had gone to church, her voice rang out
pretty loud several times, but she had no fear. Cynthy, the black
cook, was shouting, "Rock-a my soul on de bosom o' Aberham!"
in so loud a voice that nothing short of an explosion would have
attracted her attention. Miss Melissa had pleaded headache and
remained from church; or, to be fair to her, she had not used the
word "headache," but had simply said that her head "didn't feel
like as ef she could set th'ough a sermon," which was true.

It was a beautiful day in May, and the sound of bees came
floating in at the open window. Indeed, one yellow-waistcoated
fellow actually darted into the room, and flaunted his Princeton
colors almost in Miss Melissa's face. Then, seeing the red zephyr,
he buzzed about it several times, and, as suddenly as he had
come, shot upward in a shaft of sunshine, and disappeared.

Miss Melissa's eyes followed him, and when she knew that
he was gone, she suddenly realized all the outside beauty of the
spring day. In imagination she saw the opening dogwood, and
the stately spruce-trees filled to dripping with odorous sap, their

thousands of fragrant cones fairly bursting with a spicy sticki-ness. She realized the winding branch where the willows swung their light-green fringes and the clumps of wild plum were in flower. It was the plum-blossoms that decided her. She sprang from her chair and got her bonnet. Then she wrapped her knitting carefully in a fresh handkerchief, stuck it in her pocket, and started out.

It was not her fault that on her way through the cow-lot she saw the fishing-rods lying over the rafters in the cotton-seed shed. She had frankly set out to follow any vagrant impulse—to do the thing that seemed pleasantest, to go where there was beauty and unrestraint—and she had deliberately taken her work with her—on Sunday. She knew that she could not match the finished mat at home; but if she could have done it, she would not have wished to. The mat that was done was "a ravin', tearin' beauty"; and its mate would match it in recklessness, which was all she meant it to do.

But one glance at the fishing-poles made the mat seem tame. She knew as soon as she set eyes on them that she was going fishing. "No, Satan; you needn't to get behind me—not a bit of it. You can walk before me, or beside me, or any way you choose; or you can skeet off about your business. I'm a-goin' fishin'." While she was thus openly declaring herself, she had already begun climbing over the cattle-troughs to secure a rod. When she had got it down, it occurred to her that she ought to leave some explanation of her absence, and so she turned back, crossed the yard to the kitchen, and called: "Oh, Aunt Cynthy! Tell 'em all I've went out to get a little fresh air; an' whilst I'm out I'll mos' likely go an' see how old Mis' Gibbs is; an' ef I'm late for dinner, tell 'em not to wait."

In about three minutes, while the fat old woman was still drawling, "What is Miss M'lissy sayin', anyhow?" the tip of a long bamboo fishing-pole was grazing the young under leaves of the sweet-gum trees in the lane, and a middle-aged maiden was singing in a low, swinging voice:

I'm *going*, going—gone!

And Aunt Cynthy, dropping a bay-leaf into her gumbo-pot turned her head and listened. "What dat?" she ejaculated.

"Three times dis mornin' seem like I's heerd sperits. I sho trus' dey ain't come to 'nounce no harm to Miss M'lissy."

And at that moment this same reserved and orderly person was on her knees before a dirty plank at the cattle-crossing, lifting squirming earthworms out of their beds with her hair-pin, and dropping them into a little pocket she had improvised by pinning up the end of one of her broad bonnet-strings upon itself. And in a surprisingly short time this same pink bonnet might have been seen a mile away—was seen by the mocking-birds and squirrels, that came out frankly to inquire—shining through the bush that sparsely covered the jutting rock where goggle-eyed perch were known to congregate.

As Miss Melissa settled herself upon the rock, she laughed. "Reckon I oughtn't to expec' any luck to-day, jest to punish me; but I do, jest the same. An' I reckon, ef I wasn't hardened, I'd have the cold shivers puttin' these worms on the hook an' seein' 'em squirm; but I don't. Somehow, squirmin' is expected of a worm—one way or another. Well, they's one comfort, anyhow: I ain't settin' anybody a bad example. Ef they's one thing Simpkinsville can keep, it's Sunday—an' that's why this tickles me so." And she chuckled again as she added, "Like as ef the fish knew any difference!"

When she had finally dropped her line into the water, carefully baited from her bonnet-string, and when she saw that the fish were not waiting to seize it, she said: "B'lieve I'll take out the mat an' knit a few rounds while the fish are getherin' ''; and holding her rod awkwardly with her knees for the moment, she drew out the parcel. Before she was hand-free, however, the cork sank quite out of sight. There was a scramble, and in a second a fine "goggle-eye" flapped into her very lap, dropped over her shoe, and fell with a splash back into the water.

For a moment she felt as if she would never recover from the panic that it gave her—this actual, expected yet unexpected contact with the beautiful, shimmering, live thing. She thrust her work back into her pocket; then, mounting the bank, she cut a leaf from the palmetto, tore it into shreds, which she laid beside her, and set earnestly to fishing. And the tune that she thought now—thought rather than hummed it—was "Listen to the Mocking-bird":

H-h-h-h-*h*-h-h!
H-h-h-h-*h*-h-h!
H-h-h-h-h-h-*h*-h-h-*h*!
H-h-h-h-*h*-h-h-!
H-h-h-h-*h*-h-h!
H-*h*-H-H-H-H-*h*-*h*-*h*-h!

So, without vocalization, her spirit sang the sprightly measure, and she knew not at all that it was because the mocking-
bird's trill was in her ears all the time. Nor, when she smiled
down to the bank, had she the least idea that it was because the
tiny blue and purple blossoms along its margin were all in broad
grins, nodding to her. Even when she tried to fit her tune to the
funny darting movements of the black-satin-backed bugs that
went through their dance-figures for her on the water's surface,
she was consciously thinking only of her line. She had thrown
open all life's doors and windows, and was letting in light and
color and sound; and she knew only that she was out on a great
lark, and she was reckless as to where it might lead her. Of course
it was all wicked, and she would be in sackcloth and ashes pretty
soon; but she would not feel that she was there for nothing. She
was earning her penance.

The fish bit finely, after a little. Silver and speckled beauties
followed one another on the cruel palmetto strip, whose length-
ening burden kept up a perceptible movement in the water, even
though the string hung deep. In through the delicate coral gills,
and out by way of the pretty mouths, so she strung them.

There is such a thing as fishing's being *too good*. It lacks the
zest of patient angling. So Miss Melissa must have found it
to-day, for she remarked, as she sent a slim perch down the fatal
string to the number thirty-one, "I wish to goodness you-all
wouldn't bite so fast, an' give me a chance to fish."

Of course she was fishing merely for sport—a most cruel
thing to do, even on a week-day. To have carried the fish home
would have been a village scandal. Still, knowing this, she had
not the courage to throw them back into the stream. She thought
of it, but only for a moment, and her argument against it closed
with: "An' maybe ketch the same one over an' over ag'in? No, not
much. Ef I say to myself, 'I've caught a dozen fish,' I'll know I've

caught a dozen. But I'll do my best for 'em. I'll string 'em, an' hang 'em in their native element; an' ef they're lively, time I git through maybe I'll turn 'em loose—*maybe;* though I'd hate to ketch the same ones over ag'in, even ef it was next week. Ef ole Mis' Gibbs didn't have sech an inquirin' mind for scandal, an' sech a talent for distribution, I'd take 'em up an' fry 'em for her—an' I'd eat my share, too."

And here she stopped suddenly, as if surprised by a new thought.

"Wouldn't that be perfectly lovely?" she said slowly, in a moment. "But of co'se I couldn't do it—an' no fryin'-pan here, nor nothin', an' no match to light a fire, even ef the smoke could be persuaded not to rise."

Could it be possible that Miss Melissa Ann Moore, Sunday-school teacher and secretary of the Foreign Missionary Society, was contemplating a solitary fish-fry on the holy Sabbath? Perhaps not.

She fished until she was very tired, and then, fighting her fatigue as a baby fights sleep, she kept on from sheer inability to stop until she had used her last bait. Then, hastily wrapping her line, she drew up the fish and looked at them.

"Pity I couldn't send you over to the porehouse for the widders, like Deacon Tyler does his week-day surpluses," she said, addressing the fish; "but of co'se you're a Sunday ketch, an' noways fitten to nourish a Christian widder. Lordy, but what a sinner I am to be referrin' so familiar to Deacon Tyler, an' he sanctified these ten years an' over! Funny notion that was of Mis' Gibbs's thet he ain't never married because they ain't no sanctified woman fitten to mate with him! She settles everybody's hash, one way or another. But I reckon she's about right when it comes to him. Wonder what she says about me not bein' mated, ez she calls it? I'd as lief think o' marryin' that ole feller the bishop told about thet set his life away on top a pillar—St. Simon What-you-may-call-'im—I forgit his surname. Not thet I don't rever-ence the deacon—"

Miss Melissa had not had the least sense of fear, and yet, when she presently heard footsteps behind her, she felt a sudden terror lest she should fall off the bank. She was too much frightened even to glance over her shoulder when the bush against her arm trembled; but in a moment her fear was relieved in part,as she recognized the tall, gaunt figure that emerged from behind her and took a seat upon a projecting rock about a dozen yards from where she sat. It was one she had seen once before. She instantly realized it to be that of a vagrant negro, and she knew that he had come for his dinner—he or she. This very non-committal and elusive old person, whose haunts were the cane-brake and the swamp, had been in slavery days a menace to the runaway, who feared his evil and silent potency in witchcraft— for he was a mute; and when it was discovered that he frequented the brake he was not molested. The "haunt" that the negroes were afraid either to kill or to confront was better than a pack of hounds to clear the thicket, and so "Silent Si," responsible neith-er to law nor order, had lived a charmed life, done as he pleased, and was reckoned no more than the other half-shy, half-bold in-habitants of the woodland. Some said he was a voodoo woman who had escaped from the Barbour plantation seventeen years before—a woman who could cast spells at long range, and had made so much trouble on the bayou that when she ran away she was not pursued. Then there were others who felt sure he was a man who once lived on Bayou Lafourche, and who had strange white spots on his body, and claimed that God was gradually making him over into a white man, though a few feared him as a leper. And there were other stories, but none of them invited friendship with the uncanny personality that even yet chose the life of a hermit, and whose clothes, rescued from the village dumping-ground and laundered in the creek, were so freely promiscuous in their suggestions as to be entirely non-committal.

When Miss Melissa had recovered from her first surprise, she burst into a hearty, ringing laugh. "Well," she exclaimed, "ef they's one person on earth thet I'd be willin' to see me here, it's you, Silent Si."

For some minutes she sat chuckling to herself over what seemed a humorous situation.

"Don't reckon he even knows it's Sunday—or thet they is any Sundays, for that matter. Don't seem like they could be any need of religion in a cane-brake, noways, with no other sinners round. Most of our needs of grace is th'ough dealin' with our feller-man, looks to me like, though I don't know. I've been doin' pretty well to-day all by myself.

"Lordy, ef this ain't the funniest! Even ef he knew me, he couldn't tell.

"Well, they's one thing, shore: I'm a-goin' to give him my fish. Yas, I'm a-goin' to give him my fish, an' see thet he has one square meal, anyhow. He can't break a Sabbath that he ain't never heard of; an' as for me, well, maybe the good Lord'll let the charity of it balance the Sabbath-breakin'."

At this, she called bravely:

"Si! *Oh*, Si!"

"*Oh*, Si!" answered a distinct echo from across the creek.

It seemed a mocking reminder of the mute's deafness, and there was something so uncanny in it that, although Miss Melissa laughed, it was with nervous laughter.

"Well, you cert'n'y are deef in both ears, old Si," she chuckled; "for ef you couldn't hear out o' the one on this side, the echo has sampled the other for me. This would be a good place to fetch the deacon to. I wouldn't feel so called to quote Scripture to him ef I could jest locate his good ear. I know ef he ketches one word of Scripture quotation he can finish out the verse, an' I've more'n once fell back on the Bible for conversation when a worldly remark was on the tip o' my tongue. I know it's the right ear thet's good, an' yet I'm so used to makin' allowances for me bein' left-handed thet somehow I gen'ally git confused an' say things in the deef side. But out here the echo would be bound to strike it.

"I see Si is spittin' on his bait for luck. He's learned *somethin'*, ef he *is* deef. Maybe he does know it's Sunday, after all. I reckon some folks would be afeard of him, out here by theirselves, but I ain't. I recollect too well what a mild face he had the day he come out o' the bresh, that summer, when we was cl'arin' off the ground after our Sunday-school picnic, an' I give him a lot o' the scraps. I wasn't a bit afeard of him then. I jest passed the things to him on a broom because some folks said he had the leprosy. Of co'se time has proved he ain't got that. I believe I'll unwrap my line an' fling it over his, an' make him take notice."

No sooner said than done. Attracted thus, the mute turned and looked at her. With a motion of her hand she held his attention until she had drawn up the string of fish, and then by a simple pantomime she offered them to him. A difficult medium of communication seems sometimes to be conducive to a swift understanding, for in a surprisingly short time these two people, who had met only once in a twilight wood many years before, had so well understood each other without the aid of speech that the mute was building a fire under a ledge of the rock a few feet away—a secret hiding-place from which he soon brought forth a rude cooking equipment—and Miss Melissa Ann Moore was scaling fish with her own hands, using for the purpose first one and then the other blade of her scissors. She had rolled up her sleeves, and pinned up her dress-skirt to serve as apron, and while she scraped off the silver scales and trimmed the glittering fins, she hummed a tune into which she was presently fitting the words, "From Greenland's Icy Mountains."

Her song was low at first, a soft, gurgling treble; but as she went on it gradually yielded to the inspiration of the wood, abetted by the brave note of a stalwart bird that poured out his joy from a tree above her, until she was singing as she had never sung in her life before.

It was a fine duet for a while, but soon neighboring birds, hearing it, came and sang with the two until the woods rang; and no one but God heard the anthem—God and perhaps the squirrels and other voiceless creatures who came out of hiding to peep and to listen. Miss Melissa, strange as it may seem, was all unaware of aught save delight. It was as if the long-pent joy that ought to have expressed itself through years of living had suddenly burst forth, demanding right of way, and converting her, for the time, into a simple instrument of song. And the birds, knowing the life-notes, understood, and sang with her.

And all the while she mechanically continued to scale the fish. But so translated was she that when the mute came and stood beside her, she did not see him until a breeze blew his shirt across the line of her vision, and she turned. When her eyes fell full upon the slender oval face of the tall yellow "human" standing dumbly beside her, she stopped singing and withdrew her hands. He took the motion for permission, and quickly gathered up the fish and returned to the fire. His coming so near had broken the spell and brought her back to earth. She watched him in awed silence for a moment, and then she said, quite as if the circumstances were in no wise out of the ordinary:

"Well, whilst the picnic's progressin', reckon I might's well knit a few rounds on the red mat."

Suiting the action to the word, she took out her knitting, and as her needles flew she soon fell into speculative discourse with herself concerning her companion.

"I declare," she began, "I feel like as if I was jest about half in a dream, an' liable to wake up any minute; but I'd be mighty disappointed ef I was to wake up before them fish are fried an' e't. No, tain't no dream; they say you can't never dream smells. Ef anybody had 'a' told me, I wouldn't 'a' believed he'd be so clean about it—washed his hands in the branch even before he built the fire. An', come close-t to 'em, her clo'es is more faded'n they are dirty, anyhow; an' I'm shore no hair could be whiter—jest like the driven snow—"

She had dropped her knitting in her lap while she watched the silent figure at work. There was something so weird about it all that even Miss Melissa, unimaginative as she was, felt the strange spell.

"What would I give ef I could git her to come an' set down here by me an' tell me the story of her life! They can't be a life without a story, an' I reckon hers would be so unnatural thet it would make a good book. No speech—no relations—no knowledge of Gord or the devil—jest herself, day in an' day out.

"Or hisself," she added, seeing the mute break a stick of wood across his knee. "But jest to think of thinkin' thoughts with no words to think 'em in! I wouldn't undertake it, I know. Thoughtless words are common enough, but wordless thoughts—I can't conceive of sech a thing. Imagine me tryin' to think in Hindu an' not knowin' so much as *polly fronsay* in it to explain my thoughts to my mind. I often wonder what sech a one will do at the jedgment, when he's required to give an account of hisself.

"But he must have ricollections of somethin' or somebody. But I'd think even ricollections'd git to be monotonous, after a while, for a main dependence. Somehow, I doubt ef he remembers anything. I reckon he jest gits up every mornin' an' scrimmages for food, an' goes to bed at night an' rests from his scrimmagin'. Come to think of it, that's what all the world's a-doin', more or less.

"I s'pose they's any number o' places where he's got fryin'-pans an' things hid, an' little strips of bacon like that he's fryin' with now.

"Meal in a bottle with a cork in it! Who'd ever 'a' thought o' sech a thing! Well, it's a good way to keep it dry. I s'pose the annual picnic leavin's is the same as a Christmas dinner to him. They say it don't make no difference where they have the picnics—down at Silas's mill, or at the camp-meetin' grove, or up at Pump Springs—he always gits wind of 'em an' somebody sees him prowlin' round for the fragments; but from this time on I intend to see thet he finds some-thin' more'n broken victuals. I'd do that much for a dumb brute without a soul to save. What is he doin' now, for gracious' sakes? He's a-cuttin' off a bunch o' that palmetter an' tyin' it to a pole. I do wonder ef he's a-goin' to sweep the ground off before he sets the food on it. He don't know it's a sin to sweep on Sunday, I don't reckon. Ef I didn't have this mat to finish, I'd try the deef-an'-dumb alphabet on him, an' spell out the fo'th commandment."

The mute had, indeed, fashioned a rude broom from the materials at hand, and before Miss Melissa could anticipate his intention, he had taken a beautiful leaf of the green palmetto, laid it on the improvised broom, placed the fish and a corn-dodger upon it, and, standing at arm's-length, was presenting it to her.

It meant recognition.

So she had served him years ago in the twilight wood. She was much startled for the moment, but a swift glance at his pathetic face touched her almost to tears. As she looked into his eyes a flicker of servile pleasure illumined them—a flicker that she felt rather than saw, like the blink of a summer sky when one says, "Was that lightning?" and cannot be quite sure whether it was until it comes again.

When she took the fish she was so agitated that she said, "Thank you, Si," quite aloud; but the words fell upon his back, for he had not lingered.

For some minutes Miss Melissa sat and looked at the feast—it seemed a feast, for the hour was late, and she was hungry—before she could recover herself enough to touch it. But finally she drew the palmetto up on her knee, and began her novel meal, which she ate as unquestioningly as a child. She had been all her life accustomed to the negro's hand as a server of food—the negro, taken many times without question from field or forest work; and when once this sort of service is accepted, and one learns the usual cleanliness of the shapely hands of the most uncouth among them, he has arrived at a comfort point which does not always exist in more pretentious serving. The old "aunty" who shucks her roasting-ears all over her kitchen floor, and spreads her baby's pallet on the pile of bark in the corner, will make biscuits as white as snow, and her pine table will show its pretty grain even down its scoured legs. The floor is hers, but her hands and the table where she prepares his feasts are consecrate to her master's service.

It was some minutes before Miss Melissa thought of looking after the mute, and when she did look he was gone. There was not even so much as a trace of the fire he had built upon the ground. Indeed, she would not have known where it had been but for the pile of brush he had drawn over the spot.

She stopped eating, and looked about her.

"Well," she exclaimed, "I don't doubt a minute but what I'm hoodooed, an' none o' the things I seem to see are really happenin'.

"Of co'se here's the fish, an' my red mat; an' there's my fishin'-pole, layin' where I throwed it over the buckeye-bushes. That much is real. But that gray squir'l climbin' down the tree-limb, there, looks like as ef it might easy be in a dream an' suddenly dissolve. I do declare, I feel almost like as ef I was in the Garden of Eden. Ef I was to see a snake anywhere, I'd fully expect it to enlarge an' come forward an' try to tempt me. I wonder what time o' day it is, anyhow? I see the shadders is all reversed, an'—

"Why, it's gittin' dark!"

She rose to her feet and looked about her and shuddered.

"Deary, deary me!" she said, "how far wrong one bad act will take a person! Only three days ago I stopped counting my strands—an' now what an awful sinner I am! Will I ever have forgiveness an' peace of mind again, I wonder?

"What would the deacon say—or even Gord? Somehow, I don't mind the Lord knowin' it ez much as I would the deacon. He's *so* sanctified. An' of co'se Gord knows all the ins and outs of it, how werried I was, an' he's authorized to blot out. Maybe this is the real me, after all, an' I haven't been no more'n a hypocrite all these years.

"No," she added, looking upward, "tain't that. Whatever it is, I ain't a hypocrite, I *know*. Some say Gord judges us by our best days, an' some say he holds us for our worst. An' then, ag'in, some say he averages. Maybe ef he'll average up these last three days with my forty-one years of tryin' to live righteously, it'll seem like as ef I've been passable good right along.

"But I must be goin'."

II

There were bedtime twitterings in the brush on every side now, and the shaft of sunlight that had a moment before revealed the glories of the greenery all about her passed out even while she looked, and Miss Melissa realized her isolation in a momentary sense of fear. But this wood, and the banks of the stream that wound in and out of it for miles, had been the familiar playground of her childhood. She remembered it when there were tales of bears and wildcats there, and she knew where several Indian graves were, within a stone's-throw of where she sat—graves that were witnesses to some stirring times in which her grandfather had taken part. It would be hard for her to be really afraid here, even in the dense copse where she had hidden. In a moment she was smiling at the idea, and to make sure of herself she went back to the jutting ledge, and deliberately threw the fragments of her dinner into the water, so as to leave no vestige of the occasion.

She dropped them in slowly, one at a time, and watched them while they floated a minute, or sank as they fell; and her calm exterior gave no hint of a new panic that had begun to rage within her. She had felt it for a moment when the mute first disappeared, and while she stood alone in the darkening wood it came again. It was the inevitable homegoing that confronted her. She had always been truth itself, and she would have to give an account of this broken Sabbath—probably within an hour. She felt sure that her brother was already inquiring for her and watching the gate, and that her nervous sister-in-law was declaring herself "certain an' sure somethin' awful had happened"; and in all probability Sally Tolbert, and Mis' Allen, and maybe the Tompkins children, had been over during the afternoon to see how she was, having missed her at church. Possibly even Deacon Tyler had dropped in, with his ear-trumpet, so as not to miss any detail of an illness that had been serious enough to keep her from service. He always went to inquire for the sick. In imagination she could hear her sister-in-law screaming into the trumpet that "the last seen of Sis' M'liss' was thus or so. Cynthy had watched her go through the gate, and had heard her say something about old Mrs. Gibbs, she thought."

This last reflection was suggestive and helpful. She had intended to go and see how old Mrs. Gibbs was, and she would go now, late as it was. That old lady had cataracts on her eyes, so the doctors said, and she was impatiently awaiting the period of full blindness, that darkest hour before the dawn when the world might be hers again.

Miss Melissa would go now, and offer to take her to evening service; and her family, seeing her there, might assume that she had been with Mrs. Gibbs all day, and not ask any questions. Mrs. Gibbs would not see that she was not dressed for church.

How stupidly a sane person can plan when his thoughts are fixed on a single point! The whole congregation would have had to have cataracts on their eyes to make it possible for one to appear in church in a gingham frock and pink sunbonnet without creating a sensation. But she would go and see Mrs. Gibbs, anyway. It would be a safe way-station in the direction of a return, and perhaps while there something would be suggested. Of course she could not take her fishing-rod with her, but she could hide it in the brush.

There was no light in the Gibbs cottage when she arrived, which was a good omen. Mrs. Gibbs lighted up only for company, and she would find her alone—as she did.

Delighted at the sound of her voice, the voluble old lady greeted her with a characteristic welcome.

"Why, howdy, Melissy Ann! Howdy! I'm proud to see you. An' I'm glad to see you ain't expectin' to go to church, for I don't feel a bit worshipful this evenin'. Ef I'd heard a swish when you come in, I'd know it was my duty to go with you. Speak o' the devil—I was jest a-thinkin' jest now how long that bayadere silk o' yours had lasted. I ricollec' you bought it off'n yo' second mat-raffle, time the circus tent blowed away. Well, I'm glad you're better. How's yo' sis'-in-law? Got over her faint yet? Or was it the child thet fainted? Some said it was *her*, an' some *it*."

This was an unpromising beginning. It seemed at the onset

that she would be obliged to confess that she had not been at home all day. She would not be rash about it, though. If her sister-in-law had fainted in church, apparently that was all Mrs. Gibbs knew about it, and she could gain nothing by asking questions, so she said tentatively:

"Sis' Salina's subjec' to them dizzy spells sence she's stoutened up so; an' the doctor says it behooves her to take keer of herself, an' to take boneset an'—"

"An' camomile an' bitter aloways, to alleviate the boneset," Mrs. Gibbs interpolated. "Yas; you can tell her for me that I say thet when I stoutened befo' I fell away the last time, that was what brought me through.

"But some folks thought maybe it was jest fright, this mornin', thet ailed her. It's enough to scare anybody to have a cow rush into a pew du'in' services, an' to upset a whole row o' child'en, the way that cow did hers. I've always thought it was resky an' irreligious—allowin' a cow to graze in the churchyard, the way they do, whilst the gospel is bein' preached. But of co'se nobody could 'a' foresaw her takin' a notion to attend services. They say Mis' Blanks is goin' to have it out with Jim Towers—you know, it was his cow—an' she says ef he don't pay for her bonnet she'll see the reason why. Wasn't it funny for her to chew up the most expensive thing in church, which everybody knows Mis' Blanks's bonnets is—milliner-trimmed fresh every season? I ain't missed my eyesight so sence it went—never. I s'pose the cow nachelly knew straw when she saw it, an' she hadn't no respec' for a leghorn braid. Lucky thing Mis' Blanks always unties her bonnet-strings to sing, else she'd 'a' been strangled, shore. They say the cow mooed right into Deacon Tyler's ear-trumpet, an' rose him straight out of 'is pew. You know, when he sets his trumpet for the sermon he always shets his eyes; an' the first thing he heard was 'Moo!' Of co'se I knew I was safe, in the amen corner, 'cause no Durham could get over the railin', 'less she was hard pressed. I missed the sight of it all, but my hearin's better'n ever, an' to my dyin' day I'll never forget the words Brother Clayton said, an' how the cow changed things around. He was jest repeatin' his tex' for his fo'th head, an' he says, says he: '"An' Nathan said unto David"—so, Sukey, so!' Lordy! but you missed a church circus this mornin', honey, Melissy, shore.

"But I'm right glad to hear thet yo' sister-in-law ain't noways serious. Did she expect her brother Ben to come to-day, or was it a complete surprise? Mandy Jones says he's fetched a trunkful o' presents, but his sister wouldn't let him open it on the Sabbath. Mis' Jones sent Mandy down the road to see ef they was crape on the gate, not knowin' what a cow-horn might result in; an' Mandy she see the carriage at the door, an' she went to see ef it was the undertaker, it bein' a strange carriage, an' that's how it come out thet it was her brother Ben come back. Mandy didn't go in, but she counted eight child'en playin' on the po'ch, an' she see Caleb's wife rockin' the cradle with her foot, which proved it wasn't empty; so she knew they was all alive, an' she come away.

"But I don't see how you-all stand not knowin' what he'd fetched you till to-morrer mornin'. Caleb's wife is shorely a godly woman—by intention. My judgment would 'a' been to open that trunk an' have a rapid distribution. She could 'a' had it opened with prayer, ef she'd 'a' seen fit; an' then, when the things was all give out, they could 'a' been put away 'tel to-morrer, all excep' Bibles an' sech. Even a frivolous present, received an' put out o' sight, is less distractin', in my opinion, than a doubtful box with a Bible in it. They say he claimed thet none of his presents wasn't wicked, nohow, 'cep'n' the pack o' playin'-cards that he brought for the preacher, which I'm glad to see Ben ain't lost none of his devilment in his travels. But she wouldn't hear to techin' that trunk. She's got the courage of her convictions, shore. I never will forgit how she apologized for one of her babies bein' born on a Sunday, or how relieved she seemed when one o' the attendin' ladies reminded her thet all its birthdays wouldn't of necessity foller on the Sabbaths.

"But you ain't told me yet whether you-all was lookin' for him or not, or—"

Before she could answer, Miss Melissa was startled by a rap at the door, and Mrs. Gibbs asked her to light the lamp. Until now, the two women had been sitting in the dark.

The light revealed a funnel-shaped instrument thrust through a crack in the door, and Miss Melissa knew that the deacon had come, and that almost certainly he was looking for her. She knew he had presented his trumpet for an invitation to enter, and so she obediently screamed, with nervous aim—just outside the funnel: "Howdy, deacon! Come in." He caught part of the greeting, however, and while she went on to say that she was just thinking it was time to go, he came in, shook hands with the two women, and sat down between them.

"Has he got his trumpet with him?" asked the brave hostess, realizing his deafness; but Miss Melissa did not hear her, either. She felt that she must get the deacon away, if possible, before there were any revelations, and she was devoting herself to him. While Mrs. Gibbs was thinking, "Wonder ef they could be anything in him comin' here after her," that lady was screaming, in reply to his solicitous inquiry:

"Oh, yas, sir, thank you; it's a heap better. The open air—an' then, talkin' here to Mis' Gibbs. Twasn't exactly to say a headache, nohow. I reckon I ought to've went to church, by rights."

"Well," said the deacon, slowly, "I can't jedge for nobody else, of co'se, but I'd resk a good deal on yo' doin' the right thing. For myself, I know it takes all the church-goin' I'm capable of to keep me within a stone's-throw of the straight an' narrer way. Of co'se I haven't *heard* a sermon in ten year; but I go, an' set my trumpet *direc'* for the Word of God, an' that seems to be all thet could be expected of me. Some has insinuated thet I ought to keep my eyes open, an' from my experience this mornin', I s'pose likely I ought. But, exceptin' for self-preservation, I can't see no obligation to do it. Ef Brother Clayton would shave, I'd obligate myself to keep awake an' watch his lips; but they ain't no inspiration in the motion of chin-whiskers, not even ef they are dilatin' on the gospel—not to me. But of co'se I know I ain't as a good a Christian as what I ought to be noways. I don't begin to b'lieve the way I've been taught, an' I ain't got the faith on all p'ints thet folks think I have, neither. F'instance, that doctrine of 'What is to be will be,' I don't begin to b'lieve it. I don't b'lieve for a minute, f'instance, thet that fool cow was fo'ordained to moo into my trumpet this mornin', an' rouse me out of a dream o' the golden streets—which she done."

He looked at Miss Melissa and waited for a reply.

"Well, I didn't see the cow—or hear her," she began irrelevantly. "Of co'se He who created the cow, an' created you, He must have known—"

"Never mind the trumpet, Miss Melissy," he interrupted,

smiling; "you're on my good side. Come jest a leetle close-ter, please, ma'am, an' talk slow; an' hand this to Mis' Gibbs, so's she can express an opinion to my deef side ef she's so disposed."

He handed Miss Melissa the ear-trumpet, and she passed it over to Mrs. Gibbs.

"Well, I b'lieve events can be helped, or hindered," the brave hostess shouted into the funnel, glad of a chance to speak. "Ef I didn't b'lieve that I wouldn't have no courage to anoint my cataracts."

"An' I think thet nobody can go far wrong," added Miss Melissa, "Ef he jest follers the Scriptures. I know a man down here at Spring Hill, he started readin' doubtin' books, an' first thing his folks knew, he was disputin' perpetual hell an' the fire thet's never squenched; an' several of his smarty friends, thinkin' it was becomin', they started to show off in the same way. One well-raised young man thet's got two elders an' a class-leader in his family, an' is studyin' medicine hisself, why, he up an' said he doubted the story of Jonah an' the whale, jest on physical grounds—"

"I should 'a' thought he *would* 'a' been sort o' physicked with him, shore enough," shrieked Mrs. Gibbs; "Jonah, I mean—no, *the whale.*"

"An' so he was—an' physicked effectual. We've got Scripture for that. To me, the mericle ain't that. It's the two of 'em survivin'; that's what gits me. Maybe I oughtn't to say it, an' I wouldn't ef any of our young folks was around; but sometimes I've thought thet maybe the whole thing wasn't never intended for no more'n a yarn. Them apostles must've got off fakes occasional, jest to relieve the monotony, an' I don' b'lieve for a minute thet my eternal salvation has got to hinge on me a-swallerin' no fish-story over a thousand years old. Even the fresh ones we git is li'ble to suspicion—'t least, some of 'em is. I know I've been tempted myself, an' me a deacon in the church. A inch in a fish's tail, or a ounce or so of weight, or the narrerness of a person's escape from drownin', well, they seem sech harmless exaggerations, an' they give a man standin' in a community where things is pretty slow. But of co'se I ain't never done it. I've stood by my little fish all my life, an' I've had the durnedest luck, too, for a patient fisher. But of co'se you ladies ain't never tempted that-away." He looked at Miss Melissa. "You ain't never fished all day, I'm shore, an' been tempted a thousand ways to diverge. Ef *you* was to go fishin', Miss Melissy, no doubt you'd be as conscientious about yo' ketch as you are in knittin' them green mats."

Fortunately, he did not glance at Miss Melissa now, for her face was scarlet. She felt sure she had been discovered; and if she had broken all the commandments in one fell impulse, she could have not been more hopelessly criminal in her own consciousness.

"I've often thought," the deacon continued, eyeing her mischievously the while, "that ef you would make jest one crooked mat, or turn out jest one of a false color—say a red one—why, the devil might have some hope of you; but so long as you set sech a example of consistency as you do, why, ef you have even so much as a sick-headache, an' stroll away for relief, we know the place to hunt you is the bedside of the sick, an', shore enough, here you are. Well, I mus' be goin'," he added, looking at his watch. "Ef you'll accept of my company, I'll escort you home. I wouldn't advise you to pass by the willer hedge alone for a few nights, for they do say Silent Si has been seen prowlin' round for a week or so, an' you might run ag'in' him—him or his haunt. Some say th'ain't nothin' but his sperit been seen for three years—not thet you'd be *afeard* of him, exactly, either *in* the flesh or *out*."

If Miss Melissa had had a hope that the deacon knew nothing of her escapade, it was gone now; and when she rose to go, she said "Good mornin' " to her hostess, and in reply to an invitation to come again soon, she stammered, "Not at all"; and when she was outside, and the deacon offered her his arm, she actually sobbed aloud. Fortunately, though, it was in his deaf ear; and before she had further committed herself, he had passed her the trumpet, saying: "I can't offer you my good ear, lest you'd be for sale on the outside of the walk, so you'll haf to do yo' laughin' an' talkin' in this. What was you laughin' at, anyhow? A deef man can feel a chuckle he can't hear."

This was so funny that she really laughed, now, straight into the funnel. She laughed so loud and so long, and with such a growing sense of humor, that the deacon laughed with her from sheer contagion. When life's tension has been long and rigorous, and overstrained nerves recoil, it is hard to recover control sometimes. Since Miss Melissa's weeping had been translated into mirth it quite ran away with her, and it would have alarmed the deacon had he heard it all. But the snatches of it that fell into his trumpet were only sufficient to impart a sense of joyousness, and he said cheerily:

"Yo' feelin' so happy to-night is as good as a sermon to me. Notwithstandin' you haven't had the inspiration of divine service to-day, you've found the reward of doin' the Lord's work. You've found it in a merry heart."

The deacon's voice was too gentle for irony. Surely, after all, he could not know.

To feel like a criminal was bad enough, but it did not approach the hopelessness of being found out. Miss Melissa cleared her throat, and looked up a little. So long as only she and God and the speechless old negro knew, she could hope to enter her closet and have it out in confession and prayer. She had anticipated the sackcloth, and was willing to endure the sting of it; but to be whipped in the market-place, figuratively if not with bodily stripes, was more than she could brook. If the deacon knew all, and would tell, this would be her fate. But he did not know. His stumbling over the live wires that connected with her conscience was only an accident; but she was so sensitive. It was easy to turn the scales either way by a feather's weight. What could have been more innocent than the good man's next remark? And yet how easily she misunderstood it, and what despair it wrought within her! Witness his artless offense:

"Many another, in sech circumstances, havin' a headache for a good excuse, instead of doin' the Lord's work as you've done to-day, would 'a' found some fish of their own to fry."

How simple and natural the tribute to her supposed faithfulness, but how subtle and poignant the sting upon her guilty consciousness! It was more than she could bear.

"Hursh!" she screamed, clapping the funnel quite over her lips. "Hursh, deacon! Not another word! I can't stand it. Ef you've got the feelin' for me thet you'd have for a yaller dog thet was bein' pursued, you'll hursh!"

"Well, upon my word, you're purty brash, Melissy." It was her brother Caleb who stepped up from behind them, and he had heard his sister's last words.

"Don't mind her, Caleb," the deacon said mildly; "she's jest showin' her Christian humility. Whenever I refer to her good works it seems to pleg her, but I didn't have no idee of taxin' her forbearance so severe. I found her settin' in darkness, ministerin' to ole Mis' Gibbs, jest as we s'picioned she was. I s'pose you got uneasy an' come to hunt her?"

"Well, we thought we'd like to locate her befo' it got into the night. I s'pose it's foolish to be afraid of ole Si, but somehow we've been raised to fear him, an' I didn't know but maybe you might take a notion to come home the woods way, Sis, an' I'd jest as lief none o' my folks would run no resks. Sev'al of the niggers say they've saw him prowlin' aroun' our place of nights lately, but I 'spect that's jest to clair their own skirts when things is missin'. Our child'en say somebody has went off with yo' fishin'- pole, Sis. Do you know anything about it?"

"Yas, I hid it." Her voice was pretty steady, considering the pressure upon her.

"I thought likely you had. First thing when we come home from church, the young ones started nosin' round, an' they missed it. It's about church-time now, deacon, an' if you want to git in for the openin' hymn, I'll see Melissy home; or ef you—"

"No, thank you, Caleb. Not thet I'd slight a hymn because I can't hear it, but I ain't been raised to shift a lady half-way home. You go on to church, an' I'll be along d'rec'ly."

Miss Melissa dropped the deacon's arm.

"You both go," she exclaimed. "Nothin' ain't goin' to hurt me."

But the deacon held her fast.

"Go along, Sis," said Caleb, from behind. "You know he can't hear nothin', no how. He might's well be 'scortin' you home as settin' up noddin'." Caleb knew so well the range of the deacon's half-awake ear that he dared hairbreadth proximity to it with impunity. "An' ef you don't feel like comin' to preachin', which I shouldn't think you would after a whole day with Mis' Gibbs, you might let Cynthy go. She's settin' half asleep in the rocker between the child'en's beds."

"I'll stay with 'em," said Melissa. "I s'pose Saliny has gone ahead."

"Yes; she's went to the mother's meetin' in the session-room. I promised thet ef you didn't come in time I'd look after the youngsters. They're all asleep, 'cep'n' Joe an' Sallie. They're comin' straight from the Epworth meetin' to church."

As he left them, Caleb turned back and called to his sister: "Kind o' sorry you ain't comin' to church, Sis. Brother Clayton lays off to rouse the sleepers in the temple to-night. Goin' to preach on, 'Though thy sins be as scarlet'—you know the rest of it." And as he left them he said to himself: "Dear Lord! ef them two could only see theirselves as others see 'em."

Miss Melissa made no reply, but presently she said to the deacon:

"Did you ketch what Bud said to me?"

"Well, no; not exac'ly. I aimed for it, but my tube gits tangled sometimes. But I thought I caught somethin' about starlight. It *is* a-goin' to be a starlight night. Was that what he remarked?"

"No; that word was 'scarlet,' not 'starlight.' He knew you'd set out to pleg me, an' he thought he'd give me a partin' shot, that's all. He was jest repeatin' the tex' Brother Clayton has give out for to-night. I wonder you ain't mentioned it before."

She was too angry to care much what she said, and the old deacon, although he did not in the least suspect this, felt that something was wrong with her. He had known this for some time. There was a wail in the voice that commanded him to hush, and, tender-hearted old man that he was, he felt that he could not sleep until he found out what the trouble was.

When they reached her gate, Miss Melissa, instead of asking him in, extended her hand and said good night. "I know you're anxious to get to church, deacon," she began to say; but he interrupted her:

"I ain't anxious to do nothin' but to fall on my knees and apologize right an' left, Miss Melissy. Whatever I've done or said God knows, but I've hurt yo' feelin's, an' I wouldn't 'a' done sech a thing, not for nothin' on earth. Ef you'll jest let me go in an' set down a minute—I didn't ketch the drift o' what Caleb said about his wife, but I reckon she's likely gone ahead to join the other mothers, as usual; an' ef so, we'll have the parlor to ourselves, an' you kin fetch a lamp an' scan my features for honesty while I tell you *I'm innocent of whatever I've done!*"

It was rather scant politeness, but Miss Melissa said not a word as she led the way into the house.

When she had dismissed the negro, and drawn her chair beside the deacon's—one must needs sit close to a deaf man—she laid a parcel upon the center-table at her elbow, and began to speak; but the deacon interrupted her.

"Befo' we explain fully, Miss Melissy," he said, "I want to say a word. I'm afeard my talk this evenin' clair disgusted you, an' I'm sorry I said them things about the whale. I know how you feel about all Scripture, an' I ought to've kep' my mouth shet."

"You needn't feel bad about that, deacon. To be candid, after the first shock, it sort o' made me feel nearer to you to find thet you was human an' frail. Of co'se I don't share yo' misgivin's. I believe all the Holy Scriptures verbatim, word for word. But I'm of a dangerous disposition. Ef I started to doubt, they's no tellin' where I'd go. But I've always looked upon you as ef you was a sort o' stained-glass apostle with a halo on, like them two in the 'Piscopal winders. Seemed like as ef you jest lived up to everything perfect, even to yo' deefness—'scuse me mentionin' it. Am I talkin' loud enough?"

"Yas; I hear every word. Settin' so, with the house still, I can even hear that lamp sizz. Don't you reckon you better turn it down?"

She turned the wick as she went on:

"An', as I said, yo' havin' faith-weakness was a sort o' comfort to me. I don't know but it makes what I'm about to say a little easier for me. Of co'se you know all about my mats; you've showed that."

"About yo' mats? Why, cert'n'y. Everybody does; an' I think they're to be strongly recommended—both for shape an' usefulness, an' du'ability, too; an' ef anybody says I ever said different—"

"I'm not referrin' to my green mats, deacon, an' you know it. I'm referrin' to these."

She opened the parcel, and spread the scarlet mats upon her lap.

"But how you found out about 'em I don't know, but you've acknowledged you did; an' now I'm goin' to out with the whole thing. I s'pose the devil tempted me. As you said this evenin', ef I ever condescended to make a red mat, or one out o' kilter, the devil might have hopes of me. Well, here's two—both all-fired red, an' knit with no mo' conscience than a cat's got. The best part

of this last one I've knit to-day—Sunday. Not a stitch counted in
either one, an' how they turned out so everlastin' pretty I don't
know. It's like the reward of vice. Yas; every minute thet I ain't
been fishin' to-day, I've knit—pretty near. Don't put on surprise,
deacon. You've kep' a-hintin' about my fryin' my own fish, an'
throwin' up about me bein' afraid of Silent Si, so of co'se you
know about our picnic. I went fishin' this mornin', 'stid o' goin' to
church, an' happened to come up with the old nigger; an' I give
him the fish to cook, an' then, why, we picnicked. I didn't set
down to the table with him, of co'se—him or her, whichever it is.
An' I hadn't been to Mis' Gibbs's ten minutes sca'cely, this evenin', when you come, which of co'se you knew, although you
referred so sarcastic to findin' me a'tendin' the sick.

"I s'pose likely I'm goin' to perdition. I don't know, I'm
shore; but I didn't start with no sech intention." Her lip quivered
here just a little.

"The fact is, I got sick an' tired o' them green mats, an' wo'e
out with everything—all in about three days; an' ef I hadn't
started out this mornin', an' spent all the energy I had left in
Sabbath-breakin', I b'lieve I'd 'a' died. I'm forty-one years old, an'
I've green-matted tel I'm about played out.

"I ain't been to a circus, or got on a steam-car, or had a dress
made out o' the house—not for over twelve years. I ain't even had
the luxury of a spell o' sickness, with betterin' days an' neighbors'
trays sent in—not for nine years. It's jest been mat-knittin'
whenever I'd try to git a little diversion from the duties of a' aunt
an' sister-in-law, an'—an'—an'—

"Well, it broke out in me all of a sudden, this week, an' this is
what it's led to. Of co'se you can't never respect me no more; but
they's one thing: *you can't pleg me like you attempted to do to-night.*
Nobody dast to do that, not even an apostle hisself, ef they was one
alive.

"Ef I'm put out o' the church for to-day's misconduc', why,
out I go, that's all; but I'll give myself up; the conference won't haf
to summons me."

She had been borne along so fiercely by her own passion that
she had failed to see the growing distress in the deacon's face
until he laid his hand upon her arm. Then it was that she saw that
there were tears upon his cheeks.

A Note of Scarlet · 209
"Hush, Melissy, hush! For God's sake, hush!" He was obliged to take his handkerchief and wipe his eyes.

"What you've told me is all new to me—before God." His right hand trembled visibly as he held it up to give force to his words.

"Yas; it's as new to me as ef Heaven had jest revealed it; but, bless God, how happy it does make me feel! Talk about *respectin'* you! Why, honey, I wouldn't take all the money in Simpkinsville befo' the wah for what you've confessed to me. It brings you in reach of me. For ten year I've set an' contemplated you an' yore life, an' so far as I could scan it, it's been perfect, an' they's been times I'd 'a' give my head to see a flaw in you; an', bless Heaven, the time has come, an' I can speak. I couldn't ask no perfec' woman to be my wife—an' me a poor mericle-doubtin', deef old sinner like I've always been.

"I've worshipped you, Melissy, honey, same as I'd worship a saint, for over ten year; but no human man's got a right to make love to a' up-an'-down saint.

"But I can make love to you now, an' I'm a-doin' it this minute. Any dear-hearted woman thet's lived the life you've lived, an' then, when she was put to it, had the grit to kick out o' the traces—"

He put his arm about her, as if she had been a child in distress, and drew her to him.

"Did you take notice thet I never said I like the *color* o' them green mats, honey? Growin' things an' tree-frogs can have a monopoly o' that color for me, an' I don't wonder you got tired of it. But these red ones, they've got jest enough o' the ole Nick in 'em to tickle me all over.

"We'll set 'em on the mantel-shelf, an' they'll illuminate the whole house."

Miss Melissa sat quite still and looked doubtingly into the deacon's face. His words did not satisfy her. He realized the mats in their worst meaning, and yet he took pleasure in them. Her voice was almost reproachful when she said, after a while:

"You wouldn't want to illuminate the house with a reminder of my sinfulness, would you?"

" 'Tain't that, deary. It'll be as a reminder of yo' human-ness—that's all."

"An' yet they're the reverend color of *sin*, accordin' to Scripture. 'Though thy sins be—' "

"That's only half o' the tex', honey."

"Yas; that's so. Maybe it will be jest as well to keep 'em in sight. We'll try to reelize the promise every time we look at 'em—'whiter than snow.' That-a-way they'll be symbols of forgiveness."

"That cotation ain't 'whiter than snow,' honey. It's 'as white as snow,' an' it's from the first chapter of the prophet Isaiah, eighteenth verse. You're thinkin' about a psa'm verse. It's the Fifty-first Psa'm, seventh verse—seventh or eighth—thet says 'whiter than snow.' Well, *you* can read the mats that-a-way, ef you like, but don't talk too much about it, now, lessen you'll skeer me. I don't doubt you're entirely too good for me, after all. But, for better or for worse, you're mine, from this time on through all eternity, lessen you cast me off.

"Even ef I was to wake up sudden an' find I'd been dreamin' all this whole thing, I'd set out to hunt you up an' co't you now—that is, ef I remembered *all* the dream."

"Which part do you mean?" She looked artlessly into his face as she asked it.

"Put on yo' guessin'-cap," he chuckled, as he tightened his arm about her and covered her hand with his.

"All scarlet ain't sin," he added, looking down upon her. "The side o' yo' neck an' yo' ear—don't turn away, now. It's perfectly lovely. But how did you git them little black freckles on yo' wrist?"

He had lifted her hand and was turning it over. "And how red it is! The right one ain't that-a-way."

"Them's Sunday freckles," she said evenly. "You know, I'm left-handed, an' that's my fishin' hand. It's been held over the water in the sun the livelong day. I wonder you dast to hold it."

" 'Tain't no worse for me to hold yo' po little Sabbath-breakin' hand than for you to be a-listenin' to the words of my doubt-expressin' tongue, is it?" he chuckled; but in a moment he added seriously:

"But they's some precious truths I ain't never doubted, deary. I ain't never doubted the love of God, or the blessedness of livin' in Him, or the beauty of holiness.

"But"—and now he chuckled again—"come down to it, it's

only these triflin' little one-day open-air freckles on yo' hand thet brings it where I can feel anyways eligible to it—that is, it's what these dear little freckles express—God bless 'em! Seems to me you must freckle mighty easy, though."

"I always did. You know, I was sandy-haired befo' I—"

"You're sandy-haired yet, deary. The prettiest sand on earth is the white sand o' the sea-shore. It's whiter than snow, ef anything outside of a pure woman's soul is. But yo' hair ain't arrived at that stage, quite. They's a plenty of the earthly sand-color in it yet, an' I'm glad of it. Sand an' grit, you know, they're pretty nigh the same thing. I like a woman thet's got grit. It was mighty gritty the way you owned up to all you done, knowin' you'd have to face the music alone.

"Oh, what a joy this day has brought me! Yas, indeed, we'll put these red mats in sight, an' they'll be beacons to us both, each in a different way, maybe. An' nobody but you an' me an' the gatepost—"

"Which ole Si is as deaf as—"

"Will ever know the story of 'em. I'm s'prised you wasn't afeard of ole Si, though. They say he's picked up a ole stovepipe hat somewhere, an' with it an' his dress-skirts an' boots—

"I wouldn't like to come on 'im sudden in the dusk myself. You know I offered him shelter, four year ago, in my barn; but he wouldn't have it. I don't wonder you thought I knew about yo' seein' him. Every time I opened my mouth to-night, seem like I put my foot in it, as the sayin' is.

"But do you reelize thet you ain't holdin' back from me none, an' thet I'm keepin' my arm around you, straight along, an' I'm a-takin' a heap o' things for granted?"

At this Miss Melissa withdrew herself; but she was not blushing, nor in any wise conscious or confused.

"It's all so sudden," she said evenly, "seem like I can't quite git the straight of it. I feel like as ef the Apostle John had ast me to marry him, an' while I was holdin' off, half scared, he turned into Peter, an'—an'—"

"An' you give in to Peter?"

Her face was as red as the scarlet mat, but the deacon did not see it. Her voice betrayed her embarrassment somewhat, though, as she said, lowering her tone a little:

"I could take Peter easier'n I could John. He wouldn't be sech a constant reproach to me. But you've been like John to me for so long—I can't hardly—"

She laid her hand upon his arm, and putting her lips close to his good ear, continued:

"Are you shore you doubt, in yo' heart of hearts, about Jonah an' the whale—an' it all stated clair in the Bible? You ain't jest makin' pretend, jest to encourage me?"

"Why, honey, I told you about that before I knew—"

"So you did. An' you're *shore* you doubt?"

"I'm afeard I am, beloved."

"Well, *ef you're shore*—maybe we can be a help to one another."

Bibliography

I. Books by Ruth McEnery Stuart

Aunt Amity's Silver Wedding and Other Stories. New York: The Century Co., 1903.
Carlotta's Intended. New York and London: Harper & Brothers Publishers, 1891.
The Cocoon. New York: Hearst's International Library Co., 1915.
Daddy Do-Funny's Wisdom Jingles. New York: The Century Co., 1916.
George Washington Jones. Philadelphia: Henry Altemus Company, 1903.
A Golden Wedding and Other Tales. New York and London: Harper & Brothers Publishers, 1905.
The Haunted Photograph; Whence and Whither; A Case in Diplomacy; The Afterglow. New York: The Century Co., 1911.
Holly and Pizen and Other Stories. New York: The Century Co., 1899.
In Simpkinsville Character Tales. New York and London: Harper & Brothers Publishers, 1897.
Moriah's Mourning and Other Half-Hour Sketches. New York and London: Harper & Brothers Publishers, 1898.
Napoleon Jackson, the Gentleman of the Plush Rocker. New York: The Century Co., 1901.
Plantation Songs and Other Verse. New York: D. Appleton and Co., 1916.
The River's Children. New York: The Century Co., 1904.
The Second Wooing of Salina Sue. New York: Harper & Brothers, 1905.
Snow-cap Sisters. New York and London: Harper & Brothers Publishers, 1901.
Solomon Crow's Christmas Pockets and Other Tales. New York and London: Harper & Brothers Publishers, 1896.
Sonny, a Christmas Guest. New York: The Century Co., 1894.
Sonny's Father. New York: The Century Co., 1910.
The Story of Babette. New York: Harper & Brothers Publishers, 1894.
The Unlived Life of Little Mary Ellen. Indianapolis: Bobbs-Merrill Co., 1910.
Woman's Exchange of Simpkinsville. New York and London: Harper & Brothers, 1899.

II. A Note about Bibliographical Sources

Like everything else, the fashion in literary criticism has changed enormously since the time when Ruth McEnery Stuart flourished as a writer. The references cited in the theses and dissertations listed are generally biographical and uncritical, stressing Mrs. Stuart's authentic Southern gentility and charm, rather than offering real insight into her work.

There were exceptions to this fashion even in her time, and in the middle decades of the twentieth century, the revival of interest in Southern women writers and in local color literature has produced a substantial body of criticism. However, by that time, Stuart had nearly faded from the reading lists.

Consequently, the sources given here are selected for their usefulness in establishing the biographical facts of Stuart's life, or the background of the Southern local-color movement.

Manuscript Sources

A. O. Stuart Family File. Southwest Arkansas Regional Archives. Old Washington State Park.

Ruth McEnery Stuart Papers. McKeldin Library, Tulane University, New Orleans.

Secondary Sources

Fletcher, Mary Frances. "A Biographical and Critical Study of Ruth McEnery Stuart." Ph.D. dissertation, Louisiana State University, 1955.

Frisby, James R. "New Orleans Writers and the Negro: George Washington Cable, Grace King, Ruth McEnery Stuart, Kate Chopin, and Lafcadio Hearn, 1870–1900." Ph.D. dissertation, Emory University, 1972.

Hager, Esther Phillips. "Interpreters of the Mississippi: A Study in American Regionalism." Master's thesis, University of Missouri, 1932.

Howell, Ina Rebecca. "A Critical Biography of Ruth McEnery Stuart." Master's thesis, University of North Carolina, 1945.

Hubbell, Jay B. The South in American Literature, 1607–1900. Durham, N.C.: Duke University Press, 1954.

Medearis, Mary. Washington, Arkansas: History on the Southwest Trail. Hope, Arkansas: Etter Printing Company, 1976.

Mott, Frank Luther. A History of American Magazines, 1865–1888. Cambridge, Mass.: Harvard University Press, 1938.

Owsley, Frank Lawrence. Plain Folk of the Old South. Baton Rouge: Louisiana State University Press, 1949.

Skaggs, Merrill Maguire. The Folk of Southern Fiction. Athens: University of Georgia Press, 1972.

Stephens, Edwin Lewis. "Ruth McEnery Stuart." In Library of Southern Literature, edited by Edwin Anderson Alderman et al. Atlanta: Martin and Hoyt, 1909.

Williams, Charlean Moss. The Old Town Speaks. Houston: Anson Jones Press, 1951.

Woodward, C. Vann. Origins of the New South: 1877–1913. Baton Rouge: Louisiana State University Press, 1951.